THE
NEW
FAMILY

BOOKS BY VICTORIA JENKINS

The Divorce

The Argument

The Accusation

The Playdate

THE DETECTIVES KING AND LANE SERIES

The Girls in the Water

The First One to Die

Nobody's Child

A Promise to the Dead

THE
NEW
FAMILY

VICTORIA JENKINS

bookouture

Published by Bookouture in 2021

An imprint of Storyfire Ltd.
Carmelite House
50 Victoria Embankment
London EC4Y 0DZ

www.bookouture.com

ISBN: 978-1-80019-974-3
eBook ISBN: 978-1-80019-973-6

PROLOGUE

She was even more beautiful when she was asleep. The room was bathed in an early-morning light that broke in like a thief through the gap between the bedroom curtains, a triangular shard illuminating her jawline. She had taken her make-up off before she went to bed. He preferred her like this. She was so pure that it was like being taken back to the start, a kind of rebirth.

He moved soundlessly across the silent room and crouched at her bedside, her face inches from his own. Her lips were parted slightly, warm breath escaping in murmurs, whispering to him. He wondered what she might say if she was to open her eyes to find him there. He thought about how he might silence her.

He wanted to touch her, and so he did, his fingertips meeting with her soft hair, so fine that it felt scarcely different to touching the air. There were scissors in his coat pocket – he had brought them with him for this purpose, among others – and he took them out now, snipping off a two-inch lock that lay fanned out on the pillow behind her. He held it to his face, breathing in the scent of her shampoo – and he wondered whether the aroma would linger.

Beneath the duvet, her body stirred. He pushed away as he waited for her to open her eyes, but she didn't, and as she settled back into a pull of deep sleep, he watched her for a while longer, wishing they had more time. He could have watched her forever.

When he left her side, he crossed the room and opened the wardrobe door. He rifled among the softness of her clothes before he opened a drawer, looking for something more specific – a keepsake of some kind. Within moments, he found what he was looking for. He slipped the item into his pocket, putting it with the lock of hair. He would keep them somewhere special, in the place where all his other favourite memories were stored.

ONE

BROOKE
SEPTEMBER 2019

Local legend says that this stretch of coastal path is haunted by the ghosts of ancient mariners, though why these deceased men of the sea would choose solid land for their haunting ground is a detail that has remained vague as the story has passed down the generations. Today the route is open to the sky, this section of the path unprotected by trees or hedgerow, and if there are ghosts that travel alongside me, they do so silently. There are fifty-three steps down to the beach; I counted them first as a five-year-old, then repeatedly for every summer that followed. My parents never let us come here during the winter months, fearful of a landscape that both enchanted and intimidated them. As soon as we were of an age at which they allowed us freedom to roam – I, as the elder, always entrusted with my sister's safety – we would explore the web of woodland paths that led to various points of the beach, then walk barefoot on the sand until our toes hit the freezing sea. It feels right to come here on her birthday, and as I watch the ghosts of our past – two skinny little things with bare legs and dresses tucked into knickers – I wonder where she might now be.

Once on the beach, I remove my boots and socks, letting my toes sink into the wet sand. I have done this in January, when the air has been at its most bitter and the land has felt like ice beneath my bare feet, the coldness a shock to my core and a jolt to the breath that fills my lungs. I am deep within my thoughts, pressing my heels into the sand, when I spot them. They are two inert figures in the distance at first – one tall, one much smaller at its side. As I walk further down the beach, they move into life. The child stands in the shallows, throwing stones into the waves. He moves methodically, a pebble plucked from his left palm, expelled by the fist of his right. He has hair made for seaside living, sandy and shoulder-length. The boy with the sad eyes, I think, and I realise I have passed this father and son before, along this same stretch of coastal path, not really noticing the man but always the child – his head tilted to one side, glassy eyes gazing seaward as though searching for the sight of something amid the low-hanging clouds that form a perpetual ceiling over this corner of the shoreline.

I see the man properly for the first time now: tall, dark-haired. We might have said hello once, maybe a week or two ago. He stands with arms folded as he watches his son. He is wearing a thin windbreaker jacket, jeans and a pair of running trainers, the expensive type worn by people who don't run. There is nowhere to walk to other than the sea and back again, so I continue towards them, not wanting to have come here without feeling the water at my feet.

'Finley.'

The boy doesn't react to his name at first, but on his father's second call he turns his head. As he continues to throw stones, ignoring his father's suggestion that it is time for them to go, the man sees me and smiles. I sense him watching me as my toes meet the sea, probably wondering why I would be mad enough to brave its icy bite.

'Fin.'

The boy's shoulders sag, and he moves his hand to his pocket to store the remaining pebbles. As a child, my feelings were just the same; no matter how cold it might have been, I was never ready to leave.

'That must be freezing, surely?'

It takes a moment to realise he is talking to me and not his son. 'Good for the circulation, apparently,' I reply.

He pulls a face and smiles. My eyes move to the boy, who is still staring at the water, dejected. 'Do you know how to skim those stones?' I ask. The child – how old is he? Three? Maybe four? – lowers his head at the question.

'He's a bit shy,' the man explains, his tone apologetic.

Finley catches me staring, so I look away, finding distraction in a cawing gull that circles overhead.

'Come on then, kid,' he says, moving towards the boy to take his hand. 'Say bye-bye.' He stoops to pull Finley's zip closer to his chin. 'I'm guessing you live locally?' he says to me. 'Are there any pubs nearby, somewhere we can get some food?' He runs a hand through his son's hair. 'This little man must be starving.'

'There's the Ship in the village, but they won't be doing food at this time.'

'The village?'

'Aberfach. It's about a mile that way.' I gesture vaguely towards the steps. 'Where have you two come from then? People don't usually just stumble across this place.'

He rolls his eyes. 'We got lost. I said right, Fin said left... we ended up here. God knows how we'll find the car later.'

The nearest car park is at least a couple of miles away; if he didn't stop in the village, he must have parked near the diving centre.

'How far have you walked?'

He digs into his pocket for his phone and checks the time. 'We've been out a couple of hours now.' He takes his son by the hand, persuading him from the sand with a promise of snacks, and the two of them follow me back towards the cliffs.

'That's a lot of walking for little legs,' I say, smiling at the boy – a skinny child even in his padded coat – as we reach the steps. 'You'd better go first. They're pretty steep.' He makes his ascent in front of me, while his father waits to follow. 'If you're not sure where you're parked, maybe you'd better give the Ship a miss,' I say, turning to cast the words behind me. 'It might take you further away.'

'It's not a problem. I'll have to get him something, even if it's just a drink and a bag of crisps.'

'I'm heading that way if you want me to show you?'

'Thanks. It's a beautiful beach, isn't it? We're lucky to have found it.'

'You'd be surprised how many local people don't even know it's here.'

'I can't imagine many people wanting to attempt these steps too often.'

'They're what keeps it quiet. That's why I like it here so much.'

We make the rest of our way up to the top in silence, Finley's breath ragged as we reach the final steps. 'Good going,' I say, once we're back on the flat. 'He's determined, isn't he? I imagine most kids would be moaning by now.'

I notice that whenever I talk to the child, he looks away, reluctant to make eye contact. I usher him towards the path, and he leads the way, trailing his open palm through the long grasses that reach up to his waist.

'You live here?' the man asks.

'Yes.'

'I've been looking for somewhere to stay for a few months. We've been at a B and B in Fishguard for a while, but I need something more permanent.'

'I have a rental property that's empty at the moment,' I blurt, the words leaving me as though without my permission. I cringe at their desperation. The months between May and September are the busiest, even competitively cheap rental fees normally enough to see me through the rest of the year, but this past summer has been quiet, the income generated the most meagre in years. After paying the outstanding fees for my mother's care home and the rent on my own place, I've been reliant on the earnings I make from painting commissions for paying bills and buying food, but they too are sporadic. I have two bookings on the cottage over Christmas and New Year; after that, the place will be empty until April unless things start to pick up.

'Really? Whereabouts?'

'In the village. I'll show you when we get there.'

I have always referred to Aberfach as a village, despite it being too small and insufficiently populated to really be called such. Technically it is a hamlet. There is no shop, no church, no post office – just the pub, frequented by locals, walkers and tourists – and a handful of homes, some inhabited by those who have been here and will remain here forever, others rented out to holiday-makers looking for a coastal escape.

'Sorry,' he says. 'I haven't asked your name.'

'Brooke.'

'I'm Oliver.'

Finley's legs finally start to tire, and he tugs at his father's jeans as a signal of his exhaustion. Oliver reaches down to lift him and carries him the rest of his way on his hip, the boy's focus remaining on the sea view that travels alongside us, disappearing as our path dips down towards the harbour walls.

When we reach the village, I point to the curve of mountain-side opposite, and to the house, my childhood home, standing guard over the hamlet and the harbour. I try to see it now as though through someone else's eyes, that I might hide from the memories attached to the place. 'Hillside Cottage.'

Oliver raises his eyebrows. 'Impressive.'

'It's only a two-bedroom, but there's a lovely garden to the side and it's got the best views of the sea. In my opinion, obviously.'

'Can I arrange a viewing with you?'

Finley, still being carried, starts tugging at his father's arm, muttering something that sounds like 'crisps'.

'How about you take this hungry young man to the pub,' I suggest, 'and I'll meet you afterwards, unless you're in a rush to get away?'

'Sounds perfect, thank you.' He checks his watch. 'Shall we say four thirty?'

'I'll meet you outside the pub.'

Oliver prompts Finley to say goodbye, the boy responding by burrowing his head into his father's neck. I wonder why he would want to bring his son to stay in a place like this, so remote and isolated, though it was the life my parents chose for their own children. It had been my mother's dream to live by the sea. My sister and I grew up with the ocean air in our lungs and a permanent breeze against our skin, and the need for both have never left me, but for my sister, the harbour walls came to represent her incarceration, the landscape synonymous with her imprisonment.

I turn back to watch father and son as they head to the pub before making my way back across the main road to the little terraced cottage that I now call home. My thoughts stray back to the conversation just shared, filtering through the details that Oliver revealed, whether knowingly or not. He had said, 'I need somewhere more permanent.' Not 'we', but 'I'. Perhaps it was simply a misleading choice of words, though there was no mention of a partner. I wonder where the boy's mother is.

TWO
CHRISTINA
FEBRUARY 2018

Christina pulled into the driveway of Janet Marsden's house. It was a beautiful building – a sprawling detached property that somehow managed to retain a homeliness usually afforded to smaller, cosier places – and if it hadn't been for the busy main road that linked Barnet with the A1, she might have thought she was somewhere remote and rural, not just half an hour away from the centre of the capital. Although Christina saw most of her clients at her own home, there were some for whom she made an exception. Janet was one of them. She had been having chemotherapy for breast cancer for months, having already overcome the disease once years earlier. Physiotherapy was helping her to manage the pain, and though she could have completed the exercises Christina provided for her alone, it was more beneficial to both women to see each other in person.

She hid her pain behind a smile that was worn as a permanent accessory, in place as always when she opened the door to Christina. 'How are you?' she asked, as she always did, which seemed a summary of all that Janet was, forever concerned with the well-being of others despite everything that she was going through.

'I'm fine, thank you. How are you feeling this week?' Christina followed Janet through to the beautiful kitchen at the back of the house.

'The usual. Tired. But I'm okay. I've been managing a daily walk, just up the road and back.'

'That's really good progress. Can we do some of the strengthening exercises I showed you last time?'

Christina moved a couple of the dining room chairs so that they could sit side by side.

'How's Rebecca getting on with her dissertation?' she asked.

'I think she's struggling more than she lets on. She's working late into the night too often, but whenever I ask her about it, she just says everything's fine. I think she's trying to protect me, though she really doesn't need to.'

'Did she speak to Alice?'

Christina's sister-in-law was a police officer with the Met; she had offered to help Janet's daughter with any questions she might have while completing the dissertation for her master's degree in criminology.

'Yes, and she was a massive help, thank you. Rebecca's ordered her some flowers.'

'That's kind of her. She's a lovely young woman. You must be very proud of her.'

'Always.' Janet winced at a pain in her neck as she stretched. 'I'm fine,' she said, waving it away. 'Just a twinge. And how are your two doing? Is Edward sleeping any better?'

Her mention of the twins brought a tightening to Christina's throat. 'They're fine,' she managed, turning her face away from Janet's view as she stood from her chair to attend to her. 'Still a pair of little monkeys,' she added. She reached for Janet's shoulders. 'May I?' She worked her fingers into the other woman's shoulders, manipulating the muscles that had tightened through treatment and tension. 'Edward's sleep is no better, bless him. I was never a great sleeper when I was a child... he might just be following me.'

'Rebecca didn't sleep through the night until she was almost five years old.'

'God, really? Don't tell me that.'

Janet laughed. 'It's a hard phase, the toddler years. But trust me, you'll miss them when they're gone.'

They fell into silence, Christina's hands still working to ease the stress from Janet's shoulders. Beneath her fingers, the other woman seemed to have left her for a moment, her thoughts flown to some distant memory of a life that hadn't been shaped by her illness and all its consequences. She concentrated on the flexing of Janet's muscles, trying to distract herself from thoughts of her own situation.

'That hurts.'

She stepped away, lifting her hands as though Janet's skin had burned her. 'I am so sorry,' she said, moving around to face her. 'Are you all right?'

'Just hit a nerve or something.'

Christina opened the bag she had left on the table. She got out a bottle of water and took a long drink, grateful that Janet wasn't paying her any attention. She could feel herself growing too hot, a line of sweat trickling beneath her collar at the base of her neck. A burning sensation spread through her stomach, and she struggled to remember what she had eaten that morning. As the room swayed, she staggered, almost falling against the table.

The plastic bottle dropped from her hand, spilling water on the tiles at her feet. 'Oh God, I'm so sorry. That was so clumsy of me.'

There was a packet of tissues in her bag; she pulled out a handful and tried to mop up the worst of the water, managing only to make the mess worse.

'Please don't worry about it,' Janet said. 'It's just water, it'll dry.' She sat up, and Christina could feel her eyes on hers as she returned the remainder of the tissues to her handbag. 'Is everything okay? Are you feeling all right?'

Despite the heat that coursed through her, Christina knew her face had gone pale. She had felt the colour fade from it at Janet's mention of the children, the blood seeming to drain from her in an instant.

'I'm fine, sorry. I've been getting these dizzy spells, that's all. It's probably tiredness. From Edward, the lack of sleep, you know.'

The part about the dizziness wasn't a lie – the spells had been recurring for a number of weeks now, increasingly frequent and catching her off guard, with no apparent pattern to the timing of their arrival.

'It'll pass, love. Everything always does.'

The comment cast them both under a shadow for a moment.

'Should we stop it there for today?' Christina asked, noticing the wince that Janet tried to hide as she moved.

'Probably for the best. I don't want to overdo it. But this is really helping, please don't think otherwise. It's always a bit painful at first.'

'Maybe give it a few days before you attempt the upper-body exercises again,' Christina suggested. 'And if you're unsure of anything, please just give me a call, okay? Any time... I mean it.'

Janet saw her out, waiting to wave goodbye as Christina left the driveway and pulled onto the main road. She made it as far as the T-junction that took her back into town before finding the first side street and stopping the car. She checked her phone; there was a message from Joel.

Let me know when your session's finished x

Her fingers quivered guiltily over the keys as she tapped out a reply.

Now. See you soon x

THREE
BROOKE
SEPTEMBER 2019

At 4.30, as agreed, I meet Oliver and Finley outside the pub. They follow me up the narrow, winding road that leads to Hillside Cottage, and I let them into the tiny square space that almost passes as a hallway. A faint smell of damp lingers, the kind of smell that resides in places left uninhabited for too long, and yet still I can recall the scent of burning wood and home baking that would greet me whenever I came through this front door as a child. Time stops when I am here.

The house looks nothing now as it did when I was a child, back when my mother was alive with colour. It had taken years for her to get it exactly as she had wanted, the vision of a home that she had painted in her mind upon first viewing the house when I was just a baby and she was pregnant with my sister. Every room was painted in a different vibrant shade – the living room a sunshine burst of lemon yellow, the kitchen mint green, our bedroom a hot raspberry pink, and our parents' room a cheery seaside blue. She furnished the whole house with items she had bought in second-hand markets and charity shops, and some of my earliest memories are of us in the front garden, my sister and I playing on the small strip of grass as my mother sanded and drilled and painted, restoring the previously unloved and rejected pieces into things she was proud to say she had brought back to life. 'One woman's junk is another woman's treasure,' she would say, and my father would joke that she would eventually do him out of his job as a carpenter.

After his death, my mother redecorated in magnolia, painting over the memories to make them less prominent. Yet when I stand here now, I can still see it as it once was – the colour and the quirks designed by my mother's hand, the collection of nautical trinkets she had accumulated over the years lined up on the window sills, the patchwork cushion covers she had made from her favourites of our childhood clothes. I can still hear the low rumble of my father's laughter rolling into the house from the back garden, where he worked in his shed, as I know my mother must have in all the years that passed between his death and hers.

'You okay?'

'Sorry,' I say, flitting away my thoughts with an idle wave of a hand. 'I was miles away for a minute. Anyway, as I said, it's nothing special, but this is it.'

Oliver walks with me into the living room, but Finley stays by the front door. 'Don't be shy,' his father prompts him, but the boy remains frozen, making eye contact with neither of us.

'The kitchen's just through here.' I point to the door. 'Go on,' I say, when Oliver looks over to his son to check he hasn't strayed back outside. 'I'll keep an eye on him.'

By the staircase, there is a bookcase that houses things I left here for the families who stay: guides to the area, books and board games. Like a flashback from a dream, my sister appears in the corner of the room, ten years old again, her head thrown back as she laughs over the details of a game I can no longer remember. I hear her voice, hear her speak my name, about to reprimand me for some misdemeanour, and then she is gone.

I go to the bookcase and take down a few items, putting them on the coffee table where Finley can access them. 'Would you like to have a look?'

He says nothing, but when I glance away and pretend to busy

myself with straightening the curtains, he goes across to the table and starts sifting through the books. I watch from the corner of my eye as he methodically picks each one up, studying the front cover and then the back before turning the pages. He settles upon a small hardback book that used to belong to my sister, an illustrated guide to coastal wildlife.

Oliver comes back into the room and smiles when he sees that Finley has moved from his position in the doorway. 'Okay to look upstairs?'

'Of course.'

'Want to come, Fin? Brooke can give us a guided tour.'

I lead the way and show Fin the room that used to belong to my sister and me, having to fight the memories from flooding the space around me. Trying to distract myself from the past, I focus on the built-in wardrobe that is perfect for playing hide-and-seek or for setting up a den. 'Look,' I say, and I flick a switch to illuminate the space. I used to spend hours hidden away in here, usually with a book or a sketchpad. Finley remains mute and unresponsive, furtively glancing out from under his wayward hair, and I wonder just what this child has been through.

'Look at the view, Fin,' Oliver says. He lifts his son to the window and rests him on the sill so he can see the sea. The two of them look out to the greying horizon, neither speaking, and there is something intimate about the moment, something that makes me feel I shouldn't be there to invade it.

'You weren't lying about the views,' Oliver says, turning to me.

'Wait until you see this one, then.'

He sets Finley back on the carpet and follows me into the main bedroom and over to the window. Early evening is beginning to close in, yet it doesn't spoil the scene outside. The grass that borders the house merges with a low hedgerow; beyond it, the drop to the village can't be seen and a vast sweep of ocean stretches to the sky. It is a perfect evening for painting – the kind of mood that manages to lie somewhere between serene and unsettled and is my favourite to capture. The calm before the storm.

I leave Oliver at the window and go to glance back into the other room, where Finley is sitting on the bed looking at the wildlife book that he brought up with him from downstairs. When I return to the main bedroom, Oliver is still gazing out. Evening seems to have fallen upon us within minutes, and the sky outside is charcoal grey and suddenly heavy with the threat of rain.

'Do you mind me asking what brings you here?' I ask. 'This part of the world can be pretty bleak at times.'

'Pretty bleak. I like that description. The same thing that keeps you here, I imagine.'

'I've always been here,' I tell him, looking out into the greyness that is creeping towards us from the fading horizon.

A strange silence falls between us, and I feel uncomfortable, as though I have revealed something I didn't mean to. It occurs to me that he never answered my question, and I wonder whether the avoidance was deliberate.

'It's a beautiful house,' he says. 'How long have you had it?'

'I grew up here.'

He turns to me, surprised. 'A childhood by the sea,' he says, moving his hands from the window sill and folding them across his chest. 'Exactly what I want for Finley.'

'Where are you from?' I ask, noticing his neutral English accent.

'Kent originally.' He turns back to the window, his attention still tethered to the grey seascape that sweeps away from us. He is right – it is a beautiful view, haunting in its bleakness; the kind of beauty I have always believed can only be appreciated by someone familiar with its sometime hostility. 'You could lose yourself here.'

I say nothing, wondering whether this is why he has come here. Perhaps this same thing was my sister's reason for leaving.

'When's your next booking?' he asks.

'Not for nearly three months,' I tell him, embarrassed at the admission. I don't want to come across as a pauper, though at the moment I am scarcely much more. 'Demand isn't so great in the winter.'

'Can you put my name down then?'

Relief floods me, though I try to keep it from my face. 'How long do you want?'

'We'll take the three months. It'll give me enough time to sort out what I need to. I should ask how much it is, shouldn't I?'

I try to conceal my surprise. The extra income is much needed and will take a huge pressure off me, but it is unheard of to take such a long booking. No one has been here longer than a fortnight, or for anything more than a holiday.

'Are you sure this is okay?' he asks. 'Sorry... I've put you on the spot, haven't I? I mean, if you'd rather hold out for the holiday bookings or whatever, then please just say – I don't want to make things difficult for you.'

I play down my eagerness for fear of putting him off. The fact is, demand recently hasn't been what it once was – perhaps the location is too rural, the nearby tourist towns a more appealing option. If I hold out for holiday bookings, I could end up with next to nothing. 'No, it doesn't make anything difficult. It's just... unusual for someone to want to stay so long, that's all.'

There is a pause. 'We have unusual circumstances, I'm afraid.' He looks to the bedroom doorway, where Finley has appeared, still clutching the book. 'Okay,' he says brightly, changing the subject for the benefit of his son. 'I should give you my number, shouldn't I? We can sort out payment and everything then.'

I take my mobile phone from my pocket and add his number to my contacts list as he recites it. Then I call the number, waiting to hear his phone ring in his pocket so that he has mine. 'You don't need to use the internet too often, do you?' I ask him. 'Just a warning, the Wi-Fi is terrible here. The mobile signal isn't always reliable either. I quite often have to leave the village to check my emails.'

'Sounds lovely, actually. I think a break from twenty-first-century life is what we need, isn't it, kid?' He musses up his son's hair before glancing at the book he still holds. 'Be nice to spend some quality time together, technology-free.'

I follow them back downstairs.

'I'll be in touch tomorrow,' Oliver says as I lock the front door. 'That okay?'

'Whenever you're ready. There's no rush.'

'I don't know about that. We're starting to feel a bit caged in at the B and B.'

'It can't be easy for you.'

At the bottom of the hill, I remember that Oliver's car is miles away. 'Are you going to be able to find your way back?' I ask. 'I could give you a lift if you like.'

'Thanks, but we'll be okay. The pub should be doing food by now, shouldn't it? I'll get Finley some dinner before we head back.'

We say goodbye and I make my way across the road, an inexplicable sense that something is wrong taking root in my chest. Something clutches in my gut, and as I get closer to the terrace, I see it through the window, a flood of colour engulfing the wall previously muted with grey seascape paintings. I fumble with the key in the lock, my hands not working quickly enough, and when I push the door open, a wave of heat hits me, smoke flooding my lungs.

I stand unmoving, limbs frozen, as flames leap at the gallery wall and rip through years' worth of work, watching my livelihood – my life – fall to ashes. The door to the kitchen area is open, but I can't see beyond it; the doorway is a cloud of thick, billowing black smoke. I realise that everything I need – all the paperwork relating to my own life and my mother's – is beyond that door, kept in the filing cabinet in the tiny back room that acts as office and kitchen, and panic streaks through me, pushing me forward before my brain can consider the danger.

My lungs fill as I work my way through the smoke, the fire spreading so quickly that I feel its heat cutting past my clothing. The kitchen is orange with flames, fire reaching to the ceiling; I cannot go in there, yet I don't want to turn back.

'Brooke!'

I hear a voice calling my name, though I'm not sure whose. I think about the photographs in the filing cabinet just metres from me; all the memories that can never be retrieved.

'Come with me.'

There is a hand on my arm, someone pulling me back, and it is only now that I realise how light-headed from the smoke I am. I allow myself to be drawn through the flames, my senses suddenly registering the noise of the fire around me, and as I am dragged from the blaze, I watch in horror as the contents of my small existence are engulfed and destroyed.

FOUR

CHRISTINA

FEBRUARY 2018

Christina sat on the edge of the bed and looked out at the park across the road, where children ran between the trees while their mothers stood chatting in huddles. There was little green space to be found in that pocket of the city – not that it was green now, the ground awash with the remaining sludge of the weekend's brief snowfall trampled by tiny thundering wellies. She closed her eyes for a moment, wishing she could just drop off to sleep for an hour.

'One coffee, milk no sugar.'

Joel ran a palm over the bare skin of her lower back before stretching across the duvet to put the drink on the bedside table.

'Thank you.'

He sat beside her, returned his warm hand to her cool skin. 'You okay?'

She nodded, and he moved behind her, pushing her dark hair aside to kiss the back of her neck. She leaned her head back and closed her eyes, forgetting herself for a moment.

'Do you want to talk about it?'

'I'm fine, honestly.' 'It' was complex: too complicated for the time they had before she would need to pick the twins up from nursery. They could have stayed in that spot and talked until Easter, but it still wouldn't have been enough time.

She sat forward, pulling away from him. Outside, the sky was blotched and mottled, a palette of pale flesh pinched by cold. A line of thin clouds hung over the furthest rooftops, lingering like vapour trails abandoned by an absent plane. She thought about the last time she had flown: a weekend in Florence in the spring of 2015, an extravagant celebration for their second wedding anniversary. Within months, she had been pregnant with the twins. The midwives and health visitors had been quick to mention postnatal depression, or 'a bad case of the baby blues', as one woman had vaguely described it, but Christina suspected otherwise.

She recalled that evening in Florence, the two of them sitting outside a bistro on a cobbled side street, sipping chilled white wine while the sad notes of a violinist playing on the piazza two streets away drifted towards them on the air. It was a beautiful night: warm air more like summer than spring, delicious food served by friendly waiters who were keen to teach them new Italian phrases; husband and wife still in so many ways like newly-weds even two years on from the wedding day. Perfect. To anyone, it seemed, but her. Alongside warm freshly baked bread and cool dry wine, Christina tasted something else – some sickness that refused to settle. The warm air was accompanied by a chill that ran through her, and the friendliest of faces appeared distorted as though behind a mask. She could recall so minutely the feeling of being removed and disconnected, the perfect evening meant for someone else. Pregnancy hadn't changed her; it had merely brought to the surface what had already been lingering beneath.

'We could go for a walk?' Joel looked out of the window, assessing the weather. 'Rain might hold off for a bit.'

'Could we just stay here for a while?'

She rested against the pile of pillows, her head turned away from him, still focused on the world beyond the window. When he lay next to her and curled an arm around her, she allowed him to hold her. The bedroom felt like another world, a different existence, being within those four walls allowing her to escape herself for a little while longer.

'What are you thinking about?'

She felt his fingers in her hair as he lightly traced her skull, as though she might somehow transmit her thoughts through her skin and answer his question without speaking. She could hardly tell him that she had been thinking about Florence.

'Nothing.'

'Is that even possible? To think about nothing?'

'I'm managing it now,' she lied.

'No, you're not.' His hand stopped to rest on her bare shoulder. 'You can talk to me, you know.'

Over the past few months, she had talked to him while saying little. An appearance of trust had been offered; small details given up, creating an illusion of solidarity. The truth was that she had given nothing away, keeping herself hidden. Life felt safer when she was in hiding.

Joel slid away. Behind her, she heard him move from the bed and start to get dressed. 'Are you going to tell me what's wrong or leave me to guess?'

Her session with Janet had changed everything, reshaping the configuration of her brain and forcing her sense of self to the place it should have always remained: at the back of her mind. The guilt, she thought; it was always there, in so many different contexts. She worked too much; she didn't work enough. She didn't spend enough time with the twins; she smothered them, suffocating them with a love that often felt too intense to be healthy. She was a failure as a mother, as a wife, as a sister. Her life was a mess of contradictions. It had become a machine that was too powerful for her to operate.

'Nothing's wrong,' she lied. 'I'm sorry... I just didn't realise the time.'

She needed to get the twins from nursery. She needed to step beyond these four walls, be responsible again.

'You don't want to do this any more, do you?'

He was older than she was, nearing forty, and yet there was

something younger about him that might well have contributed to her initial attraction. Irresponsibility, perhaps that had been the draw. He still lived as a man in his mid twenties, carefree and independent, unstrung from the trappings of the suburban life that had dragged her into seeming obscurity. He was alive, while she was... what was she?

Was this what a midlife crisis looked like, having snuck up on her a decade earlier than might be expected? The cliché of the middle-aged man was a sports car and a younger woman, but what about crises for females... did anyone ever talk about that? She was only thirty-three, but had she been ten years older, might this be how she could explain away her decisions and her behaviour?

'I never said that.'

'You didn't have to.'

She finished dressing. She could sense him silently watching her, as though knowing this was the last time he would do so. 'I've got to go,' she said. 'Sorry.'

He got up, crossed the room to intercept her at the doorway, and when he reached for her shoulders, she allowed herself to be held. She felt his hand move across the back of her head, his palm smoothing her hair. He smelled of the aftershave he always wore, and as its strong scent caught in the back of her throat, she felt an inexplicable urge to cry. Instead, she pulled away from him.

'I'll call you,' she told him, knowing this was a lie.

He reached for her arm, his fingertips digging into her skin. 'I'm not ready to let you go.'

She looked at his fingers, at the whitened knuckles. A sudden fear crept through her, icy and unnerving. She barely knew this man. He had allowed her to temporarily escape herself, yet she had no idea who he really was.

He seemed to be suddenly aware of what he was doing, and his grip loosened. When he stepped aside to let her pass, Christina said nothing.

She made her way alone down the staircase to the communal

front door, stopping once it was closed behind her and she was out on the street to take a deep breath of cold afternoon air. Nausea rolled in her stomach. Something had reached an end, yet she was filled with an inescapable sensation that something else had yet to begin.

FIVE

BROOKE

SEPTEMBER 2019

'Christ, what were you thinking, going in there?'

Sylvia sits beside me, her hand resting lightly on mine. From her house on the other side of the main road she can see everything that goes on here, and at the right time of day – any mealtime or tea break – her perch in the window of her first-floor living room makes her unelected chairwoman of a neighbourhood watch scheme no one asked for or probably wanted. At times, though – like now – her nosiness seems a blessing of sorts.

'The photographs,' I mutter. I might have said it a hundred times already, I don't know. The last few moments seem to have blurred and distorted.

'They might not be lost, love,' she tries to reassure me, but as we watch the fire blaze on, her optimism seems misplaced.

We are sitting on a wall near the harbour, watching my life go up in flames. The paintings I sell, gone. My life's few possessions, gone. I live in one of the smallest villages in the UK, yet I have never seen so many people here at one time. The neighbours from the terrace are out in the road, fearful that the fire might spread to their properties. A group of boys on bikes, no older than fourteen, has stopped to witness the gallery's demise, some having taken out their phones to record the blaze, revelling in the drama of someone else's tragedy. Even the pub seems to be unusually busy for a weekday afternoon, customers spilling out to watch the action, drinks still in hand. Someone called the fire service, but they're not here yet. By the time they arrive, it will be too late. It is already too late.

'All that matters is that you're safe,' Sylvia says, and her fingers tighten around my hand. 'Who was that man?'

'What man?'

'The man who went in after you.'

I don't remember seeing the person who was in there with me. Someone spoke my name; after that, there was a hand on my shoulder, and I was pulled away. I came out of the building coughing and spluttering, my lungs thick with smoke. Then I saw Sylvia crossing the road towards me, moving faster than I have ever seen her move.

'I don't know.'

'Dark-haired. He went chasing after a little boy.'

Oliver. I turn to look at the harbour, and at the route that leads to the coastal path, but if he was there before, he is gone now.

'Brooke.' Sylvia gives my arm a gentle shake, rousing me from my trance.

'Sorry. I'm fine.'

I hear the distant scream of sirens, and within moments a fire engine appears at the turn in the road that leads into the village square. It stops outside the terrace, and a team of firefighters emerge. I watch as though observing the unfolding of someone else's day, floating above my own life. Sylvia has wrapped her thick cardigan around me, despite me already having a jacket on. She starts to talk to someone – one of the fire crew, I think – yet their words pass me in a blur of sound.

Someone brings me a cup of tea, sweetened. I feel another hand on my shoulder as the mug is passed to me, and I sip it without tasting, my senses numbed. I try to think of all the things that could have caused a fire: kettle, toaster, hair dryer. I haven't used the hair dryer for a couple of days, and it was up on the mezzanine floor by my bed, nowhere near the hub of the fire. Was the kettle faulty? Did something spark in the toaster – a piece of bread left stuck between the metal bars?

'Are you the owner of the property?'

The man has taken his helmet off and is carrying it under one arm. I nod and look over to the building, where a few of his colleagues are now gathered outside. The fire is out. The damage is done.

'No. I mean, I live there, yes. I rent it.' Behind him, I see a flashing blue light. A police car has pulled into the village. 'Why are the police here? Is this normal procedure?' I turn to Sylvia.

'What's your name, love?' the firefighter asks.

'Brooke. Brooke Meredith.'

He looks at my smoke-stained trousers, visible between the folds of Sylvia's cardigan. I know that my hair is scorched on one side, and I have no idea what my face must look like, but it occurs to me now that I must be a mess.

'Okay, Brooke. Do you think you need to get checked over at the hospital?'

'No, really. I mean, I'm fine. Thanks.'

I can feel Sylvia looking at the side of my face, throwing an unspoken question to my response. 'Do you know how it might have started?' she asks.

'Not yet. We'll make a start on investigations now the fire is out.' He turns to greet an approaching police officer, and my mind switches off from the sounds around me once again.

I'm not sure how long we sit there. The boys on bikes grow bored of the spectacle once the fire is diminished, and disappear as quickly as they arrived. People return to the warmth of the pub, and the other people from the terrace seek temporary shelter elsewhere as the fire crew and police carry out their work. The last of the evening fades to darkness. Someone brings another cup of tea.

In the unnerving silence that falls upon us, I occupy my mind with a calculation of how many hours' work has been lost in less time than it would take to prepare a palette and a canvas. I lose

track of the numbers, like misplacing counted sheep before sleep
has been found, and am left with a void – a vacuum of time now
absent, spent on nothing. I want to cry, but I can't. The fire feels
like a last kick in the stomach to a life already on the ground.

'Why don't we go over and wait at mine, love?' Sylvia suggests,
not for the first time.

'You go. Honestly, I'll be fine.' I stand, realising I am still
wearing her cardigan. 'Here,' I say, pulling an arm through a sleeve.
'Have this back.'

'No, you keep it. I'll pop over and get another one. Will you be
okay?'

I manage a smile. 'I don't know. Anything might happen out
here now.'

Sylvia squeezes my arm affectionately before heading back to
her house. As I wait, a black Toyota pulls up near the harbour, and
a moment later Oliver gets out from the driver's side. I watch him
ease the door shut gently, careful not to make a sound; Finley must
be sleeping in the back.

'I am so sorry about earlier,' he says, coming over to me.

'Sorry? You got me out of there, didn't you?'

'I mean sorry for leaving like that. Fin just ran off – I think the
fire must have scared him. Are you okay?'

'I'll be honest, I've had better days.'

He sits on the wall beside me, filling the space that Sylvia left
empty. 'What made you go in there like that?'

'I don't know. I wasn't thinking straight.'

He looks for too long at my burned hair, his expression filled
with pity. I wonder whether he can smell it, and whether it will
ever wash off me. 'Where are you going to stay tonight?'

It's something I haven't yet considered. 'Over at the house, I
suppose. I don't know.' Then I remember our earlier arrangement,
that Oliver wants to move in there. 'I'll find somewhere. You still
want to rent the house, don't you?'

'Well, no. I mean, we can't stay there now. You're going to
need it.'

I need the money more, I think, but I say nothing. I see Sylvia returning, now wearing a thick winter coat to protect her from the chill of the night air. 'I'll make arrangements,' I say quickly, not wanting Sylvia to hear the details of the conversation. 'Honestly, the house is still yours if you want it.'

Oliver looks at me with concern. 'I don't think it's—'

'Please,' I say, trying to keep the desperation from my voice. 'Honestly, it'll be best all round.'

He looks away, made awkward by the indirect admission that I need the money. As Sylvia approaches us, so does the firefighter I spoke with earlier.

'Brooke.'

I stand nervously, as though I am still at school and have just been summoned by the head teacher. 'Any news?'

'We'll have to wait for the evidence to go off to the lab,' he says, 'but it looks as though some sort of accelerant has been used. I'm sorry... we think the fire was started deliberately.'

SIX

CHRISTINA
FEBRUARY 2018

She had parked the car three streets away from Joel's flat, as she always did, and there was now little under an hour before she had to pick the children up from nursery. The thought of them made her stomach lurch, and as she made her way along a pavement that seemed too overcrowded, dodging people in her hurry to get away from the scene of all her crimes, she thought she might be sick with the guilt. She had never intended to live two lives. An initial flirtation had developed into something she should never have allowed to happen, and yet there had been times with Joel that she had felt more normal than she had in a long time. It wasn't just sex. Something in her had died – some desire for life and for living that had been lost somewhere years earlier, its absence unnoticed until it had become seemingly irretrievable.

In the car, she realised that she had forgotten her scarf. It was silk, embroidered with blue butterflies; Matthew had bought it for her as a birthday present a couple of years ago. She couldn't go back for it, not now. Was it likely that he would remember it at some point, realise that he hadn't seen her wearing it for a while and ask her where it was?

She stemmed the sickness that rose in her chest until she was back at the house, where she raced along the hallway and threw up in the downstairs toilet. When her stomach was emptied, she sat with her back to the cold tiled wall and cried with a self-pity that was at once alleviating and repulsive. Was it possible to put right everything that she had done wrong? If she told Matthew, would he forgive her?

Ten minutes later, she pulled into the car park of the nursery that the children attended four days a week. The large double-fronted townhouse had been converted ten years earlier and had been recommended to Christina before the twins had been born. The first morning she had taken them there, she had sat in the car two streets away and cried into a takeaway coffee cup. She felt that she was betraying them, worried that they would be scared or feel alone, though she was reassured by the thought that, as twins, they would never be by themselves. After the initial shock at that first scan where a twin pregnancy was confirmed, this was the thought that had comforted her. Amid all her concerns over whether she and Matthew would cope with the care of two children – when just one had at times seemed an overwhelming prospect – she had sought solace in the fun they would share, the bond they would have; that instant, exclusive relationship known only to such siblings that would grow and strengthen over time.

As expected, Elise had settled at nursery quicker than Edward, who had cried for the entirety of the first week and hadn't been much better during the second. The staff had been brilliant, updating Christina regularly throughout the day with both children's progress, offering her reassurance and sending photographs to confirm that they were both not only doing fine but enjoying themselves, yet it didn't alleviate the inevitable brew of emotions that she wrangled with on a daily basis. She loved her children, but she loved her career too. She loved the independence that her job afforded her, and she enjoyed the work she did, and yet she wanted to be with her children every moment of the day. She was worried she would miss something – first steps, first words – and when she did, with Edward, those first wobbly steps taken from the edge of a seat to the arms of his key worker, the guilt that had eased to become more manageable during the previous months resurfaced tenfold.

She loved collecting them from the nursery, seeing their little faces light up when they saw her there waiting for them. There was nothing quite like the feeling of them running into her arms, or the little squealed 'Mama!' that would pass their lips. Today was no different. Elise appeared first, as always, running from the day room in her winter coat, her hat pulled down too far over her forehead so that it was almost covering one eye.

'Mama,' she called excitedly, flinging herself at Christina, who almost fell back against the weight of her daughter's adoration.

A moment later, Edward followed. For months after finally taking those first steps, he had tottered behind a more confident Elise, who had been running around while her brother still coasted the living room furniture. He had been tentative on his feet, his thought processes seemingly more deliberate than those of his sister, who now, at almost two years old, would throw herself at – and from – everything, heedless of the possible dangers. He was getting better at running, Christina thought as he neared her – stronger and more confident.

After embracing them both, she took each by a hand and led them out to the car park. She got Edward strapped into his seat first, then Elise, and after getting into the driver's seat, she turned to smile at them both. Gosh, they are beautiful, she thought, and they really were. Not just the kind of beauty only visible to a parent, but the kind other people commented on, strangers in the street who would stop to peer into the double buggy and coo at the pink cheeks and beaming smiles looking back at them. Yet she had never felt that she deserved them. From the moment she had first seen their scrunched red faces, the first time she had held them as they screamed against her chest, she had felt a detachment that she could never tell anyone about for fear of being judged, as though in seeing her children into the world she had watched herself leave. Every time she held them a little closer, a voice in her head told her they deserved better.

As she pulled out of the car park, an involuntary image flitted in front of her: Joel, half dressed, standing in the doorway of his bedroom. Shame flooded her. What sort of mother was she? She had two beautiful children, a husband who loved her, and she was risking it all... for what? They had never spoken of what came next, yet he must have known that what was happening between them was only temporary, a phase that she couldn't even explain to herself, though he had never asked her for any explanation as to where it was going, or when, or how.

A phase, she thought. Toddlers went through phases. Teenagers. Not grown women with families and responsibilities.

Elise kicked the back of the driver's seat, her little feet stamping an irregular heartbeat into Christina's spine. When she turned to look at them, Edward had fallen asleep, the exhaustion of the day proving too much for him. His sleeping face wrenched her heart, and she pulled the car over, saying nothing as her daughter continued to kick the seat.

She took her mobile from the glove box and tapped out a message.

This isn't how I wanted to go about things, she wrote, *and I know it's the coward's way out. I think we both knew this was coming. I'm sorry. I don't want to hurt you, but what we're doing is wrong. I am wrong. Please forgive me.*

SEVEN

BROOKE

SEPTEMBER 2019

I stand in the doorway, staring at the charred and broken carcass that was once my home. I can only say 'home' rather than house – a 22 foot by 16 foot living space that doubled as my studio, with a small mezzanine floor above holding a mattress and a suitcase of permanently creased clothing. The gallery of paintings that once adorned the back wall is now a blackened mess of burnt canvas and rotten wood, interrupted only by the door that leads to the tiny shower room and toilet, and to the glorified cupboard that acts as office, storeroom and kitchen. This area is a shell now, destroyed by the fire that was started at the back door.

This row of terraced cottages – four in total – once housed the families of fishermen, the wives and children all living and sleeping under these small roofs, their existence dependent on the ocean just two hundred metres from their front doors. I am often met with the same questions from visitors and tourists – 'You live here? But how?' – and though even to me it seemed impossible at first, life has moulded to fit my needs, and it turned out that those needs are few.

The fire investigators concluded that the blaze was started by a petrol-soaked rag that was shoved through the window left ajar in the kitchen. It was a deliberate and targeted attack, and when I was

asked by police if there was anyone I knew of who could be responsible, the truthful answer was no one. I live a quiet life in a quiet
village. I speak to very few people. The thought that there is
someone who wants to hurt me in this way – to destroy my home
and my livelihood – crushes me, a tower of bricks stacked on my
heart.

Despite my fears, the contents of the filing cabinet survived the
fire, the metal withstanding the heat to protect the photographs
and paperwork stored within. There are still forms relating to my
mother's financial issues that need to be completed and sent off,
despite her death being almost a year ago. She left only a savings
account with a little over a thousand pounds in it. She had already
signed over Hillside Cottage to me, long before the Alzheimer's
made its inevitable turn from bad to worse, and the few other items
she owned – the collection of faded clothing, her television and her
radio – I donated to a charity shop in Fishguard. There are a
handful of cards, letters and school reports that she kept in a folder
– they moved with her from the house to the nursing home – now
tucked away in a drawer in the back room, too painful yet to look
through.

I remember the final signing of her will, when she knew that
her condition would deteriorate and there would come a time
when she might no longer be able to hold a pen. With every day
that passed during her long and debilitating illness, my mother's
hand started to feel different in my own. It grew softer and smaller,
and as her grip started to weaken, I felt her slipping away. I was
losing her, though in so many ways she had already been lost. We
had been lost to each other. She was too young, at just sixty-five
years old, to be diagnosed with Alzheimer's. I was too young to say
goodbye to her. We had lost half our time together to someone
else's sin, never able to rebuild what had been destroyed so many
years earlier.

'You're grieving,' Sylvia said to me one Sunday afternoon as I
was peeling carrots at her kitchen sink. 'I know she's still here, but
at the same time, she's not, my darling, is she?'

I said nothing, my back turned to her, head dipped to the task in hand. I caught my thumb with the blade of the peeler, winced as a line of blood surfaced on the skin, and then I cried, still facing the window, silently weeping for a truth I had until that moment not allowed myself to accept.

I am woken from my thoughts by a tap at the open door behind me. In the spring and summer months, when the weather permits it, the door to my gallery is always open, ready to welcome dog walkers and ramblers and the lunchtimers who stray over from the pub on the other side of the harbour. Quite often I sell nothing – people just want to browse and chat, and sometimes they do not want to speak at all, drawn by curiosity to the funny little ramshackle row of tiny cottages – but it is always nice to have the company, silent or otherwise, as though the space within these walls only comes to life when there is someone else here. During the winter, the village goes into hibernation. Visitors at my door are rare.

Outside, Oliver and Fin are standing on the pavement, the boy clutching a soft toy that looks as though at some time in its history it has been mauled by a dog. His head is lowered, his sandy hair covered with a thick bobble hat. The mild air that we have enjoyed these past few days has been replaced with a biting autumnal breeze, the skies drenched in grey as the seasons make an obvious shift. I wonder whether the scene here frightens him, remembering that Oliver said he had run at the sight of the fire.

'I would invite you in,' I tell them. 'But...' I gesture behind me. Oliver leans in to inspect the disarray, glancing with concern at the dropped beam above my head.

'Should you be in here?' he asks.

'I'm not staying. I just came to assess the damage.'

'Where did you stay last night?'

'At Sylvia's. My neighbour. She's said I can stay there as long as I need to while this place is sorted out.'

I see Oliver's focus rest on what used to be my gallery wall. He is staring at what was once a painting of a stormy sea, all blue-blacks and greys, a tiny boat caught on the crest of a bucking wave. Now the scene is one of devastation, a depiction of destruction.

'Maybe I could start a new movement,' I say. 'Fire art. Or ash drawings. There's probably an arsonist somewhere who already does it.'

The word 'arsonist' throws us into an uncomfortable silence, neither wanting to address last night's revelation. Oliver says nothing and looks away from the wall, the sound of my voice breaking the invisible spell under which he was caught.

'I confess,' he says, 'I had a look on your website last night. Your paintings were amazing.'

I am grateful for the compliment, but the inescapable use of the past tense leaves me feeling hollow.

'How do you capture the water like that? It's as though it's moving.'

I don't tell him that I'm an artistic one-trick pony, failing to mention that if I were given a face to replicate on paper, I couldn't draw a nose distinguishable from an eyebrow. I have never had the patience to capture the human form. People don't interest me, not in the way that nature does. 'Thank you. A lot of practice. Do you like to draw, Finley?'

As always, the boy says nothing. His head is lowered, face turned from the door; we shouldn't keep him here any longer, breathing in the burned air that still lingers around us. I cast an apologetic glance to Oliver, who shakes his head as though to reassure me that his son's silence isn't my fault.

We step outside and join Finley on the pavement, where the air is clean.

'Fin can draw, can't you?' Oliver says. 'Wait until I unpack, we'll get some of his masterpieces up on the fridge. Brooke can come over to see your gallery then.' He looks up at me before adding, 'If she'd like to.'

'I'd like that very much,' I say, and I smile at Finley, wondering at the same time what I'm doing. His father's invitation is loaded with more. I know nothing of these people, nothing of their circumstances, yet I sense enough to realise that their history includes some form of tragedy. My own life has already seen sufficient, and selfishly it occurs to me that it doesn't need to be exposed to any more.

'Anyway, I'm sorry for dropping in without warning. I just wanted to give you this.' He reaches into his coat pocket and pulls out a thick white envelope with an elastic band looped around it. 'There's three months there.'

And the first thought that passes through my mind, as unexpected as it is, is not of the cash that is inside this envelope, or even that his staying has made my life financially easier for a while, but just that he is staying.

'Okay. Thanks.'

I take the envelope from him and smile awkwardly. Payments for rent are usually made online; a lot of the time I never even come face to face with the people who stay at the house. I clean before they get there, open the windows wide to air the place, lay out fresh towels on the beds. I always leave a welcome hamper with essentials: tea bags, a loaf of bread, half a dozen eggs. I make sure there is milk in the fridge. I sometimes get a thank you message upon departure day; sometimes not. I have never spoken to a guest for as long as I have already spoken to Oliver.

An uncomfortable silence has fallen over us, the kind of awkwardness only generated by conversations involving money, and I smile at Finley, who has raised his head enough for me to see his face, his wind-pinched cheeks flushed pink against his pale complexion. His name suits him. There is something traditional about it, old-fashioned, and there is something of this about the child himself, his face stolen from a sepia photograph and placed into a world unknown to him.

'Anyway,' Oliver says, 'we should leave you in peace. Thanks again for letting us stay.'

'How soon do you want to move in? I can get the place ready by tomorrow, if you like.'

'You're sure that's not too soon?'

'It's no problem. I'll go over there later this afternoon, get it cleaned ready for you.'

'You don't need to worry,' he says. 'You've got enough to think about. It looked perfectly clean when we went there yesterday.'

'It's been empty for a while,' I admit. 'It'll need freshening up. Come back tomorrow for the key. About eleven-ish, will that be okay?'

Oliver musses his son's hair. 'That'll be perfect, won't it, Fin? Thank you.'

He takes Finley by the hand, and I follow them outside. His car is parked near the harbour, and I head back into the house as he gets his son into his car seat.

In my pocket, my mobile starts ringing. The sound is unfamiliar in this room – signal in the village is intermittent and unreliable – and I answer it quickly, keen to cut off its noisy tones.

'Hello?'

No one speaks, but I hear breathing at the other end of the line.

'Hello?' I say again.

As I move the phone from my ear, about to end the call, I hear her voice.

'Brooke.'

A single word, distant down the line. My stomach lurches, my heart tripping in my chest at the sound of my sister's voice speaking my name. I cling to the word, fighting for breath as I drown in air. I want to reply to her, but my own voice has been strangled. I would be talking to a ghost. My sister died a year ago.

EIGHT

CHRISTINA

FEBRUARY 2018

The morning before a night shift, Christina and Matthew would take the twins to the park. She found it difficult taking them on her own: Elise was a daredevil who would climb far too high, and as Edward was a tentative child who wanted assistance and constant reassurance, he would cry whenever his mother had to leave his side. It meant a choice between a wailing Edward and an injured Elise, and as neither was a desirable prospect, Christina took advantage of Matthew's help whenever it was available.

Besides that, she had been feeling unwell all morning. She had been suffering with dizziness and nausea again, and despite not being sick, she had the constant feeling that she was about to be. She had forced herself from the house hoping that some fresh air might ease her symptoms, knowing they wouldn't be eradicated.

Joel had called her twice that morning, on the cheap pay-as-you-go mobile she had bought at the start of their affair, not wanting her personal life to merge with her profession. She kept the phone with her, paranoid that if it wasn't on her person, it might somehow be discovered. She was going to have to find a way of destroying it so that the messages were irretrievable, but she hadn't had a chance to do it yet. If Matthew was going to find out at some point, she wanted it to come from her.

She pushed Edward on a swing and watched as Matthew helped guide Elise across a rope bridge. Though it was intended for children far older, Elise would push her father's arm away, fiercely independent, and a couple of times Christina winced as her daughter wobbled and seemed about to fall. Each time, Matthew caught her, and Christina felt a stab of guilt that seemed to pierce her heart. What had she done?

A memory took root at the forefront of her mind, transporting her away from the park in which she stood. Joel behind her, his strong hands holding her hips. A glass dish that had been used to hold keys and business cards for local tradespeople smashed on the wooden hallway floor, its contents littered at her feet. Her hands gripping the edge of the table as it shook with the rhythm that he pounded against her. It had been the first time she had been to his flat, and they hadn't made it as far as the bedroom. Later, on her way to the bathroom, she had cut her bare foot on a shard of glass that had sliced her skin at an angle, the incision deep and painful. She took the wound home with her, a punishment. She felt sick at the memory, having to force back tears as she returned her focus to her son.

She looked over to Matthew. Elise had moved from the rope bridge and was climbing the steps to the top of the slide, still shoving his hand away every time he tried to assist her ascent. He was a good father. Even at moments when things between them had been strained, Christina could never have accused him of being anything but brilliant where the children were concerned. He had woken night after night to settle a fractious teething Edward, and when Elise had discovered her voice – and with it the word 'no' – he had been the better of the two of them at soothing her tempers. He had never tried to shirk his share of nappy-changing or dealing with reflux – an unfortunate ailment that both twins had suffered with – and he had taken an interest in the things she suspected some fathers left to their wives or partners: Christmas presents, colour choices for their bedroom walls, first pairs of shoes.

So why did she feel so detached from him?

'Would you like to play with your sister on the roundabout?' she asked Edward, bringing the swing to a stop. He reached for her, and she lifted him out. She stooped to pull down the leg of his puddle suit, which was halfway up his calf, and as soon as she was done, he ran, wobbly in his wellies, to join Elise at the roundabout.

'You cold enough yet?' Matthew asked, pulling a face. 'Here.' He retrieved his wallet from his jacket pocket and pulled out a ten-pound note. 'Don't fancy popping over to the café, do you?' He tilted his head and smiled coaxingly.

Christina gave a mock sigh. 'The usual, is it?'

'Your mother's a gem,' he said, scooping Edward up and helping him onto the seat of the roundabout. 'Right then, hold on tight...' And with that, he started pushing the children in circles, running faster as their laughter grew louder. Christina waited a moment, convinced that Edward would start crying or call to his father to stop, but when he did neither, she left them, heading out of the playground and making her way to the café on the other side of the main road.

She was greeted inside by a blast of warm air from an overhead heater and the aroma of fresh coffee and newly baked treats. She scanned the fridges at the counter and picked out chocolate cookies for the children before ordering two takeaway Americanos. As she waited for the drinks, she checked her mobile. She had heard a message notification as she was pushing Edward on the swing, though she hadn't yet checked it.

You could have told me in person. That was it. Somehow the message said more for having so few words than had he constructed a tirade of angry recriminations. She had taken the coward's way out. She felt guilty for it, but it was nothing compared to the overwhelming shame that consumed her every time she looked at her family.

Your mother's a gem. Said so casually, and with such unthinking conviction. And yet Matthew was more wrong than he could ever have imagined.

'Two Americanos?'

She snapped her phone cover shut, collected the drinks and headed back to the park. When she got there, Matthew and the children were at the climbing frame, where Matthew was holding Edward around the waist as he attempted to tackle the monkey bars. Elise was clinging to her father's right leg, apparently trying to climb it as she filled the air with manic whooping noises.

'I would offer you a hand, but...' Christina raised the cardboard cups in her hands and shrugged a mock apology.

'Snack,' Elise said, her little voice clipping the word with a command, and she let go of her father's leg to follow Christina to the nearest bench, clapping her hands with excitement as the paper bag emerged from her mother's pocket, its rustling teasing the promise of a sugary treat.

'Edward,' Christina called. 'I'd come and get your cookie before your sister eats them both.'

'Come on, little monkey,' she heard Matthew say, and he carried a giggling Edward over to them, arms outstretched as though he was flying. 'What, none for the grown-ups? That's the last time I send you.' He winked as he took his coffee from her, and they sat like bookends, the twins wedged on the bench between them.

Elise had somehow already managed to get chocolate in her hair, her cookie half eaten, while Edward nibbled at the edge of his. 'Mmm,' she said, dragging the sleeve of her puddle suit across her mouth. 'Yum!'

Matthew laughed and caught Christina's eye, giving her a look so filled with contentment it made her want to cry. He was happy with what he had – with what *they* had – in a way that she had taken for granted. Her stomach churned, carving emptiness into her insides, and she felt a swell of recurring nausea course through her.

'You okay?' Matthew asked, and she realised she had been staring at the top of her son's head, at the light catching on his hair from the winter sun that was struggling between the clouds.

'Fine.' She sipped her drink, wished she had added sugar before leaving the café. 'What time do you need to go to work?'

Matthew worked as an air traffic controller at Heathrow Airport, a job that involved long shifts often with antisocial hours. Christina had never minded his work patterns – she had always been busy with her own projects and had quite enjoyed having the house to herself some evenings – but since having the children, the nights had grown longer, and she sometimes found herself dreading the solitude. There was always something to do – ironing, tidying, admin – but by the end of the evening, once she had settled the twins, she quite often found that all she could manage was to sit in front of the television or go to bed.

Or, in more recent months, message Joel.

'We should get going soon,' Matthew said, tilting his head to the sky. 'It looks as though it's going to pour down.'

'No,' Elise said, her face contorting into an exaggerated pout, and she slid from the bench before stamping her foot like an enraged rabbit.

'Two more minutes,' Christina said, delaying the inevitable tantrum that would ensue. 'Then Daddy has to get back for work.'

Elise ran back to the climbing frame while Edward stayed at his mother's side, still eating his cookie. Matthew smiled and rolled his eyes before getting up to supervise her.

'Would you like to play on anything else before we go?' Christina asked Edward.

He said nothing, his answer offered in a cuddle as he shielded himself from the growing cold.

A minute or two later, Matthew was able to quell Elise's tantrum before it escalated to a scale sufficient to draw the full attention of the park. They took a child each, pulling off muddy wellies and stripping off damp puddle suits before strapping them into their car seats and tucking them in with blankets. Just a normal family having enjoyed a trip to the park together. A normal, happy family.

When they got home, there was a parcel waiting on the doorstep.

'Why do they insist on doing this?' Christina sighed, pushing Elise up on her hip. 'Anybody could just walk past and...' She recognised the company name on the side of the box – a local florist who had a shop on the high street.

'Everything okay?' Matthew asked, stopping just behind her.

'Fine. I'll come back for that.'

She nudged the box to one side with her leg before unlocking the front door and setting Elise down in the hallway. Her daughter shot off to the living room, and once Matthew and Edward were also in the house, Christina went back to the doorstep to retrieve the box.

Rather than go to the kitchen, she took it into her treatment room and put it on the desk in the corner. She grappled with the tape at the edges before tearing it loose, then pulled open the top. It was a beautiful bouquet of cream roses and blush-pink lilies, no expense spared. She moved some of the flowers aside as she searched for an accompanying note, finding a small card propped on a stick among them. With a glance towards the living room, she took it out and tore it open.

You don't get to do this xx

NINE

BROOKE

SEPTEMBER 2019

Sylvia is in the garden pegging out washing when I tell her I'm going out for a walk. It looks as though it is going to rain, though I don't have the heart to tell her.

'You okay, love?' she asks.

'Fine. Just need a bit of fresh air.'

She stops what she's doing, a damp tea towel gripped in one hand, a plastic peg clutched in the other. She looks at me with a pinched expression, something she wants to tell me held back.

'What's the matter?' I ask.

'I saw Tom just now.' Tom is the landlord of the pub, another resident who has been in the village for as long as I am able to remember.

'Okay.' I wonder where this is leading.

'There was a break-in over at Jean Miller's place last night.'

'Really? Is she okay?' Though she has said some terrible things about me in the past – awful, unforgivable things – I wish Jean no harm. She lives a quiet life now, even quieter than mine, and we manage to keep a respectful distance from each other, our paths never needing to cross.

'Shaken up by it, but otherwise fine. She didn't see or hear anyone. Wouldn't have her hearing aid on in bed, would she?

Came down in the morning to find the place smashed up. Strange thing, though: by all accounts they didn't seem to take much. Bit of cash that was in the kitchen.'

First the fire, now this. Aberfach has a tiny population. Our closest thing to a crime wave is a bit of selfish parking by tourists during the summer months. It seems too much of a coincidence that there would be a fire and a robbery in the space of just a few days, and that the two would not be connected.

'This never happens here,' I say quietly.

'Exactly.' Sylvia pegs her tea towel on the line. 'Kids, I reckon. They've been having that trouble over in Fishguard with all the antisocial behaviour, haven't they? Only a matter of time before it spills over, I suppose.'

'Maybe. Anyway, she's okay, that's the main thing. I'll see you in a bit.'

I leave the house and make my way to the coastal path, where I take a route I usually avoid, along a section of cliff edge I haven't been to in years. All night I heard my sister's voice repeat my name, the single word looping on a taunting, eerie cycle, and when I eventually found sleep, she was there with me, her face resting behind my eyes as my sleeping brain tried to chase her away in dreams. I awoke with the sound of her voice in my ears, the bitter taste of smoke still clawing at my throat.

I can make no sense of what happened yesterday. My sister is dead. She has been dead for a year, and yet I know that was her voice I heard, as familiar to me as my own.

But was it, really? I had moved the phone from my ear – I was about to end the call, believing it to be a mistake of some kind. Did it really happen, or was my mind playing tricks on me, tiredness making me hear things that weren't real? The fire has thrown my life off balance, thoughts of Delta dominating my mind during the first anniversary of her death. Perhaps my subconscious simply gave me what I had been hoping for.

When I get back to the village, I see Oliver and Finley near the path that leads up to Hillside Cottage.

'Oliver. Oliver!' He turns and sees me waving, and they wait for me at the bottom of the hill. 'Everything okay?' I ask.

They came to meet me a few hours ago to collect the key, Oliver asking me again whether I was sure I wouldn't need the property. But even if money wasn't an issue, I couldn't return there, and besides, I think Sylvia is secretly enjoying having the company. I presume that since I saw Oliver and Fin earlier, their time has been spent unpacking and making themselves at home. The thought is a strange one. People come and go – they pass through. They never stay, not for periods of time such as Oliver has planned.

'I think we've had a power cut,' he explains. 'I'm sorry, I'm probably being thick, but I just can't work it out.'

I realise that in my haste to get him moved in and secure the rental, I have forgotten to tell him that the electricity and gas run off a meter. I apologise and explain that the card needs topping up. He looks at me, bemused.

'It should be on top of the meter,' I tell him. 'I'll show you.' Then I smile at Fin. 'What have you been up to this morning?' I ask. I know he is unlikely to answer me, but I don't want him to feel ignored either. I wonder whether he speaks to his father when it's only the two of them there, or whether this is his default setting, muted to a life of silence, communication stretching as far as a nodded head or the gesture of a raised arm. It must be incredibly isolating for him, and for Oliver too.

Oliver smiles that apologetic smile he has offered before in the aftermath of his young son's non-response, and answers for him despite his obvious reluctance to do so. 'Fin's been helping me unpack, haven't you? We've been setting up a den in that walk-in wardrobe.'

'Best use for it. That space is wasted on clothes.' I smile at Fin again, but he lowers his head, clutching his father's hand. 'I think I just saw a dolphin,' I tell him. 'You catch glimpses of them every now and then when it's clear enough. You'll have to get your dad to take you out on a boat one day, to see them up close.'

'You can do that?' Oliver asks.

'There's one company that has a glass-bottomed boat. Brilliant as long as you don't get seasick.'

'We'll have to go,' he says, giving his son's arm a gentle shake to encourage some enthusiasm from him.

When we reach the house, I expect to see piles of boxes in the living room, but other than a few of Finley's toys, it's just as I saw it last. I imagine that living in a B and B means they haven't been able to accumulate much in the way of material things. I wonder what has happened to the possessions accrued in their previous life, wherever that may have been. Perhaps they are all in storage, or maybe Oliver decided to cut loose to save himself from the emotional pull of the past.

Fin's toys are spread out on a play mat in front of the television – a collection of wooden trains and a plastic track that winds to a halt at the skirting board. He returns to them, occupying himself while Oliver and I go to the kitchen.

'He wanted to watch a bit of TV,' he explains. 'It was the end of the world when I couldn't get it working.'

'I'm really sorry,' I say again, as I gesture to one of the cupboards. 'I don't know how this slipped my mind.' There is a box in the cupboard that hides the meter. I take out the card that sits on top. 'This needs topping up – I usually do it at the Londis in Fishguard. There should be backup credit on there, but maybe it's been used up. I'll go and do it for you now.'

I catch him looking at my arm, and realise that my sleeve has risen to reveal the burn beneath. I didn't feel it at the time, my jacket alight; the pain came later, delayed like grief.

'You don't have to do that. I can go.'

'No, honestly, it's my fault – there should have been enough to see you through a week. I'll have to get it changed,' I add. 'I mean, it works well when the house is only in use for a week or two at a time, but long-term these things are a bit of a pain.'

'I'm really embarrassed,' he says, taking a step back and folding his arms across his chest. 'I'm sorry... I should have been able to work that out for myself, shouldn't I?'

'I should have mentioned it, don't worry.'

'Are you okay?'

I pull my sleeve down. 'I'm fine.'

'Have the police said any more about the fire?'

'Nothing more than what they said the other night.' Nausea rises in my throat.

'God, I'm sorry.'

Behind him, I notice that he has already stuck a couple of Fin's drawings to the fridge. One looks like an attempt at a dinosaur; the other is a person, stick legs and a round body. They are accomplished efforts for a child so young.

'He's good, isn't he?' I say, pointing to them, hoping to change the subject. 'You've got yourself a budding talent there.'

He smiles. 'He doesn't get it from me.' The smile fades, and an awkward silence falls between us. Where is Finley's mother? I wonder. Why are they here alone, so far from where they must once have called home?

In the corner of the kitchen, I see the ghost of Delta, a fleeting memory of her, eight years old, sitting on the worktop singing a Madonna song into a wooden spoon my mother has been using to mix batter for Yorkshire puddings.

Brooke.

'Are you okay?' Oliver is looking at me with concern.

'Sorry. I'm fine. I'll go and top this up,' I say, keen to avert my mind from where it has drifted. 'I won't be long.'

'Thank you.'

I go to leave, and he steps aside, but I step the same way so that he is blocking my path to the door. He hesitates for a moment, looking at me – a moment in which too many unuttered words are granted exchange – then apologises and moves. I say goodbye to Finley on my way past, but he doesn't look up from his toys.

Outside, I wonder whether I imagined the moment that just passed between us. I couldn't decipher the way Oliver looked at me if I tried, though perhaps I am now remembering more than was really there. It has been so long since anyone looked at me in any way other than 'Brooke from the terrace' that maybe I am allowing myself to imagine something more. Perhaps he is just lonely.

If he is searching for an escape, it seems to me that he has chosen the wrong place. This is a landscape characterised by isolation, the miles of coastline interrupted only by little pockets of civilisation that exist within their own limited bubbles. This is a beautiful part of the country, rugged and wild, but you can only survive here if you have the armoury of family, or if you have chosen loneliness as a way of life. Maybe Oliver has made that choice, or perhaps, I think, he has been forced to it through circumstance. Either way, there is something about him that inexplicably makes me long to learn more.

At the bottom of the hill, my attention is drawn to the pub near the harbour. I see someone going inside – tall, dark-haired; too familiar. A shiver passes through me. He hasn't been here in so long – not to my knowledge, at least. I head for the pub, not knowing what I would do if I was to come face to face with him. He can't do anything to me, not with other people there, and yet I find it hard to believe that he would do anything again, not after all this time. He took what he wanted a long time ago. At the top of the steps that lead to the pub's front door, I stop. Beneath my jacket, my heart races, and my mind has taken me to a place I have for so long tried to avoid.

You have put yourself back there, Brooke – not him. Stop it. Stop it.

With a deep breath and the knowledge that my resilience is stronger than I credit it, I go inside the building. It is quiet – it is always quiet on weekday afternoons – and the only people here are the landlord and a man sitting in the corner, a dog resting at his feet.

'Brooke,' Tom greets me. 'Don't see you in here often.'

I smile awkwardly, realising that I have no reason to be in here.

I can hardly ask if Lewis just walked in before me; it would make me look as though I was stalking him. Besides, everyone knows our history – everyone thinks they know it, at least – and it would only serve to draw negative and unwanted attention to myself.

I cannot think of anything to say, no reason to have come in here simply to walk out again, so I order a drink, using the excuse that I need a change of wallpaper for ten minutes.

'Feeling a bit cooped up over at Sylvia's, is it?' he asks as he pours me a glass of wine. I wonder what I am doing, drinking mid afternoon; even one will probably result in a headache tomorrow.

'Something like that,' I say as he passes me the drink. 'Thanks.' Then I realise I haven't got my purse with me and have no money to pay for the drink. I sigh, embarrassed. 'I've forgotten my purse,' I say, making a point of checking pockets I already know are empty. 'Sorry. Can I pop it in later?'

'Have it on the house. You've got enough to worry about.'

Then I see him. Tall, dark-haired; so similar that from a distance he looked exactly like Lewis. But it isn't him. Relief makes my body sag, and the held breath that leaves my lungs is audible. The man passes me as he makes his way to the corner of the room, where he sits opposite the man with the dog.

I drink my wine at the bar, alone, too quickly. When I leave the pub, sea air hits me, making my head whirl. First Delta and now Lewis. I am hearing things. I am seeing things that aren't real, haunted by shadows. I am living with too many ghosts.

TEN

CHRISTINA

A week passed before Christina was able to begin to focus on repairing a marriage her husband hadn't even seemed to notice was damaged. Packing the twins and their overnight things into the car was a process made more difficult than it might already have been by Elise's recent tendency towards obsessive routines. That afternoon, the twenty-two-month-old decided for the third time that week that she wouldn't get into the car until each and every one of the fourteen soft toys that sat lined up against the wall beneath her bedroom window had been put into a bag to make the journey with her, and Christina didn't have the energy to argue against it.

Once Mr Ted had been pulled from the bag and reunited with his red-faced owner, Christina was able to make the journey to her brother's place with little further fuss. Leighton lived with his girl-friend, Alice, in a flat in Hampstead, not far from the park. The twins had been over a year old when Christina had first dared to leave them for an evening, and Alice and Leighton had enjoyed having them there so much that they had decorated the spare bedroom as a nursery/playroom, insisting that should Christina and Matthew ever feel the need for a night off, they would be more than happy to have Edward and Elise to stay. Christina suspected they were broody – Leighton perhaps even more so than Alice –

and the twins offered an opportunity to find out how they might adjust to life as a family. They had probably reasoned that if they could cope with two, then one would be a breeze, though Christina had no idea whether this was an accurate assumption.

Leighton and Alice were waiting in the parking area when Christina arrived, ready to help with getting the twins and the assortment of bags that inevitably accompanied them up to the second-floor flat. Alice picked up Elise, while Leighton went to the boot.

'Got toys,' Elise said, wrapping her arms around Alice's neck and squeezing her tightly.

'So I see,' Alice laughed.

'Thanks so much for this,' Christina said. 'I really appreciate it.'

'Probably a bit overdue, by the looks of things,' Leighton said, lifting open the boot. 'You okay? You look exhausted.'

'Thank you. Nice to see you too.'

He pulled the remaining items from the car and put them on the ground, waiting for Alice to guide the twins away before turning to his sister. 'Honestly, though. Is everything all right?'

'Everything is fine, baby brother, thank you. Wait until you've got kids of your own – you'll realise this look is normal.' Christina closed the boot and put her arms around her brother to hug him. It wasn't something she usually did, and she realised as soon as she'd done so that it might only heighten his suspicions that something was wrong. They hadn't hugged in years, not since the aftermath of Bethany's funeral. The thought of her sister caught her off guard, filling her chest with sadness.

'Eat something,' Leighton said, jabbing a finger to her ribs. 'You're wasting away.'

Christina rolled her eyes. 'Good luck,' she joked, pressing the thought of Bethany to the back of her mind. 'Call me if you need me, okay?'

She checked her phone repeatedly in the car on the way home, half expecting Leighton and Alice to have decided within moments of the twins being there that they had changed their minds. The first thing that greeted her when she arrived back at the house was the vase of flowers on the hallway table. She couldn't throw them away – that would have only looked suspicious – and she didn't want to put them in the kitchen or living room where she would have had to see them regularly, so they had ended up near the front door, a reminder every time she left and entered the house of the type of person she had allowed herself to become. She couldn't wait for them to die so she could dispose of them.

She went to the kitchen and set to work on dinner with the reassurance that it wasn't too late to make her marriage work. Small steps – a meal together, a few child-free hours, more effort on her part. She would gather up the frayed and faded pieces and stitch them back together, colour life back into them one at a time. She and Matthew had more history in their seven and a half years together than many couples accumulated over several decades. He was a good man. She was going to be a better wife.

She prepared the lasagne, then set to work chopping salad ingredients. It was nothing too complex, but it was Matthew's favourite – the first meal they had shared at a restaurant after reuniting seven years earlier. By 8 p.m., the kitchen was filled with the warm scent of tomatoes and Italian herbs. After setting the table, she went to the fridge and took a chilled bottle of white wine from the shelf. She left it unopened, expecting that when he came home, Matthew might want to go for a quick shower first, then change into more comfortable clothes.

By 8.15, he was still not back, probably caught in evening traffic on the M25. She tried his mobile, but it went straight to answerphone. The lasagne was keeping warm in the oven, and she put the salad bowl in the fridge. The waiting bottle of wine proved too much of a temptation, so she opened it and poured herself a glass, taking it to the living room, where she turned on the television. She flicked through channels aimlessly as she drank the wine, its sweet sting burning her throat. At 8.40, she tried

Matthew's mobile again, but again it went straight to answerphone.

She poured herself another glass and drank it while she ate her portion of lasagne, now blackened at the edges and barely warm. At some point after finishing her food and leaving her plate on the coffee table, she fell asleep on the sofa with the television still on. She was awoken by the sound of the front door.

'I am so sorry.' Matthew was in the doorway, framed in the darkness by the light in the hall.

Christina sat up and pressed her fingertips to her eyes. 'What time is it?'

'Just gone eleven.'

'You said you'd be back by eight.'

'I know, and I'm really sorry. Things overran and I had to stay later. I should have messaged.'

She stood and picked up her plate. 'Everything okay at work?'

'Engine failure on one of the planes.'

'I had to eat, sorry. I couldn't wait any longer.'

'Don't apologise, it's fine. I'm sorry I couldn't call.'

'Do you want yours?' she asked, passing him to go through to the kitchen. 'I can reheat it in the microwave.'

'It'll keep for tomorrow, won't it? I'm not really hungry. Sorry.'

She took the plate to the sink, where she washed it and placed it on the dish rack.

'Hey.' Matthew stood behind her, his hand on her arm. 'Are you mad at me? I'm really sorry.' When she turned to him, he kissed her, his mouth open against hers. It took her by surprise. She couldn't remember the last time they had kissed in such a way. She thought of Joel, of his hands on her skin, and a hot guilt coursed through her. It was her fault, obviously.

She kissed him back, willing herself to feel the way she knew she was supposed to. 'Are the kids at your brother's?' he asked, and when she nodded, his hand snaked beneath her top. As it moved to her breast, an involuntary flinch shuddered across her body. She was sure he had felt it too, thrumming through the fingers that caressed her flesh. Thoughts of Joel flooded her senses, and she closed her eyes, trying to push him to the back of her mind. He was a thing of the past now. Gone. She could still put things right.

With this thought in mind – hope for the future temporarily replacing her regret of the past – she began to reciprocate. She reached for the back of her husband's head, locked her fingers in his hair, tilted her head back as his mouth moved down towards her throat. This was Matthew, the man she had married – the man who loved her and the children more than anyone ever had or could. Matthew, who had saved her all those years ago, who had been there – and stayed – at a time when so many others might have walked away. He knew her better than anyone. She knew him better than anyone.

So why did it feel so difficult to just *be*?

Later, as he slept with one arm still draped across her body, Christina wondered what was happening to her. She had watched them as though from outside her own body, an intruder on an intimate moment – a peeping Tom. She felt disconnected from herself, removed from him in a way that felt disloyal and yet somehow normal, resetting her own reality to the format in which it should always have played out. She was a performer on a stage, working through the actions of her character, reciting her learned lines.

She should be happy here, she thought. This life should make her feel complete.

So why did everything feel so forced? And if everything was really as it was meant to be, why did she feel like she was acting?

ELEVEN

BROOKE

SEPTEMBER 2019

Unable to sleep, I leave Sylvia's house and go down to the harbour, where I sit on the solitary bench that looks out over the sea. The sound of the water lapping at the harbour walls is rhythmic in its repetition, and the light of the moon draws shadows from the boats that sit docked and purposeless. When I close my eyes, my senses are overrun, the smell of the evening air bringing with it a comforting familiarity. As teenagers, my sister and I would come here regularly on weekend evenings to have the conversations we didn't want our parents to overhear. We would watch boats leave the harbour and make up stories about the men who steered them, the families they left at home; we would wait for a glimpse of Lewis, the Millers' son – away at technical college somewhere but home during the holidays, daring each other to speak to him, both knowing that we would never be brave enough. We would share our dreams and swap our secrets, the only interruptions those made by people leaving the pub across the road. We would long for the day we were old enough to get served at the bar, wishing the years to pass so that we would no longer be trapped by the restrictions of our age. Now, I would give anything to go to that place, to that naïve feeling that the future was a place filled with better things.

'You so fancy him,' Delta had said, her legs swinging against the harbour wall, her long hair lifted by the breeze that swept in from the sea behind her.

'No I don't.' I remember blushing, always useless at lying.

We had watched Lewis go into the pub with his father. He was five years older than me, and as teenagers, that gap had felt like an uncrossable chasm.

'What if I speak to him for you?' she said.

'Why would I want you to do that?'

'Because you'll never do it.' Delta jumped up onto the wall and stuck a long leg out in front of her before pivoting carefully on one foot. 'But then what if he likes me more?'

She was goading me; she was always goading me. She knew she was the prettier of the two of us, the more confident, and she had no problem with reminding me that despite being older, I was very much in her shadow.

'He wouldn't,' I said, chewing my lip at the possibility that once Delta was a little older, he might. 'You're just a kid.'

She smiled. 'Not for much longer, though.' She paused, stuck her hands on her hips and pouted. 'Which is my best side, do you think? This one?' She pivoted again, spinning too fast; so fast that I feared she would lose her footing and fall. 'Or this one?'

'Shut up,' I said with a small smile. 'He wouldn't like either side – not with that stupid face you're pulling.'

Delta thrust a dramatic arm in the air before putting her hand on her chest. 'Aargh... I'm bleeding. Your words have struck a fatal wound through my heart.' She jumped from the wall and dropped against my legs, a fallen heroine from a Shakespeare play. Her head tilted to the dark evening sky as she laughed, her long, soft hair in my lap, and I laughed with her, both of us oblivious to the real-life tragedies that awaited us. Later, she got back up and returned to the wall, resuming her role as tightrope walker, once again precariously close to the edge. She stretched each leg in front of her as she walked its length, raising her feet and pointing her toes like a ballerina, like a gymnast navigating a bar.

'Stop being silly,' I told her. 'You'll fall.'

At the thought of a fall, I am transported to another memory, of my mother's room at the nursing home, the depressing beigeness of it all and the unmistakable smell unknown to any other kind of place. I see my mother sitting in her chair at the window, looking but not really seeing; myself at the edge of the bed, stalled by the frailty of a woman once so strong and capable.

'Look after her.'

'Who?'

'Your sister.'

It had been one of my mother's lucid moments, a glimmer of clarity amid the confusion that characterised much of her dialogue.

'She's old enough to look after herself now, Mum.'

'That may well be so,' she said, turning her face to the window. 'But she can't, can she?' Her eyes narrowed, focusing on something outside. 'Tell her to get down from there. She's going to fall.'

And just like that, lucidity was lost again. My mother was pointing to the small square of garden outside her window, her fingers dancing erratically as she gestured to something unseen, some delusion or memory that kept her stolen from real time.

I had recalled the conversation on repeat after their deaths. *She's going to fall* – as though she had known what would happen. Afterwards, in those drawn out, eye-blink days between Delta's death and her own, I wondered whether my mother had somehow been aware of what had happened, a maternal instinct having awoken some shift in her. Had she felt her younger daughter's soul escape the air somehow, the physical miles that rested between them no barrier to the connection that had kept child tethered invisibly to mother? Had she just known, somehow, that Delta would be taken from this world, her death played out in the garden that day, a hellish waking nightmare that I had explained away to myself as a hallucination?

I allow my focus to rest on the row of terraced cottages, on the abandoned half-shell that used to be my home. For a moment, I imagine the heavy scent of smoke still in the air, its smell continuing to linger with me. I wish that Delta was here with me now. She was the stronger of us in so many ways. Would she know what to do? She was always smarter than I was, more confident. Would she find a way to work out who was responsible for sending my life and my work up in flames?

There are lights on up at Hillside Cottage. From here, the window of my childhood bedroom can be seen, its views casting over the Atlantic Ocean as it pushes out into the distance and merges into a sky of grey. Though it is late, the bedroom light is on. I imagine Oliver in there now, sitting beside Finley's bed, the boy raised from sleep by some noise outside his window. In my mind, he is sitting on the carpet, an arm resting on the duvet, the other hand holding a book that he reads aloud, his voice low and melodic as it soothes Finley back to sleep. I wonder what he does once his son is asleep – just how lonely the evenings might sometimes become. I am thinking about him more than I should, and yet there is nothing about any of my thoughts that makes me want to stop them.

Music floats from the pub across the street, distant and upbeat, distracting me. The sound of voices chatting and laughing grows louder as the door is opened, a cluster of drinkers spilling out into the night. I watch them make their way down the steps that lead to the road, couples exchanging hugs and saying their goodbyes, and as they branch away from one another, I see him again. He heads across the road alone, his hands thrust into his jacket pockets, his head dipped slightly. The same man who looked so much like him before? But no.

A pain rips through my chest as I realise that this time there is no mistake. It *is* Lewis. I should go back to Sylvia's house – though I would have to pass him now to get there – yet I sit here trans-fixed, my eyes not moving from him. And then he looks up. Looks up, sees me, and stops. We stay as we are for a moment, both of us inert – two night creatures sizing each other up, each silently calculating the possible danger presented by the other. My hand tightens around my phone; I remind myself that Oliver is just a minute away. He could be here in less than that if I need him to be.

Lewis's face is expressionless, and when he starts walking again, there is an awful moment in which I think he is going to make his way over to me. He doesn't; instead, he heads for the main road leading from the village, presumably returning to his mother's house. But not before he glances back to the terrace. He knows, I think. He knows about the fire. As I watch him grow smaller as he gets further away, I realise I have frozen. He did this to me once before, years ago. I cannot let him do it again. With a heart that beats so hard it is painful, I get up and hurry across the street, back to the safety of Sylvia's house.

TWELVE
CHRISTINA
MARCH 2018

It was a dry day, so Christina took the children out in the garden to let them burn off some energy. Matthew was on a day shift and would be home within the hour, and on such days, he liked to give them a bath and put them to bed while Christina took the opportunity to catch up with any housework that needed to be done. It was mild for early March, and as the twins ran in and out of the pop-up tent that she had retrieved from the shed, she took the opportunity to just *be* for a moment, with nowhere to go and nothing to do other than listen to the sounds of her children shrieking and laughing as they chased each other in circles.

Matthew had left early for work, despite having got home so late the night before. He had fallen asleep not long after sex, leaving her lying beside him staring at the darkened ceiling as she tried to make sense of everything that plagued her mind. When she went downstairs to make herself a cup of peppermint tea, she took the flowers from the hallway table and threw them in the bin before washing out the vase.

You don't get to do this xx

She hadn't heard from Joel again, and though she had been

tempted to text him, she hadn't done so. She was worried that a response from her might lead to something more; if she ignored him, maybe he would take the hint and leave her alone.

She crouched to hide behind the tent before jumping out at the children with an exaggerated roar. Elise screamed with excitement and Edward ran to the end of the lawn, and Christina caught them in turn, scooping Edward up under her arm before chasing a squealing Elise into the corner. The three of them fell onto the grass, giggling, and as Christina looked up at the sky – a wash of pale blue and smudged grey – she was suddenly overwhelmed by the vastness of the world around her, and the infinite everyday details of the comparatively tiny life she had taken for granted.

As she tried to drag her thoughts away from those that persisted in racking her with guilt, she heard the house phone ringing. Leaving the twins to return to the tent, she went into the kitchen and picked up the phone from its stand, taking it into the garden as she answered.

'Hello?'

'Chrissie? How are things?'

It was lovely to hear Ollie's voice. They hadn't spoken since Christmas, distance and lifestyles making face-to-face meetings rare and phone conversations fleeting. There was always something comforting in just hearing her brother-in-law speak – an audio link to the past, as though if she tuned in a little closer, somewhere alongside his voice she would also hear her sister's.

'We're all okay, thanks. Just out in the garden getting some fresh air while the rain holds off for five minutes. You both okay?'

'Yeah, not bad. We're at the park. Fin's been asking about you and the twins – we're wondering if you've got any plans for their birthday?'

'Not yet,' Christina confessed. There it was again – the stab of guilt that pierced like a blade. The twins' birthday was in little over a month's time, yet she had barely given it a thought. 'We'll definitely be having a party, though, and it'll be here at the house. I'm just not sure what day yet – their birthday is on a Wednesday, so it'll have to be one of the weekends either side. Do you think you'll be able to come? I know it's a long way for you.'

'Count us in,' Ollie said. 'Fin would love to see you all. And me too.'

'Is he sleeping any better?'

The last time they had spoken, Ollie had told her that Fin was waking up frequently in the night, crying.

'On and off. He still won't tell me what the nightmares are about, though.'

'Poor kid. I wonder if he's trying to protect you. I mean, I know he's still so young, but children are sharper than we sometimes give them credit for, aren't they?'

Ollie sighed. 'I wish I knew what it was. Anyway, wait until I tell him about the party – it'll give him something to look forward to. Hopefully it might settle him a bit.'

'I hope so.' She was distracted by the twins; mainly by Elise trying to drag the tent to the floor while her brother was still inside it. 'Elise! Don't do that, please.' She wedged the phone between her chin and her shoulder while she rescued her son, and Elise ran down to the far end of the garden, dodging any further scolding.

'Give him a big hug from us,' she said. 'And you can stay here, you know that. Why don't you come for a while, if you can – make a holiday of it?'

'Thanks, Chrissie, I appreciate that. Matthew okay?'

'Yeah, he's all right. Busy with work, as always.'

There was a pause that Christina didn't know how to fill. This void inevitably rested between them at some point during every conversation, when neither of them was sure what to say to the other or how to speak without giving way under the weight of all the things left unsaid. Neither of them ever mentioned Bethany's name, afraid it may break the other, though she was the person who held them together, the reason they kept in touch. Speaking to Ollie, just hearing his voice, felt like being transported back to the past, and Christina would have given anything she had to go back there, just for a moment.

'If you think of anything the twins might like for presents, can you send me some ideas?' Ollie asked.

'Don't worry about presents. You and Fin just being here will be the best present for us all.'

'Thanks, Chrissie. It'll be lovely to see you all. Let me know when you've decided the date and we'll go from there, shall we?'

'Will do. Don't forget to give Fin that hug, okay? And one for you, too.'

'And one for the twins from us. Speak to you soon.'

She said goodbye and they ended the call. The twins' birthday would give her something to focus on, she thought – it could be a fresh start for them all. She would speak to Matthew that evening, decide which weekend they could hold the party. She would have to write some invitations and ask the nursery to pass them on to the parents of the children the twins played with. Perhaps she could do something themed, she thought – a dinosaurs and unicorns crossover to keep both Edward and Elise happy.

She called the children into the house for dinner, trying to occupy her thoughts with party planning, but no matter how much she tried to distract herself, it was impossible to avoid what haunted her. Speaking to Ollie had brought everything back, his voice alone enough to resurrect the grief she had tried to bury. She ushered the children into the kitchen and closed the patio doors, knowing that once they were safe in the house, she could let the tears flow.

The police investigation into the fire delivers glimmers of answers before each is snuffed out. A few teenage boys are questioned, but no charges are brought against anyone. Fingerprints were recovered from the window frame in the kitchen, but a match hasn't yet been found. A lack of evidence makes anything difficult to prove, and with the village as it is, there are no CCTV cameras about to help identify the culprit. It makes me wonder again about those boys I saw on their bikes the evening of the fire. I didn't recognise any of them, but would they really have been bold enough to hang about to watch the fire crew put out a blaze that one of them had started? Perhaps it wasn't so unheard of. Last year, in some of the inland towns not far from here, there was a spate of fires started by youths who thought boredom was an excuse for arson. But why target me? If a disgruntled teenager was looking to make some sort of statement, setting fire to a tiny art gallery in one of the quietest villages in the world was hardly likely to make him front-page news. It seems far more likely that the fire was started by someone I know, and there is still only one person who is capable of such cruelty.

Among the photographs and paperwork that were stored in the filing cabinet in the back room, I find a paint set – a small rectangular tin with six watercolours and two brushes. It was left at the house by a family who came to the village on holiday last summer, and though I meant to put it out for anyone else who might like to use it during their stay, it got mixed up in my things somehow and ended up back here. I wonder whether Fin might like it.

In what was once my makeshift kitchen, I look at the window where the petrol-soaked rag was thrown into my home, wondering whether Lewis's hand might have started the blaze. I might have been inside when it was done, I think. Though it was afternoon when the fire was started, I may have decided to go for a lie-down. I might have been unwell and asleep, oblivious. Had the person who lit that rag and pushed it through the window considered the fact that I could have been here? Had that, in fact, been their intention?

Thoughts of the fire have become obsessive. I have gone through it over and over, detailing the moments before I opened the front door. Was somebody still there, just beyond those walls? Did I see something I might have missed in the panic of the moment – something that might later return to me like the detail of a distant dream? I have racked my brain to think of someone – anyone – I might have upset, but there is no one. No one except Lewis, but why would he do this now, after all this time? And if he was in some way involved, that would dismiss a link between the fire and the break-in at his mother's.

I return to Sylvia's house to join her for lunch as I promised, and afterwards, I take the paint tin over to the house. Oliver and Fin have been here for over a week already, that time having passed so quickly. I feel I have known him longer, as though we had already met before that afternoon on the beach.

When I get to the house, they are outside, heading to the car.

'I won't keep you,' I say. 'I just found something I thought Finley might like.' I hold out the tin of paints to him, and after looking at his father for confirmation that he can accept the gift, he takes it from me. 'They were left here by another family,' I explain.

'I've seen how good your drawings are, Fin, so I'm sure you'll be brilliant at painting too.'

Fin sneezes, then covers his face with his arm, embarrassed.

'I think he's coming down with something,' Oliver says. 'He had a bit of a temperature this morning – I was going to stop and pick up some Calpol after I've been to the bank.'

'That's where you're heading now?'

Finley does look pale, despite his complexion always being quite pallid.

'I've got an appointment.'

'I'll let you get going.'

'What do you say to Brooke, Fin?'

Finley looks up, almost makes eye contact, but says nothing. His shyness is so severe that it is impossible not to feel sorry for him. I would offer to stay with him while Oliver goes to the bank, but they barely know me, and anyway I have no idea how to look after a child even for a couple of hours, so I say nothing.

'Sorry,' Oliver says, apologising for his son's quietness. 'Thank you – that's really kind of you.'

I return to Sylvia's house and go upstairs to the spare bedroom that was once her son's. A solitary canvas leans against the wardrobe – the only piece that remained intact following the fire. I say 'intact'; it is charred and blackened, though otherwise whole. It was a landscape ordered for a golden wedding anniversary. The couple stayed in the house last year, and their daughter contacted me last month to say that her parents had spoken of my paintings and she wanted to surprise them with one of their own. Nothing too dark, she said, clearly having visited my website and seen for herself the kind of landscape that characterises my work. I sent her some sketches of different ideas, and she got back to me with the one she thought her parents would prefer: a midsummer sunset fading into a greying sea, the harbour in the foreground, a solitary fishing boat moored to its wall. Despite the lightness of the palette, there managed to be something bleak about the image even before the smoke soaked through it – some darkness that seems to be inherent to the place and is therefore unavoidable in its re-creation on canvas.

My phone pings with a message, the Wi-Fi deciding today that it will function as required. It is from Oliver.

Sorry to rush you out earlier. Errands all complete and now on way home. I was wondering if you're not busy later if you'd like to come over to show Fin how to use the paints? Don't worry if you can't make it.

I leave the phone at my side for a while as I continue to stare at the painting, wondering whether I have the heart to start it again or to contact the customer and explain what has happened. I don't want to appear too keen to reply. Besides which, I am not sure *how* to reply. I would like to go over. I would like to see him. But that may not be a good thing. He is someone I know nothing about – someone whose past may be littered with even more tragedy than my own. It would be foolish to enter the unknown without caution, and yet it is that same caution that has kept me tethered here, bound to the village as the fishing boat in the painting is moored to the harbour wall.

I pick up the phone.

I would love to, I type. *What time?*

And then I delete it. There is keen, and then there is desperate.

I'm free after 5.30, I write. *Is that too late for Finley, and is he feeling better?*

Better. I'm focusing on Finley and not on Oliver – nothing to suggest that I am going there to see him. I read it again, checking for any ambiguity, for anything that might be misconstrued. Happy that there is nothing open to misinterpretation, I press send. Within minutes, I receive a reply.

Thank you, that'll be great. Usually start settling him for bed at about 7. He's feeling much better and looking forward to it. See you later.

I lock my phone and push it to one side. Though I need to focus now on my work and how I am going to complete this commission in time, my thoughts cannot be dragged from Oliver. There has never been a man in my life – no one serious, at least; for the past sixteen years I have avoided relationships, with few opportunities coming my way. Locals marry locals, that's the way things have always been here, and there are no eligible locals left. Besides, I have never moved on from what Lewis did. He is there in the shadows, always at the back of my memory, and every relationship that has been started has been abruptly ended by the thoughts that have followed me for all my adult life.

I stand and go to the window, open it and allow a blast of fresh air to circulate around me. The world outside my door is small and contained, my horizons stretching as far as a house I cannot return to and an ocean I cannot cross. Echoes of an argument sound in the whistle of the wind as it cuts past my ears. *You will die here, Brooke. You will stay here and die, having never lived.*

I slam the window shut, cutting dead her voice. There were times I believed I might hate my sister, and I resented her for leaving me. But alongside the echo of her voice, there is another: my own, telling me that she was right.

My mobile starts ringing. I pick it up and look at the screen. Unknown caller. The sight sends a chill through me; I hold the phone at arm's length, as though it might explode in my face. I don't want to answer it. I can't not answer it.

'Hello?'

Nothing. No breathing, no sounds; no voice.

'Hello?'

And then it comes to me, as soft and distant as the first time.

'Brooke.'

My body weakens at the sound of her voice, as though my bones have been reduced to nothing. 'Delta?'

She is dead, I tell myself. She is gone; she is not here. This is not real. This is not her.

And yet it is her voice.

'Who is this?' I say, my voice shaking. 'This isn't funny. Just stop it. Leave me alone.'

I wait for a response, for a repetition of my name, but nothing comes. When I cut the call, I am shaking, my knuckles white with their grip around the phone. Then the tears come, hot and fast. She is not there, this is not her, and yet I want so much for the opposite to be true.

FOURTEEN

CHRISTINA

The call from Ollie had left Christina feeling detached from the day, unable to focus on anything other than the past. She had cried at the sink, her back to the children as they played on the floor; then, once she had allowed her body to drain itself of a grief that had been stored and silenced for too long, she set about preparing dinner. It was as she was peeling potatoes – the twins pushing giant puzzle pieces around the floor, not really knowing what else they should be doing with them – that there was a knock at the door. When she went to answer it, a delivery driver was standing there with a large box in his hands. Christina's heart sank. It was the same florist that had sent the other flowers, the ones she had disposed of in the early hours of that morning.

'Christina Hale?' the man said, thrusting the box towards her.

'Thanks.'

Heart hammering, she closed the door quickly and took the box through to the kitchen. She would have to find somewhere to dispose of it before Matthew got home, but that wouldn't be easy while the children were in her care. She took a pair of scissors from the drawer and used them to slice through the tape that sealed the box, which looked as though it had already been opened and resealed. What was Joel's plan? she thought – to keep sending her flowers until she caved in and contacted him? It was never going to be the response he seemed to hope for, and bombarding her like this was only going to make things worse.

She opened the box and pulled out the plastic wrapping, wondering why it felt so light. At first there appeared to be no flowers inside, but as she lifted out more plastic, a burst of colour could be seen at the bottom – creams and pinks, just like the flowers that had been sitting in the hallway. Only these had been bludgeoned. There were no stems or leaves, just petals, all of them torn and shredded.

She searched the box for a card or a delivery slip, but there was nothing. She looked at the children. Edward had pulled a book off the table and was amusing himself with turning the pages and pointing to the pictures, muttering away as he identified the animals on each page. Elise was still engrossed with the puzzle pieces, now trying to force the letter J to join the C.

She looked back at the desecrated bouquet and went to get her secret phone from the filing cabinet in the treatment room.

Please stop sending things to my house, she wrote. Then she went back and deleted the word *please*. Her thumb hovered over the arrow that would send the message, but instead she left the thread and called him, her heart hammering in her chest as she waited for it to connect.

There was a pause, then a beep, and she was taken straight to answerphone. She hung up without speaking.

After the twins had been fed, she put them in the car. She put the box of flowers on the passenger seat and drove three streets away, where she dumped them in the first wheelie bin she saw. When she got home, she realised she had left the house without locking the front door. Anxiety flooded her. What if someone had come in while they had been out? They had only been five minutes or so, but someone could have taken a chance on the door during that time and might still be there now, some-where in the house. An uncomfortable heat coursed through her as she checked every room, starting downstairs and working her way up, going so far as to open wardrobe doors and look beneath beds. Elise watched her questioningly, while Edward acknowledged the ritual silently, apparently accepting of her neuroticism.

'That was a fun game,' Christina said, getting up from Elise's carpet. 'Shall we go back downstairs now?' She smiled, too enthusiastically, suspecting that it might border on a look of mania.

She reached for Edward's hand, Elise already at the bedroom doorway, and as they made their way down the stairs, she was jolted by the sound of the front door. Matthew came in, smiling as he saw them on the staircase.

'You're back early.'

'Only by ten minutes or so,' he said. 'Roads were pretty clear.' He looked at their feet, and it was only then that Christina realised they were all still wearing their shoes. They never wore shoes upstairs; it was a house rule.

'Been out somewhere?'

'Only the garden,' Christina told him, letting go of Edward's hand as they reached the bottom of the stairs. She smiled, but it felt forced, and she could still feel the flush in her cheeks.

'Are you okay?' Matthew asked. He opened the living room door for the children, ushering them inside.

'Um... actually, no. I don't feel very well again. It's just... I don't know. It's this nausea again – it just won't go away.'

'You need to call the doctor.'

'It'll pass,' she said with a wave of a hand, feigning nonchalance.

'You just said it won't go away.'

'Turn of phrase. You know what I mean. Are you hungry? You've still got that lasagne from last night.'

Matthew glanced into the living room to check the children were occupied. 'I haven't been able to stop thinking about last night,' he murmured, putting a hand on her hip. 'You might have caused a plane crash today and I wouldn't have noticed.'

He leaned in to kiss her, but she moved away, immediately

regretting the abruptness of the action. He looked at her as though she had burned him.

'Not in front of the kids,' she said lightly, leaning into him and kissing his cheek.

He smiled. 'Fair point. Do you want a cup of tea? I'll put the kettle on.'

She watched him as he made his way to the kitchen, oblivious to the secrets she carried with her through their home. She felt weighed down by them, exhausted by carrying the invisible burden alone. Taking a deep breath, she tried to compose herself. She had to stop this, she had to act normally – if such a thing were at all possible – for Matthew's sake and for the sake of the children.

'I spoke to Ollie today,' she said when she went into the kitchen.

Matthew stopped what he was doing and turned to her. 'You called him?'

'He called me. He asked about plans for the twins' birthday.'

'We haven't discussed that yet.'

'I know – that's what I told him. We'll have to organise something soon.'

'Is he coming here?'

'I think so. I said he could stay, make a bit of a break of it.'

Matthew turned back to the kettle. 'Is that a good idea?'

'What do you mean?'

She knew exactly what he was referring to. The last time she had seen her brother-in-law and nephew had been the Christmas before last, when the twins were just babies. It was an already emotional time of year for her, the season highlighting the absence of her sister, but she had been unprepared for the onslaught of grief that their visit brought on, which lasted long after they had physically departed. It had led to arguments between Matthew and Christina, who had accused him of being completely removed from the memory of Bethany.

'It took you months to recover.'

'So what do I do – never see them again?'

'I didn't say that.' Matthew crossed the room and took her hand in his. 'I know you love them,' he said. 'So do I. But you need to consider the timing, that's all.'

He was right. Perhaps it wasn't a good idea after all. Seeing Ollie and Fin was painful, and though she wanted to keep in touch with them, to see Fin grow up and be a part of his life, maybe it would be better for them to meet up another time, when her emotions could be left unchecked without running the risk of ruining another celebration.

'Why not suggest the summer holidays?' Matthew said, reading her mind. 'They could come and stay then.'

He pulled her to him, and she let him hold her. She closed her eyes as the memory of Bethany engulfed her: the feel of her fragile arms draped around her shoulders, the touch of her soft hair against her cheek, the floral scent of the perfume that was her favourite. It had been almost eight years since she had left them, yet there were moments when Christina felt she had seen her just the week before, the music of her laugh still playing clearly in her memory. She leaned into her husband, resting her weight against him.

'I miss her,' she said quietly. 'I let her down.'

Matthew took her by the shoulders and gently pushed her back from him. 'Don't say that. It wasn't your fault. You did everything you could for her – more than anyone. She couldn't be saved. You didn't let her down.'

Unable to look at him, Christina rested her head against his chest. Nausea rolled through her again, and as she closed her eyes, a thought occurred to her. She moved a hand to her stomach, passing a palm across its curve. *No*, she thought. *No*.

FIFTEEN

BROOKE

At 5.20, I get changed, deliberating over the limited items of clothing that I managed to salvage from the house. I settle for a black denim dress over a long-sleeved sweater, still wondering whether Oliver's reasons for inviting me to the house are really anything to do with helping his son learn to paint, and whether I mind if they are not. When I step outside, it is colder than I had realised, and a chill sends a shiver tripping through me. There is music on the air, some tune drifting from the open doorway of the pub, and as I breathe in a lungful of October evening air and head up to the house, I feel strangely alive, as though the possibility of something new may be just around the corner.

The thought stops me. What am I doing?

The question of where Finley's mother is hangs over me, stopping me on the lane. I am cast into shadow by the hedgerow beside me, shrunk in size as all the possible what-ifs re-emerge to remind me that impulsive decisions rarely lead to anything but disappointment. I am woken from the thought by my phone; when I answer, the caller introduces himself as DS Jones.

'We have a witness,' he tells me. 'A delivery driver from the brewery says he saw a teenage boy on a bike hanging around near the end of the terrace. He says he was behaving suspiciously.'

'What does that mean?'

'He says he might have been acting as a lookout.'

Or he might just have been a kid on a bike hanging around, I think. Sylvia's comment about the recent antisocial behaviour in Fishguard preys on my mind. I remember the group of boys I saw in the village on the evening of the fire and mention them to the detective.

'Can you describe any of them for me?'

'Not really. I'm sorry – they were too far away, and I was a bit preoccupied at the time. All kids that age look a bit the same, don't they – the way they dress and everything.'

'What age would you say they were?'

'Fourteen? Fifteen, maybe. There were four or five of them, I think, but most had their hoods up. I'm sorry I'm not being more help.'

'It's fine,' he says. 'Leave it with us.'

'I've heard about the break-in at Jean Miller's house,' I tell him. 'Do you think there might be a link between the two?'

'I'm sorry – I really can't discuss anything about other investigations. We'll be in touch.'

Frustrated by the lack of developments, I turn round and go back to Sylvia's, wanting to shut myself away again. Outside the house, I tap out a text message.

I'm sorry, I've got a terrible headache. We'll have to do another time. Please say sorry to Finley for me.

It feels wrong to let a child down, but I press send and turn my phone to silent, not wanting to read a reply if one should come this evening. I doubt Finley will even notice my absence; I suspect, if anything, that it may be felt more greatly by Oliver. Perhaps he just wanted some adult company. His love for his son is obvious, but it must be lonely for him, just the two of them, especially in a place that can feel so isolating to those who are unfamiliar with it.

'Back so soon?' Sylvia is at the bottom of the stairs when I go back in, her dressing gown already on and a steaming mug of tea in her hand.

'Headache.' I hadn't told her where I was going, and she didn't ask; I suspect she had already guessed.

'There are some paracetamol in the bathroom cupboard if you need some, love.'

'Thanks.'

'I'm just going to watch a bit of TV. There's that quiz show on with whatshisname in a minute, if you fancy it?'

'I think I might just go for a lie-down, if you don't mind.'

'Course not.' But she looks disappointed. Sylvia likes having me here, but I don't want her to grow too comfortable with the idea. It wouldn't be healthy for either of us to have me living in her pocket, and the sooner I am able to go back to the gallery, the better.

The landlord is sorting out the buildings insurance while I deal with the contents. I owned little, but I still find it all confusing enough, grateful that I don't have to manage the myriad of hoops he will likely be made to jump through before restoration work can begin. I hadn't realised how much I loved the place until it was taken from me; or at least, not loved, but depended upon. It felt like some sort of home. Safe.

I go upstairs to my room and get changed into a pair of pyjamas. The painting taunts me from where it is propped against the wall opposite, its half-finished cliff edge glaring back at me, an accusation against my own lack of productivity. I need to order more supplies, contact the customer and start again. Perhaps this painting could mark the start of something new for my work – something brighter, more optimistic to counteract the darkness.

I think about Oliver, about what he might be doing now. I want to rewind the past twenty minutes: walk backwards out through the front door, unwrite that text, continue along the hedgerow until I reach the house. I want to sit with company that is not my own, surrounded by possessions that belong to someone else.

What are you scared of, Brooke? That living might be fun?

I hear her voice as clearly as though she stands beside me; I remember that argument like it happened just this morning. Delta had come home for the weekend, gracing us with her presence for a couple of nights before she headed back to London. I found out later – Mum inadvertently slipping me the details of a conversation that had been kept from my ears – that Delta had asked for money, but by that time our mother had been no longer able to take care of her limited finances, and I had been added as a signatory to her accounts. Delta never raised the subject with me, but her abrupt departure was evidence enough of her feelings about the set-up.

'Come to London for a weekend.'

It was her first night back; we were sitting at the kitchen table eating a salad Delta had barely touched. I glanced at Mum, who was pushing a piece of lettuce around her plate as though expecting a foreign object to appear from somewhere beneath it.

'I don't think that's a good idea.'

'Why not?'

I raised my eyebrows, dropping a subtle nod in Mum's direction.

'Surely there's someone who can watch her? What about Sylvia, she won't mind? She wouldn't have to stay here, would she? She could just pop up to check on her.'

I hated the way Delta talked about our mother as though she wasn't just across the table from her. She had no idea how challenging her behaviour had become either; there was no way I could have left her alone.

'She's not safe on her own.'

Delta tutted beneath her breath. 'Excuses,' she muttered.

I didn't want to get into an argument, not there and then with Mum sitting beside me.

'What are you scared of, Brooke? That living might be fun?'

She could never just leave things – she always had to push and push, always needing the final word, and a single word rarely enough for her.

I close my eyes, trying to force Delta's face away. My God,

despite everything, I miss her. In this moment, I would rather have her here, angry and full of recrimination, than just this void where a person so full of character and life once resided. And yet at times, I hated her. She hated me. We were opposites – the daredevil and the scaredy-cat: she alive and fully charged; me too tentative to step beyond my own shadow.

I lie on the bed, trying to chase away the living memories that play out in my head. We did what we did, whether rightly or wrongly; Delta made her choices, and I made mine. I chose to stay, and I accepted what that meant.

I think of Oliver again in the house up on the hill, getting Finley ready for bed before preparing for another evening alone. Perhaps I haven't accepted this life with everything it promised, not entirely. I thought I wanted to be alone, to remain in a self-imposed isolation where nothing and no one could cause me further harm. Caring for someone hurts. Loving someone brings an exposure to a type of pain nothing else is capable of inflicting. Yet it seems to me now – a year on from the deaths of my remaining family, but much longer since they had both begun to leave – that loneliness is worse, and that in trying to protect myself, I may be achieving the opposite.

In the living room across the landing, with her evening view of the harbour, Sylvia watches television on her own, her only company the photographs that line the window sill and the mantel-piece: her husband's sixtieth birthday celebrations, their wedding day, their ruby anniversary, holidays they took abroad. For the first time, it occurs to me that she is not alone. She has accumulated a lifetime of memories – days and years that are the source of her continued optimism, the things that keep her going. I could still have that, if I give myself the chance; if I allow myself to believe that I am deserving of such happiness.

I get up to turn the light off before climbing back into bed. Lying in the darkness, I have the absurd urge to pinch myself, to make sure that I am truly still here. Perhaps there is good reason for this, the impulse justifiable. I may be alive, but sometimes I am not sure whether I am living.

SIXTEEN

CHRISTINA

Christina and Matthew lived in a terraced house in the suburbs of north Barnet, a street characterised by large bay fronts and traditional sash windows. The back room, once used as a dining room before the extension on the kitchen had been added, now functioned as Christina's treatment room. Clients would often comment on her home as they entered the hallway, passing favourable opinion on her choice of artwork, or on the tall, exotic house plants that sat just inside the porch. Once the twins had arrived, the wall art was replaced with studio portraits – Edward and Elise sitting side by side on a plush cream blanket, their chubby hands clasped in one another's – and the house plants were removed before crawling limbs were able to reach up and root among the soil. Now, clients passed comments on the babies – little dolls, as one woman had called them – and Christina experienced a surge of pride that felt at once fulfilling and undeserved.

As she led the client through to the treatment room, she cringed at the thought. She had offered all of herself to someone else, a person who should have been kept off limits.

'How have you been since your last appointment?' she asked.

'Good. The first couple of days were much better, then the pain started to come back.'

'It'll take a few sessions.'

She pushed open the door to the treatment room and stepped aside to let the client enter. 'When you're ready,' she said, gesturing to the coat rack where the woman could hang her things. The client took off her jacket and then removed her jeans, under which she wore a pair of skin-tight running shorts. Christina waited as she stepped up to the treatment bench and lay face down on the sheet that she had spread out ready.

She reached for the client's ankle, checking the back of the heel for inflammation. It was a little improved since she had seen her three weeks earlier. The same thought occurred to her now as it had then: the woman's legs were flawless. All of her, in fact, was flawless – the lithe limbs and grace of a dancer. Christina felt a stab of jealousy jab at her side. The twins had battered her body, both physically and mentally, and though she loved every hair on their heads and every breath that was expelled from their perfect little mouths, she couldn't escape the feeling that as they grew, she continued to diminish. She had lost a part of herself when she had given birth to them – a natural labour, despite the horror stories about twin births that so many people had been keen to share during her pregnancy – a piece of her personality pushed out with the placenta and the afterbirth.

As she worked on the woman's calves, Christina couldn't help but notice the smooth and unblemished thighs. Her own were laced with silver threads, stretch marks she had developed long before pregnancy, when yo-yo dieting and a misguided student lifestyle had caused her weight to fluctuate. The skin of her inner thighs was loose and pale, the colour of raw chicken flesh; a world away from the taut, toned legs in front of her. She remembered the first night she had slept with Matthew – a couple of months on from reuniting after all those years, having last seen each other as teenagers – and was unable to recall even the slightest sense of shame or embarrassment about her appearance. At the time, she had been caught up in too many other emotions to worry about a thing as inconsequential as the way she looked.

The doorbell pulled her from thoughts of the past. Matthew was at home, so she wouldn't need to get it. She never liked to leave the room during a session; having to do so was one of the downsides of working from home. It always seemed unprofessional to be interrupted by the door or the phone when she was with a client.

It rang again. Where was Matthew? In the attic, presumably, though she had thought he would still hear the bell.

'Do you need to go and get that?'

'It's okay,' Christina said. 'My husband's here, he'll get it.'

There was another ring, followed by knocking. Christina's sigh was audible.

'Go on, it's okay.'

'I'm really sorry about this. I'll just be a minute.'

As she left the treatment room, she looked down the hallway and into the kitchen, but there was no sign of Matthew. Perhaps he was in the garden, though it had been raining quite heavily not long ago. She went to the front door. On the doorstep was a box. A delivery driver was at the pavement, getting back into a van.

It was addressed to her, as she had known it would be. There was no company name on it this time – nothing by which she might have been able to guess at what was inside. She wanted to leave it where it was, to not have to so much as touch it, but she couldn't allow Matthew to find it there. She carried it into the house and closed the front door, grateful now that he hadn't responded to the sound of the bell.

She took the box with her back to the treatment room and put it in the corner. 'Sorry about that. Right... let's get you sorted.'

At the end of the session, once she had seen the client from the house, Christina returned to the treatment room. Her first thought was of the box waiting in the corner, and she felt her heart hammer in her chest before she had even begun to tear it open. The smell hit her first. It was the smell of something rotting in a fridge, a stench of decay and death. She lifted the lid to find a protective layer of bubble wrap. When she pulled that away, the stench intensified, tying her stomach in knots. There was a second box inside, and when she lifted it out, she felt something wet on her hand, something leaking from the cardboard. With trepidation, she opened the box, realising as she did so that the fluid staining her hands was blood.

She took a step back and retched. Inside the box was a pile of raw meat, small red-brown chunks of shiny flesh and pale gristle. The stench was overpowering, and she raised an arm to cover her nose, breathing momentarily the scent of fabric conditioner that was embedded in her blouse. It wasn't enough to take away the smell of decay that had settled at the back of her throat, and when a watery sensation began to fill her cheeks, she rushed to the downstairs toilet, barely making it in time.

She had hardly eaten that morning, unable to face anything other than a dry piece of toast, yet despite this she was sick with such force that it made her head throb. Why was he doing this to her? She had done wrong, she knew that, but it wasn't for him to punish her in this way. He was hardly an innocent party himself, and to subject her to this barrage of cruel attentions was sinister. He must have seen the remorse that had already consumed her. She didn't need to be punished more.

'Chrissie? You okay?'

'I'm fine.' She got up and sat on the closed toilet lid, resting her head in her hands for a moment. When the wave of sickness subsided, she stood and ran the cold tap, splashing water on her face to revive herself.

'Have you been sick?' he asked when she opened the door.

'I'm okay,' she said again, the words sounding less convincing than the last time she had spoken them.

'Come here.' He opened his arms to her, and she moved against him, resting her head on his shoulder. He put a hand to her head, checking for a temperature. 'Maybe you should make an appointment with the doctor.'

'I'll do it later.'

'Chrissie...'

'Okay, okay. I'll go and do it now. Let me get some water first.'

'I'll get it for you. Why don't you go for a lie-down. I can pick the kids up later.'

She shook her head. 'I've got another couple of clients. Honestly, I'm fine – just a funny five minutes. I'd better get the room ready.'

'I'll bring you that water.'

She was about to object, but realised she couldn't, not when it meant having to find an excuse to keep him from the treatment room. The more she acted out of character, the more suspicious he would become, and it seemed it would be only a matter of time before one of these parcels fell into his hands.

She went to the treatment room and put the box under the table, then took a clean towel from the shelving unit and used it to cover it. Hopefully it would ward off the smell until Matthew left the room, though it would need to stay there until she had finished work for the day.

He came into the room and handed her a glass of water. If he smelled anything untoward, he didn't mention it. 'Please call the doctor,' he said, looking at her with concern.

'I will. I promise.'

'Do you mind if I go back upstairs for a bit?' he said.

She laughed and pulled away from him.

'Of course not, you geek,' she said, her standard response whenever he spent time in the attic with his model railway – something she had playfully teased him about since they had met. 'What are you building up there this time, a full-scale cinema complex to go with your high street?'

His face changed. 'I'm just really missing him. You know what it's like – some weeks are worse than others.'

'I'm sorry,' Christina said, feeling guilty for having teased him. The railway and all its accessories had belonged to his father, who had died before she and Matthew had got together. She knew it was the place he returned to when he wanted to feel close to him. 'I didn't mean anything by it.'

'I know.' Matthew smiled. 'The geek bit still hurts, though.'

He leaned in to kiss her before heading back upstairs, and she closed the door behind him, trying to steady her breathing to calm the quickening beat of her heart as she realised she had to find somewhere to dispose of the box and its contents.

SEVENTEEN

BROOKE

OCTOBER 2019

The following morning, I leave the village to do a food shop. I have always done Sylvia's along with my own anyway, but this week, over breakfast, we compile a list together to save us from doubling up on items that we may end up having too much of. Once I'm about half a mile down the country lane that leads to the main road to Fishguard, my phone begins to ping with notifications. I stop near a gate that leads on to farmland, knowing that one of the messages may be from Oliver.

There is a text from him, a response to the message I sent yesterday evening with my white lie about a headache.

Don't worry. Hope you're feeling better soon. Take care.

There is nothing to read between the lines, and yet I still search them for hidden meaning, hoping to find something that says so much more. And then there is the disappointment. Perhaps I should have gone over there last night; maybe I missed something I might have enjoyed. I hear my sister's voice in my head, her presence here with me, responding to my thoughts. *You'll spend your whole life running away from happiness, then blame everyone else for your loneliness.*

I hover over a reply before I start texting. *Feeling a lot better this morning, thank you. Hope you had a good evening. If you're free later, I could help Finley with the paints, if you'd still like me to?*

I press send, for once not allowing myself to find a reason why I shouldn't do the thing I am drawn towards. I wait, as though Oliver has spent all morning sitting beside his phone, awaiting my response, and then I find myself drawn to the internet browser and to Facebook. My account has been deactivated for a while now; I hardly used it, and for the past year other people's happiness has been something I've wanted to avoid. The last photograph I posted is still there on my timeline: me and Mum, sitting next to each other in her room at the nursing home. I rarely posted photographs, especially not ones of myself, but it felt fitting at the time, my subconscious realising that it would be something I would need to look back on later. Five weeks after the photograph was taken, my mother was no longer with me.

I type Oliver's name into the search bar at the top of the page. As I scroll the list of people, I look for his face – for his eyes looking back at mine – but it doesn't appear. There are a couple of people with the same name who have inanimate objects as their profile pictures, but when I click on to them, neither seems to be Oliver. It occurs to me that it is a strange world we live in where we stalk new acquaintances online, trying to find out the details they may prefer to hold back. Perhaps it is better that I find nothing, because I know that what I'm really looking for – *who* I'm really looking for – is not Oliver, but Finley's mother.

I give up my search and fling my phone onto the passenger seat before making my way to Fishguard. By the time I leave the supermarket, Oliver has replied. He and Finley have been for another walk along the coastal path, and they will be home this afternoon if I would like to go over at three o'clock. I load the shopping into the car first, not wanting to appear too keen by replying too quickly, and then I text back, telling him I will see them then.

It is as I'm sitting in the car, having just replied to Oliver, that I see Lewis again. I have to remind myself that I know it's him, my brain still trying to convince my heart that I'm seeing things. These past couple of weeks have played tricks with my mind, raising the voices of the dead and bringing ghosts I would rather not be reacquainted with. Without thinking about what I'm doing, I get out and cross the car park.

'Lewis.'

He turns at his name; he looks surprised to see me, though perhaps it is more the case that he didn't expect me to confront him.

'Brooke. How are you?'

'What are you doing here?' I ask, ignoring his pretence at pleasantries.

He glances at the carrier bag in his hand before raising it with a shrug. 'Shopping.'

I blink, fighting back the darkness that has crept into my brain: the overhanging trees, the night air, the fallen leaves beneath my feet. 'Back in Aberfach,' I say, hating the shake in my voice that has become evident.

'It's still home. It'll always be home.' Even now, after all this time, he is taunting me. It hasn't been his home for years; he never comes back here. 'I suppose you've heard about the break-in at my mother's house?'

'I suppose you've heard about the fire.'

He nods, but says nothing. No question as to whether I am all right; no attempt at a kind word of consolation. Nothing.

A skittering among the branches; a screech somewhere overhead. I close my eyes for a moment, fighting the sounds away.

'Was it you?'

He raises an eyebrow, his lip curling into a smirk. 'What? The fire?'

A teenage boy may have been seen near the terrace before the fire started – that same boy may have been responsible for igniting the rag – but that doesn't mean Lewis couldn't have instigated it.

He laughs, as though there is anything amusing to be found in the situation. 'I'm being accused of that as well? What will it be next, Brooke?'

'It can't be a coincidence, can it? A fire and then a break-in. Nothing ever happens in Aberfach, you know that.'

He steps closer and I feel myself freeze, just as I did all those years ago. 'I know that, Brooke. Everyone knows that nothing ever happens in Aberfach, not unless you've invented it.' He opens his mouth in faked horror, mocking me. 'Was it you, Brooke? Did you start the fire? Did you break into my mother's house as well?' He sighs and looks at me pityingly. 'It could have been you. You know how muddled up you get about things.'

I feel tears at the corner of my eyes; I hate that they are there and that he can see them. He is humiliating me all over again, and all over again, I am allowing him to.

'Fuck you, Lewis,' I manage, my voice trembling on the words.

He laughs. 'Already been there,' I hear him mumble, and when he gets into his car and drives away, I am left standing there, inert with shame and anger.

Driving home, I have to fight my brain to keep it from returning to that place. *He isn't doing this to you*, I tell myself. *You are doing it to yourself.* When I get back to the village, I take Sylvia's shopping to the house, stopping to have a cup of tea while she puts the food away. I don't tell her that I've seen or spoken to Lewis, as though keeping him hidden might send him back to wherever he came from.

I make an excuse to go upstairs, and just before three, I head to the house. Oliver is outside, pulling shopping bags from the boot of his car. 'Everyone does their food shop on a Thursday then,' I say.

'You've been as well?'

'Always on a Thursday. I'm a creature of routine.'

He has his hands full, so I take the last bag from the boot and follow him into the house.

'How's the head?' he asks.

I stumble on an answer, forgetting for a moment that I lied about a headache. My thoughts are now consumed with Lewis, and with everything he may be responsible for. 'Much better today.' I am useless at lying, so am grateful that his back is to me as he puts the shopping on the kitchen worktop. 'Where's Finley?'

'He's gone up to his room to get the paints.' He pulls a plastic bottle of milk from one of the bags and turns to me. 'Thanks for this. I think he's looking forward to it. I mean, he doesn't really get excited about much... you might have noticed.'

Well, he's been through a lot, I think, then realise I don't even know this yet. It is just the impression Finley gives – the way that sadness seems to hang around him, enveloping him in an invisible bubble that keeps him removed from the rest of the world.

'Has he always been quiet?'

Oliver nods and steps past me as he goes to the fridge to put the milk away. There is an awkward moment in which I feel I have said something I shouldn't have. He doesn't look at me, avoiding eye contact as he continues to put the shopping away.

'Would you like a tea or a coffee or anything?'

'Tea would be great, thanks. No sugar, just milk, please.' I could do with something stronger, though I can't say this without having to explain why, and I would then have to explain who Lewis is. I would have to talk about what he did, and I don't want to go back there, least of all with Oliver.

While he makes tea, Finley comes in carrying the paint tin. Oliver musses his hair in the way he so often does, and once again I feel as though I have interrupted a moment for which I shouldn't be present.

'I brought some paper,' I say, gesturing to the folder I'm still holding. 'I wasn't sure you'd have any.'

'Actually, we don't, do we? Thank you, that's really kind. I'm going to have to get a bit more organised now we're settled in.'

'I always used to have a roll of cheap wallpaper to draw on when I was a kid. My parents would have ended up bankrupt if they'd kept buying me drawing pads.' I take out the paper and put it on the table, then sit and wait for Finley to join me.

'Do you have something we can put some water in?' I ask

Oliver. He gets a bowl from the cupboard and takes it to the tap. 'What would you like to paint? Your dinosaur on the fridge is impressive. Shall we do another one, or something else?'

I already feel as though I'm talking too much, trying to shake off the earlier events of the day with some effort at normality. I open the paint tin and hand Finley a brush, keeping the other for myself. I share out the paper between us and then I dip the brush in the water Oliver sets on the table. Perhaps if I just show him rather than talk, I will make him feel more at ease.

'Watch this. Always squeeze the brush off a bit first, otherwise you'll have too much water.'

I swirl my brush on the circle of red paint before sweeping it in two curves over the right-hand side of the paper. Then I add some blue haphazardly – a swirl within the upper curve and a squiggle within the lower. I put the brush down and fold the paper in two. 'Can you give it a good press-down for me?'

Finley leans forward to press on the paper.

'Open it up.'

When he pulls back the paper, the paint has smudged within the outline of a butterfly.

'What do you think?' I ask him. 'We could make more of them, if you like. You could hang them from the ceiling.'

'I can make one.'

I am so surprised to hear his voice that I say nothing, aware that a response might render him silent again. I glance at Oliver, who smiles at me as he sets down a cup of tea next to me.

'Thank you. So, Fin, what colour is yours going to be?' I watch as he folds his paper before reaching for his brush. 'Good idea to fold first. I should have done it that way.'

His tongue pokes from the side of his mouth as he concentrates on his task. He dips his brush in the water and then the green paint, managing a big semicircle on the paper. When he returns for another colour, he forgets to squeeze off the brush as I showed him, and the red paint merges with the green to make a smudgy brown mess. He lets out a little cry of frustration and I place a hand on his arm.

'Don't get stressed about it. Take a breath and try again. Look.' I catch the running paint with my own brush, dragging it into a curve so that a butterfly shape will still be seen when the paper is folded. 'Try it now.'

I watch him reach to fold the paper together, fascinated by the concentration that imprints on his face. He is a handsome little boy, unruly hair and long eyelashes, and I wonder not for the first time what his mother might have looked like. There are no photographs of her around the house, though I suppose that in coming here for a fresh start, Oliver wanted to leave the past behind. Maybe having to look at her is too painful for him.

'Good job, Fin!'

Finley beams proudly at his father, who leans across the table to give him a high-five. It is the first time I have seen the child smile, and though there is something gratifying about the moment, I yet again have that feeling of being an intruder.

Fin reaches for another sheet of paper, enjoying himself far more than I anticipated he might. I sit back and allow him to take over, reminding him occasionally to squeeze the water from the brush.

When I glance at Oliver, he is looking at me. He mouths the words 'thank you', and I shake it off, not wanting to embarrass Finley or myself.

'Actually,' Oliver says, his voice breaking the silence that has fallen over us as Fin paints, 'there was another reason I asked you over. I was hoping I might pick your brains.'

'About what?'

'The area, really. I just want to find out more about the place. Is there a leisure centre where I can take Fin swimming? And where are the best parks? I mean, I know I can look it all up on the internet, but it's not the same as getting the opinion of a local, is it?'

'There's a leisure centre in Fishguard – it's just got a standard pool, but it's decent enough. The next best would be in Tenby –

they've got a play area there as well. As for parks... I'm not sure. I don't really remember playing in parks as a kid. The beach was our playground growing up.'

'Sounds like a good childhood.'

'It was.' And it had been, once upon a time.

Beside me, Finley puts down his brush and leaves the room.

'He's okay,' Oliver says when I look at him. He tilts his head to check the living room. 'He's just gone upstairs to play. Three-year-olds don't have the greatest attention span, do they?' He sips his tea. 'Where did you go to school?'

'Fishguard. Primary and high school. Are you looking for Finley?'

'Well, I've already been to school once... I don't really fancy it again.' He smiles. 'I'm just weighing up our options.' When he looks at me, there is something more behind his eyes, something he manages to say without vocalising. 'I've been applying for jobs,' he adds. 'Locally, I mean. I think this place might suit us.'

'What do you do?'

'I work in computers. Exciting stuff. I'd been doing a bit from home before we came here, but I need something more reliable.'

He is thinking of staying, a voice in my head says, and though a part of me would like to listen, I push it to one side, silencing it. I feel a hot flush fill my face. 'Do you mind if I use the bathroom?' I ask, sounding embarrassingly like a child asking permission from a teacher.

'It's your house,' he says with a smile.

When I go upstairs, Finley is sitting cross-legged on the carpet in his room. He has his back to the door, an array of soft toys lined up in front of him, arranged as though they are in assembly. I stop to watch him for a moment, knowing that I probably shouldn't. He is talking quietly, and at first I can't make out what he is saying. Then I realise that he is introducing the toys to one another. *Hello,* his little voice says, his hand resting on a small brown teddy bear, *my name is Ted.* He moves to the next, passing his attention along the row as though they are shaking hands, repeating his introduction to each in turn. He stops, sensing me there behind him, though he doesn't turn to look at me. When my mobile starts ringing in my pocket, I swear beneath my breath and hurry into the bathroom, closing the door behind me. I answer quickly, not checking the caller ID on the screen first.

'Hello?'

As soon as I speak, I realise my mistake. There is nothing. And then, as gentle and distant as ever, her voice comes to me from the other end of the line.

'Brooke.'

I fling the phone into the sink. If it wasn't for Finley in the next room, I might be tempted to scream at it: *Leave me alone. Whoever you are, just leave me alone.* I look at myself in the mirror. When I left the house to come here, I thought I looked okay, yet in the flood of natural light that bursts in from the bathroom window, I realise my reflection fooled me. With my paleness, the sunken, tired eyes, I could join the ghosts of the past; I could become one of them.

When I close my eyes, Lewis is looking back at me, smirking. I rub the heel of my hand over each eye in turn, forcing back unwanted tears. He won't do this to me again, I promise myself. I can't let him.

When I leave the bathroom, Finley is no longer in sight, having perhaps retreated into the den in the walk-in wardrobe. Downstairs, Oliver is sitting at the kitchen table waiting for me.

'Are you okay?'

'Fine.' I reach for my jacket, which is hanging over the back of one of the chairs, and shove my phone into a pocket.

'Has something happened?' he asks, standing. 'You look a bit pale.' He puts a hand on my arm. His fingers feel somehow weighty, comforting, and I find myself retreating to my seat, allowing myself to be guided there.

'I'm fine,' I say again, not believing my own words. 'I just came over a bit light-headed, that's all.'

'Another cup of tea? I could put a spoon of sugar in it for you.'

'Thank you.'

A voice in my head tells me I should go back to Sylvia's, but she has gone to visit a friend in Fishguard this afternoon and I don't want to be alone. Besides, I am done with listening to the voices that tell me what to do, especially now that there is only one voice that I need to pay attention to. How would someone get a recording of Delta speaking my name, and why would anyone be so cruel as to use it in this way? If Lewis is responsible, why is he tormenting me now, after so long?

EIGHTEEN

CHRISTINA

On Saturday, Christina made an excuse about needing to pop into town for a birthday card. She took the box from the utility room where she had hidden it and put it into a supermarket bag before driving into town and finding a parking space as close to the butcher's as she could get.

She hadn't contacted Joel after he had sent the flowers to the house, and could only now imagine the reaction that her non-response had caused. Was he so angry with her – so affronted by her rejection – that he had felt this to be an appropriate way to retaliate? She would never have thought it of him, and yet she realised now, too late, that she was really in no position to consider how he might react to any given situation. She had known him for merely a matter of months, and she had seen what she had wanted to see, using their attraction as a means of escaping the tedium of her reality.

She called him, but it went straight to answerphone. She knew that the number she had was for the phone he used for everything, for work and his personal life – unlike her, he'd had nothing to hide from anyone. He would need it for work, so why was it switched off in the middle of the day? Frustrated, she went to the boot to get the box. Its contents were by now rotting so badly that she was sure the smell of decay followed her as she carried it down the high street. She kept her head turned towards the shopfronts, not wanting to make eye contact with anyone she passed, and by the time she entered the butcher's shop, she felt flushed with embarrassment and anxiety.

There was a young man working behind the counter, hacking through what might have been a pork loin but could have been anything. Christina stood and watched as the cleaver sliced through the flesh and slammed into the chopping board beneath before the man looked up from his task and noticed her waiting there.

'Can I help you?'

'Actually, yes.' She nodded to the box she was carrying. The counter was too high and there was nowhere else to put it. 'I was hoping you could tell me what these are.'

The young man looked questioningly at the box before raising an eyebrow sceptically. 'What's in there?'

'Well, I'm not sure – I was hoping you might be able to tell me that. I took my dog for a walk and he got distracted by something near some wheelie bins... I think he might have eaten some of it. I just wanted to find out in case I need to take him to a vet.'

She smiled, knowing how useless the lie was and how strange she must appear. The boy glanced through to the side room before wiping his hands on his apron and raising the counter end to step out into the shop. 'Let's have a look, then.'

Christina put the box on the floor and opened it. The young man peered down into its contents, holding back as though half expecting something to jump out at him. He went back to the counter and ripped a length of plastic wrap from a roll before returning and scooping a handful into it. 'Give me a sec – I'll just double-check for you.'

He disappeared into the back room and she heard lowered voices as he spoke with someone else. Christina couldn't tear her eyes from the rows of raw meat lined up behind the glass counter. A metallic tint of blood was in the air, as though she was breathing in death.

'Yep,' the boy said, coming back through the doorway. 'What I thought. Chicken hearts.'

'Chicken hearts?'

'You don't want them back, do you?' he said, raising his hands, and when Christina shook her head, he turned and dropped them into a bin.

Christina could feel the blood draining from her face as the boy looked at her questioningly. She thought she might throw up.

'The good news is, he should be fine.'

'Sorry?'

'Your dog. Shouldn't be anything to worry about.'

'The dog. No. Okay. Thank you.'

She felt dizzy with sickness as she made her way back to the car.

Chicken hearts. Why chicken hearts?

There was the childish association of the word chicken with cowardice, and if that was his intended implication, he was right – she was a coward. Was that what all this was about – the way in which she had ended things? She should have spoken to him that morning at his flat when she had had the chance, though it was pointless to linger now over what should have been. She should have stayed away from Joel after that first meeting, even if it had meant finding an excuse not to continue treatment for his injury. Like so many other things, it was too late to reverse now.

She got back to the car and rested her head on the steering wheel. The vehicle still smelled of rotting meat, so she opened the windows wide despite the chill of the afternoon air. Hearts. Why hearts? Hearts sliced in two. Broken hearts. She hadn't broken his heart – he hadn't loved her. Had he?

She wrote several long-winded and grovelling messages that she then deleted before, exhausted by it all, texting a simple three-word request.

Please stop now.

He wasn't going to listen – why would he now, when he'd had other opportunities to stop what he was doing? She took out her work phone and began to cancel the patients she was due to treat that morning. She used Edward as an excuse, explaining that he had been sick that morning and that there was no one else available to look after him. She was very sorry, but she would book them in for the following week. She wasn't sure how she was going to manage that with an already full diary, but she would have to work it out somehow.

She parked where she had always parked when she had gone over to his flat, three streets away. She felt sick with anticipation as she got out of the car, knowing exactly what she wanted to say but unsure whether the words would leave her in the way she wanted them to once she was in front of him. Knowing what she knew about him now, would she even feel confident enough to confront him? He had persecuted her, stalked her; made her feel like a victim inside her own home. Was she even safe going to see him?

But she knew that if she didn't face him, he wouldn't stop. Each parcel he had sent to the house – each message he had left for her – had become more sinister in intent, and her only other option was to go to the police. She wasn't sure whether accusations of stalking were even taken seriously, not without real concrete evidence to substantiate them. Then there was the fact that going to the police and filing a complaint would mean admitting to her infidelity, and it would only be a matter of time before she would have to tell Matthew what she had done. Every time she had gone through the scenario in her head, the same outcome had prevailed. She would lose her family. She might lose the children. It wasn't a chance she was prepared to take.

The door to his building had an intercom, each buzzer linked to a different flat. She pressed number four and waited, glancing at the For Sale sign that had been there for months. She had no idea whether he would be there; as a lawyer, he was sometimes at the office and sometimes worked from home. After pressing the bell for a third time, she stepped back and looked up at the first-floor window. The curtains were drawn. She wondered whether he was behind them, peering out to get a glimpse of her, too much of a coward to come outside and admit what he had been doing. It was far easier to persecute someone from afar than it was to face the repercussions.

She returned to the step and pressed the buzzer again. Then she held her finger to it, letting it ring without pause. She stopped. Repeated. Stopped again and then repeated, each time allowing the buzzer to ring for longer, so that it couldn't be ignored.

She heard a catch being opened, and a dark-haired woman appeared at the ground-floor window.

'I can hear that through the ceiling,' she snapped. 'Just a thought, love, but I'm guessing he might not be in.'

The woman was older than Christina, possibly early forties. She was olive-skinned and attractive. Christina wondered whether Joel had ever had sex with her, before realising how ridiculous the thought was. And why did she care?

'Have you seen him?'

'I'm not his mother,' the woman said. 'I'm just the poor cow who lives downstairs and has to put up with the noise.'

Christina felt her face flush. What exactly was this woman referring to? Who else had Joel had in his flat?

'I take it neighbourly relations aren't that great?' Christina pried.

'I'm sure he's fine to get on with as long as you don't disagree with him about anything,' the woman replied curtly.

'If you see him, can you tell him I've been here? My name's...'

The woman stared at her, eyes widening as she waited. 'Your name is...?'

'It doesn't matter.'

The woman sighed and pulled the window closed.

Christina was left feeling humiliated and foolish, a realm of new possibilities taking form. What if she hadn't been the only one? *You don't get to do this* took on a new meaning in the light of the woman's words. Had she shunned someone who was used to getting his own way? And just how dangerous might that someone become?

NINETEEN

BROOKE

I contact the police on several occasions, but there is never any progress. No teenage boy has been identified; no further witnesses have come forward to offer anything that might be of use to the case. Village gossip says that fingerprints were found at Lewis's mother's house following the break-in there, but whether this is true or not, I don't know – the police still refuse to tell me whether they think the two incidents are linked in any way. Work at my house is yet to be started, so for now my life feels on hold once more, thrown into a state of limbo by someone else's crimes.

I am sitting on the sofa in the living room of Hillside Cottage drinking a cup of tea, when Oliver tells me he has an interview.

'Great. Whereabouts?'

'It doesn't matter, I can't make it anyway. It's this afternoon; it's too short notice.'

'Why, are you supposed to prepare something?'

'No.' He looks at Finley, who is playing with some toys on the rug near my feet, and then I realise. He has no one to look after his son. 'Can't really leave him in the car, can I?' he says, his voice lowered.

'What time is the interview? I can look after him if you like.'

I make the offer without a clue as to how to look after a child, but then I remember the box of paints. So long as Finley is happy to put up with me, I am sure we will be able to muddle through together somehow. It will give me something to do other than sit in Sylvia's spare room and obsess over Lewis's return to the village.

'I can't ask you to do that.'

'You didn't ask me. I offered.'

He glances at Finley, who is now sitting watching a cartoon. I say watching, but I'm not sure he is – rather, he is staring at the screen, seeing but possibly not taking anything in; lost in his own world, as he so often appears to be. If the painting doesn't keep him occupied later, there is always the television as a backup.

'It's at two thirty. Are you sure? I know it's a big ask.'

'It's fine, honestly. I don't mind. As long as Finley's okay with it.'

My motives are not entirely altruistic. If Oliver decides to stay in the area for longer, he may want to extend his rental on the house. But he might not be able to do that if he doesn't have a job and the money to pay for it.

'Thank you,' he says, and his hand slides across the sofa, his fingertips gently touching mine. 'I really appreciate it.'

He doesn't move his hand, and I don't pull away from him. There is a moment that lasts a beat too long, and for the first time I see how dark his eyes are, the pupils merging with the irises. He smiles, and the moment is broken; I move my hand, flustered.

'Fin. Finley.'

The boy turns his head.

'I have to go somewhere in a bit,' Oliver explains. 'I won't be long. Brooke is going to be here with you. Is that okay? You'll be a good boy for her, won't you?'

Finley looks away, but the word 'yes' is just about audible. There is something endearing about the fact that this child who seems so wary of everything and everyone has come to accept me.

'We'll be fine,' I tell Oliver. 'We can always get the paints back out.'

A couple of hours later, that's exactly what we do. I sit with

Finley at the kitchen table, the paints and brushes in front of us, and watch him as he smooths out the paper with his palm before he begins. He is a cautious child, methodical in his approach to anything he attempts, and I wonder whether this is a common trait in children of his age, or whether his almost obsessive movements are the result of his past.

And here the thought returns to me. I know nothing about him. I know nothing about his father. And yet the need to know has filled me in the same way as an ambition does, relentlessly and with passion.

I watch as Finley dips his brush in the water and presses it against the side of the bowl without being reminded to. There is a satisfaction in the moment, a sense that he has developed and learned something from me, and I wonder whether this is the same feeling I might have experienced had I gone into teaching years ago. It was the suggestion of the school careers adviser, though at the time I could think of nothing worse. I wanted to escape school, not go back there; I wanted to pursue my own creativity, not nurture other people's. Yet now, watching Finley and taking pride in the way he responds to my example, I wonder whether I might have gained fulfilment from it.

Finley is hard at work, dragging impressively straight lines along the page. 'A house,' I say, watching the form take shape. 'Good job, Fin – that looks great. Is it this house?'

He doesn't answer, and I take no offence from his silence; I have learned that he will speak when he is ready, and it is best not to push him into doing so. I wonder where he goes when he falls into this quiet world of his, whether the land that lies beneath his feet there is solid stone or sand that sinks beneath him. He seems such a sad little boy that I can't imagine anyone looking at him without feeling their heart ache for all the weight his poor little soul must carry.

He has painted in bold black lines, his grip assured for a child so young. There are windows, a front door – he has now even added a chimney. I watch him paint the door in red, the watery colour bleeding beyond the lines so that it inadvertently looks as though he has attempted detail of brickwork.

'Do you enjoy painting?'

Beside me, Fin leans across to the paint tin and rubs his brush in the orange paint. He returns to the paper to smear streaks across his work, his arm moving wildly as he drags the paint up and down the page, and when I look at his face, it has become expressionless, as though he isn't even here.

'Oh Fin, why did you do that?'

I don't mean the words to leave me so abruptly, and they need mere seconds to take effect. He is back, the momentary distance in his eyes gone, and now his pupils are enlarged, present, and he is on the verge of tears. His right hand grips the paintbrush, his knuckles whitened.

'I'm sorry,' I say, feeling terrible for snapping at him. 'It was just such a lovely painting, that's all. It's okay. It's still lovely.'

He turns and looks at me. 'It's not lovely. It's on fire.'

He drops the brush onto the page, pushes his chair back and leaves the table, his feet pounding the stairs as he runs up to his bedroom. I wait a moment, allowing him time to be alone. I study the painting, his lovely little house burned in frantic streaks, reduced to a Hallowe'en smudge of black and orange. Is this how Finley views the world, as everything destroyed? Did what happen at the gallery frighten him so much that he now can't erase the memory of it?

When I go upstairs, he isn't in his bedroom. I check Oliver's room, feeling uncomfortable being there. The bed is neatly made, a pair of checked pyjama trousers folded and placed at the bottom of the duvet. There is a wash bag on the chest of drawers and a towel hanging on the radiator. His suitcase is on top of the wardrobe, but other than these things there is little that belongs to Oliver – no more than there might be if he was staying here for a fortnight's holiday.

Where are all their things? I wonder.

I go back out onto the small landing, realising now where

Finley is. Back in his room, I stand near the walk-in wardrobe. The sliding door is partly open, allowing for light and air.

'Is there room in there for two?' I ask him. When he says nothing, I move a little closer and sit on the carpet. Fin is on the other side of the door, just inches from me, though we cannot see each other. 'When I was a little girl, I used to play a game with my sister. Do you want to play it?' He says nothing. 'I would think of a word, usually something I loved. So, say I said ice cream. My sister would then have to say the first thing that came into her head when she thought of ice cream.' Still he says nothing. I am probably getting on his nerves, I think, but I vow to try just a little longer. 'She would say sunshine, because ice cream would make her think of the summer. Then sunshine would make me think of holidays, so I would say holidays.'

'I don't want to play.' His voice is so small and sad that it makes me want to cry for him.

'Okay, Fin,' I say. 'You don't have to play. I'll just sit here quietly, okay. If you want to talk to me, you can.'

I don't expect him to talk to me, and he doesn't. When Oliver gets home, we are still there, sitting either side of the wardrobe door. I hear him call our names in turn, and it sounds odd somehow, as though we are a family – like he has just got back from work, a man returning home to his wife and son. The strangeness of the thought jolts me, and I go to the landing to wait for him.

'Everything okay?' he asks as he heads upstairs.

'He's in the wardrobe,' I say quietly. 'How did it go?'

'I'll hear from them next week. What's happened?'

I gesture to downstairs. I don't want to have this conversation where Fin can overhear us. In the kitchen, I show him Fin's painting. 'He drew a house,' I explain. 'And then he scrawled all over it. He said it was on fire.'

I watch Oliver's face, see the sadness that creeps into it. 'He keeps having nightmares. Fires, monsters, witches... he's always crying out in his sleep.'

'Since the fire?' I don't know how much Finley is aware of, or whether he saw anything that evening.

'No, they started before that. He won't speak to me about it, though,' he admits. 'I try, but... he's just shut himself off. How is a three-year-old supposed to articulate everything he must be feeling?'

'Do you think perhaps he might need to see somebody? Someone professional who can help him?'

Oliver raises an eyebrow. 'Like a shrink, you mean?'

His phrasing surprises me. It seems uncharacteristically insensitive. 'If he's struggling as you say he is, I just thought maybe he needs someone he can talk to.'

'He can talk to me. He just doesn't want to. So he's not going to talk to anyone else, is he?'

I look for my bag, collecting it from the back of the chair where I left it. 'I didn't mean any offence,' I say, feeling myself bristle at his reaction. 'I just thought that a professional might know how to help him.'

'Are you saying I can't look after my son?'

'That's not what I'm saying at all. It's just, he's very quiet, you've said that, and maybe a professional might have methods of getting him to open up.'

Oliver's face has changed, the sadness dropped to make way for an expression I haven't seen before. 'Fin will speak when he's ready to. You don't even have children, Brooke, so please don't give me advice about mine.'

His words affect me more than I should let them. I barely know this man, and yes, he is right, it is none of my business, but still the statement cuts, and worse than his words is the way he looks at me.

'You asked me to look after him for you,' I say curtly. 'That's what I was trying to do.' I step past him and go to the living room, retrieving my jacket from the sofa. I pull it on as I walk out, stepping into the cold afternoon, not bothering to turn as he closes the door behind me.

I should go back to Sylvia's, but I don't. It isn't home. I have no home. Instead, I find myself heading for the coastal path, my legs offering little resistance. The wind picks up as I near the sea, its cries interspersed with the voices in my heads: Delta whispering my name; Oliver's words on repeat; Lewis's still deafening despite the time that has passed. With every quickened step, my heart beats harder, and I find myself taking a route I haven't chosen in years. My surroundings change, the overgrown hedgerows and well-trodden path giving way to an expanse of long grass and exposed horizon, the cliff edge just metres ahead of me.

The tide is in, waves crashing against the rocks below. I stand near the edge and close my eyes. Sixteen years ago, this same stretch of sea had been pulled back by the tide, the rocks below exposed, jagged and black. I remember standing as I do now, teetering at the edge, a voice inside me, its mantra on repeat, taunting me. I could do now as I did then – just step off into the darkness. Just one step and then nothing. One final breath, one carefully executed rote of last things.

Before I open my eyes, I hear my father's voice. I don't hear what he says, and yet I feel him beside me, somehow, a hand pushing me away from the edge.

In the hospital, it was my mother's voice I heard first: a sharp intake of breath that preceded a shrill cry, and I realised I had been given a second chance. A moment later, the room was alive with people and sound, Mum and Dad both there, the relief on their faces tangible. Delta was there too, though I couldn't bring myself to look at her.

I step back from the cliff edge, a lungful of breath sucked down into my chest as I touch the scar on my forehead. I could never have returned to this place before now, not while there was my mother to look after. I had made a promise to her that I would never do it again, that I would never leave her, despite everything, and I had carried that promise through, even when living felt like the hardest thing to do.

TWENTY
CHRISTINA
MARCH 2018

Matthew waited in the surgery car park, the twins both fast asleep in the back seat. Christina turned to look at them before she got out of the car, taking a mental snapshot of their sleeping faces, an image she could return to later in moments when she might need the comfort of the memory.

'You'll be fine,' Matthew said, as though reading her thoughts. He touched her knee gently. 'Just go and get it sorted.'

She nodded and opened the car door, closing it carefully behind her.

The surgery was busy, as she had known it would be on a Monday. She went to reception and gave them her name and date of birth before taking a seat near the far wall. Expecting to be there for some time, she took her phone from her pocket to occupy her while she waited, knowing exactly where it would inevitably take her. She opened the internet browser and typed Joel's name into the search bar. What was she expecting to find? Evidence that affairs with married women were a regular hobby for him? Or that he was the type of man who might send an estranged lover a box of severed chicken hearts?

'Gillian Healy to room seven, please,' said the computerised voice from the speaker overhead. 'Gillian Healy to room seven.'

Christina glanced up from her phone to see an elderly lady wearing a rain mac and shoes that were too tight for her swollen feet push herself up from her chair and hobble to the corridor that led to the GPs' rooms. She looked back down and scanned the search results. She had already checked out Joel's social media profiles, months earlier. He wasn't particularly active on any of them, posting the occasional thought about a Netflix show and retweeting random sports-related news articles. There was certainly nothing that had flagged any warning signals.

Fifty minutes after arriving, Christina's name was called. She made her way to room three, where Dr Kane – a female doctor she had seen before, during her pregnancy – was waiting.

'Take a seat,' she said as Christina closed the door behind her. 'How are you doing?'

'I've been having a problem with nausea. Well, not just that. Headaches and chest pain too.'

'Okay. How long have you been getting these?'

'The nausea maybe a month or so. The headaches and the chest pain longer.'

'Any pattern you've noticed? Do they get worse after you've exercised, or do they happen at any particular time of day?'

Christina shook her head. 'I mean, I don't get enough regular exercise now, not with work and the twins, but there doesn't seem to be any pattern I've noticed. They just come on randomly.'

Dr Kane glanced at the notes on her computer screen before picking up her stethoscope from the desk. 'I'll just listen to your chest and then do your obs, if that's okay?'

When she had finished, she checked the screen again.

'How is your menstrual cycle since having the twins? Your periods were a bit erratic before you got pregnant, weren't they? And was that around the same time you were prescribed medication for migraines?'

Christina nodded. 'It's been about the same as it was before. My cycle has never been regular.'

'Okay. And when was your last period?'

'I don't know. Five weeks ago? Maybe six.' She felt herself growing frustrated. This was nothing to do with her periods.

'Is there any chance you might be pregnant?'

'No,' she answered, too quickly.

She noticed the doctor's lips purse. 'You're using contraceptives?'

She felt her face flush. She was being spoken to as though she was some naïve teenage girl, not a thirty-three-year-old woman who was quite aware of how to prevent herself from getting pregnant.

But had she been careful enough? The possibility had already occurred to her, though she had tried to push the thought to the back of her mind.

'We haven't been having sex,' she said, her voice clipped. 'With two children who don't sleep well, it hasn't really been at the top of my priorities.'

Dr Kane was silent for a moment, allowing Christina time to feel embarrassed by her reaction.

'This chest pain you mentioned. Whereabouts do you get it exactly?'

'Right in the middle, here.' She gestured with her hand and pushed her fingers to the bone.

The doctor nodded. 'I think it could be anxiety. You've mentioned the children's sleep too. Are you working full-time?'

'Yes.'

Dr Kane nodded again, as though this fact confirmed her diagnosis.

'If you'd like some help with the sleep issue, it might be worth you making contact with the health visitor. She might be able to give you some suggestions. Other than that, what I'd like you to do for now is just keep an eye on the symptoms. If they get any worse, get in touch again. And I'd like to see you again if you haven't had a period within the next month. Would that be okay?'

Christina stood and put her jacket back on. 'Thank you,' she said, not feeling particularly thankful. She was no nearer help than she had been when she had arrived. The doctor thought there was a chance she might be pregnant, and that the symptoms she had mentioned were all related to that, but she had never suffered chest pain when she was pregnant with the twins, or any other time for that matter. It felt like a fist gripping her sternum, clenching and twisting until she became dizzy.

She stopped in the empty corridor, put her head against a wall and took a deep breath. She had told the doctor her last period had been five or six weeks ago, but she wasn't sure. It could well have been longer. It had been a month since she had finished things with Joel. They'd had sex just a week before that.

No. She wouldn't allow herself to even consider it a possibility. They had been careful; she had always made sure of that.

She fell through the doors of the surgery and out into the car park, gasping for a lungful of fresh air. When she reached the car, Elise was sitting in the front passenger seat, watching *Peppa Pig* on Matthew's phone. Edward was still sleeping. That was no surprise, not after the terrible night he'd had.

'Everything okay?' Matthew mouthed as she opened the door.

'Mummy!'

Elise's voice, always a boom, jolted her brother from his slumber, and he opened his eyes with a look of creased confusion, his mouth quickly contorting to form a wail. Christina sighed and leaned into the back seat, stroking her hand gently down his cheek to soothe him.

'Right, you,' Matthew said, lifting Elise from the passenger seat. 'In the back you go, missy.'

Elise wriggled and kicked in protest, and soon the two children were wailing in competition with one another, their frustration and over-tiredness creating a wall of sound that lined the car.

They made the journey home without conversation, neither Matthew nor Christina able to hear the other above the noise. Christina rested her forehead against the cool window, hoping it might ease her headache a little, but there was no chance of that while the screaming persisted. Anxiety, she thought. Perhaps Dr Kane had been right after all.

'Can we stop at the chemist? The doctor has given me a prescription.'

The possibility of a little life growing inside her took root in her stomach, gnawing at her insides as though they had been starved. Matthew would know he wasn't the father if the timings didn't add up. There would be no way of convincing him that the baby was his. She screwed her eyes tightly shut, wishing the past few months could somehow be undone. The noise from the back seat kept her in the present. She had got herself into this mess, and now she was going to have to find a way out.

TWENTY-ONE

BROOKE

I am sitting out on the narrow strip of pavement, watching a burnt-orange sun bleed into a darkening horizon. When the evenings are dry, I like to sit outside and listen to the sounds of the sea, to the water lapping at the harbour wall and the distant caw of gulls circulating in their search for the day's leftovers. This place is just as beautiful when it is cold as when it is warm; in fact, I think I prefer it at this time of year, when the sharp-edged air is at its most raw. There is a haunting bleakness about the landscape, something final in the curve of the mountainside that lunges down to the sea. Beneath it, I am minuscule. Nothing. I am reminded of how fragile and precious all of life is.

I'm sitting where I usually would, in front of the terrace. Building work started this morning. As I watched the men clearing timbers and removing shards of debris that I recognised as former paintings, I studied their faces, considering them possible suspects, wondering whether in a life lived so quietly and inoffensively, an incident such as this might make me wary of everyone. Worse has happened, I think, not for the first time. But what if worse is yet to come?

With the house just there, on the hillside above me, I sit in the shadow of my former life. My childhood plays out in the woodland behind, our voices still tangled in the winds that whip out to the ocean; we are all there, the four of us, ghosts. And then there is that night, the most vivid memory of all.

Though I am the last of us living, I sometimes feel spirited away already, that if I sit here long enough – if I focus on the house and allow myself to be lost to my surroundings – I am already gone, the four of us reunited, together in the way we once were. *You live in the past*, Delta once said to me. It was easy for her to say, when our pasts had been built on the same foundations and had yet been so very different. She was the good girl. The one who had told the truth. No one would have guessed that in our house of cards, I would remain the last one standing.

Despite having previously told Delta that I would never go to London, I did. I think now of watching her on that stage just a month before her death, bathed under a sun of warm spotlights, oblivious to the fact that I was there. I had resolved not to tell her that I was going or that I had been, believing at the time that it was better for us both if my visit was a silent and distanced one. A month later, upon receiving that call, I wished I *had* told her. I wish now that I could tell her just how brilliant and beautiful she was.

I wish I could tell her that I forgive her.

When I next saw my mother, the first person she asked after was Delta. I was used to that – her younger daughter was quite often her first thought, regardless of the time that had passed since we had last had a visit from her. I had been standing by the door, poised to take the coward's route and leave having only just got there, but then we had been interrupted by one of the carers popping her head around the door to ask if either of us would like a cup of tea. Forced to stay, I watched as my mother nibbled the edges of a custard cream, methodically turning the biscuit until she reached its final corner.

There were times I was tempted to remind Mum of how little we had both at times seemed to mean to Delta. 'Look after your sister,' I had always been told, as though being the elder sibling meant Delta was my responsibility, and I had silently accepted a role I had never been given an opportunity to refuse. I never did remind her, though; not then, and not after. We hadn't had long after. Within three weeks, my mother was also gone. I never told her about the accident, allowing her to believe instead that her younger daughter's star continued to rise in the capital, on a stage flooded by spotlights and to the rousing applause of an audience who adored her almost as much as she had. 'My little starlet' she had always called Delta, and yet now it had become my turn to perform, putting on an act during every visit to the nursing home, and stripping off my costume once I stepped back outside.

My phone ringing breaks the trail of my thoughts. I move further beneath the comfort and warmth of the blanket thrown over my knees and search my pocket for my mobile, finding it just as Oliver hangs up. I haven't seen or spoken to him since I was last at the house, and I am in no hurry to do so. He made his views clear enough.

And yet I keep my phone here in my lap, clutching it as though expecting him to call again. Though why would he? He will wait for me to return the call, or try me again tomorrow. I lean my head back and close my eyes, allowing the night air to cool my skin. His words return to me – *you don't even have children, Brooke, so please don't give me advice about mine* – and I wonder whether he realises just how deeply they cut. It occurs to me that I don't want to wait until tomorrow to know what he wants to say to me, and so my fingers tap in my passcode and retrieve his number, unsure whether I am doing the right thing.

'Brooke,' he says, answering after the third ring. 'Thanks for getting back to me.'

'Everything okay?' I ask, trying to sound as casual as possible. 'It's pretty late.'

'Yeah, I know. I'm sorry. It's just... it couldn't really wait.'

'The meter's not playing up again, is it?'

'No, I... Look, could you come over? I'm sorry to ask. I'd come to you if I could, but Fin's asleep and I can't leave him, so...' He trails into silence, waiting for my reply.

'It's late,' I say again.

'Okay. Of course. Sorry I disturbed you. I'll let you get on. Um... yeah. Bye.'

After he hangs up, the cool air doesn't seem so appealing. I realise I am now cold, and though I pull the blanket closer to warm me, it cannot keep out the chill that seems to reside within my bones. I see the figure of a twelve-year-old Delta dart from the harbour wall, dancing in the darkened shadows. I hear Lewis's words, a distant echo, taunting in my ear. Tired of being cold and alone, I push the blanket from me, bundle it under my arm and head across the street.

Sylvia's house is darkened, dead to the night. I should go inside and go to bed, but I don't.

The path to Hillside Cottage is coated in a heavy blackness, and when I look at my phone, it is later than I realised – almost nine thirty. Doubt creeps into my chest, but my feet continue to move, carrying me onwards, and I allow them to do so, powered by the feeling of needing five minutes' company. As the path turns to the left and the house comes into sight, the light from the kitchen window casts a glow along the driveway. I don't see him at first, but then there is movement, a shadow at the glass, and I wonder whether he has seen me. I don't want to knock and wake Finley up. I am deliberating whether to call Oliver or to risk giving him a heart attack by appearing suddenly at the window when the front door opens.

'I saw you on the path,' he says, as though he needs to explain himself. 'Come on in, it's freezing.'

I follow him into the house and find myself lingering in the hallway, as Finley did when I showed them around the place nearly six weeks ago. It seems strange to feel so hesitant in my own home – and yet this is no longer my home, and it hasn't been for quite some time now. I have made it, even if only for the time being, someone else's home. Another family, not my own.

'Is everything okay?' I ask.

'Yeah. Come in.' He steps further into the living room and I wait for him to gesture to the sofa. 'Look, I...' He is still standing, and then, as though realising it is making him look awkward and uncomfortable, he drops into the chair opposite. 'I'm sorry. I'm really sorry for what I said before, when, you know—'

'It doesn't matter.'

'No, it does matter.' He tilts his head, urges me to make eye contact with him, then stands again. 'I got you something.' He goes to the sideboard, opens a drawer and takes out a black jewellery box. 'It's a thank you,' he says. 'For everything you've done for Fin.'

'I haven't done anything.'

He comes closer and extends an arm, offering me the box. I don't move at first, almost as though my body has frozen and doesn't know the appropriate way to react.

'You don't have to accept it, of course,' he adds.

'I'm sorry.' I reach and take the box from him. 'It's just... it's been a long time since anyone gave me a gift. Thank you.' I don't need to open it to see that it is jewellery. I try to remember the last time someone gave me a piece of jewellery. A boyfriend, years ago. It was supposed to mean something, but at the time, all I saw was an unspoken expectation that I knew I wouldn't be able to live up to.

Oliver watches me as I flip up the lid. Inside is a necklace, a delicate silver chain with an aquamarine jewel in a teardrop pendant lined with tiny diamonds. It is beautiful. 'Wow,' I say, not really knowing what the right thing to say is. 'This is certainly an elaborate way to say thank you. I usually just get a box of After Eights or something.'

'Is it too much? It's too much, isn't it? Sorry... It's just that I was in Fishguard and it caught my eye in the shop window and it was too lovely to leave there, and it was sort of spur of the moment, you know, and...'

If my awkwardness is visible, Oliver's is currently doing a dance naked around the living room. He stops talking and bites his lower lip as though to prevent himself from saying anything more, before sitting back down in the chair opposite me.

'It's beautiful,' I tell him, which it is. 'But I can't accept it.'

He doesn't ask why. 'That's okay,' he says, but he doesn't move to take it back from me.

'It's just... It's really kind of you, but...' I wonder why neither of us seems able to construct a coherent sentence, like two awkward teenagers fumbling their way through a first date. Because the necklace might be a thank-you, but it is also something else, something I am unready for; something I may never be ready for. The woodland returns to me, dark and enclosed. Lewis's face is there again, so close to mine that I can smell the alcohol on his breath.

'You don't have to explain,' he says, and he reaches to take the box from me. 'I'm sorry. I didn't want to make you feel uncomfortable.'

'I should get back,' I say.

He follows me to the front door. It has started raining. 'Wait,' he says. 'You can borrow an umbrella.'

He is gone before I can object, returning a few moments later. When he passes me the umbrella, his fingers touch mine. He looks at me a beat too long. 'I'm sorry again.'

'It's okay.'

'Goodnight, Brooke.'

'Goodnight.'

I step outside, open the umbrella and head into the darkness without looking back. At the turn on the driveway, I sense him still there, the light from the open doorway illuminating the path ahead. He wanted to kiss me, I think, replaying those last few moments. At the bottom of the hill, I make my way to Sylvia's. As I get ready for bed, moving through the motions of my evening ritual, I wish I had let him do it.

TWENTY-TWO

CHRISTINA

MARCH 2018

Once they got the children home, Matthew bathed Elise while Christina played in the living room with Edward. It was sometimes necessary to separate the twins when things became too chaotic, and baths in the middle of the afternoon had become a regularly employed method of calming flared tempers. The pregnancy test that she had bought in the chemist's was still in the paper bag she had asked for, tucked into the waist of her jeans and concealed beneath her oversized sweater. She had been tempted to do the test as soon as they got back, but she knew that the results would be most accurate first thing in the morning. As she couldn't risk Matthew finding the box, it meant keeping the test on her person until he left for work, with a long night of anxiety and uncertainty ahead of her.

'Where does the sheep go?' She passed her son a puzzle piece, and watched as he moved it from space to space on the farmland cut-out puzzle board, wiggling it about until he found the right place. 'Good boy!' She mussed his hair, smiling at the little frown that curled his mouth. His thinking face. 'What about the pig? Where's the pig?'

They were interrupted by the doorbell. Christina got up to answer it, finding her brother's girlfriend on the doorstep. 'I hope it's not too late for popping round,' Alice said. 'You're not getting the kids ready for bed yet, are you?'

'No, you're fine. They'll be excited to see you.'

She followed Christina through to the living room. 'I was just on my way home from work,' she explained. 'Leighton's out with a friend tonight. Hey, little man!'

She held her arms out to Edward, who ran into the cuddle. Alice put her face against his, nuzzling into his soft hair. 'Stop getting so big,' she said. 'I swear you've grown two inches every time I see you.'

Christina smiled, moving a hand to her waistband to check that the box hadn't slipped when she'd got up to answer the door. 'Do you fancy a cup of tea?'

'Only if you're having one. Right then, why don't you show me what you've been doing with Mummy?'

Christina went into the kitchen to put the kettle on. Upstairs, she could hear the hair dryer as Matthew dried Elise's hair. She put a hand to the curve of her stomach. What had she done? She loved her children, but a third had never been part of the plan. Matthew would leave her, and she would be a single parent to three; either that, or he would try for custody of the twins. Maybe, with everything she had done, he would stand a good chance of winning. She would be deemed selfish, irresponsible, unfit to be a mother.

She made the tea and headed back to the living room. Matthew was helping Elise down the stairs. 'You okay?' he asked. 'Headache gone?'

'Yes,' she lied. 'I'm fine, honestly. Don't worry. You'd better go and get some sleep, hadn't you?'

'Do you mind?' He glanced at the two cups in her hand. 'Is someone here?'

'Alice has just dropped round.'

He looked at the living room door. 'Say hi for me. I'll leave you to it.'

Elise, all glossy-haired and newly calm, ran to Alice when she saw her, wrapping her little arms around her waist for a hug before going to the toy box and pulling out a wooden tea set.

'I'm glad you're here,' Christina said. 'I wanted to speak to you about the twins' birthday.'

'Not far away now, is it?' Alice said, helping to direct Edward's puzzle piece to the right space. 'Made any plans?'

'Not yet. But I'd like to. Ollie and Fin were going to come, but...' She trailed off, not knowing how to explain the decision that had been made without Matthew coming out of it unfavourably.

'But what?'

'Matthew doesn't think it's a good idea.'

'How come?'

Christina lowered her voice. 'Christmas.'

Alice said nothing, maintaining what Christina assumed was a diplomatic silence. She had been a witness to that particular festive season, though she had never passed comment. Christina got up to close the living room door.

'I'm probably being silly here, but do you think Matthew likes Ollie?'

'What's not to like? Ollie's lovely. Everyone likes him. Don't they?'

'I don't know. Matthew's always been a little bit... I don't know... off around him. Have you ever noticed it?'

'Not really. Perhaps he feels a bit left out; do you think that could be it?'

'What do you mean?'

Alice pondered the question. 'Male pride, I reckon. You and Ollie share something that Matthew's not a part of. He doesn't have the memories of Bethany that you two do – perhaps he feels excluded by that. I don't know, I'm just going on what I've seen. Matthew loves you. I think he just feels this need to be the one who puts everything right, but where Bethany's concerned, he can't.'

'So he's jealous of Ollie then?'

Alice pulled a face. 'In a way, I suppose.' She clapped as

Edward found the right place for the horse he had been shoving into various incorrect spaces for the past few minutes. 'Is he working tonight?' she asked, taking a sip of tea.

Christina nodded. 'He's gone to get a couple of hours' sleep.'

'Are you okay? You look a bit pale.'

'I'm fine. It's just a headache, that's all.'

She watched as Alice helped Edward complete the animal puzzle with one hand while pouring Elise an imaginary cup of tea with the other.

'Leighton's worried about you.'

'Why?'

'He thinks you've not been yourself.'

I'm not, Christina thought. I haven't been myself in a long time. I'm not even sure I know who I am any more.

She had to tell someone, get it all out in the open, no matter what the cost. She could be honest with Alice, she trusted her; she would admit all her failings and feel lighter for having done so. Carrying the secret alone was breaking her.

But just as quickly as it had come, the feeling passed. She couldn't do it to Leighton; he had already suffered enough. And what would telling Alice achieve? It would only be passing the weight of the burden on to someone else, and that would just be selfish.

She smiled. 'My brother is a worrier, isn't he? Honestly, I'm fine. As soon as this little one starts sleeping,' she said, gently mussing Edward's hair, 'I'll be a new woman, just wait and see.'

'We don't need a new you,' Alice said kindly. 'The old one will do just fine.'

'She's still here, I promise. Somewhere. Just, you know... young kids and all that. Anyway, work busy?'

The question lit a spark, and Alice came alive in its glow, embracing the opportunity to share what that week had brought her. Christina listened with a mixture of interest and envy as Alice regaled her with an anecdote about an arrest that hadn't quite gone to plan. There had been a time when Christina had felt this way about her own job, her own life. She listened and nodded, wondering where and when her spark had gone out, grateful that she had found a way to divert the conversation from herself.

'I'd better let you go,' Alice said after they'd been chatting for a while. 'You've probably got plenty to be getting on with.'

'There's no need to rush off.' Christina made no attempt to sound casual. It was lovely having the company, and she didn't want Alice to leave. 'We're not going anywhere. Stay for another cuppa?'

'Only if you let me make it.'

'Mine's that bad, is it?' Christina smiled and pulled a face. 'I'm sure the kids would rather have you stay and play than me.' She took Alice's empty cup. 'I think there might be some cake left somewhere too – I'll have a look.'

She went into the kitchen and flicked on the kettle again. As she waited for it to boil, her work mobile sounded from the top of the microwave, where she had left it plugged into its charger. She went to check it. There was a message from an unsaved number.

Your secret's out.

Attached to the message was a photograph. When she saw it, Christina felt ice pass through her, as though her veins had been frozen, and her blood stopped in its flow. The image was grainy, though it was clear enough to see that it was her, naked from the waist down, lying on Joel's bed. He was in front of her, his back to the camera. She remembered that afternoon vividly, and as it played out as though in front of her, she tried to swallow down the panic that lodged in her throat.

Why was he doing this to her? What sort of person installed a secret camera, filming someone without their knowledge?

And then another thought occurred to her. What if Joel wasn't responsible for this? What if someone else had been watching them together and he hadn't known that camera was there? Her mind returned to the day she had gone to his flat, to what the neighbour had said. If the flat was noisy, had Joel been there with other women? What if one of them had found out about Christina and had planted that camera there to catch him out?

She ran a hand across the back of her neck, wiping the sweat that had pooled there. This person had her work number; they knew exactly who she was. *Your secret's out.* Out where, exactly? How long before this image ended up in Matthew's hands, or on the internet, where anyone might be able to access it? Her marriage, her career... everything would be ruined.

With fumbling hands, she tapped out a reply. *Who is this? Just tell me what you want from me.*

TWENTY-THREE

BROOKE

OCTOBER 2019

On Sunday, I cook the weekly roast dinner at Sylvia's house. Ever since I've been living at the gallery, she has allowed me to use her washing machine. She also lets me have a bath whenever I fancy one; showers are fine, but it's nice to have the occasional option of soaking in a tub of bubbles and losing myself in a book for an hour. In exchange, I have been cleaning her house weekly and doing her food shopping for years now. She insisted on me coming here once a week for a 'proper' meal (she seemed convinced that I didn't eat anything between Monday and Saturday), and I have always agreed, providing that she allows me to do the cooking. Now, with her house my temporary home, I don't need to get changed out of my pyjamas to prep the vegetables.

There is a storm forecast for later today; the sky has already turned dark and heavy. Light rain begins to fall as Sylvia and I work together in the kitchen.

'How long is Oliver staying at Hillside Cottage?' she asks, trimming runner beans at the table as I prepare the roast potatoes. 'Been there a while already, hasn't he?'

I haven't spoken to Sylvia about Oliver, though there doesn't seem to be much she misses. The village is so small that the arrival of a new face constitutes an event worthy of teatime gossip, and someone staying at the house for longer than a fortnight is unheard of.

'Until Christmas,' I tell her.

'Working locally, is he?'

'Not yet.'

'So he hopes to?'

'I think so.'

I am being purposely evasive, and I feel Sylvia eyeballing me as she assesses my abbreviated answers. 'Good-looking, isn't he?'

'Is he?'

She drops the beans into a saucepan. 'Don't tell me you hadn't noticed.'

I say nothing, but I see Sylvia smile wryly as she stands and brings the saucepan to the stove.

'He gave me a present.' I've been wanting to tell someone, if only for a second opinion. I like him, though liking people – liking men – has brought me little good luck in the past. I barely know him, yet there is something that draws me to him, something I haven't felt or allowed myself to feel in a long time. The timing of our meeting feels significant somehow. The fire. Lewis's arrival back in the village. What if Oliver was sent at a time when I needed him?

'A present?'

'A necklace.'

She smiles that same smile, an eyebrow raised inquisitively. 'Well, come on, let's see it then.'

I turn the potatoes in their oil and lift the oven tray from the worktop. 'I gave it back.'

The eyebrow drops, as though it has been released from an invisible string. 'You gave it back?'

'There's an echo in here.' I stoop to the oven and slide the tray onto the shelf before turning up the heat.

'I always said you were a strange one.'

'And I've always known I can come to you for a compliment.'

Sylvia returns to the table. 'You didn't want to give it back, did you?'

'I don't know anything about him.'

'That wasn't what I asked.'

'Do you fancy a cup of tea?'

'Always,' she says, giving an exaggerated sigh.

I put the kettle on and go to the fridge to get the carrots while it boils.

'And have you asked him?' she says as I put the bag on the table.

'Asked him what?'

'About himself. You said you don't know anything about him. Seems to me you'll never know if you don't ask.' She drops a carrot on the floor. I move to pick it up, but she ushers me away, fiercely independent as always. 'Well... have you?'

'There are certain subjects that are difficult to broach, aren't there? I mean, I can't really just come out and say, so where's Fin's mother, can I?'

Sylvia pulls a disapproving face, the one that always emerges when she finds me flippant. In my mother's absence, she has been the one person I can rely on to not tolerate my abrasiveness.

'Just talk to him. You won't have to prompt it. If you talk to him, it'll come. What's he like with his boy?'

'Lovely. Fin's a quiet little thing, but they seem very close. I suppose they have to be, if it's just the two of them.'

'Do you know,' says Sylvia, 'whenever I met a new boyfriend, I always judged him on how he treated his mother. You can tell a good man that way. The same applies to fathers, doesn't it? Good dad... good man.'

I take one of the carrots Sylvia has peeled while we've been talking and chop it into pieces. 'It must be hard for him, though, being on his own with his son. No man is an island, as they say.'

'And no woman is an island either,' she says, trying to catch my eye. 'You mustn't go through life believing every man is like Lewis.'

The room falls into silence at the mention of his name. As brief as our past conversations concerning him have been, they were all I needed – sufficient to let me know that unlike everyone else, Sylvia believed me. She must know he is back, but she hasn't mentioned it. Perhaps she is staying silent in the hope of keeping me protected.

'Don't be alone all your life only to get old and regret it. I can confirm that being old and alone isn't much fun.' She passes me a carrot. 'Anyway,' she says, her sing-song tone an attempt to lighten the tension, 'what's a woman got to do around here to get a cup of tea?'

I had forgotten I had put the kettle on, and go to make the tea, grateful for the opportunity to hide my face for a moment, aware that Sylvia can read my thoughts.

'He's back,' I say quietly.

The room falls silent again. At last Sylvia sighs deeply. 'I had heard, love. I'm sorry.'

'I saw him come out of the pub, and then I saw him in Fishguard.'

'Must be the break-in at his mother's.' She gets up from her chair and comes over to me, putting a hand on my arm. I am unsure which of us she is trying to steady. 'Son of the year now, is he? Do you want me to go over there and speak to Jean?'

'No.' I turn sharply. 'I know you mean well, but please, don't do anything. Don't mention this to anyone either. He probably won't be here long – he'll be gone again in no time. But I did wonder...' My words fade as I struggle to find the end of the sentence.

'What?'

'The fire.'

She studies me intently, concern etched on her kind face. Her brow furrows. 'You don't think he would have... But why?'

'I don't know. It's stupid, obviously. I'm just tired, that's all.'

Her fingers tighten their grip on my arm before she lets go and returns to her chair. 'Should have been in prison a long time ago.'

I say nothing and finish making the tea, taking a cup over to her. We sit side by side in silence, separate with our own thoughts. I hear Delta's voice on repeat in my head, that single, breathless word – my name on her lips – and I wonder, not for the first time, could he be responsible for that too? I, better than anyone, know just how cruel Lewis Miller can be.

After dinner, Sylvia and I do a crossword from her newspaper together, and then I leave her reading while I go for a bath. I can focus on nothing other than her words, his name echoing, taunting me. I lie back and close my eyes.

I am sixteen years old, my birthday just a few days behind me. Delta will be fifteen in a few months' time, yet to look at her, to hear her speak, anyone would think she is far older. We have been drinking a bottle of vodka in the woods together, the two of us light-headed and giddy, finding humour in the inane. We have never done this before – we have never done anything like this before – but Delta dared me to take a bottle from the top cupboard in the kitchen, and I did it just to prove I wasn't the chicken she claimed I was.

We've had an argument. It was so stupid, so inconsequential, that afterwards I can't remember how it started or what it was about. All I remember is that she left me. After swigging her last mouthful from the bottle, she threw it onto the leafy ground at my feet and said she was going home. *Go*, I told her. *I don't care.* But once she is out of sight, I care far more than I claimed.

I don't know the woods as well as I thought, or perhaps the alcohol has disrupted my sense of direction. After fifteen minutes of walking, I don't recognise where I am, and where I expected to hear the roar of the sea, I am met with trees that scrape the sky and a whispering wind that taunts me, telling me I'm lost and alone. My head is spinning; I feel sick at the prospect of being on my own somewhere so remote and isolated. It is getting dark too quickly, the grey afternoon that could be glimpsed between the trees not long ago now dulled into a darkness that seems to close in around me.

Panic has already set in by the time I hear the footsteps.

Someone is running, snapping twigs and rustling leaves under feet that are moving quickly towards me. It is only then that I realise how cold I have become, as though the alcohol that has filtered into my bloodstream, warming me from the inside out, has suddenly left, draining me to a chill that permeates every bone.

I turn. When I see it is Lewis, relief floods through me. He will know his way back to the village. He will help me find my way home.

'Brooke.' He looks at the vodka bottle in my hand, his lips curling into a sneer.

'It's not mine,' I say, feeling stupid and childish. 'It's Delta's.'

He nods, disbelieving. 'Look at you,' he says, his voice strange. 'All grown up.'

I feel myself blushing. I don't want to be here; I want to go home. Where is Delta? Did she find her way back? Why has no one come looking for me? 'Are you heading back to the village?' I ask.

'At some point,' he says. 'But there's no rush, is there?' He steps towards me and holds out a hand. 'Any left for me?'

I pass him the bottle. He takes a swig, screwing up his face as the sharpness of the alcohol hits the back of his throat.

'Have a bit more,' he says, holding it out to me.

I shake my head; I've had enough.

'Have a bit more,' he says again, and this time I understand that it is not a request but an instruction. I look past him, into the darkness that lies behind him and all around us, and realise I have nowhere to go. He is so close to me, yet he looks nothing like him. His voice sounds nothing like his.

I allow the liquid to touch my lips, trying to avoid having to swallow any more of it.

'Relax,' he says with a smile. 'Loosen up a bit.' He takes the bottle from me and puts it on the ground. He is standing too close to me, so close that I can smell the sweat from his T-shirt, and when he reaches for my shoulders my body freezes.

Run, Brooke, I tell my younger self, my insides screaming, begging for her to hear me. *Run. Shout. Do something.* I open my mouth to scream, as though my voice will become hers, but nothing escapes me. And then I realise that I cannot make a sound. No words can leave my mouth. I cannot breathe.

Water cascades from the bathtub as my body heaves upright, and as I splutter and fight for air, I realise I have no idea how long I was submerged beneath the surface. I must have made more noise than my own ears heard, because within moments Sylvia is at the door, knocking a warning that she is going to enter the room.

'What's happened, love? Are you all right?'

I must look a mess. I put make-up on this morning, an attempt to hide the tiredness that hangs around my eyes; it must now be staining watery black streaks down my face. I am drenched, drowned; disorientated.

She moves to the side of the bath, keeping her eyes averted politely as she sinks to sit on the bathmat. 'Oh sweetheart,' she says, and her fingers move lightly across my wet hair, working to free the memory that lies beneath. 'Let me speak to the police for you. If they don't know what happened, someone should tell them.'

'They didn't believe me the first time. Why would they now?'

We sit in silence for a while, and if Sylvia sees my tears, she makes no mention of them. 'I'll go and put the kettle on,' she says eventually, and after she has gone, I get out of the bath, my limbs turned purple with the cold.

TWENTY-FOUR

CHRISTINA

MARCH 2018

It was 5.15 a.m. and the twins were both still sleeping. Matthew wasn't due home until lunchtime. Christina sat on the edge of the bath, looking at the unopened pregnancy test. She didn't want to do it. She had to do it. She opened the box, ripped the top of the foil packet and pulled out the white stick. She couldn't do it. She felt sick.

Was the nausea the same as it had been in those early months of her pregnancy with the twins? She had tested positive just days after her missed period, her hormones already in overdrive, finding out at the first scan seven weeks later that she was carrying not one but two babies. The morning sickness had stayed with her for the next four months, refusing to fade out after week twelve as had been promised by all the online and magazine articles she had read. It had been gruelling and relentless at the time, and yet now that she tried to recall how it had felt, she found the memory blurred by everything that had happened since.

Her work phone was resting on the sink nearby. She had looked at the image that had been sent the previous afternoon over and over, sickened by the sight of it yet unable to turn away. Eventually, in the early hours of the morning, she had deleted it, hoping to obliterate the reality of it. If it had been from Joel, why had he sent it to her work number rather than the mobile she had used for communicating with him during their affair? It didn't seem plausible that it had come from him, yet that left the question of who *had* sent it.

How had she made such a mess of her marriage? She and Matthew had been at school together, but had been reunited at the age of twenty-five, seven years after last seeing each other. Christina had been sitting on a bench on Hampstead Heath, not far from the flat where she was living. A voice had said her name, twice; she had been miles away, in some other world: a distant, far-off life that she had had to say goodbye to the previous afternoon.

A tall young man wearing a green parka had stopped a few feet from her. He smiled, his eyes widening in expectation – she was supposed to recognise him – and she had apologised, hoping that she wouldn't be dragged into a conversation she didn't want to engage in. She had gone there to be alone, and she wished to remain that way.

'Matthew,' he had said. 'Matthew Hale. From school.'

It had taken a further moment, but then she had made the connection. He looked completely different. The hair that had once been worn long had been cut short, the face that had been kept hidden all those years earlier now on show.

'I'm so sorry,' she had said. 'I didn't recognise you. How are you?'

'Good, thanks. Really good. I just moved to the area a couple of months ago. How are things with you?'

She had nodded. 'Fine,' she said, swallowing down the truth, its taste sour in her throat. She had been as far from fine as she thought it possible to be.

'Are you living around here now?'

She had nodded. A lump had formed in her chest, pulling her voice away from her throat.

'Is everything okay?'

Try as she might, she had been unable to keep the pain from showing, the corners of her eyes damp with tears she was determined to keep back. A sudden embarrassment had flooded her, rushing to her cheeks in a burst of colour. 'Sorry,' she had said, and she had run her thumb under her right eye, taking a deep breath of crisp autumn air to calm herself. 'I'm fine, honestly.'

An awkward silence had followed, Matthew seeming uncertain whether to say goodbye and resume his walk or to stop and sit with her, and Christina unsure which she would prefer. She had wanted to be alone and yet she hadn't; she had wanted to talk and yet she couldn't. The person closest to her was Leighton, and he was the very person she couldn't speak to. Her brother had shut himself off from the world, shielding himself from everything that might possibly cause him further pain.

'We cremated my sister yesterday.'

The words left her as though involuntarily, and hearing them out in the open didn't make them sound any more real. Bethany was supposed to be there that afternoon, walking with her, as they had done once a week for the past year. They had taken that same path, stopped to sit on that same bench, followed the same pattern, never diverting from the routine for fear that the change would set something in Bethany reeling. But it had already been too late for that. Something had embedded itself within Bethany's brain, some parasite that had eaten through her happiness, and nothing was going to bring her back to them. But Christina could only see that now.

'God,' Matthew had said, shifting his weight uncomfortably. 'I'm so sorry.' He hadn't known where to look, and as she had wiped her eyes with her sleeve again, Christina had been grateful that his focus hadn't rested upon her.

'No,' she had responded hurriedly, '*I'm* sorry. I don't know why I told you that. You're just taking a walk, minding your own business, and I offload my problems onto you. Sorry.'

Matthew had acknowledged an elderly couple walking their dog, giving them a faint smile and waiting for them to pass before he sat at the other end of the bench.

'Don't apologise. I can't imagine what you must be going

through. Was she unwell? Sorry,' he had added quickly. 'I shouldn't have asked that.'

'No, it's fine. Yes, she was unwell. Not in the way you probably mean, though.' She had pushed her hands into her pockets. 'Anyway,' she had said with embarrassment, blinking back tears. 'There's probably somewhere you need to be, isn't there? Where were you heading?'

'Only home. I've got the day off.'

Another awkward silence had followed. Christina had wished she was wearing something warmer; she hadn't realised how cold it was.

'Do you fancy—'

'I'd better be—'

They had spoken at the same time, each simultaneously cutting short the other's words.

'Go on,' Christina said. 'Sorry.'

'I was just going to suggest we go for a coffee somewhere. You don't have to talk – we could just warm up a bit. Don't know about you, but I'm freezing.'

She had been about to say that she had better be heading home, though there was no reason to, with nothing and no one to go home to.

'Okay,' she had agreed. 'Yeah... why not?'

And they had gone for coffee together, walking to the nearest café in a companionable silence that she recalled as comforting. She hadn't felt the need to fill the air between them with words, and it was this she remembered all these years later, sitting on the edge of the bathtub with a pregnancy test in her hand, wondering if she was carrying another man's child. Matthew had made her feel safe and secure. He had anchored her when life had cut her adrift, yet somewhere during these past seven years she had become untethered. Now she felt as though she was sinking.

She got up and moved to the toilet, knowing that she could no longer delay the inevitable.

TWENTY-FIVE
BROOKE
OCTOBER 2019

Ignoring the forecast and Sylvia's advice, I head out for what I know will be a long walk. I feel I will go mad if I stay in the house any longer, and there is nothing I need more than sea air in my lungs and the wind against my face. The sky darkens as I get further along the coastal path, a mass of black clouds looming over-head. When the rain comes, it is relentless and unforgiving, yet there is something about its sharpness and its driving iciness that makes me feel alive. I should turn around, but I don't.

Where the hedgerow tapers off and the land merges with the sky, the force of the wind almost knocks me from my feet. I stand my ground while I look out to sea, watching in awe as the waves break and crash, the water in turmoil with itself. The wind screams past my ears, drowning out everything else that tries to fight for prominence in my cluttered brain, and for a moment there is nothing but the sea and me: no fire, no Lewis, no one.

I have my head down against the hammering rain when I hear his voice. He is calling someone's name, and when I look up, I realise he is shouting to a dog that is too close to the cliff edge. I'd had no idea he was still in the village. The dog must be his mother's.

There is no way to avoid him unless I turn and walk back the way I've come. The path is barely two feet wide, though he at least steps to one side when he sees me, finding a gap in the hedgerow where he can leave room for me to pass. He is wearing unsuitable clothing for this weather, his coat soaked through and his jeans clinging to his legs. The dog, finally listening to instructions, runs to join him. The poor animal is clearly distressed by the weather; I feel its anxiety transfer to me as a warning that I should go home, yet the thought that I have no real home to go to sounds like a klaxon in my brain, drowning out what might be regarded as common sense.

'You shouldn't be out in this,' he says, wiping rain from his face. 'It's too dangerous up here.'

I narrow my eyes, waiting for what comes next. Nothing comes but a surge of wind, and the dog starts howling in competition with the growing storm.

When I move to pass him, Lewis puts out a hand and grabs my arm. 'Seriously, Brooke, don't be stupid. I'll walk you back to the village.'

Rivers of rainwater streak his cheeks and trail down his chin. His dark hair is flattened beneath the hood of his coat, which is soaked through. I wonder what he is doing here; the storm has been forecast for days. What am I doing here? What if our reasons for being here are the same?

I yank my arm from his grip. 'You could have done that sixteen years ago.'

I expect some sarcastic remark, something flippant that manages somehow to shirk all responsibility or blame. It is what he has always done; what he will always do. 'I know,' he says instead. 'And I should have. But I can do it now.'

Still waiting for the punchline, for the comment that belittles me and reminds me of everything he is, I stand my ground against the wind and the rain. Just metres from us, the cliff edge curves to a drop, the ocean crashing against the rocks thirty feet below. Its noise competes with the storm that breaks overhead, and in the distance, there is a low rumble of thunder.

'Come on,' he urges me again. 'Please.'

'Admit it.'

'What?'

'Admit what you did.' I raise my hands to show him that they are empty, that this isn't a trick to gain a recorded confession. 'I just want to hear you say it. All these years I've lived with what happened that night, when you got to walk away from it. There's no one else here, Lewis – I'm not trying to catch you out. I just need to hear you say it.'

He grabs the dog's collar as it tries to make a dash for it. He struggles with the animal for a moment before returning his attention to me. 'I'm sorry,' he says, and my heart thunders in my chest at the thought that he is on the brink of an apology. Then he shrugs. 'I can't do that.'

Another roll of thunder – this one much louder than the last – shudders through the air. In the distance, a crack of lightning splits the sky. The dog breaks free from Lewis's grip and charges for the cliff edge, rendered senseless with fear.

'Bertie!'

Lewis chases after it, lunging to grab it as it nears the edge. He misses his footing and stumbles, and I watch in horror as the animal slips from the edge of the cliff, the ground seeming to fall away beneath it.

'Bertie!'

I can still hear the dog's whimpers. Tentatively moving closer, I watch as Lewis wriggles to the edge, trying to coax it from the ledge where it has landed. I am struck by the thought that this man now trying to rescue his mother's pet is the same man who raped me and then lied to everyone about what he had done. Who tried to gaslight me, making me question everything that had happened that night, things I knew to be true. Perhaps we are all contradictions; all capable of good and evil, some more predisposed to the latter than others.

I watch in horror as he starts to lower himself over the edge.

'What are you doing?' I cry out, my words stolen by the storm. 'This is madness!'

Down on the ledge, Lewis loses his footing, pieces of rock and grass breaking loose and falling thirty feet into the sea below. I drop to the ground and grab for the dog as he pushes it up towards me. The animal is weighted with fear, and it takes every ounce of strength I own to drag it onto the grass beside me, sodden and trembling. I hear more of the cliff edge breaking away beneath Lewis's feet, and when I reach to him, he grabs for me, his fingernails catching on the sleeves of my rain jacket.

'Hold onto my wrist,' I tell him, and as I take his weight, I claw at the ground with my free hand, trying to find something solid to anchor myself to. He screams as a piece of rock breaks away beneath him, crashing to the water below.

'I've got you,' I shout, knowing that it isn't true. I can't pull him up – I can't drag myself backwards – but when I heave myself with all the strength I have, it feels for a moment that I might be wrong. He looks at me, eyes wide with fear, before the last piece of ledge that is keeping him there shifts beneath him. I keep his hand in mine for as long as I am able, the water making the grip impossible as his fingers slide from mine.

I don't hear his body hit the water. The storm that rages around me drowns out the sound of my scream, and when I dare to open my eyes, he is nowhere to be seen.

I don't know how long I stay like that, the rain battering my back, but when I finally manage to push myself up, I feel drunk with adrenaline and fear. Bertie has disappeared; I call his name, but he has run away. I just hope he is able to find his way home.

By the time I get back to the village, the storm has peaked. I'm hoping to avoid Sylvia, but she is in the hallway when I go inside, returning the vacuum cleaner to the cupboard under the stairs. 'Christ,' she says when she sees me. 'What happened to you?'

I glance down, considering for the first time what a mess I must look. My hands are red and raw with the cold and my jacket is ripped and covered in mud. There is a tear in the knee of my trousers.

'Brooke?'

I can't tell her. I can't tell anyone. Everyone knows my history with Lewis, and no one will believe that I tried to save him. What if people think I pushed him? It only takes one person to plant the seed of an idea, and in a village such as this I know only too well just how quickly that seed can grow into a fully formed truth.

When I shake my head, Sylvia seems to understand. She comes to me and helps me out of my sodden jacket, and I tell her that I am going upstairs for a shower. In the bathroom, I strip off all my clothes and bundle them into a pile before taking a long and too-hot shower. My skin glows red in the heat, yet I barely feel it. I keep seeing Lewis's pleading eyes. I feel his hand in mine as though he is still holding on to me.

It is my fault. He is dead and it is my fault. If I hadn't left the house, if I hadn't gone for that walk; if I hadn't tried to get him to admit what he did all those years ago, he would still be alive now. It shouldn't have mattered that he didn't say the words: I already knew what had really happened, and so did he. I go over and over those final moments, replaying them like the details of a nightmare, but whichever way I try to pick them apart, Lewis is dead, and it is my fault.

When my skin is too red and I am unable to see through the steam, I turn the shower off. I go to the bedroom to dry off, and once I am dressed, I take my wet clothes to the kitchen and put them in the tumble dryer, planning to burn them later, after Sylvia has gone to bed.

When I go back into the hallway, she is waiting for me. 'That quiz show with whatshisface was on,' she tells me gently. 'There was a man from Surrey who did really well, managed twenty thousand on his own before the team took home forty-five. Beat that other bloke, the one with the hair, with three questions still left when the time was up.'

I wonder why she is telling me all this, and why she looks at me the way she does, her face pinched as though these details are paining her. Then I realise that she is giving me an alibi.

'There was a question about a durian, which is a popular fruit in South East Asia. Apparently it smells really bad, like rotting onions. Denmark won the Euros in 1992, and Charles I is still the only king of England to have been executed. There were three women on the team – one of them was a music student who wanted to start a theatre academy for children with learning difficulties.'

She comes to an abrupt stop before taking me by the hand. We stand there saying nothing, and in the silence, I allow myself to cry, feeling undeserving of her hand in mine.

TWENTY-SIX

CHRISTINA

Christina's heavy heart lightened when a single line emerged on the pregnancy test and wasn't followed by a second. Negative. She rested the test on the window sill and sighed with relief as she put her head in her hands. It felt as though she was being given a second chance, as though fate was allowing her the opportunity to put right her wrongs. Thoughts of Joel flooded her. Where was he? How had it been so easy for him to evade explanation for everything he was now putting her through?

After collecting her thoughts and washing her face with cold water, she left the bathroom. She took the test with her and put it in her handbag, planning to dispose of it later, once she was out of the house. She was seeing Janet Marsden again that morning, and after what had happened during their previous session, Christina knew she had to appear more composed. She was there to support her client, not the other way around.

Once again, visiting Janet was a stark reminder of all the things Christina took for granted. When the older woman answered the door, her smile was there, ready and in place as always, but it couldn't hide the pain that lay beneath it.

'How are you feeling?' Christina asked.

Janet shrugged. 'Not one of my better days, but it'll pass.'

Christina tilted her head. 'You don't have to pretend with me.'

She watched Janet's face change, seeing tears glisten at the corner of her eyes for the first time. It was so unexpected that at first she didn't know how to respond. 'Let's go through,' she said. 'Come on.' She put a hand on Janet's arm and led her through to the living room. 'Where is everyone?'

'Robert is at work and Rebecca's gone to meet a friend. She didn't want to go, but I insisted. She'll be a hermit if she stays cooped up in here much longer.'

'So you can tell me honestly, now they're not here,' Christina put her bag on the sofa, 'how are you really feeling?'

Janet nodded as she fought back tears. 'It's been a bad week,' she admitted. 'The pain just seems to be right through me.'

'If you're not feeling up to it, let's give today a miss. Perhaps you need a break.'

'You've come all this way.'

'It's not far, and that really doesn't matter.'

'I should have called you earlier. I've had this headache all morning and... Sorry.'

'Stop apologising. We can rearrange for when you're ready.'

Janet sighed. The rough, rattling sound that came from her chest was impossible to ignore. 'Stay for a cup of tea, at least?'

'You've twisted my arm.'

They chatted while Janet made the tea. They talked about Rebecca and about the twins, and as they spoke, Christina realised that this was what she had been missing. Her life had become a carousel of parenthood and work, with no diversion from the cycle and no time just to take a minute for herself. She missed having a friend – someone outside the family she could confide in. Bethany had been her best friend, the person she would have done this with before. Now she found herself cut off, stranded in a house that had become more of an island than a castle.

'I'm sorry,' Janet apologised again. 'You've come all this way. I'm wasting your time.'

'You never waste my time. I really don't think you should overdo things, though.'

The older woman gave a knowing smile, one eyebrow raised. 'Says she. When are you going to take your own advice then?'

'A good question. Probably never.'

She poured water into the mugs, then put a hand on her hip. 'Mind if I say something?'

'Depends what it is.'

'You need a break. You look exhausted. You looked tired the first time I met you, but now you're more of a corpse than I'm becoming.'

'Wow,' Christina said with a laugh. 'Thank you. And don't say that about yourself.'

'Dying does funny things to you, you know. I feel as though I can speak the truth, possibly for the first time.'

'You're not dying.'

Janet tilted her head in a cautionary gesture. 'I am. I wouldn't say it to Robert or Rebecca, but I can to you. You've been a good friend to me, and that's why I'm being honest with you now. I don't know who or what is making you unhappy, but I've been around long enough and seen enough to know when someone is papering over the cracks. You don't have to tell me what it is, but I want you to know that you deserve to be happy. If there's something about your life that you don't like, change it. Do it now, while you still can.'

Christina smiled. She appreciated Janet's concern, but the woman couldn't begin to imagine what was going on. 'I'm fine. Nothing that a bit of sleep won't sort out.'

She stayed and drank the tea, changing the subject quickly and moving the focus to Rebecca, to her dissertation and her mother's hope for her future. By the time she left, she had managed to distract herself from the continuing echo of Janet's words.

But not for long. As soon as she was alone in the car, she realised what she had to do. She would face Joel head on, put an end to things before they escalated. She knew where he worked, though she had never been to his office. He was a partner with a law firm in Edgware, less than fifteen minutes from Janet's house.

As she drove, a yet-unspoken exchange played out in her head.

'Leave me alone. Stop sending things to my house. Were you filming us together? I'll go to the police, I swear I will.'

'But then Matthew will find out everything.'

'You can't hold that over me any more, Joel. I'll tell him. He'll forgive me.'

'But what if he doesn't? You'll have thrown away your marriage over what? A few gifts delivered to your door? I'm not hurting you, am I, Christina? Are you really going to risk everything for a few flowers?'

As the conversation progressed, she realised she wasn't having it with Joel. She was arguing with herself, weighing up every possibility to prepare herself for something she knew she couldn't predict. By the time she reached the address she had tapped into her sat nav, she had exhausted herself with all the potential arguments.

The office was on a main road, between an estate agent's and a hairdressing salon. Outside, parked at the kerb, was a police car. She drew up ahead of it, getting out and feigning interest in the window display of a children's boutique clothing store as she watched two uniformed officers go into the building where Joel worked. She waited a moment before walking past, taking out her mobile and holding it to her ear, pretending to be engaged in conversation.

The officers were at the reception area, talking with an attractive Asian woman who was sitting at the desk. Christina stopped at the estate agent's next door, scanning the properties on sale before returning her attention to the neighbouring window. She had to look for a moment longer than was comfortable, unsure at first that what she thought she had seen was real. But it was. The receptionist was crying.

She crossed the road and went into a café, not wanting to draw unwanted attention to herself. She chose a table at the window, ordering quickly when a young woman came over to ask what she would like. When the police left the solicitors', the receptionist followed them to the door, wiping her eyes as she watched them get back into their car.

Christina took a five-pound note from her purse and left it on the table as payment for the coffee that hadn't yet arrived. In the solicitors' reception area, the woman was now on the phone, her conversation brought to an abrupt pause when she heard the door.

'Can I help you?' she asked, her hand held over the receiver.

'I was wondering if Joel is in today, please.'

The woman faltered. 'Um, I'm sorry, he's not here at the moment.' Her voice was uneven, unsettled by the visit from the police. 'Do you have an appointment?'

'No. I just... He was recommended to me, that's all.'

'Um... excuse me, just a minute.' The woman's hand slid from the receiver as she returned it to her ear. 'I'll have to call you back. Sorry.' She ended the call, then looked up at Christina. 'If you leave your name and number, I'll get Mr Cooper's colleague to give you a call.'

Christina took the pen from the receptionist and wrote down a false name and number. As soon as she left, the woman returned to the phone. Where was Joel, and what was going on?

TWENTY-SEVEN
BROOKE
OCTOBER 2019

I spend Monday in the bedroom, pretending that I am working. Sylvia comes up to me at one o'clock with a cup of tea and a sandwich, but I touch neither of them, unable to stomach anything. All night I saw Lewis's face, his eyes pleadingly helplessly; felt his hand still in my own. Every time I drifted into something that resembled slumber, I woke in a sweat watching him fall.

For hours I deliberated over whether to go to the police. I would tell the truth, be honest about what happened; they would understand that there was nothing I could do. I tried to save him. I tried.

I cannot go to the police. They will never believe me. Other people will talk, there will be too much gossip; it will be my word against everyone else's. They may think I pushed him from the cliff edge. At best, they might believe that I just left him there to die.

I should have got help straight away. What if he had still been alive? If I had called 999, he might have survived the fall. But in my heart, I know this speculation is futile. I waited to see him, to catch a glimpse of his body in the water, but there was nothing. He was gone. But still, the fact that I didn't go for help will make me look guilty.

Oliver calls me, once, but I ignore it. He doesn't leave a

message and I don't call him back. How can I even look at him now, knowing the secret I will be keeping? I want to go for a walk, but I can't bring myself to leave the house. It is only a matter of time before Lewis's body is found or someone reports him missing, and what then? I am a terrible liar, and I hate secrets. Living with the guilt and shame of what I have done – of what I didn't do – will kill me.

Sylvia comes to my room on Tuesday morning to tell me that a man's body has been found washed up on one of the beaches a couple of miles away. It is all over the local news – nothing like this ever happens here. Though the person has yet to be identified, she doesn't need to ask me whether I know who it might be. She wouldn't ask me anyway. Yet again, we are bound by an unspoken pact, and I lament the fact that she has once more been dragged into the mess my life seems to be without me even having to try.

By the evening, I think I might be losing my mind. I put on a pair of leggings and a sweater and go up to Hillside Cottage, hoping that Finley will be asleep. The kitchen light is on. I see Oliver pass the window, so I go around to the side door.

'Sorry to just show up,' I say when he opens it. 'I tried to message you, but it wouldn't send – you'll probably get it the next time you drive out of the village.' I stop talking, aware that I am close to rambling.

'Do you want to come in? It's a bit cold.'

I follow him into the kitchen, which suddenly feels like a different place – no longer a part of the house in which I grew up. It is someone else's home now, temporarily at least, and I feel like an imposter here, as though I have no right to be invading Oliver's privacy.

'I'm sorry,' I say.

'What for?'

For not telling you the truth, I think. For the lies I am about to tell you and the secret I am about to hide. 'The way I reacted. To the gift.'

'You have nothing to apologise for,' he says. '*I'm* sorry. Maybe it was inappropriate of me. I didn't mean it to be.'

'It just caught me off guard, that's all.'

'Do you feel you need a guard up? With me, I mean.'

I feel a need to keep my guard up with everyone, I think, and with no idea how to answer the question, I say nothing.

'I'm sorry for what I said. I shouldn't have reacted the way I did. I know you were only thinking of Fin.'

'You don't need to apologise,' I tell him. 'You were right – it's nothing to do with me.'

He gestures to the sofa, and I sit down. He sits beside me, keeping a respectful distance, both aware of the space between us. 'You've already been through enough these past weeks,' he says. 'I didn't mean to make things more difficult for you.'

'You haven't.' I've done that all by myself. I should have stayed home, I should have stayed away from Lewis; I should never have left the house.

'I feel as though we should start again. Hi,' he says, extending a hand to me. 'I'm Oliver.'

'Nice to meet you, Oliver.' I shake his hand. 'I'm Brooke.' But I don't want to be Brooke any more. I want to be someone else, anyone else; my history erased, my mind wiped clean.

'It's a pretty name – Brooke. Are you named after somebody?'

'My mother was obsessed with anything and everything to do with water. It was her dream to live by the sea – that's how she ended up here. She used to tell my sister and me that she was really a mermaid.'

Oliver smiles. Sylvia was right about his looks.

'What's your sister's name?'

I pause at his use of the present tense. I might tell him one day, but not here. Not now. 'Delta.'

He smiles. 'Because of the water thing.'

'Because of the water thing.'

He goes to the drawer and takes out the jewellery box. 'I've tried this on, but it just doesn't suit me. Nothing to go with it.' He smiles and holds it out to me. 'No strings. I'm not asking for anything in return. You can call it a peace offering, if you prefer.'

I take it from him. My hand is shaking, the thought of Lewis still holding me captive in its grip. 'Thank you. It's still too much, but it is beautiful.'

He smiles again and looks at me for a moment that draws on a fraction too long. I feel warm beneath my clothes, transparent, as though everything I am thinking may be crossing my forehead like an autocue that Oliver is now silently reading. If this had happened just a few days ago, it might have been near perfect. Now, tangled with the awful truth of what happened on the clifftop, it is tainted by my secret.

'And you were right, anyway,' he says.

'About what?'

'About Fin. He does need help. I've known it for a long time – I just haven't wanted to accept it. I'm going to take him to see someone as soon as we're registered with a doctor.'

'Do you know which one you're planning to register with?'

He nods. 'I've got all the forms, I just need to fill them in. I had another job rejection today.'

Oliver's first interview here has been followed by a string of rejections.

'Sorry. That's annoying for you. Something will turn up.'

An involuntary image flits into my mind: Lewis's face emerging from the waves, his pallid skin shimmering wet and his still-open eyes sunken in his skull. Bile rises in the back of my throat.

'Are you okay?'

'Fine,' I say, too quickly. He is looking at me intently; he will see the lie as though it has a face of its own.

'Can I ask you something?' I say, desperate for a distraction.

'Anything. Go ahead.'

'Where is Finley's mum?' I regret the question as soon as it leaves me. I needed a diversion, but this shouldn't have been it.

'She died. You'd probably already guessed that. Suicide.'

I open my mouth to say something, but nothing comes out. I have already said too much. 'Oh God,' I eventually manage. 'I'm so sorry.'

He shakes his head. 'She hadn't been well for a long time. No one would have known it to look at her...' He turns to check that Fin hasn't come downstairs without either of us hearing him. 'I think pregnancy might have made her condition worse, you know. I'd obviously never want Fin to know that, though.' He exhales slowly, a long breath through pursed lips, then smiles at me sadly. 'He was only a baby at the time. He doesn't really talk about her, so I don't push it. I'm guessing that when he's ready, he'll let me know.'

I wonder if Fin remembers her, or at least some aspect of her presence. A part of his life has been taken from him, and no matter how young he was when his mother died, her loss must have impacted upon him in ways no one might be certain of. No wonder he is quiet, I think. His sadness has formed a cocoon around him, whether he is aware of it or not.

And then there is Oliver. A widower in his thirties. A single parent. I know about loss and grieving, but our experiences are far from comparable.

I picture myself on that clifftop, my feet precariously close to the edge. My mother's voice plays on a loop. *Did you stop to think about anyone but yourself?* Colour rushes to my cheeks; I can feel it there, burning, and I know that Oliver notices it too.

'I shouldn't have asked you,' I say. 'I'm sorry.'

He shakes his head again. 'You have nothing to be sorry for. I've asked you to come here, to paint with Fin. You've looked after him for me. You have a right to ask questions.'

'How come you've waited until now to come here?'

'I tried to make it work where we were, but there were too many memories. Maybe it was selfish of me, but I couldn't stay living in the past any more.'

'I understand that,' I say, although perhaps it isn't true. How many times did Delta accuse me of living in the past? Perhaps the fire marked a turning point. When the gallery is restored, perhaps I shouldn't return there. I can't stay in the village now anyway, after what happened to Lewis. But where else would I go? My entire life is here, and I don't know how else to live.

'Will you try it on?'

He gestures to my hand, to the necklace I am still holding. We are both looking at my whitened knuckles, my grip around it too tight. 'Oh. Um... yeah, of course.'

I stand, and when he reaches for the necklace, I hand it to him. He opens the clasp and moves behind me; his fingertips brush my neck as he pushes my hair to one side. I feel heat rise in my neck as I start to panic.

He isn't Lewis, I tell myself. *You are not there.*

It takes just seconds for him to close the clasp and step away from me.

'Thank you,' I say, putting a hand to the pendant. My collarbone feels too hot, and I wonder whether my anxiety is visible. He is too close, not close enough; I want him to touch me again, to take the necklace back off.

'You don't have to wear it,' he says. 'But it does look beautiful. I knew it would suit you.'

He looks at me as he did the other night, and when he steps towards me, I move closer to him. When we kiss, his hands move to my shoulders, the back of my neck, my hair. Lewis's face, grey and lifeless, returns behind my eyes, and I pull away sharply, burned by the memory.

'Sorry,' I say hurriedly. 'I shouldn't have come so late, I—'

We are interrupted by the doorbell. Oliver swears beneath his breath, glancing at the staircase in the hope that the noise won't wake Fin, and when he comes back from the front door, there are two men with him: DS Jones and an officer in uniform.

'Miss Meredith,' DS Jones greets me.

'What's happened?' I say, feeling heat rise in my throat. 'Have you arrested someone?'

'We're not here about the fire, I'm afraid. We're investigating a recent death in the area. Lewis Miller.'

He waits for a reaction to the name and offers no further details. He is trying to catch me out.

'God,' I say. 'What happened?'

'That's what we're trying to find out. You knew Mr Miller then?'

'Yes.'

He nods. 'His mother tells us there was an historic sexual assault allegation made against Mr Miller by you.'

Beside me, I sense Oliver's reaction. This wasn't how I wanted him to find out.

'It wasn't an allegation,' I say. 'He raped me.'

I hold DS Jones's eye; I cannot bring myself to look at Oliver.

'No charges were brought against Mr Miller.'

I am unsure whether this is said as a question or a statement of fact. 'It happened sixteen years ago. I don't see why it's relevant now.'

Oliver's hand slips into mine. I see both officers take note of the gesture, and I wish I could take some comfort from the knowledge that he is here beside me. But I can't. I am about to tell lies – huge, irreversible mistruths – and I know it will be only a matter of time before one of them trips me up and brings me crashing to the ground.

TWENTY-EIGHT

CHRISTINA

When Christina got home, Matthew and the twins were in the living room. The place was in chaos – plastic building blocks and books littered the floor, a half-eaten pear had been abandoned near the doorway, and a piece of toast was stuck to the wall, cemented by butter that was beginning to turn orange at the edges. Christina never usually minded the mess – toys were a sign that they had been having fun, and the clear-up operation never took as long as it often looked it might – but that day she felt herself recoil as she stared at the disorder that greeted her arrival home.

'I'll tidy up,' Matthew said, as though reading her mind. He looked up at her apologetically as she stood in the doorway and surveyed the scene.

'Mama!' Elise ran over to her and flung her arms around her legs.

'Don't worry,' Christina said, stooping to hug her daughter. 'It looks as though you've been having fun.'

Elise wriggled free of her mother's grip and ran back to the rug to join Edward, who was quietly stacking a tower of building blocks, his tongue poking from his mouth as he concentrated on his construction.

'I'm going to make some lunch,' Christina said, forcing herself into normality. If she smiled enough, made enough cups of tea, that morning might be erased. Janet's words might be undone. 'Do you fancy a cup of tea?'

'I'll do it,' Matthew said, following her through to the kitchen. 'How was your morning?'

'Fine. Yours?'

He ran a hand across her shoulders as he passed her to get to the fridge. 'The kids have been good as gold. You okay? You look tired.'

'I couldn't get back to sleep after Edward woke up last night.' Their son had had another bad night, waking with a nightmare and taking almost an hour to get back to sleep. After that, Christina had found herself unable to drop off again. 'Do you mind if I pop upstairs to get changed?' She had felt unusually warm all morning, sweating though she was only wearing a thin blouse. It was probably now marked, and she didn't want to look scruffy when her next clients arrived. 'I'll only be five minutes.'

She went upstairs, used the bathroom, and stripped off her blouse before going into the bedroom. At the wardrobe, she rifled through her tops, opting for another loose blouse that would allow her skin to breathe. She checked her make-up in the mirror and tucked a few loose strands of hair back with grips. She still didn't look right. Her eyes were too dark – not the kind of shadows that hinted at a night of broken sleep, but something that suggested a disturbance that was deeply rooted. Could guilt and anxiety really be responsible for all the physical ailments she was experiencing?

Downstairs, Elise began to wail. She heard Matthew say something to her, and though she knew she should go down to them and take over, her head swelled at the thought of having to endure a tantrum while she was feeling so terrible. Thankfully, the noise subsided quickly, Matthew having apparently quashed the outburst before it became explosive. Christina sat on the edge of the bed and put her head in her hands. She took a deep breath, fighting against the sickness that threatened to overwhelm her, and resolved to go back downstairs with a smile that would hide what she was really feeling.

It was then that she saw it. Poking from beneath the duvet, something she recognised instantly. She pulled the duvet back. Lying on the sheet was the scarf with the blue butterflies that Matthew had bought her as a birthday present. The one she had left at Joel's flat. It was stained with blood.

She recoiled from the bed as though she had been scalded, then closed her eyes, willing herself back to the bedroom she had for weeks been trying to forget. Forcing herself to remember the details, she scanned the room as though watching a video of the place, as though she was viewing it online for potential purchase. The black leather bedhead, the dark curtains that were too long for the windows, the abstract grey and silver artwork, the naked light bulbs that hung in the place of lamps. The scarf that had slipped from where it had been left at the end of the bed.

A chill snaked down her spine. Joel. Somehow, he had been here.

She snatched the scarf from the bed, stood and turned, half-expecting to find Matthew in the doorway. Panic began to bubble in the pit of her stomach. What if she hadn't come upstairs to change? He had been about to go to bed to sleep before his night shift. What if he had seen it first?

As she looked around for somewhere to hide it, she realised her hand was wet, her fingertips sticky. Bile rose in the back of her throat. Was this animal's blood, like those chicken hearts he had sent her? What sort of man would be sick enough to do something like this?

In a panic, she checked the bed again, making sure there was no blood on the sheets. Then she went into the twins' bedroom and put the scarf on top of the wardrobe, covering it with a folded blanket. She would have to come back while he was sleeping, take it with her when she took the children to nursery; dispose of it somehow.

She realised that in her haste, she had got blood on one of

Elise's baby blankets. Leighton and Alice had bought it for her, one of the many items that had been in the beautiful gift box they had put together when the twins had been born. She felt sick at the thought that it was now ruined forever, that she would never be able to use it again even if the stains came out, and her eyes filled with angry tears.

He had been in her home. The flowers, the chicken hearts. Now this. He had been here, in the house with her family. While she had been out looking for him, he had been right here.

TWENTY-NINE

BROOKE

News of Lewis's death dominates conversation in the village, and the rumour mill goes into overdrive with talk of how he may have come to fall from the clifftop. Bertie made it back to Jean's house alone – the first indication that something was wrong – and when Lewis failed to come home that evening, Jean called the police to report him missing. The police apparently took little notice – a thirty-eight-year-old man had no obligation to report in with his mother – but their response changed when his body was washed up on the beach, discovered by a young wetsuit-clad couple who had been about to go surfing.

After the police left Oliver's house, I had no choice but to tell him about that night in the woods sixteen years ago. I kept my account as brief as possible, excluding Delta from the details, and when I had finished, he said nothing, respecting my need to keep myself as distanced from the memory as is ever possible. We sat together on the sofa, and he held me, neither of us speaking, and it managed to be everything I needed.

In the days that follow, I keep myself to myself, filling my time with painting and with Oliver. As the shift into autumn makes itself more apparent, we go on long walks together with Finley, and I introduce them to the hidden footpaths that line the land like an intricate map. We get nets and go searching in rock pools for crabs and shrimps, and on Saturday – a beautifully sunny day for November – we take the glass-bottomed boat from Fishguard that goes in search of seals and dolphins. Much to my disappointment, we spot neither, but Finley seems in awe despite this, amazed at the life that floats beneath his feet. As he watches his son point and gasp at the fish that swim below us, Oliver reaches silently for my hand and gives it a gentle squeeze before letting go. 'Thank you,' he mouths, and I feel grateful that they have let me into their lives; that it was Aberfach they chose to come to and my little house they picked to call their own, if only for the time being.

I am pretending to be normal. Time with Oliver and Finley makes it feel possible somehow – that the Brooke who couldn't hold on to Lewis for long enough to save him is a different Brooke to the one who catches crabs in nets and bakes trays of cookies and paints countless rainbow butterflies.

There have been no more phone calls, which makes me more convinced that Lewis was the perpetrator. I am relieved to be free of them, though I would rather have the torture of hearing Delta's voice on repeat than be cursed with this guilt of the secret I now carry. How did he get Delta's voice like that? Why did he do it?

The following weekend, I take Fin and Oliver to St David's. I show them around the shops and Oliver buys Finley a new pair of shoes, then we stop at the cathedral, listening at the doors to the service that is taking place inside.

'Are you religious?' Oliver asks me.

I shake my head. 'You?'

'No, though I sometimes wonder whether life would be more simple if I was.'

'What do you mean?'

'I just wonder whether it makes grief easier to bear.'

There is silence between us for a moment before Finley wanders off towards the graveyard and Oliver runs to stop him.

'There's a park just a few streets away,' I suggest.

They follow me back through the church grounds and out onto

the main road. Once at the park, Finley has space to roam. Oliver watches him climb the steps of a slide before turning to me. 'You never talk about your family,' he says.

'What would you like to know?'

'It's not about me wanting to know anything. I was just thinking for you, you know...'

I glance at Finley, who is now at the bottom of the slide and planning his next move.

'They're all dead.' I say it quietly, not wanting anyone around us to hear, but once the whisper has left my tongue, it sounds more sinister than I had intended it to.

'Shit,' Oliver mutters beneath his breath. 'I'm sorry, Brooke.'

'You weren't to know.'

I follow Finley to the see-saw; he will need someone to sit at the other end for him. It gives me a perfect excuse to leave the conversation. We might have it one day, but not here and now.

'I need to go to the bank before it closes,' Oliver tells me. 'Shall I meet you back here?'

'We'll come with you.'

'No, honestly – Fin would rather stay here, wouldn't you?' He looks at his son, who says nothing. 'If you don't mind, that is?'

'No,' I say. 'It's fine.'

'Thank you. I won't be long.'

We play on the see-saw for a while before I push Finley on a swing. Twenty minutes later, I realise that Oliver has taken Fin's backpack containing his snacks and drink with him.

'I'm hungry.' Fin swings his legs, his mouth downturned as he laments his empty stomach.

I check my phone. It is gone midday. 'No wonder. It's lunchtime. Shall we get some chips? I'll call your dad to tell him to meet us there.'

Fin holds out his arms to me and I lift him from the swing. I try Oliver's phone, but it goes straight to answerphone. 'Come on,' I say to Fin, reaching out for him to take my hand. 'We'll have to go and find him.'

Fortunately there aren't too many banks in the town centre and they are all within close proximity of one another, so it shouldn't take us too long to find him. Finley grips my hand tighter as we leave the park, sensing the danger of the main road. I try not to think about Lewis, though not an hour passes when this is possible.

We go back past the cathedral to get into town, which means passing the graveyard once again. Finley's pace slows, his attention stolen by the rows of headstones, so many of them untended and left to grow green with ageing moss. 'What happens when you die?' he asks.

The question throws me into an uncomfortable silence. How do I answer it without telling him that his mother is gone forever? That he will never see her again? I stand to one side, leaving room on the pavement for people to pass us. Crouching to Finley's level, I let go of his hand for a moment. 'People go, but they don't really go. They stay here,' I say, touching my chest where my heart is. 'And here.' I tap my head, though he is looking at me perplexed, as though I am speaking in a foreign language. 'If you ever want to be close to someone who isn't here any more, all you have to do is think of them. Then it's like they're with you.'

I muss his hair in the way I have seen Oliver do so many times, then stand and take his hand in mine again. Despite the apparent conviction of my words, I don't believe them. Grief is a slow and painful torture, and the adage that time is a great healer is the cruellest falsehood fed to anyone in the crippling grip of loss.

'Ice cream,' he says suddenly, stopping on the pavement.

'Maybe later. Better have some lunch first.'

'No,' he says, pulling on my arm. 'You say ice cream.'

It takes a moment for me to understand. What did I tell him that day he hid in the wardrobe? Whenever I was sad, my sister and I would play a game. I squeeze his hand in mine and smile down at him, wondering at the marvel that is his little brain. 'Ice cream,' I say.

He pulls a thinking face, his mouth twisted as he contemplates his first choice of word. 'Chocolate flake.'

'Chocolate flake. Good one. Um... strawberry sauce.'

'Cheese.'

'Cheese?!'

He giggles, the first time I have ever heard him laugh. My heart soars at its beautiful sound.

'Toast.'

'Pizza.'

'You're just shouting out random foods now, Fin.'

He laughs again, and his little hand tightens around mine. The weight of responsibility feels almost too much to bear. He trusts me, I think. I have earned his trust and he has let me in. I give his hand a squeeze back. 'Come on then,' I say. 'All this talk of food is making me hungry. Let's go and find your dad and get those chips.'

We find Oliver sooner than I expected to, near the car park. He is with a boy who from this distance looks no older than fifteen, and as we get closer, I realise he has his hand on the youth's jacket, gripping him by the chest. I stop and pull Finley to one side, but it is too late: he has already seen him.

'What's Daddy doing?' he asks.

Good question, I think. 'Just chatting with someone.'

Whatever he is doing, they are not chatting. The boy tries to push Oliver off him, but his grip is too tight. Oliver pulls the boy closer and says something in his ear before shoving him away; the boy hurries off, but not before shouting something inaudible back at him. And then Oliver turns and sees me. His face is fixed with anger, and there is an uncomfortable moment that passes between us before it eases. He smiles at Fin as he approaches us, greeting me as though everything is normal.

'Who was that?'

'Just some kid,' he says, taking Finley by the hand.

'You know him?'

'No. I just caught the little shit putting a scratch down the side of my car.' He shakes his head and looks down at Fin before apologising. 'Sorry. I shouldn't have sworn like that.'

'There'll be CCTV here,' I say, looking around for signs of a camera. 'You should report it.'

'I've dealt with it now.'

'He might do it again—'

'I said I've dealt with it,' he snaps.

Finley looks at the ground, unsettled by his father's tone.

'I'm sorry,' Oliver says. 'Let's just go.'

'I want chips,' Finley says quietly.

'We'll get something at home now.'

Neither Finley nor I argue with him, and I wait in the passenger seat as he puts Fin into his car seat. We travel back to the village in silence, and when I get out at the house, I see the ten-inch-long scratch that has been etched into the driver's side of the car. He catches me looking at it, and I quickly look away. He is lying. We are both lying.

THIRTY
CHRISTINA
MARCH 2018

The hot sweat that Christina had experienced earlier had turned into a chill, and as she went back downstairs to join her family, she knew that any pretence at being fine would now be immediately transparent.

'Your tea is over there,' Matthew said, gesturing to the mantelpiece but not looking up. He was helping Edward with his construction, the tower now transformed into a robot. 'Look out! He's going to get you!'

Elise squealed and grabbed her brother's arm, and the two of them ran to the window, where they hid behind the curtains. Matthew followed slowly, stomping out the robot's footsteps on the living room floor. An overenthusiastic Elise got herself tangled in the curtains before falling to the floor, but the noise and excitement barely registered with Christina as she thought of the scarf upstairs and of Joel in her bedroom. Joel standing beside the bed she shared with her husband.

Matthew laughed and turned, his smile fading as he looked at her. 'Is everything okay? What's happened?' He scooped Elise up and brushed her off before going to Christina. He reached for her shoulder. 'Chrissie,' he said, lowering his head, urging her to look at him. 'What's happened?'

She was still sweating. She could feel it running down the length of her spine, soaking into her shirt. 'I'm sorry,' she said, her head spinning with a dizziness that was threatening to pull her legs from beneath her. 'I really don't feel very well again.'

'Sit down.'

Matthew sat on the sofa next to her and put an arm around her shoulders. 'You're burning up. Shall I get you something?'

'No,' she said, shaking her head. 'Thank you. Maybe just a glass of water? I'll be fine in a minute.'

She didn't deserve his sympathy. This was her fault, all of it. Where would Joel stop? She had got herself into this mess, but she could never tell Matthew what was going on, not when telling him would mean admitting to her infidelity. There had never been anything about Joel that had suggested he might be this kind of person – but then she had never really known him, had she? She had seen what she had wanted to see, ignoring anything that would disrupt the fantasy she had created for this alternative existence, when the truth was that he could have been anyone, capable of anything.

Matthew came back into the room with two paracetamol and a glass of water, which Christina downed within seconds. 'You're dehydrated,' he said. 'You should have another one.'

'I'll get it in a minute,' she said, putting a hand on his arm to keep him there. 'Matt...'

'Yes?'

She looked at the children before reaching to the coffee table for the remote control. She doubted they would pay any attention to the conversation, but she didn't want to risk the possibility. 'Did anyone come to the house today?'

'No. Why do you ask?'

Joel couldn't have let himself into the house; it was impossible. She had thought back on all the times they had met, and though there might have been opportunity for him to take her keys from her bag or from her coat pocket, there had never been a chance for him to have a copy cut and return the original. They had never spent more than a few hours together, and during those times they had always been with one another – he had never had to pop out anywhere or made an excuse to leave her alone while he went off to do something.

That left only one other possibility – someone had let him into the house. And if it hadn't been her, it could only have been Matthew.

'I just...' She paused, allowing time for the lie to come to fruition. 'There was something left in the treatment room, that's all. A scarf. It must have been one of the women I saw yesterday, but I only noticed it this morning. I thought she might come back for it.'

'She'll probably collect it during your next session,' he said, taking the glass from her hand. 'You stay there. I'll get you another drink.' He got up and went to the door, stopping before he left the room. 'Actually, someone *was* here earlier. A man came to read the meter. He didn't really seem the type to wear women's accessories, though.'

Uncertainty stirred in the pit of Christina's stomach, threatening to resurrect the sickness that was only just beginning to die down.

'Did you see his ID?'

Matthew pulled a face. 'Have you ever asked to see a meter reader's ID before?'

It was the first time she had ever considered the fact that she hadn't. Men came to the door, came into her home while she was alone, while the children were there, and yet she had never once asked for them to prove that they were who they claimed to be – she just allowed them in acceptingly, believing without question what she was told.

The children. They had been there all afternoon with Matthew. Had Joel seen them, or had either of them seen him?

'What did he look like?'

'Chrissie, what's this about?'

'What did he look like, Matt? Please.' The question was fired at him, a command.

His eyes narrowed with scepticism, but he gave her an answer anyway. 'Tallish, I suppose. Probably about my height. Skinny. Dark-blond hair. I don't know, I only saw him for a minute.'

Her stomach churned. He had described Joel. 'Why?'

'Why what?'

'Why did you only see him for a minute?'

Matthew exhaled loudly, his patience beginning to fray. 'Jesus Christ, Chrissie – what's all this about? He was just a bloke who came to read the meter.'

'Yes, but why did you only see him for a minute? Weren't you there when he was checking it?'

He sighed. 'Elise started kicking off about something in here – I had to go and deal with that.'

Christina looked away, trying to conceal the panic she knew she was unable to keep from her face. Joel had been here, in her home, and if Matthew had come into the living room, there had maybe been sufficient time for Joel to go upstairs, find her bedroom and slip the scarf under the duvet. Perhaps he had intended for Matthew to find it, or maybe this was what he had wanted, for her to see it there. The flowers, the chicken hearts, the footage of them together – and now this. One step closer every time.

'What the hell is going on, Chrissie?'

Was this why the police had been to the solicitors' firm? Had he done this to someone else and been caught out?

'Nothing. I'm just over-tired and I feel terrible.' She looked at him, forcing herself to make eye contact. 'I'm sorry.'

He looked back at her sceptically. He didn't believe her, and he had every reason not to. 'You should put your head down for an hour before you start work again. Let me take the kids to nursery after lunch – I'll have plenty of time to sleep when I get back.'

'No,' she said, too quickly, thinking about the scarf on top of Elise's wardrobe. 'I mean, thanks, but I'll be fine. The tablets will kick in soon. Honestly, you go and get some sleep.'

She waited until he had gone upstairs before going to the hallway and getting her mobile from her bag. With shaking hands, she searched for Joel's number. *This has to stop*, she wrote, *or I'm going to the police.* She pressed send. She meant it. What if Joel got even closer next time – did something to scare or endanger one of the children? She could never take that risk, even if it meant losing her marriage.

THIRTY-ONE
BROOKE
NOVEMBER 2019

I see Jean as soon as I leave Sylvia's house; she has been sitting on the low stone wall opposite, waiting for me. Bertie is beside her, lying stretched out on the cold ground. There is nothing I want more than to turn and go back inside, but I can't; it is too late for that now.

'You know something,' she says venomously, approaching me with a finger that is wagged in my face as soon as she gets close enough. The poor dog is being dragged by its lead, and as soon as it comes near me, it starts whimpering pitifully. 'See?' She jabs the finger in Bertie's direction. 'He knows what happened, doesn't he? Listen to him.'

'I think you're pulling his lead a bit tight,' I suggest quietly.

She glares at me, her expression hate-filled, her eyes rimmed with imminent tears of anger. 'First the fire, then the break-in, and then Lewis. It's no coincidence, is it? Everything comes back to you somehow, and it's only a matter of time before the police see it.'

We have gained an audience already, I notice: a couple in their forties making their way into the pub have stopped to play witness to the awkward scene that is unfolding in front of them. If Jean has noticed, she doesn't care. Bertie's whimpers have developed into distressed yelps, and I wonder if he really does remember me from that night.

'I bet you're happy now, aren't you?' she spits. 'It was never enough for you to try to ruin his reputation – did you want him dead as well? Did you see him that Sunday? You're not going to tell me the truth anyway, are you? You were a liar as a child and you're a liar now.'

'That's enough now.' Sylvia has come out of the house. 'This isn't going to help anyone, Jean.'

'That's it,' Jean says bitterly. 'Defend her like you always have. What is it with you two, eh? Thick as thieves and twice as devious.'

'Go inside, Sylvia. Please. I can fight my own battles.' I turn back to Jean. 'Your son raped me, Jean. I know it's not what you want to hear, but that's the truth. I'm sorry that he's dead and I'm sorry that you're suffering, but it doesn't change the facts.' When I turn away, Sylvia is still on the front doorstep. I hurry past her and go back inside, hot tears streaking my face.

Jean mutters something to Sylvia; I don't hear what it is. When Sylvia closes the door, I can't bring myself to look at her.

'What happened on Sunday, Brooke?'

'I tried to help him,' I tell her, the words barely audible through the tears. 'I couldn't cling on.'

I hear her sigh – hear the disappointment in her exhalation as she realises that I lied to her; that I have lied to everyone. She gave me a chance that evening to tell her, but I didn't. Now I've left her burdened with it, an impossible decision to make.

'Go to the police,' I say. 'I'll tell them what happened. You believe me, don't you?'

She refuses to make eye contact with me, her focus fixed somewhere on the wall to my side. 'Sylvia, please...'

'I just don't know what to believe any more.'

She heads upstairs, leaving me alone in the hallway. I run my sleeves across my eyes, snot and tears staining my sweater, then leave the house via the back door, cutting through the garden to get to the path to Hillside Cottage. If Jean is still out the front, I don't want to have to face her again.

When I get to the house, I let myself in, not bothering to knock. I can hear Oliver's voice upstairs, splashing from the bathroom.

'Jesus,' he says, when he sees me at the top of the staircase. 'You almost gave me a heart attack.' He stops when he notices my tear-stained face. 'What's happened?'

I glance into the bathroom and shake my head; this conversation isn't for Finley's ears.

Oliver guides me into the bedroom, leaving the door open so that he can still hear Fin splashing about in the bathtub. 'What's happened?' he asks again. I don't want to speak, so instead I kiss him. My hands are insistent, finding the skin beneath his T-shirt, and when he pulls away, he looks at me as though he doesn't quite recognise me. 'I've got to get Fin out of the bath and put him to bed,' he says. 'Will you wait for me?'

'Here?'

He nods. 'I won't be long.'

When he is gone, I go to the window. The night is black and heavy, the sea merging with the sky, no line to divide them. I pull the curtains shut, blocking the past from view, and as I lie on the bed, I listen to Oliver reading quietly to his son, his voice changing for the different characters. When the story ends, there is silence for a while before the bedroom door eases quietly open and he comes to join me on the bed. He looks at me intently, neither of us speaking until he breaks the silence.

'How did you get this?' He runs a finger along the scar at my temple. I expected the question at some point, surprised it has taken him this long to ask.

'Tripped and fell when I was kid,' I lie. 'Hit my head on the grate downstairs.'

'Ow,' he says, wincing. His finger lingers there, smoothing my skin as though he could erase the scar. 'Why do you stay here?'

It seems a strange question to come from nowhere, yet in light of recent revelations, perhaps not. After telling him in the park that all my family are dead, it might seem there is nothing to keep me here. He now knows about Lewis and what happened that night, and I suppose that to an outsider my staying here is difficult to understand. 'I like it here. I like being by the sea. I'd never want to live in a city – I don't think I could handle it.'

I can do it again, I think, touching my temple. Any time I choose to.

'Which bit do you think you couldn't handle?'

'All of it. The noise, the pace, the busyness. I just want a quiet life.'

He props himself up on an elbow and looks down at me, his face inches from mine. 'Me too.' He leans down and kisses me. 'Does it get lonely here?'

'Sometimes.'

'Are you happy?'

I was, I think. Before the fire, before Lewis's return. Before I couldn't save him.

'This is starting to feel like an interrogation. You just need one of those lamps.'

He kisses me again before pushing himself up. 'There's a bottle of wine in the fridge. Want to help me with it?'

I shouldn't – I should keep a clear head – but the thought of escaping for a while makes the decision for me.

He returns to the bedroom with a bottle and two glasses. He pours me a glass and passes it to me.

'What happened to your mum and dad, Brooke?'

I sip the wine. It is sweet and strong and its warmth flows through me. 'Dad had a heart attack when I was sixteen. Mum died last year. She had Alzheimer's, among other things.'

'Were you close?'

I wouldn't know how to even begin with an honest answer to this question. We were close because we had to be. We were all we had left, whether we liked the fact or not. 'I lived here with her until she went into a care home. I didn't want her to go. It never felt right, even when I couldn't manage on my own any more.'

'You shouldn't feel guilty. I don't really know much about dementia, but no one can cope with someone's care on their own.' He runs his fingers through the hair at the back of my neck as I take another sip of wine. 'You didn't answer the question, though.'

'What question?'

'Were you close?'

'We only had each other. We had to be close.'

'But you mentioned your sister before. Delta.'

'She moved out when she was young.'

I already know what is coming next. He is remembering our conversation in the park; he is piecing together the separate parts of what I have revealed to try to form a picture of the whole.

'What you said in the park, though... about your family...'

I nod for an answer. 'Yeah,' I tell him. 'Delta too.'

He puts an arm around my shoulders and says nothing, and the silence is comforting – there is reassurance in being able to stay quiet and to not feel awkward while doing it. He doesn't ask what happened to her, and I am grateful for not having to discuss it. I rest my head at the top of his chest.

'What was Finley's mum's name?' I ask.

'Bethany.'

'It's sad, isn't it, that this is what we've got in common?'

His arm closes tighter around me. 'I'm sure there's more than that.'

We drink our wine, and when my glass is empty, Oliver refills it. It has gone to my head. I rarely drink alcohol – there seems something sad in drinking alone, and so I gave it up, rationed to the occasional glass with dinner on a Sunday at Sylvia's house.

'What happened to Delta?' Oliver asks.

'There was an accident.' I catch a sob in the back of my throat, gulping it down like something that has nearly choked me. 'I'm sorry,' I say, waving a hand as Oliver begins to apologise. 'She fell. At a Tube station. She fell down a set of steps.'

I see Lewis again and feel a wave of nausea rush through me.

Oliver looks down. 'I'm so sorry. I shouldn't have asked you about her.'

'It's fine.'

'What was she like, your sister? Were you close?'

'She was beautiful and funny and fun to be around. We were completely different in so many ways, but we were always the best of friends. Until we weren't, I suppose.'

'What do you mean?'

'Nothing.'

He tilts his head, smiles affectionately, as though to suggest there is no point in trying to mislead him. 'Did something happen between you?'

I turn to him. His face is inches from mine. I have never looked at him this closely. I have never had anyone look this closely at me.

'We were just two different people. You can get away with that when you're kids, can't you? You don't really notice so much.'

'But *you're* beautiful and funny and fun to be around. You can't have been that different.'

He is watching me intently, and when I cast my eyes down to the duvet, I feel his attention still resting on me, gauging my reaction. No one has ever called me beautiful, except maybe my father, back when I was young enough to fool.

'We fell out over my mother,' I tell him, though we had fallen out long before that, right after she had left me alone in the woods that evening and then lied to everyone about what had happened. 'Well... not so much my mother, really. Her illness, I mean. It happens, doesn't it?' I say, trying to brush it away casually, as though my mother's Alzheimer's wasn't a parasite that had gnawed through every aspect of her being until all she was left with was a shadow of what she had once been. 'But my sister couldn't cope with it. She did what she always did whenever there were problems. She ran away.'

'She left you to deal with it on your own, you mean?'

'Pretty much.'

He raises a hand and pushes a strand of hair from my face,

tucking it behind my ear. His touch sends a shiver through me. 'Sorry,' he says. 'I'm staring, aren't I? There's just something about you, Brooke.'

When he kisses me again, all other thoughts leave me for a moment. Delta, my mother, my father, Lewis... We are alone in the moment, just Oliver and me, and the ghosts that have for so long tormented me evaporate and are gone. A different thought takes their place, something that has circled my mind since our trip to St David's. That boy in the car park. The look on Oliver's face. I cannot be sure, but I don't believe that the scratch on his car was there when we left that car park. He must have done it himself, either after getting Finley into his seat, or here, before taking him out. But why would he have done that, and why would he have lied to me about it?

THIRTY-TWO
CHRISTINA
MARCH 2018

It was gone ten o'clock when Ollie called. Christina was already in bed – she had stayed upstairs once the twins had fallen asleep, her energy drained so that she was good for little else – but she had forgotten to turn her phone to silent, and its ringtone was loud as it vibrated on the bedside table. She was grateful for the noise, a distraction from the echoes of what had happened earlier in the day.

'Sorry for calling so late. Are you okay to talk?'

'Yes, fine.'

'Were you asleep?'

'No, no. Is everything okay?'

'Fine here. I was calling to ask you the same.'

His voice came to her as though from a dream, and as the thought crossed her mind, she realised that she had been dozing, and that Bethany had been there. She herself had been a teenager again, Bethany no older than ten, and they had been sitting together in the garden of their childhood home, legs curled beneath them as they sought shelter from the rain in the wooden playhouse.

It was almost as though he had known to call, to wake her from the dream before she became too immersed in the memory.

'Everything's fine here,' she lied, wishing that she could tell him what had been going on. 'How's Fin doing?'

'He's good. There have been some signs of improvement, actually – he's started to come out of his shell a bit. Look, Chrissie... there's something I need to tell you.'

'Okay.'

'I, uh...' There was a lengthy pause. She sensed what he was going to say before he said it, as though the end of this chapter of their lives could already be anticipated in the silence. 'I've met someone.'

She had known it would happen at some point. It was right that it should happen. Ollie was only in his thirties; it wasn't fair that he should have to spend the rest of his life alone. And Fin was still young – he needed someone to be a mother to him. She just wished that that someone was Bethany, that she was still there for him; for them all.

'Okay.' She wanted to say something more, but she couldn't find the words. Though there was no reason for it to, it had still come as a surprise. 'Good. That's good. I'm happy for you.'

Silence again. She didn't sound happy. She sounded as she felt, like someone whose last tether to the past was being cut away. Everything was falling apart, and there seemed nothing she could do that would stop it.

'Has Fin met her?'

'Yeah, they've met. They get on really well.'

The words felt like a knife in her side, though she knew there had been no intention for them to injure her.

Ollie cleared his throat awkwardly. 'Look, I, uh... I don't know if we'll make it over for the twins' birthday. I just think we need a bit of time to, uh, you know... We will come to see you, but I, uh, I just think—'

'It's fine,' Christina said, saving him the awkwardness of having to explain. He had a new relationship. He was trying to move on. She was his past, and he didn't want the two to merge; not yet at least. After speaking with Matthew about it, and then with Alice, she had been planning to find a way to deter Ollie from coming for the children's birthday – she just hadn't got around to it yet. She supposed she should have been grateful that he was saving her the task.

'I'll always love Bethany.'

The words came from nowhere, knocking her sideways. She felt tears catch at the corner of her eyes and she wiped them away quickly, though there was no one there to witness them.

'And we'll always be your family, me and Fin, even if we're miles away. You're stuck with us if that's okay?'

'Always. You know that.'

'I just, while we're—'

'You don't have to explain.'

The silence that followed lasted longer than was comfortable for either of them. It was Oliver who eventually broke it. 'Look after yourself, okay? And if you need me, I'm still at the end of the phone.'

'I know. Give Fin a big hug from us.'

Once the call ended, Christina got out of bed and went into the twins' bedroom. Edward was sleeping with his back to the door, his blanket rising and falling with the gentle motions of his breathing. Elise was a sprawl of limbs, her arms flung to the sides, her head tilted back as though she had fallen asleep amid planning an escape. Even in sleep, their different personalities were already visible.

In the half-light, Christina's eyes moved to the top of the wardrobe. She felt sick now at the thought of her children sleeping in the same room as the scarf. Careful not to disturb the silence, she felt beneath the blanket. The silk should have been soft against her skin, but her fingers met with a patch of hardened fabric, stiff with blood, and she recoiled. The blood of an animal, or so she had thought earlier. Drained from a plastic supermarket meat tray, or from raw steaks purchased from a butcher.

But what if it wasn't either of these? Her heart stuttered at the possibility that this was something else. A warning. Had the police been looking for Joel? Just what was he guilty of? Her focus moved back to her sleeping children, her own blood running cold at the thought of what might happen next.

On Thursday, I stop a couple of miles outside the village and park the car by a gate that leads to farmland. Years of testing Aberfach's surrounding areas for the strongest Wi-Fi point has proven this to be the nearest place at which I am able to gain a connection decent enough for my search not to buffer every few minutes. I tap the passcode into my phone and open the internet browser.

Bethany Scott. I feel disloyal for even typing her name, wondering what Oliver would think if he could see me doing this. But it has been so long since I allowed someone into my life. I just want to know him. I want to know about the life and the circumstances he has come from; I want to know his secrets, despite hiding my own.

There are LinkedIn profiles and Facebook accounts belonging to women with the same name, and then, midway down the page, I find her. *Young Mum Dies After Overdose*. Her photograph is here; she is smiling at me from the screen of my phone. She is young – younger than I had imagined her, maybe even early twenties – and the light that catches her eye and brightens her face disguises the pain she must have been carrying with her for longer than those around her probably realised.

I click on the headline.

The death of a 22-year-old north London woman was yesterday ruled as suicide. Mother of one Bethany Scott was found last month by her husband, who returned to their home after taking their young son to a doctor's appointment to find his wife dead in their bed. A toxicology report stated that Mrs Scott had consumed a cocktail of prescription medication shortly prior to her death.

I stop reading. Sadness rises from the screen, their story gripping me with all its inescapable tragedy. Oliver found her dead. He had Finley with him. I am unable to think past this: that they were both there. It is an unspeakable horror, something no husband – no child – should ever have to endure.

I think of my parents sitting at my bedside in the hospital, the relief in their faces at my open eyes. Less than six months later, a massive heart attack killed my father. Too much pressure on his heart. Too much stress and sadness. What I did had killed him.

I click back out of the article, feeling sick with the words I have read.

I scroll further down the search results, stopping at a GoFundMe page. I click on it and am met with a photograph of the same young woman, this time holding a baby in her arms. She is so slight and fragile, though she smiles for the camera, her head tilted to one side and her eyes bright. She is sitting on a sofa, the light from the window behind her creating a glow that seems to embrace her. The baby is wearing a white sleep suit, his tiny fingers clutching his mother's thumb. Finley.

Though I never met this woman – despite the fact I had never heard of her until this week – this image of her with her newborn son brings tears to my eyes. No one would ever have known, I thought. To look at her, no one would think there was anything but joy filling her head and love residing in her heart. Though painfully thin, she looks happy, her smile shrouding the multitude of agonies she must have been carrying. From what Oliver has told me, she was already leaving them when this photograph was taken. Not long afterwards, she was gone.

I picture Oliver in a living room that my imagination paints in colourful detail, smiling back at her as he stands behind the camera and takes the photograph – ignorant to the fact that just a year later, he would be a single parent, a widower, raising a young son on his own.

Fund total, I read, £31,452.

In May, our beautiful sister Bethany took her own life. She was intelligent, funny, kind, loyal – a brilliant wife and a loving mum to Fin. But she had demons she couldn't shake off – demons that in the end she only saw one way of escaping from. Her husband, Ollie, found her dead at their home – a house he can no longer face going back to. Bethany's family will miss her every day and will love her for the rest of their lives. Ollie is too proud to ask for help, so here I am doing it for him. He and Bethany share a son, Fin, who deserves a fresh start and the best life we can give him. Please help me make that start possible by donating anything you can.

Thank you.

Alice x

Now the cash that Oliver gave me makes sense. He must be temporarily living off this money, funding their fresh start through the kindness of others. It explains his trips to the bank, but also why he has been silent on anything finance-related, too proud to admit that while he cares for his son and navigates them through this period of grieving, he is living off what he perhaps perceives as charity. It explains why he was so insistent on me not going to the bank with him that day, repeatedly suggesting that Fin and I stay at the park instead. Perhaps he is worried that I will judge him for accepting the generosity of others.

I have been so engrossed in the contents of my phone screen that I hadn't realised until now just how cold it has become in the car. I restart the engine and turn the heating up full, willing it to hurry up and blast some warmth against my legs. No wonder he has come here, to somewhere as remote and isolated as Aberfach. Everywhere he went, the memory of Bethany and of how she left this world must have haunted him. Staying where he was must have been impossible, made even more so by the fact that everyone would have known what had happened. Here, he can start again.

You did this. My mother's words rise from a badly covered grave, pushing up easily through the earth I have tried to bury them with. *If you hadn't done what you did, your father would still be here.*

A headache swells behind my eyes, and I push back against the headrest, fighting off the memory, desperate for some respite from the shooting pain that attacks my skull. I killed my father. I have carried the weight of responsibility for his death my entire adult life, and now I am responsible for another. Already the guilt of Lewis's death feels too much to bear – another weight that I will carry alone. I return to thoughts of Oliver. It feels like a form of betrayal, being here and reading into the details of his life, and yet now, having done so, I feel somehow closer to him, that in knowing more about him I have a greater understanding. I don't want him to leave Aberfach. I am scared of being on my own.

A car pulls up in front of mine and a man gets out of the passenger seat. I recognise him as DS Jones. He is alone, and when he comes to the side of my car, I wind down the window.

'Miss Meredith,' he greets me.

'Just Brooke is fine.'

He looks around the inside of the car, glancing at my phone. 'Everything okay? You've not broken down?'

'No. Everything's fine. Just something I'd forgotten to do.' I gesture with the phone as though this explains everything, before throwing it onto the passenger seat.

'I'm on my way to see Jean Miller. Post-mortem results came in this morning.'

He probably shouldn't be telling me this, so I wonder why he is. Is he still trying to catch me out? I say nothing, waiting for whatever else he wishes to reveal.

'It makes for interesting reading,' he says, keeping his eyes fixed on mine as he speaks. 'There were fibres found under Mr Miller's fingernails, you see. Quite specific fibres – ones used for wet-weather gear. You know... rain jackets, that sort of thing.'

The pause that follows is uncomfortably long. 'I still can't believe what's happened,' I say, knowing he will wait for me to be the one to break it. 'His poor mother.'

'Quite,' he says. 'Anyway...' he taps the top of the car with his hand, 'I'd better be going to give her the news.'

I watch him return to his car and wait for him to drive away. When he has disappeared around the bend, I press my skull into the headrest again and close my eyes, willing away the surging headache that pulses at my temples and thinking about the jacket burned to cinders with the rest of my clothing from that night, the ashes from the fire in a carrier bag in the boot of my car.

THIRTY-FOUR
CHRISTINA
MARCH 2018

The house was too quiet. Christina had done the food shopping after dropping the twins at the nursery, disposing of the bloodied scarf on her way home. Though she hadn't touched it – merely transporting the plastic carrier bag that held it from the car to the industrial-sized wheelie bin at the side of the supermarket – she felt dirtied, criminal in some way, like she would never be clean again. When she got home, Matthew was nowhere to be seen. He must have been held up at work again; either that, or the traffic had been worse than usual that morning. As she put the shopping away, she battled against the headache that sat right behind her eyes. All she wanted to do was go back to bed.

When she went upstairs, the folding steps to the attic were pulled down onto the landing.

'Matthew?'

His face appeared at the open hatch.

'Everything okay?'

'I didn't know you were already back.'

'I thought you had clients this morning?'

'I rescheduled them for next week.' She didn't want it to become a habit, particularly as she had now cancelled sessions for the second day running, but she just didn't feel up to facing people.

Her heart hurt, her eyes hurt... everything ached in ways she had never felt before. 'How's everyone in Toytown doing?' she asked, with a nod towards the attic.

'Very funny.' Matthew climbed down the ladder. 'You don't look well, Chrissie. Do you feel okay?' He put a hand to her forehead, checking her temperature as though she was one of the children. 'You're not getting anywhere with our doctor. Perhaps you should go somewhere else – get a second opinion?'

'I'm fine, honestly. Stop worrying.'

'You're obviously not fine. Is it stress, do you think? There's no point running yourself into the ground with work only to be unwell all the time. Look, I've been thinking about this for a few weeks – why don't you take a break? Have a few weeks to get back on track, look after yourself for a change?'

'I couldn't. I'd lose too many clients.'

'You're good at what you do,' he tried to reassure her. 'They'll come back.'

'It doesn't work like that. Clients don't owe me any loyalty. It would be too much of a risk.'

Matthew tucked a stray strand of hair behind her ear. 'Why don't you go back to bed for a bit?'

There was something off about his voice – not anything obvious, but a subtle difference, a shift in tone sufficient to suggest that not everything was as it had been the last time they had seen each other. Did he know that she hadn't slept in their bedroom last night? Perhaps she had left the bed too neat, or he had been into the spare room and noticed that someone had slept in there. Or perhaps she was imagining it. She was tired. She felt disorientated. She was looking too deeply into things.

'Someone called for you earlier,' he told her, pushing the steps up into the hatch. 'Joel something... I can't remember if he gave his surname, sorry. He just asked if you could call him back. He said time was running out.'

Christina turned away, pretending to be preoccupied with

something in her pocket. The performance wasn't enough. She could feel Matthew watching her, sensing her discomfort.

'Everything okay?'

'Yeah. Just looking for my mobile. I've got a client called Joel. I don't know why he called the house phone, though – he should have my work number.'

She could feel her heart hammering in her chest with every word she spoke. Why was he doing this to her?

'What did he mean?' Matthew asked. '"Time is running out"?'

'No idea. Something relating to his injury, perhaps. I'll call him back.'

'What injury?'

'Sorry?'

Matthew held her eye. 'I'm just wondering what injury he has?'

'Oh. Sorry. Yeah... he, um, it's a football injury.'

The first time they had met, Joel had come to her with an injury to his ankle, gained during a five-a-side so-called friendly.

Matthew nodded slowly. 'That's why I've always avoided sport.'

'What do you mean?'

'Well, it's a bit too dangerous, by the sounds of it.'

She laughed. The sound came out too loud, too high-pitched. Forced. 'Exactly. You've got the right idea.' She smiled and gestured to the stairs, realising that even this was awkward. 'I'm going to make some lunch for the kids before I go and pick them up.'

Matthew was still looking at her strangely. He was watching her for signs of lies, she thought, reading her eyes as though every word of every mistruth she had ever uttered might become legible there if he were to just look hard enough. He knows, she thought.

'I'll put the kettle on,' she added.

She went downstairs and into the kitchen, stopping at the doorway and resting against the wall. Her heart was hammering so hard it was making her feel sick. A thin trail of sweat was trickling down the centre of her spine. She breathed deeply, trying to keep it silent for fear that Matthew would be able to hear it from upstairs. She had to focus on the here and now: making food for the twins, collecting them from nursery. She could get through this – she could get through anything – one thing at a time.

She reached for her phone and accessed the internet, typing Joel's name into the search engine. She needed to know why the police had been to his office. Had he done this before, to someone else? Had another woman come forward to report his stalking? Her hands shook as she scrolled the screen.

It didn't take long to find him. When she did, the result was not what she had been expecting. His face looked back at her with a half-smile, a self-assured pose for an image that had probably been used as a profile picture. Beneath it were words that threw everything she had thought she'd known on its head. *Joel Cooper, 39. Missing.*

'What did you and your sister argue over?'

Oliver and I are lying on the sofa together, soft voices whispering from the television, neither of us watching. My continued pretence at normal life has pushed me closer to him, my desire to be someone else – anyone other than myself – driving every decision I now make. I can lose myself when I am with Oliver, as though everything else disappears when we are together.

'When?'

'You said something before, about an argument before your mother's illness. I just realised you'd never said what it was about, that's all.'

I turn my head to lie on his chest so that I don't have to look at him, feigning interest in the scene that is unfolding on the television screen. I don't remember ever making the comment, though we have talked about so much that it will have been easy for details to have been missed.

'We just... It was that night, that's all. She said one thing and I said another. We could never recover from it.' I can feel Oliver's eyes on me, waiting for more, and for the first time in forever, I feel ready to talk about it. 'That night in the woods. Lewis. Delta was there before he showed up. She and I had been out together, but we argued, and she left me. Later, she didn't want to admit that she'd just run off – that would have got her into trouble. So instead she told my parents that *I'd* left *her*.'

'And then what happened? After she left you?'

'I lost my bearings. It was dark, I was disorientated... the drink didn't help. I mean, it was one of the reasons why no one believed me.'

'Believed you about the assault?'

Oliver seems to hear what I cannot speak, and his arm folds around my shoulders, closing me closer.

'What was he doing there anyway?'

'Running.'

'I'm sorry. You don't have to talk about it.'

'I'd always had a crush on him,' I admit, 'and everyone knew it. He told his parents that it was consensual, that I'd instigated it. I saw a doctor afterwards, you know, at the police station, but there was no physical evidence of an assault.'

'So it was your word against his?'

I nod. 'I started to doubt myself. Nobody believed me... I started not to believe myself. I hadn't tried to fight him off. I hadn't screamed for help. I just froze. And what people were saying was true – I did fancy him. I'd liked him since we just kids, and everyone knew it.'

'But your parents believed you when you told them what happened after Delta left, didn't they? When you told them what he did to you?'

I cringe at the words. *What he did to you*. Afterwards, when the police were no longer involved and the incident had been swept over the edge of the harbour wall as something the locals no longer wanted to acknowledge, I had to relive the memory of that evening in the woods over and over, to remind myself that I wasn't a liar. Had I inadvertently done something to lead him on? Had I encouraged it in some way, given the impression that I had wanted him to do what he did? It was all my fault, it must have been, and for a while I fell under an awful persuasion that allowed me to believe that everything Lewis had claimed about that night was in fact the truth after all.

'I think my father did, but my mother wanted it hushed up. He let her deal with everything.'

'What do you mean, "deal with everything"?'

I look him in the eye, deliberating over a final truth from that night that I have kept to myself all these years. No one knows, not even Sylvia. Delta didn't know. My parents took it to their graves, and now I am alone with the secret. 'I had an abortion. No one ever knew I was pregnant, not even my sister. Just my parents. My mother organised everything.'

Oliver says nothing, and for once I am grateful for the silence.

'I lied to you about the scar,' I tell him, touching my temple. 'I didn't fall over. I tried to kill myself. I went up to the coastal path, found an exposed bit of cliff edge and stepped off.'

'God, Brooke.'

'About six months after that, my father died. He had a massive heart attack. It came without warning – he was gone by the time the ambulance arrived. I killed him. If only I hadn't taken that step. If only I hadn't put him through everything I had. That pressure on his heart. My mother never stopped blaming me for it.'

I spent the next sixteen years paying back a debt that had been silently written and passed from her to me without words, one that no matter how much I did for her could never be written off. I stayed here in the village, the cause of all my family's suffering, and my mother held the noose of my guilt around my neck, tightening it a little more each day until I became irreversibly tethered to the place. But how could I explain to Oliver that I chose to stay here knowing that I could go back to that cliff edge at any given moment and do it all over again – that just knowing this made me feel powerful, as though the only element of control I had over my life was my death?

'And yet you were the one who did everything for her. The one who stayed.'

'I didn't really have a choice.'

'Of course you did. You always have a choice. You could have just walked away, but you didn't. You're a good person, Brooke. Only someone selfless would stay to care for a woman who hadn't believed her about something so terrible and life-changing.'

I've never thought of it in that way, as life-changing, but I suppose Oliver is right. What happened in the woods that night did change my life – there was a before and after, when one version of me ended and another came into existence. Lewis was responsible for that, and now, sixteen years later, he has managed in death to do the same to me again.

'Maybe Delta was right, though. Maybe I'm just scared of living.'

'That's what she said?'

'Plenty of times.'

Oliver reaches out a hand and places it over mine, saying nothing. I realise that most of our conversation has been for myself, a cathartic process of self-explanation, though I still keep so much hidden.

'It sounds as though she was a good actress, your sister.'

I look up at him, shaken by the words. 'What do you mean?'

'Well, everyone believed her. About what happened in the woods. She must have been convincing, that's all.'

My thoughts are interrupted by my phone; I answer it quickly, not wanting the noise to wake Finley.

'Sylvia?'

'The police have been here,' she says hurriedly. 'With a search warrant. They've been through the whole house – I couldn't stop them. They're on their way up to you now.'

As though on cue, there is knocking at the front door.

'I am so sorry,' I tell her, but we are cut off from one another. I'm not sure whether one of us lost signal or she has hung up on me. I wouldn't blame her if she did.

Oliver answers the door and returns with DS Jones and another plain-clothes officer who introduces himself as DC Chapman.

'We have a search warrant.'

'For this place?' Oliver says. 'What for?'

'We'll tell you when we find it,' DS Jones says, as DC Chapman begins rifling through the bookcase at the bottom of the stairs.

'My three-year-old son is asleep,' Oliver says sharply.

'We'll be as quick as we can, sir,' DS Jones tells him, the word 'sir' oozing sarcasm. 'But we'll have to search his room as well, I'm afraid.'

I look at Oliver apologetically and mouth the words 'I'm sorry'. Oliver goes upstairs and a few moments later returns carrying Finley, still asleep, in his arms. 'We'll wait in the car,' he says, and I follow him outside, helping him open the car door and get Finley inside.

'I don't know why they're doing this,' I whisper. 'I am so sorry.'

Oliver holds Finley to his chest and rubs my arm with his free hand. 'Just keep an eye on them. I don't trust them.'

When I go back inside, DS Jones is in the kitchen, rummaging through the cupboards. 'This is ridiculous. If you're looking for my things here, you won't find any. I don't have whatever it is you're looking for.'

'A pale blue rain jacket, you mean? North Face?' He stops what he's doing and looks at me with raised eyebrows, as though expecting a confession. 'The coated nylon used in the fabric made it pretty easy for forensics to identify. You don't have that jacket any more, you mean?'

'I have one jacket. It's red. It's by the front door – take a look for yourself.'

He studies me impassively, still waiting for me to slip up and expose the secret I am carrying. 'The thing is, Miss Meredith, there are a number of villagers who've come forward to say they've seen you wearing a pale blue rain jacket on a number of occasions.'

'I'm sure they have,' I say, turning at the noise as DC Chapman begins to empty the contents of Finley's toy box onto the floor in the living room. 'I used to have a blue rain jacket. It wasn't a North

Face one – I can't afford anything that pricey. It was destroyed in the fire, along with most of my possessions.'

'How convenient for you,' he remarks casually.

My heart stutters in my chest. 'What's that supposed to mean?' The comment doesn't make sense: the fire happened before Lewis's death. He is just trying to unsettle me, waiting to see me trip up on a lie.

He steps past me, saying nothing more, and I stand and watch as between them they turn the rest of the house upside down.

THIRTY-SIX

CHRISTINA

In her mind, Christina went through all the things she might have said or done to make Matthew suspicious of her. Perhaps she hadn't done anything; maybe her guilt had radiated from her in a layer of air that had become increasingly toxic and visible. Did he know who Joel was? Did he know that he had been reported as missing? Nothing made sense, not when Joel had been there in her home, and had left that bloodied scarf as some kind of warning sign.

Matthew was upstairs. Christina went to the house phone and checked the call history. No one had called since she had got back to the house, so unless someone had phoned after Joel, his should be the last number logged. She tapped it into her mobile and searched for it in her contacts list. Then she did the same on her work mobile. Neither of them recognised it.

She dialled the number on the house phone and let it ring. Would Joel answer? she wondered. Had he called the house from an unknown number so that she wouldn't know it was him? If the police were looking for him, they would have checked his call history and messages. They would link him back to her. Panic rose in a swell of confusion, and she tried to focus on her breathing while she realigned her thoughts. She was his physiotherapist. Any personal messages that had been shared between them had gone to the pay-as-you-go mobile, never to her own number.

'Hello, Lakeside Dental Surgery.'

She hung up. The dentist must have called sometime before she had arrived home, presumably for Matthew. Had it been for her, he would surely have mentioned it to her.

The number before that was a mobile number. She did the same again, tapping it into her personal mobile and then into her work mobile to see whether either of them had it stored. The latter did. Her eyes narrowed questioningly as she stared at the name on her screen.

Delta Meredith.

It had been weeks since she had last treated Delta, and she was due for another appointment. Why had she called the house number? There had been no need for her to do so, not when she had Christina's mobile number. And anyway, Christina had never given her the number of the house phone; she never gave that to clients, not even Janet Marsden.

Confused, she moved to the outgoing calls, wondering whether Matthew might have returned any of them. There was only a limited list of numbers stored, and it took just moments for her to realise that Delta's number was among them. Ten forty-nine that morning. He had called her back.

Later, she wasn't sure why she had done it, but she pressed the green button and waited for the call to connect. No one answered, and the call rang through to answerphone. After a click, Delta's voice spoke, lilting and chirpy, like an overly excitable children's television presenter.

Christina returned to the incoming calls to double-check her assumption. There was something wrong, something that didn't add up and made no sense. The timings of the calls didn't correlate. Matthew hadn't called her back; his call had come first. Delta hadn't called the house until eleven fifteen. How did he even have her number, and more to the point, why had he called her?

She went into the kitchen, where his iPad was on the worktop, his emails open. With a shaking hand, she took it through to the living room, scrolling his inbox as she went. There was little of interest; it looked as though he rarely bothered to clear out the plethora of junk mail that was sent to him.

Then something made her stop. Ticket confirmation. She tapped on the email, her heart racing as she scrolled its contents. He had ordered a ticket for *Cabaret*. She remembered wanting to go the previous year, but Matthew didn't 'do' theatre. He hated musicals. She had taken him to see *Les Misérables* once and he had fallen asleep within twenty minutes of the curtain going up. When she had mentioned this more recent show, he had suggested she would be better off going with a friend, but that was the thing – she didn't have any friends, not any more. She had lost contact with her former colleagues, and everyone from school had long since gone their separate ways. Her job meant that she no longer attended any toddler groups or play sessions, so there had never been a chance to meet other mothers that way. She hadn't wanted to go to the theatre alone.

And yet looking at this email, that was exactly what Matthew had done. The purchase of a single ticket. She looked again, double-checking that she hadn't made an error, but there was no mistake. He wouldn't have gone to the theatre alone, so that left only one possibility – he had gone with someone else, who had also purchased a single ticket. And why would two people do that and book separately, unless, of course, they had something to hide?

Stop it, Christina, she told herself. It could be a surprise – a present that he hadn't yet given her. She would have to act as though she knew nothing about it, though she was certain she would be useless at maintaining the pretence. Her own betrayal was now making her suspicious of Matthew, as though doubting him would justify her own wrongdoings.

And then she checked the date of the performance. It had already been and gone.

'Christina!'

Matthew's voice travelled from the hallway; moments later, she heard his footsteps on the stairs.

'Shit.'

She logged out of the emails and hurried back to the kitchen, putting the iPad back on the worktop where she had found it.

The twenty-sixth of February. Had he been working that night – or had he claimed to be, at least? She wished now that she had started recording things, keeping a check on dates so that she could go back and try to recall where everything had started to go wrong. But she had never thought to suspect him of anything, not when she had been so consumed with thoughts of her own betrayal.

'Everything okay?' he asked, appearing in the doorway.

'Fine,' she said, knowing that her voice sounded odd. She glanced at the iPad, realising now that she shouldn't have logged out of the email. When she had found it there, the account had been open. Would Matthew notice, and would he realise what she had been doing?

'You seem flustered,' he said. 'It isn't about that phone call, is it? This Joel person? Is he giving you trouble?'

'No, of course not. It's just the headaches and everything, you know.'

'You know what you need,' he said, moving closing and putting his arms around her waist. 'A break. A weekend away somewhere, just the two of us. What do you think?'

'We can't leave the kids for that long.'

'We never do anything for us any more.'

'They're still so young,' Christina said, not sure why she needed to defend her objection. 'It won't be like this forever.'

There was a lengthy pause. 'It sometimes feels as though I'm losing you. Am I losing you?'

Her smile felt forced; she could only imagine how it must look to Matthew. 'Of course not.' She put her arms around him, reciprocating his embrace. She was doing it again, she thought. Needing to justify herself in the face of his secrets; feeling guilty though it was his lies that were at risk of being exposed.

Yet she must have still felt something for him, or the burning sense of betrayal that had sparked inside her at the thought that he had called Delta would have died out much quicker, replaced with relief that now he would be the cause of their demise; his affair would be the reason for their separation. Or was there something else? she wondered. Was he doing this as revenge, having found out about Joel?

Despite her suspicions, she leaned into him and rested her head on his shoulder, the question she wanted to ask him left unspoken on her tongue.

Why did you call Delta Meredith?

I am woken by banging at the front door. Before I get out onto the landing, Sylvia is already there, her tired eyes adjusting to the artificial light. 'It's three a.m.,' she says.

'Stay here.'

I go downstairs, where the banging continues, and head to the kitchen to check through the window. Oliver is on the doorstep, a coat worn over his pyjamas, and I hurry back to open the front door.

'Help me, Brooke, please. It's Finley.'

'What's happened?'

'He's been sleepwalking again. He's fallen down the stairs.'

'Christ.' I am awake now, his words chasing away any slumber that may have been left in me. 'Wait here.' I run upstairs to grab the cardigan I left last night at the end of the bed, and briefly explain the situation to Sylvia. She doesn't reply; I haven't spoken to her since the police were here. The house is still a mess, the chaos unavoidable as I make my way back downstairs.

I pull on the walking boots that I left by the front door. 'Where is he?' I ask, wondering why Oliver is here and not with his son.

'In the car. I couldn't get a signal to call an ambulance, so I was going to take him myself, and then the bloody car wouldn't start.'

I grab my keys and slam the front door shut behind me while Oliver runs ahead. I almost lose him to the darkness of the silent road as he races to get back to his son.

'I shouldn't have moved him,' I hear him say to himself as I catch up, and perhaps he is right. Isn't the advice not to move someone who has suffered a fall? An involuntary image of Lewis haunts me once again. And then there is Delta, and I try to fight her face from behind my eyes. She appears to me now as I do not want to see her, broken and lifeless, nothing like the young woman I watched on that stage. Did anyone try to move her? If they had, would she have stood a chance?

There are no street lights at this end of the village, one of the few places where the night sky can still be viewed in its true form, unaffected by the light pollution of life below. Oliver finds the torch on his otherwise redundant mobile phone, flashing it with arm outstretched to light the path ahead. His ragged breaths lead us to the car. The back passenger-side door is open, and Oliver swears into the night air.

The car is empty. He bumps against me as he backs away from it, turning to me, his expression racked with panic. 'He was here,' he says, pointing to the booster seat in the back of the car. 'I left him here, he was unconscious. Finley!'

'He can't have gone far,' I say, putting a hand on his arm to calm him. In truth, I fear the opposite. The field behind the house, overrun in recent years with brambles, leads on to the woods that characterise the hillside, difficult enough to navigate during the daytime. At the ages of ten and eleven, Delta and I spent months familiarising ourselves with the intricacies of their connecting paths, picking circles through fallen leaves and dodging the roots of ancient oaks as we lost our way again and again. At three years old, and a stranger to the land, Finley will be lost within minutes if he has ventured further than fifty metres from where we stand.

'Finley!'

'Oliver,' I say, keeping my voice steady to try to calm him. 'Let's check the house first, just in case.'

I am closer than he is, so I let myself in, the door left unlocked in the earlier panic. I step into the living room, and a noise greets me as my eyes adjust to the darkness.

'Oh God,' I say, my hand flying to my heart.

Fin is sitting in an armchair in the darkness. His hands grip the arms as though he might fall if he lets go, and when I flick the light switch, I see that his cheeks are red and his eyes wet with tears.

'It's only me, Fin, don't be frightened. It's just me.' I turn back to the front door. 'Oliver! He's in here.'

He is beside me in moments.

'Where did you go?' Fin asks. He stares past me at his father, who drops to his knees and traps him in an embrace that almost pulls him from the chair.

'Oh God, you're okay. I am so, so sorry, Fin, the car wouldn't start and then I panicked, and...' Oliver rests back on his haunches, his hands still grasping Finley's arms as he checks him over. 'Is anything hurting? Have you hurt yourself?'

Finley shakes his head. 'I was in the car.'

'I know, you were sleepwalking again. Did you have a bad dream?' Oliver turns to me. 'He used to do it all the time back home – he'd always come into my room. Maybe that's why he fell – he didn't remember where we were.'

'We should still take him to the hospital. Just to make sure.'

'Could you take us? I'm sorry, I hate asking for favours.'

'Of course. Give me five minutes, I'll be outside.'

I go back out into the darkness and return home to fetch my car. I drive it up to Hillside Cottage, then sit with Fin in the living room as his dad moves his booster seat from their car to mine. He doesn't speak to me, but while we wait, he reaches out and takes my hand in his, the gesture unexpected. I squeeze his fingers gently, a silent reassurance that everything is going to be okay.

At the hospital, they find no worrying symptoms, though every question they ask Finley goes unanswered, the child muted by trauma. When we return home I wait outside while Oliver carries his son from the car.

'He's asking for you.' He reappears at the front door, his face pale with tiredness and worry. 'Do you mind going to see him?'

'Of course not.'

Fin is sitting up in bed, his little face exhausted. 'Why don't you close your eyes now?' I say. 'You need to catch up on some sleep.'

'Stay with me, Brooke.' His tired eyes plead with his father.

'Brooke needs her sleep too, kid. I think we've kept her up enough already, don't you?'

'Dad,' he says, giving the word two syllables, and I turn to look at Oliver.

'I don't mind if you don't,' I tell him.

'Are you sure?' He looks at Fin. 'You little charmer.'

I glance at the shelves near the window, unable to stop myself from picturing the room as it was when it was mine. If I were to close my eyes now, I would see the hot-raspberry walls and the dreamcatcher that hung in the window, its pinks and purples as delicately threaded as a spider's web. 'Would you like me to read you a story?' I ask, dragging myself from the past.

Finley nods.

'Thank you,' Oliver mouths, and he leaves the room, pulling the door gently behind him.

I slide a book at random from the shelf and show Fin the cover. 'This one?'

He nods again, having fallen back into silence.

I pull the duvet up to make him warmer and more comfortable, then turn to the first page and begin reading. By the second page, he is murmuring at my side, reciting the book word for word. Oliver must read to him a lot, I think – but not only that, Finley must always be listening. He may speak infrequently, but he is more aware than I – than perhaps his own father, even – have realised.

We finish the story together.

'Try closing your eyes now.'

'I see her sometimes.'

'Who?'

'The little girl.'

'This one?' I ask, pointing to the book that still lies open in front of us.

Finley shakes his head, his eyes fixed on the room ahead of him. 'No, not that one. The little girl who stands at the end of my bed.'

THIRTY-EIGHT

CHRISTINA

The doorbell rang while Christina was still with a client.

'Please excuse me.'

When she went to the front door, Delta was there. Christina had called her after finding her number on the house phone, using the excuse of checking that she could still make her appointment. There had been no mention from either of them of Delta calling the house phone. She was wearing skin-tight leather trousers and boots that elongated her already impossibly long legs, and she shifted her weight from one foot to the other as she apologised for being early.

Christina hesitated. The thought that this woman might be involved with her husband brought a heat to the back of her neck that snaked around to her throat. Delta was probably not much younger than her, though she could easily have passed for early twenties. She was slimmer and her skin was clearer, and the pang of jealousy that Christina had felt when treating the other woman previously returned now, inappropriate and unsettling.

'I have a client still with me,' she explained. 'Would you mind waiting in the living room?'

'Thank you,' Delta said, following her through.

'I won't be long.'

When she left the room, Christina waited in the hallway for a moment, wondering what Delta would do. Would she sit down, or would she stay standing like that in the middle of the room, perhaps assessing the place as she waited? Just how much attention had she paid to the house on previous visits? Christina had been so tangled up in thoughts of her own infidelity that she had never considered the possibility that Matthew might be guilty of the same. And yet so much now made sense. His long work hours and all the overtime he had been doing. The extended time spent up in the attic, needing to 'unwind'. Had he been on the phone to her up there? Had they laughed and joked about Christina's naïvety while she had been just downstairs, looking after the twins?

And when exactly had they met? She had agonised over this one detail, obsessing about the potential ways in which her husband and her client had come to cross paths. Had it been here, in their home? Had they had a chance encounter elsewhere, finding out only later that they were already connected through his wife? As she considered the various possible scenarios of their first meeting, one involuntary image had kept recurring, taunting her with its simplicity and its implications. That day the chicken hearts had been delivered to the front door, when Matthew hadn't been available to answer the door, Delta had been alone in the treatment room, half her body exposed on the table. Had he seen her that day? Had he approached her after that, or was it she who had pursued him?

She wondered whether Delta had been to the house on other occasions. Had Matthew had her over here when Christina hadn't been home? The thought filled her chest with a pulsing anger. It was impossible, though. She was always home, and when she left for any reason, it was never for long. It was Matthew who spent hours away from home. He hadn't needed to bring Delta here, not when there was so much opportunity elsewhere for them to be together.

She grappled with an endless cycle of what-ifs as she closed the session with her current client, returning to the treatment room to prepare for the next before going to fetch Delta. The woman walked ahead of her, and Christina realised as she followed that the pangs of jealousy were something greater. She had resented this woman even before she suspected she might be sleeping with her husband. Delta was younger, slimmer; beautiful. She had a career that seemed glamorous and exciting, and she was enthused by life, not ground down in the way Christina must so often seem, exhausted by routine and lacking in energy for anything more than an hour of television by the time evening arrived. Perhaps Delta softened to Matthew's touch, where Christina flinched. What wouldn't he had found attractive about her?

Delta sat at the edge of the treatment table and rested her foot on the chair Christina had put in place for her. 'I'm starting to worry this is going to affect me long-term,' she said.

Christina met her eye, imagining for a moment that Delta was referring to the affair.

'It's still only been a matter of months,' she said. 'I know it must be frustrating, but it will improve. Does much of your current role involve dancing?'

'Most of it. I get a lot of chorus parts. I won't if this keeps playing me up, though.' Delta studied her leg as though it was something unconnected to her, resentful of the limb that had until now aided her career. Christina could sympathise: a calf injury to someone who earned their living as a dancer would have the same impact as she herself suffering damage to her hand. We take so much for granted, she thought. Health. Limbs. Marriages.

She carried out some manipulation of the strained muscles in Delta's leg before talking her through some of the exercises they had gone over during their previous session.

'Which show are you in? Sorry, I know you've told you before. I'm so forgetful.'

'*Cabaret.*'

Christina felt the breath leave her lungs. Matthew had been there. He had gone to her. Had they met up after the show, going on together to a bar or a hotel?

'Ow, that hurts.'

She loosened her grip around Delta's leg, realising her finger-tips were digging into her calf muscles.

'Are you married?' she asked, trying to make the question sound a natural part of the conversation.

'No. I haven't really got time for that.'

But time for sleeping with other people's husbands, Christina thought, an image of Matthew and Delta together flashing involuntarily into her head. She forced it down, wrapping her hands around the throat of the thought until she had squeezed the life out of it.

'You've probably got the right idea. It's not all it's cracked up to be.' Take that back to Matthew, she thought.

Delta glanced at Christina's left hand. 'How long have you and your husband been together?'

'Too long.' There was an awkward silence for a moment before Christina smiled. 'Just kidding. Eight years. I'd get less for murder, right?'

Delta laughed, though the sound was short-lived, her expression changing when she looked at Christina to find her gazing solemnly back. She shifted uncomfortably, disconcerted by what Christina realised was strange behaviour. She wanted her to feel discomfort. She wanted her to know how it felt to be scorned, deceived, humiliated. She wanted to see how far she could push her before she would fall.

'You must have a partner, though?'

'Why must I?'

'Well... you're successful, young, attractive.'

'That's kind of you to say, I suppose, but I don't need another person to validate any of those things. A man, I mean.'

'Of course not. I'm sorry if I've said too much. I meant nothing by it.'

Delta brushed the comment aside. 'There are a couple of people. No one serious.'

The conversation returned to the nature of her injury and the time frame she could expect for it to begin to see signs of improvement. The session continued in a tense silence, and when Delta left, Christina regretted her behaviour. She went back to the treatment room, closed the door and cried hot, angry tears. She wasn't angry at Delta; she was angry at herself. She didn't behave like this. Joel's disappearance had sent everything she thought she had known into freefall. If Matthew was having an affair with Delta, then her issue was with him. They had been lying to each other, deceiving one another for longer than either had realised. Delta had been dragged into their mess of a marriage, possibly under false pretences. If it hadn't been her, it would likely have been someone else. Taking her frustrations out on the other woman was going to achieve nothing. At some point, Christina was going to have to speak to Matthew.

THIRTY-NINE

BROOKE

Finley's words are spoken so matter-of-factly, with such innocence, and yet they turn my blood to ice. I look to where he still stares, as though I may see another child looking back at us. Though I know I imagine it, I feel a cold breeze brush the back of my neck. Delta, I think, and the thought sparks tears that I quickly blink away.

'I used to dream like you,' I say, trying to draw him from the memory, whether real or imagined. My heart beats too quickly as I try to reassure him. 'I used to dream about all kinds of girls and boys and animals and places. All the people you meet in your dreams are your friends, did you know that?'

He is looking at me with the eyes of someone who is far older – someone who knows that I am talking nonsense to appease him but doesn't have the heart to tell me that he knows. *Dreams*, he seems to be saying. *I didn't say anything about dreams.*

'Come on now, tired eyes. Time to catch up on some sleep.'

As I reach for his duvet I hear a noise on the landing, someone moving from the door, and it occurs to me that Oliver has been standing there this whole time, listening. Does he not trust me with his son? And did he hear Finley mention the little girl?

I go to the door and pull it open, allowing a shard of morning light to soften the room with its glow, and Fin calls out, his voice frantic. 'Don't leave me.'

Poor little man. He must live with a weight of uncertainty, never sure when someone leaves a room whether they will return. How much of his mother does he remember? I wonder.

'I'm not going anywhere,' I tell him, and return to his bedside. In the half-light, I pull his duvet up again so that it is snug around his shoulders. 'Are you warm enough?'

He gives a little purr, like a contented cat.

His eyes begin to flicker, but before he succumbs to sleep, he slips his hand from beneath the duvet and reaches for mine. His palm is hot and clammy, yet when I reach to touch his forehead, it is cold.

'You're okay now,' I tell him, rubbing his knuckles with my thumb. 'Everything's going to be all right.'

I wait with him until his breathing deepens and I know he is sleeping, then I gently ease my hand from his. When I go out onto the landing, I hear movement in the other bedroom. I go to the door and tap gently, not wanting to intrude.

'Sorry,' Oliver says. 'I never thought it would take him that long to drop off.'

The room is a mess – less consideration was given here than in Finley's. The contents of Oliver's drawers are strewn across the floor, his clothes abandoned in piles he hasn't yet attempted to tackle.

'Don't worry. He's had an ordeal, hasn't he – he was probably over-tired, bless him.'

'You're so good with him. Thank you.'

'It's fine. I'm sorry about all this, though.'

'Forget it. I'll sort it later.'

'I'd better be getting back.'

Oliver reaches for my hand. 'Stay with me,' he says, repeating the words Finley used. He pulls me closer, and I respond to his body when his lips crush against mine. He draws me into the bedroom and closes the door behind us, and I allow myself to forget where I am as his hands roam to my waist and lift away my top.

Afterwards, he falls asleep beside me, his body turned into mine. I can't go to sleep now. I am too unsettled by the events of last night, and now the room is closing in on me, a reminder of a past life that still lives within these walls. As I watch Oliver's chest rise and fall, I think of Finley, gone from the car when we returned from Sylvia's, and of all the nightmarish outcomes that might have transpired if things had taken a different turn somewhere.

As events play out in my memory, something seems wrong. Finley's face in the darkness when I came into the house. He was disorientated, that much was obvious, but there was something else too. What, I don't know. Had his skin felt cold enough to have just come from outside? In the greyness of a room lit only by moonlight, had his face looked pinched by the night air?

I push the duvet back gently and get out of bed, each move made carefully so as not to disturb Oliver. When I get downstairs, I put my shoes on and pick up his keys. I open the door slowly, trying to avoid breaking the silence of the sleeping house. The mid morning air greets me with a cool kiss upon the cheek, a welcome respite from the heat that my anxiety has generated.

Oliver's car is parked just along the sloping driveway, and when I press the key fob, its side lights flash yellow. I get into the driver's seat and turn the key in the ignition. I expect nothing. Instead, the car starts with my first attempt.

I cut the engine, not wanting the noise to disturb either Fin or Oliver. Beneath my clothes, my heart stutters in my chest, uncertainty swelling and bringing a return of the heat that earlier burned through me. It might have been a lucky one-off, but I don't want to try again. It wouldn't start last night... Oliver couldn't start it – and as I return to the house, the mantra continues in my head, taunting me.

I push the door closed gently and return the keys to where I found them. I know the staircase well enough to know which steps are the creakiest, so I navigate them as though I am dodging jellyfish on the beach, and when I get to the landing, the house is still as quiet as when I left it.

In the bedroom, daylight spills through the partly opened curtains. Oliver's eyes are open; he is looking right at me. 'I couldn't get back to sleep,' I say, hearing the guilt in my voice. He says nothing for a moment, as though he is sleeping with his eyes open, looking but not seeing, and I am just about to leave the room again when he says, 'Come back to bed.' I cross the room and get in beside him, the heat from his body warming me quickly.

'You're freezing,' he says, and he puts a hand on the side of my face before kissing me. Despite being exhausted, I respond to him, our bodies finding each other's. I push to the back of my mind the thought of the car starting, the little girl in Fin's room, Lewis, the woods – everything. As Oliver's lips find my throat and move down my body, he makes me forget it all, and once again I allow him to.

FORTY

CHRISTINA

APRIL 2018

On Thursday morning, Christina returned to Janet's house. She parked in her usual place on the driveway, alongside Janet's husband's car, and turned off her phone. She had tried calling Joel a couple of times since finding the scarf in her bed, but each time the line was dead. A part of her had clung onto the idea that the police had got it wrong, that perhaps Joel had chosen to disappear, hiding after what he had put her through, though the more she considered it, the more unlikely it became. He had professional responsibilities – a livelihood that would crumble in his absence.

She rang the doorbell, and Robert answered. She had met him during one of their more recent sessions, but it was only when she saw him there that day that she realised why he had been around more often. Despite her smiles and her optimism, Janet's condition had been getting worse.

He looked confused for a moment, as though he had never seen her before and didn't know who she was. 'I forgot to call you, didn't I?' he said, the words barely audible. His face crumpled, and he didn't need to say anything more.

'Oh Robert. No.'

He started to cry. This strong man, all six-foot-plus of him, stepped back into the hallway as he sobbed, and Christina dropped her bag on the doorstep, reaching out to steady him.

'Dad.' His daughter, Rebecca, appeared in the living room doorway, watching her father as he folded against Christina.

'I am so, so sorry,' Christina said, feeling the weight of him press upon her shoulder. She looked past him to Rebecca, and saw that she was crying too. She wanted to hold them both, to make everything better, to bring Janet back to them, and yet all she could do was stand there and allow him to expel his grief.

After a minute, Robert stepped back, embarrassed. 'I'm sorry,' he said, wiping his eyes with the palm of his hand. 'I thought I'd be prepared... you know... when the time came. But you never really think it's going to.'

'Please don't apologise. I'm so sorry I came this morning. If I'd known...'

'That's my fault,' Rebecca said. 'I was supposed to go through her calendar.'

Christina shook her head. 'Nothing is your fault. If there's anything I can do, for either of you, you have my number, so please just call me, okay?' Robert nodded, though Christina knew she wouldn't hear from him. She put a hand on his arm. 'Janet was a lovely woman. She wasn't just a client – I considered her a friend. She spoke of you both so much.'

Robert nodded again, swallowing down any further sobs. 'Thank you. You really helped her, you know... to manage the pain.'

Christina gave them her card so that they were sure to have her number. She left the driveway and made it as far as two streets away before pulling the car to the side, her vision already blurred with tears. She had worked with patients who had passed away before, but it had never affected her like this. Janet had held up a mirror to her, allowing her to see her life and her choices for what they had become. Without her, Christina might have continued her affair with Joel, mindlessly bringing ruin on whatever was left of her marriage. Janet had been a good woman – honest, hard-working, loyal – and yet that goodness had been repaid with pain and suffering.

But there was something else she had made Christina face, something she had been hiding from for a long time now. She wasn't happy. She believed she should have been – that she didn't deserve not to be – but for reasons she still couldn't isolate, her heart felt sad, an incompleteness residing there. Janet, a woman who had known her for merely a matter of months, had been able to see it. Now it was up to Christina to do something about it.

When she got back home, she couldn't hide the fact that she had been crying. Matthew was in the hallway when she opened the front door, trying to grapple a plastic pram from the twins, both seeking victory over the other in their quest for ownership.

'What's happened?'

She pursed her lips as she tried to fight back the tears, but they were stronger than she was.

'Chrissie, what's happened?' Matthew gave up on the pram, leaving Elise to chase down the hallway with it before Edward had a chance to claim it. He went to his wife and put his arms out to embrace her. She laid her head against his chest and sobbed as he held her in the way she had not long ago held Robert.

'It's Janet,' she told him. 'She's gone.'

'The cancer patient? God, I'm so sorry. I thought you said things seemed better for her?'

'They did, for a while. But things just turn, don't they? Life is so unpredictable.'

Matthew said nothing, but ran a hand across her hair as she composed herself. She took a breath as she stepped back from him, shaking herself from the sadness that gripped her. She reminded herself of what he was doing; of what she suspected he had been doing.

'Can I ask you something?'

'Of course you can. What's the matter?'

Are you sleeping with Delta Meredith? The words wouldn't leave her, trapped in her head and held hostage on her tongue.

Aloud, a different question escaped. 'If you ever start to feel differently... you know, about me... would you tell me?'

He pulled a face. 'Where has this come from?'

'I just... I don't know. I need to know, that's all. People change. People's feelings change.'

'You've known me since we were kids,' he said. 'Do you think I've changed?'

She would never have told him so, but the truth was, she wouldn't have known. She had never paid him much attention at school. He was just one of the quiet boys, one of the ones who never got into any trouble but never stood out for any reason either, seemingly happy to fade into the background. He could have changed ten times over between sixth form and their meeting at twenty-five, and she wouldn't have known a thing about it.

The half-smile that had rested on his face fell from view. 'Have *your* feelings changed?'

'No,' she answered, too hurriedly. *I'm not sure*, a voice in her head said. *I don't really know what they ever were*. She silenced the voice, shutting the words in a corner of her brain where she might ignore them. Ending things with Joel had been evidence that she loved Matthew. 'I'm sorry. I'm being silly. It's just that everything with Janet... it makes you think, doesn't it?'

Matthew put an arm around her waist and pulled her closer. 'Come here,' he said, and he kissed her forehead. 'That's always been your problem, over-thinking. It's much safer not to.'

FORTY-ONE

BROOKE

It is a windy Wednesday evening in late November; a storm is forecast for overnight. Oliver has invited me to Hillside Cottage for dinner, so I wait at home for him to settle Fin for the night. We have agreed to dress up as though we are going to a restaurant – Oliver's idea; he claims he feels guilty for never having taken me on a proper date – and I feel a fraud walking the path from Sylvia's to the house in a dress and heels I had to order especially for tonight, hoping that no one from the village sees me. I want to feel normal, to pretend that my business isn't burned, and that Lewis didn't die; that the police aren't watching me, waiting for me to trip over my own lies. But normal is something that hasn't applied to my life in a long time.

It starts to rain just as I reach the house, but Oliver is waiting at the door, having seen me from the window. He is wearing tailored trousers and a crisp shirt, far smarter than I expected him to be and impossibly handsome in a way I hadn't quite realised he was.

'Storm tonight,' he says, closing the door behind me. 'You might not be able to get home.' He grins and kisses me, and I take off my coat, feeling self-conscious and wishing I could get away with keeping it on while we eat. 'You're definitely not leaving now.' He takes the coat from me, the perfect gentleman. 'You look beautiful.'

'Thanks. You scrub up all right as well, I suppose.' I run a finger along the edge of his collar. 'Impressive skills with the iron.'

He looks at the necklace around my throat and smiles. 'You wore it.'

'I heard this is quite a posh restaurant. I thought I'd better make an effort.'

He kisses me again and ushers me through the living room and into the kitchen. 'Wow,' I say, genuinely impressed at the effort he's made. The table is decorated with candles and flowers, the cutlery set out with the precision of a Michelin-starred restaurant. I feel heat rising in my neck at the thought that none of this is deserved. I am a liar. I let a man die. I deserve nothing.

'Don't be too overwhelmed,' he warns. 'You haven't tasted the food yet.'

There is something in the oven, and whatever it is, it smells delicious.

'How have you had time to do all this while you were getting Fin ready for bed?'

'He was my sous chef.'

'Bless him.'

He pulls out a chair. 'Madam,' he says, with an exaggerated wave of his arm.

'Okay, you can stop now.'

'Wine?'

'Daft question.'

He goes to the fridge to get a bottle and pours us both a glass. We chat while he prepares a starter, and I wish so badly that this could really be my life, the normality of food and company, an honest existence. If I play this part for long enough, might it eventually become reality?

'Explain something to me,' he says. 'What time is dinner?'

'Depends when you're hungry, I suppose. Twelve thirty? One?'

He turns to look at me, bemused. 'That's lunch. Dinner is about seven-ish.'

'That's tea.'

'But tea is tea. You know, a cup of tea. You can't have a drink that's tea and a meal that's tea, it's just confusing.'

'There's nothing confusing about that.'

'You're strange,' he says, placing a plate in front of me before leaning down to kiss me. 'I like strange.'

The food is delicious, despite him continuing to play it down. As we eat, we talk about everything and nothing; all the small details of our days while avoiding the still-untouched territories between us. We are midway through the main course when there is a sound at the kitchen door.

'Daddy.' Finley stands in the doorway in his pyjamas, a teddy bear clutched in one hand while the other rubs at his tired eyes.

'You okay, mate?' Oliver goes to him, crouching down to give him a cuddle.

'I had a bad dream.'

Oliver turns and gives me a look, worry etched in his expression. He has made no further mention of getting Fin professional help for his anxiety and his sleep problems, and after what happened the last time I passed comment, I haven't wanted to ask about it.

'Come on, little man,' he says, scooping Finley up. 'Let's get you back to bed.'

'Can Brooke take me?'

Fin is looking right at me, wide-eyed and expectant, more vulnerable than I have ever seen him. I wonder what the dream was about, and how real it must have seemed to him.

'Not tonight, mate,' Oliver says.

'Please.'

'I don't mind.'

Oliver turns to me. 'Are you sure?'

'Of course.'

Finley reaches out his arms to me, and it fills me with a warmth unlike anything else. He has accepted me here, their double act now a trio, and I am at once both thrilled and terrified at the prospect of being a regular feature in his life. I haven't earned the position; it was simply left vacant.

When I hold him, he feels hot and clammy. He puts his arms around me and clings on like a baby koala, nestling his head against my neck.

'Thank you,' Oliver says, before mouthing, 'Sorry.' I shake my head; he has nothing to feel sorry about.

I carry Finley upstairs and lay him down in his bed. 'Drink some of this,' I say, offering him the cup of water left on his bedside table. 'What did you dream about?'

He gulps the water and then lies on his back, staring bleary-eyed at the ceiling. 'I don't know,' he tells me, and yet I sense that he does and that he doesn't want to share it with me. 'I'm cold.'

I put a hand to his forehead, suspecting a temperature. 'Let me tuck you in. You should keep warm.'

He wriggles his body down the bed and I pull the duvet up around his shoulders. He reaches out for my hand and holds my fingers in a grip that is surprisingly tight.

'I think I must have dreamed it.'

'Dreamed what?' I ask him.

'Falling down the stairs.'

We haven't spoken of that night since it happened. Nor have I mentioned the little girl at the end of his bed, though she has stayed with me like some invisible presence at my side, acknowledged silently and kept a secret.

'Why do you think that?'

'I don't remember.'

Does he mean he doesn't remember why he thinks that, or that he doesn't remember actually falling? Either way, I have already thought back on that night and wondered at how he ended up in the living room the way he did. There is nothing surprising about a child sleepwalking, and yet there is something about that evening that has always seemed strange.

'Don't worry about it any more,' I tell him, putting a hand to his forehead again. I stroke his head gently and wait for him to close his eyes before turning out the light. 'Sweet dreams now,' I say, my voice hushed and soothing.

He continues to murmur, snatches of broken thoughts and displaced dreams escaping him. I hum softly, hoping to distract him from whatever thoughts still plague him.

'Hell is on fire,' he says, the words cutting through the air between us, sending a chill through me.

'It's okay, Fin,' I say, moving my hand from his forehead and placing it on his arm. 'It's just a dream. The fire has gone now.'

His eyes open; in the darkness, he is looking right at me. 'You're going to leave me, aren't you?' he says. 'Bad things happen to all the girls.'

FORTY-TWO

CHRISTINA

Joel Cooper, last seen three weeks ago. Colleagues and friends concerned. Anyone with any details, please contact Met Police.

Christina stared at the photograph that accompanied the tweet, Joel's face looking back from her phone screen. She was shaken from her thoughts by the sound of the doorbell. Every time her phone rang or there was someone at the door, she expected the police to come questioning her.

Matthew was upstairs, getting ready for work. Supposedly. She knew it was a lie because she had phoned the airport to find out whether he was scheduled to be there that evening, which, after a little persuasion with a person reluctant to believe she was really his wife, she found out he wasn't. There was a risk he would find out that she had checked up on him, but it was one she was willing to take.

Alice was at the door, earlier than expected. 'Are you sure you don't mind doing this?' Christina double-checked. She had asked Alice to lie for her, having told Matthew that they were going to have a girls' night in once the children were asleep.

'Of course not. I'm intrigued, though.'

'And I'm not giving anything away,' Christina told her breezily, faking a smile.

She had told Alice that she was arranging a surprise for Matthew's birthday, which was not long after the twins'. She hoped that a few weeks down the line, she would be forgiven for the lie. No one knew what was around the corner, least of all her, but there were things she could do to help herself prepare for the future, and the first of them she was going to do that evening.

'I won't be too late,' she said, knowing she couldn't guarantee that.

She had to wait until Matthew had said goodbye and left the house before going to her car. Worried that she had already lost him, she caught a glimpse of his car at the end of the next street, turning left on to the main road that led towards Barnet town centre. Keeping him in sight, she followed him along the main road before he turned on to a side street and into a hotel car park.

Christina felt her heart race. Surely he wouldn't stay here with someone – with Delta – so close to their home? She had to stop on the side street, hoping that Matthew wouldn't notice her car. She watched as he walked away from the hotel and headed on foot along the pavement, heading for the Tube station. Panicked that she would lose him, Christina pulled her own car into the hotel car park and hurriedly got out, having to run. She caught sight of him again on the Tube station steps, hanging back and waiting as he made his way to the platform.

She followed Matthew to Covent Garden, managing to keep him in sight during the change to the Piccadilly Line. As they neared the West End, she had felt her heart sink. She knew where they were going, and though she had wanted this outing not to prove a waste of time, she had also clung to the hope that she might later reprimand herself for her foolishness, having followed him to a meeting with a work colleague or to collect a surprise birthday gift for the twins.

The Tube shuddered to a halt, and Matthew stepped towards the doors at the far end of the carriage. Christina bumped into someone as she struggled to keep her husband in sight. She mumbled an apology before pushing through the crowd of people and hurrying towards the exit. There were too many people. She could no longer see Matthew – there was no flash of the khaki jacket he was wearing, its colour too muted amid the evening rush of commuters and restaurant-goers. She glanced at the winding staircase that seemed to go on forever, then opted for the lift. If Matthew had taken the stairs, the lift would reach ground level before he did; she could find a corner in which to conceal herself and wait for him to make a reappearance.

She was bustled into the busy lift, barely having to move her feet as she was transported with the crowd. She was grateful not to find that Matthew was in there with her, doubtful that she would have been able to keep herself hidden had he turned to look in her direction. The air was thick and hot, and she felt herself beginning to burn up. It wasn't the conditions, she thought; it was him. The affair. The lies. Joel's disappearance. The blur of deceit between them.

She was glad of the rush of cold air that greeted her once the lift doors yawned open. She followed the crowd out of the exit, all the while scanning faces and clothing. But Matthew was no longer with them. Her heart raced beneath her clothing and a headache pulsed at her temples, and as she moved aside to free herself from the thickening throng of people still filtering from the Underground, she took a deep breath and sank into the shadow of the station wall, wanting to disappear into it. It was easy to get lost in the city, she thought. Was this what Joel had chosen?

The theatre was three streets away. She and Matthew had been there years earlier – the infamous *Les Misérables* experience that had been their first and last theatre visit together. They had had an early supper before the show, then afterwards had gone back to the ludicrously overpriced Shaftesbury Avenue hotel that they had booked on a whim for the kind of sex Christina could never imagine them having again. The thought jarred in her head. Was that what he was doing with Delta? she thought. All those nights and weekends she had thought he was at work, had he really been with her?

She thought about that night in the hotel. Snapshots of memories flicked into her head as though she was flipping through a photo album. The images became blurred, the faces changing. Matthew was older. Delta's face took the place of her own, Christina's body replaced with the lithe limbs she had treated in the back room of their home.

As she neared the building, faces smiled down from the huge images fixed to its facade. Delta's was not among them. These days, so many of the starring roles were taken by famous faces from the television – reality stars and former members of pop groups. Delta had told her she often took chorus parts, and it had been easy enough to find her with a quick internet search. She looked strikingly beautiful in the background of the publicity photographs that appeared on the show's website, and Christina doubted it would be long before producers were booking her as a leading lady.

She stopped on the opposite side of the street, waiting with others at a set of traffic lights. She caught sight of Matthew by the main entrance; he was looking down at his phone, scrolling something that had stolen his attention from the world around him. He had got better-looking with age. At school, he had fallen somewhere between popular and geek, getting lost in that mid-section of boys who might have been nice enough but weren't sufficiently interesting to be noticed. And then he had been there for her that day in the park, and everything had looked different.

She felt sick. The guilt she had carried about her relationship with Joel had consumed her for the past months, and she had been doing everything she could to try to make things right again. Now he was missing, and the threat of police involvement hung over her daily, casting a permanent shadow of uncertainty over her life.

When the pedestrian lights turned to green and the traffic stopped, she crossed the road. She watched her husband go up the theatre steps and disappear into the building, and waited a while, letting crowds pass by her before she approached a member of the theatre staff who was standing near the entrance.

'How long is the performance?' she asked him.

'About two and a quarter hours,' he told her. 'With the interval.'

'And it starts at seven thirty?'

He nodded; Christina thanked him and stepped aside, allowing a young couple to pass her as they made their way into the building. She glanced at her phone. The show was starting in less than fifteen minutes. She might have bought a ticket – there were still seats available – but she didn't want to risk Matthew spotting her in the audience. Not only that, but she didn't think she could bear to watch Delta on that stage, not when doing so would mean having to watch everything that she herself apparently wasn't, being reminded of what her husband had chosen over her.

Instead, she went to a coffee shop in the next street. She ordered a drink and found a table in a quiet corner before taking out the book she had brought with her, having known she would have time to kill. None of it would be read – she couldn't concentrate on anything other than the thought of Matthew watching his lover on that stage, and of the things they might have planned for afterwards.

After an hour, she left the coffee shop and walked around the neighbouring streets, idling away the time by browsing in shop windows and going into those that were still open. She returned to the theatre fifteen minutes before the show was due to end, staying on the opposite side of the street, where she was close enough to see people leaving but far enough away to keep herself hidden from sight.

She caught her breath when she saw Matthew walk down the steps from the entrance and head around the side of the building. He had sat through the performance on his own, she thought, Delta's presence on the stage company enough for him, knowing that she would be waiting for him once it was over. That was where he was heading now, the stage door. She felt sick. The thought that she deserved this, that it was karma for her own affair, swept through her, making her feel even worse.

They waited for Delta, both of them, on opposite sides of the street. Matthew lingered against the wall of the theatre, leaving room for people to pass on the pavement. Christina stood in the shadows, transfixed by the imminent union despite not wanting to be subjected to it. After what felt like hours, Delta appeared in the doorway. Her dark hair was swept back loosely at the nape of her neck, her face perfectly made-up and glowing from the exhilaration of the performance.

Christina forgot to breathe. Her lungs failed to function, her heart stopping in her chest as she waited for Delta to hurry to Matthew, to throw her arms around his neck or press her mouth against his. But they would be more discreet than that, she thought. There would be a smile, perhaps a brief touching of hands, some acknowledgement of the thrill of their meeting, then they would walk away together, to a hotel or to her place, and the rest was something Christina didn't want to have to think about.

What she hadn't imagined or prepared for was that Delta would walk past Matthew without so much as a glance. She watched as the other woman pulled the collar of her plush coat higher around her throat before heading off along the street. Matthew was looking right at her. He watched her as she passed him, yet Delta seemed oblivious, allowing her bag to drop from shoulder to hand as she searched for something within, then disappearing around the corner.

Christina waited for Matthew to follow, but he didn't. When he turned, she was snapped from her trance and moved closer to the wall, turning her back to the street and pretending to write a text message. She felt a lump lodge in her throat. What she had just witnessed – the exchange that hadn't taken place – had stolen everything she'd thought she knew and tipped it inside out, making it unrecognisable. Matthew wasn't having an affair with Delta. Delta didn't even know him. He had come all that way just to watch her.

FORTY-THREE

BROOKE

On Thursday, when I do the food shopping, I stop in Fishguard to go to the post office. I feel bleary-eyed and weighed down with tiredness as I park the car in the town centre, wishing that I had been able to find some peace last night. I didn't stay at the house with Oliver, the evening drawing to a seemingly inevitable halt after I had settled Finley back to sleep. When I returned downstairs, the mood had shifted. I wondered whether Oliver had listened in on my conversation with Finley, sure I would have sensed him on the landing, and when I got back to the kitchen, he looked as though he hadn't moved from the table. He looked tired too, the sharp outfit no longer able to distract from the heaviness of his dark eyes.

I didn't mention to him what Fin had said. I wasn't thanked the last time I passed comment on his need for professional intervention, and I didn't want to spoil the evening. Oliver has already said he is looking into getting help for his son, and how he chooses to go about that is none of my business. He didn't say much when I told him I wasn't feeling too well – an excuse he was likely to have seen straight through – and when I left, he didn't try to kiss me, disappointment placing a distance between us. At home, I didn't sleep well, my thoughts preoccupied with all the things that still fail to make sense: the car engine that started after Oliver claimed it hadn't; the fall that Finley seems to have no recollection of.

Across the road from the post office, I stop outside the jeweller's. The window display is adorned with tiers of engagement and eternity rings, the large cardboard banner that hangs behind them boasting an early winter sale. I think of the necklace I wore last night. I felt ridiculous when I got back to the house, for reasons I was unsure of. Cheap – as though I had been humiliated in some way. I couldn't get changed out of the dress quickly enough, and the pendant felt cold against my skin, as though it had chilled through to my throat.

I put my hand into my coat pocket to touch its coolness now.

There is a woman inside the jeweller's, watching me through the window. She smiles when my eyes meet hers. I go inside and she greets me with a cheery hello, and I waste no time in producing the necklace, still uncertain of how I am going to get the answers I am looking for.

'I'm looking for the person who sent me this,' I tell her. 'I know it was bought in Fishguard, but I'm not sure which jeweller's.'

It doesn't take her long to inspect the necklace. 'We've never stocked anything like this,' she tells me. 'Beautiful, isn't it? Looks antique.'

'Thanks. So there's no chance it was bought here?'

She shakes her head. I thank her again and leave, making my way to the next jeweller's. The same happens there – they have never stocked such an item. As I head for the third and final shop, I run an internet search for the necklace. Too many results are thrown up, and when I scan the images, I find nothing that exactly resembles the item in my pocket. I don't know what I'm looking for, or what I'm hoping to find. If I found the item for sale elsewhere, it wouldn't answer anything for me. The question would remain: why would Oliver lie about where he bought it?

I am greeted by a young male shop assistant when I enter the third jeweller's. He looks barely out of school, and bored, his attention distracted by a magazine that rests on top of the counter. I repeat my story to him, pretending that I am looking for the person who might have sent me the necklace.

'Can you wait for my mam to get back? I'm just covering while she pops out.'

He could have told me that five minutes ago, I think, and saved me having to repeat myself. As I wait, I browse the engagement rings on display in the window. I wonder how Oliver proposed to Bethany, and whether it was planned, ring in hand, or something more spontaneous. She must have been so young when they got married. I've never asked about the age difference; there's never been an appropriate moment to drop the subject into conversation. His past is none of my business, yet I wonder when they first met, and how, and it raises so many questions that at some point will need to be answered, for my own peace of mind if for no other reason.

The bell ringing above the shop door wakes me from my thoughts. The woman smiles and greets me before asking her son whether everything is okay. I repeat my request to her before handing her the necklace.

'This is an unusual piece, isn't it?' she says, turning the necklace in her hand. The comment gives an immediate answer to my question. The necklace wasn't bought here. 'Sorry, love. Not one of ours.'

I thank her and leave, thoughts of Bethany plaguing me as I make my way back to the car. If the necklace didn't come from Fishguard as Oliver claimed, then where did it come from? And why would he lie about it? No matter how I try to swerve the possibility, one thought keeps making a return. Did I wear his dead wife's necklace to dinner last night? Did I sit across the table from him, smiling and laughing, oblivious to the fact that his gift to me had been passed on from another woman, the mother of the boy I then tucked into bed and comforted when he was scared?

It is like something from a tabloid column, an agony-aunt letter written by a bemused lover who needs no real confirmation of the inappropriateness of the gift yet still desires reassurance that her reaction isn't the issue here. I have overlooked things that haven't made sense and avoided questions that should be asked, my own secrets holding me silenced against the possibility of Oliver's. One thought pushes itself through the swamp of the others, rising to the surface in all its ugliness. If Oliver has lied about this, what else has he been lying about?

Christina had avoided Matthew since that evening in the West End, immersing herself in work and the children, and using the excuse of not feeling well to go to bed early on the nights he had been home. She couldn't stop thinking about Delta, and about what she had seen outside the theatre. What she hadn't seen. And then there was the conversation she had had with him, one that at the time hadn't seemed as significant as it did now, replayed and analysed until there was nothing left but a truth that she had refused to consider a possibility.

You've known me since we were kids.

He was wrong; she hadn't. When they had met again in that park, at twenty-five years old, Matthew Hale had been little more than a stranger. Yet when he talked about it, he made it sound as though they were already so much more. Perhaps they had spoken at school more often than she remembered. There was a great deal about that time that she didn't remember, including half the names of the teachers and the other kids in her year group. The details of her life preceding Bethany's death had been lost in the vacuum that had followed, everything that she had been until that point lost with her sister's passing.

She stood on the landing and looked up at the hatch that led to the attic. When they had viewed the house together, the attic space had been among the first things that had appealed to Matthew. Within minutes he had claimed it for himself, despite not having got as far as discussing making an offer. But Christina had already known by then just how important his model railway was to him. What was it he had said the first time she had gone to his flat and seen it there in the spare bedroom? That it was the only way he could feel close to his father. That just being there, among his father's things, was like being a boy again.

She remembered the first and only time she had gone up to the attic. She had taken Matthew a cup of tea and some cake, struggling on the steep staircase as she tried to balance the two without losing her footing. He had heard her and come to help, though the interruption hadn't been welcome. He didn't want food and drink around the model village, he'd said, in case anything got stained or damaged. They were better off going back downstairs.

It had been a while since she had seen the railway, though she had caught a glimpse of it then: the buildings and the people laid out precisely, hours of time and concentration spent creating this inert world. She had pictured Matthew as a child, sitting beside his father and watching in awe as his fingers deftly added intricate features to a tiny face. Now, standing on the landing and looking up at the closed hatch, her imaginings offered her something very different.

In the cupboard on the landing there was a pole to pull down the hatch. She flinched when it dropped down, reaching out to steady the ladder as it descended to the landing floor. She climbed the steps slowly, careful not to lose her footing. It was dark in the attic, and she fumbled for the light switch. Beneath the glow of a naked bulb, the model railway and the village through which it wound lay silent.

Tiny little houses. Tiny little people, frozen as they went about their tiny day-to-day lives. A woman carrying a brown paper bag of shopping. A man with a newspaper tucked under his arm. Two children playing hopscotch on a chalk-lined pavement. There were a thousand stories within those streets, and Matthew's hands moved the sequence of each, shaping every narrative.

Like God, she thought. Like playing God. The thought sent a chill through her.

She had never known anyone else with a hobby like this, and when he had first mentioned it to her she had pictured old-age pensioners wearing corduroy trousers and smoking pipes, consigned to the garden shed by wives who had almost forgotten what their husbands looked like and wished to reclaim use of the spare bedroom. She had told Matthew this and he had taken it light-heartedly, but then he had mentioned his father and the pastime had made sense. It was an anchor to the past, and Christina understood the need for this better than most.

Grief was the thing that had brought them together during that reunion in the park and in the café, where they had shared coffee along with the details of their pasts. Now it seemed that grief would also be the cause of their undoing. Christina was still grieving Bethany; it was a process without end. Loss changed a person, taking away pieces that could never be restored or replaced. When she had met Matthew, she had been altered – or if not already altered, in transition. He had entered her life when she was between selves.

She moved to take in the details of a tiny shop window adorned with old-fashioned sweet jars. Her thigh knocked against the table, but instead of the buildings and figures wobbling with the impact, she noticed that everything stayed unusually still. She reached out to pick up one of the houses, only to find that it was fixed in place. She tried another house, and then a figure – an elderly woman pulling a tartan shopping trolley – but none of them could be moved. What was the point of this, she wondered, if everything was immovable and nothing could be altered?

She sat in the only chair in the room, where Matthew spent so much of his time. What did he do there? she wondered. There was nothing to move, no trains kept on the railway line, so what did he spend all his time up here doing? As she sat there, looking around, she noticed the lip at the edge of the tabletop on which everything was set. She felt around underneath it, and found a small handle. When she gripped it, she realised that the top of the table could be raised. There was something beneath it, something inside.

It took both hands to lift it. Inside, there was an arm that could be extended to take its weight. Christina barely managed to push it into place, too preoccupied with what she had found. Inside the hidden panel were a number of books laid flat, each with a patterned cover. When she took one out, she realised they were photograph albums.

She felt a tide of sickness wash over her as she opened it. Delta Meredith looked back at her. It was a promotional image from what looked like a professional photo shoot, Delta resting against a plain white wall, her body arched, lips parted slightly. On the next page there were more photos from the same shoot: Delta straddling a chair provocatively, smiling at the person on the other side of the camera. There were photographs that had been cut from magazine articles and printed from websites; others that looked as though they had been taken from Delta's social media pages. She had been listed as one of 2017's 'Ones to Watch' by the *Guardian* newspaper, with a biography detailing her acting experience to date.

And there weren't just photographs. There were theatre tickets, more for the same show.

Just how many times had he been to watch her?

She flinched at a noise downstairs. The front door.

'Shit.' She closed the book and returned it, hastily fumbling to close the lid of the hidden compartment. Then she hurried to the steps and back down to the landing. Downstairs, Matthew was talking to someone on his phone. She went into the living room, fighting to catch her breath. What the hell was going on? What had she just found? Delta didn't seem to know her husband, and yet it seemed that Matthew had been following her closely.

'Everything okay?'

She started at the sound of his voice behind her. 'I thought you were at work.'

'Forgot something.' He narrowed his eyes. 'Are you all right, Chrissie?'

'Fine. Just a bit of a headache again, that's all.'

'Where are the kids?'

She glanced at the clock on the mantelpiece. She had lost track of time and was due to pick them up in less than ten minutes. 'Oh, shit.'

She went into the hallway and fumbled in her coat pocket for her keys. 'Are they still going over to your brother's tonight?' Matthew asked. 'Probably for the best. You need an early night and some rest.' He put a hand on her lower back, and Christina felt herself flinch. It was obvious that he must have felt it too.

'I'm going to take them straight over there now.'

'Chrissie.' Matthew reached for her hand and pulled her to him. 'I'm worried about you. You haven't been yourself for ages.'

'I'm fine,' she said, giving a forced smile. 'I'll message you later.'

She left the house and felt instantly better for the blast of fresh air that greeted her. Amid the discovery she had made and the chaos it had left her mind in, she had forgotten to pick up the bag of overnight things that had been waiting outside the children's bedroom door, where she had left it that morning. She would stop to buy some nappies after picking them up; the rest they would have to manage without.

She got in the car and started the engine. Matthew's words echoed in her mind, repeating on a loop. *You haven't been yourself for ages.*

No, she hadn't. She had put it down to having young children, the sleeplessness and the consequent lack of energy. Her old self would reappear once the twins were a little older and less dependent on her, as though it had simply been lying low for a while, hibernating in order to replenish itself. It wasn't the children, she thought; it had never been them. What if the real cause of her absence was Matthew?

With thoughts of him embedded at the front of her mind, she felt a lump of dread lodge in her throat. She realised that she had left the folding stairs of the attic on the landing.

FORTY-FIVE

BROOKE

Over the next few days, I manage to avoid Oliver. He texts me and I make an excuse about work, though the truth is, I have little to work on. Commissions have been scarce, though I have feigned busyness to avoid Sylvia too, our relationship still injured by the police search at the house. The investigation into Lewis's death has fallen silent, presumably no new evidence arising, though I can't allow myself to believe that it is over. I am not ready to face Oliver yet. I need to ask him about the necklace, about why he lied, but there is no way of raising the subject without appearing suspicious of him. Worse still is the thought of where the necklace might really have come from.

After two days of relentless rain, the weather finally eases, and I go for a walk along the coastal path. When I get back, Oliver is at my front door. I can't turn and head back the way I came, not now that he has already seen me.

'Where's Finley?' I ask when I reach him.

He gestures to his car, which is parked at the side of the road. 'Fell asleep on the way back from the shops. Bad night.'

'He okay?'

'More nightmares.' He shifts his weight from one foot to the other and glances back to the car. 'Look... Brooke. Have I done something?'

'No. Why?'

'I've not heard from you, and—'

'I've been busy,' I say, a little too quickly. I put my hand in my pocket. The necklace is still in there after my visit to Fishguard. 'I had a painting to finish.' He must know I am lying; I am a terrible liar. 'Actually, it's this,' I say. I hold the necklace up, my thumb moving across the tear-shaped pendant. 'Where did you say you got it again?'

'Jeweller's in Fishguard. You don't have to wear it, Brooke. It's not a commitment to anything.'

'I know. I don't have to do anything.'

His expression changes as my voice does, and he eyes me questioningly. I hold his gaze, wondering whether he will admit the truth or if I will be forced to nudge him there.

'What's the matter, Brooke?'

'I know you didn't get it in Fishguard. There are three jeweller's, and none of them sold it to you.'

He studies me for a moment. For the first time ever, I feel uncomfortable beneath his gaze. 'You've been checking up on me?'

'You lied.'

He glances again to the car. 'Can we go inside?'

'No. Where's the necklace from, Oliver?'

He looks at the floor, like a guilty child who has been caught stealing sweets. 'It belonged to my wife.'

I throw the necklace at him, as though it has burned me. His reactions are quick, and he catches it.

'Your dead wife.'

'Thanks for the reminder. There's only been the one, so yes.'

'I don't believe this,' I say with a quiet sigh.

He says nothing, but has the good grace to look as uncomfortable as I feel.

'Why did you lie?'

'I knew you wouldn't accept it, and...'

'And what?' I say when he falls silent. 'You thought you'd just give it to me anyway. And lie about it? You realise how weird that is, don't you?'

'I'm sorry. I realise now it was an inappropriate thing to do.'

'Inappropriate?'

'Yes. Stupid, okay? I know. And I'm sorry. I just... I wasn't thinking. It was there, and I wanted to give you something, I just wanted you to know that I was grateful for everything you'd done for Finley, and—'

'You know that the more you say, the worse this sounds, don't you?' My heart is hammering in my chest, adrenaline running through me as though I've just finished a sprint. 'What is this, Oliver? Do you want me, or do you just want a replacement mother for your son?'

An uncomfortable silence falls between us.

'I'm sorry you feel that way, Brooke. I never meant it to come across like that. Things have moved quicker than perhaps we've both realised, but it's never felt wrong, not to me anyway. I wish I hadn't given you the necklace. If I could undo it, I would.'

There is a knocking at the car window; Finley has woken up. Oliver goes and lifts him from his car seat. Fin looks hot, his hair tousled and matted against his forehead as though he is coming down with something. He manages to give me a smile.

Am I a replacement? Is Oliver simply looking for someone he can offload the weight of his solitary responsibilities onto? If so, he didn't need to buy me. I enjoy spending time with Finley. I've never had any intention of having children of my own, but the thought of being involved in his life has never once deterred me. The opposite, in fact.

And perhaps that is the truth of this, that despite knowing them both for just a matter of months, it has been a sufficient period for me to fall in love. But perhaps it is little Fin, and not his father, who has stolen my heart.

'Miss Meredith?'

I turn at the sound of my name, recognising the voice without needing to see the detective's face. He gestures to his car, parked at the opposite side of the square, where his colleague is waiting.

'I'd like you to come to the station with us.'

I look to Oliver, panicked. 'Why?'

'I'm sure you'd rather we had that conversation there.'

'I'm asking now,' I say, unable to hide the fear from my voice. 'What's going on?'

'Brooke Meredith, I'm arresting you on suspicion of murder. You do not have to say anything, but it may harm your defence if you do not mention when questioned...'

FORTY-SIX

CHRISTINA

Christina stopped at a petrol station after picking up the twins from nursery. She was returning to her car after paying when she heard a voice call her name. A tall, slim woman was filling an Audi at the opposite side of the pump.

'Christina? Christina Finley?'

She knew immediately who the woman was; she hadn't changed a bit since school. Sarah Dickinson, one of the pretty, popular girls, whose elite group, made up of other pretty, popular girls, had never broken ranks to bother with any of the mediocre crowd. She looked as beautiful as ever, her highlighted hair styled as though she had just left a salon, and her knee-length coat belted around a waist that was as tiny now as it had been when she was a teenager.

Christina was surprised that she remembered her name, considering they probably hadn't spoken to one another through the whole of sixth form.

'How are you doing? You look so well.'

Liar, Christina thought. Edward had woken her up at 3.15 that morning, wet with a cold sweat and whimpering about a nightmare involving a dragon. She had gone back to bed after eventually settling him, but she hadn't been able to drop back off and had applied two coats of foundation and extra eyeliner that morning in an attempt to disguise the appearance of sleep deprivation.

'Fine, thanks. But it's Hale now, actually. Christina Hale.'

'You got married! Great!'

'And how are things with you?'

Christina knew that Sarah wouldn't pass up an opportunity to talk about herself. She braced herself for at least twenty minutes of the other woman's history, reminding herself that she should nod every now and then to make it appear that she was listening. After a while, she switched off, lost in thoughts of Matthew and whether he was still at home. Whether he had been upstairs and seen the loft ladder.

'... so yeah, it's going really well, it's been a crazy couple of years, but then running your own business is so much better than being employed, isn't it? Sorry... what was it you said you did?'

She had zoned out to the extent of not knowing what Sarah had been talking about. She had said something about running a business, but it might have been anything from a casino to a hotel for cats for all the attention she had been paying.

'I'm a physiotherapist.' She opened her phone to glance at the time, as though she might be able to make an excuse about needing to be somewhere.

'Oh my gosh, are they your kids?'

Christina's phone cover had a montage of photographs of Edward and Elise; it had been a Christmas present from Matthew.

She nodded. 'These are my twins. They're in the back of the car.'

Sarah glanced in the direction of the car without bothering to look. 'Twins? God... well done you. Rather you than me. I don't think I could cope with one, let alone two. Anyway, did you say Hale?'

Christina nodded again and saw the realisation creep in. Sarah had obviously paid greater attention to her classmates than she had given her credit for.

'Not that boy from school?' she said, returning the petrol hose.

'God... what was his name now? Matthew? Not Matthew Hale from school?'

'Who would have thought it, right?'

Sarah threw her head back with an exaggerated laugh. 'Well, it was obvious, wasn't it? Actually, I think Fiona Benton owes me a tenner.'

Christina smiled awkwardly. 'What do you mean?'

'There were bets riding on you two back in sixth form,' Sarah said. 'I mean, he was never going to give up, was he? "Find someone who looks at you the way Matthew Hale looks at Christina Finley", that was our dating mantra. And now look at you guys. It's like Romeo and Juliet.'

Christina felt the forced smile fade. 'Except they both died,' she said flatly. 'Anyway, I'm glad we were the subject of so much discussion.'

Sarah's face flushed slightly, something Christina wouldn't have previously thought it capable of. 'Sorry, it was only a bit of a joke, you know what kids are like. Anyway,' she said, nodding at the car that had just pulled in behind hers and was now waiting for her to leave. 'Better dash. It was lovely to see you.'

Christina watched her as she made her way to pay, her long coat flapping behind her as she strutted across the forecourt.

As she pulled out of the petrol station and joined the main road, she noticed a florist across the street, an array of colourful blooms set up in buckets in front of the shop. She pulled over at the next available opportunity and retrieved her phone from her bag, using it to find the phone number of the florist that had delivered the bouquet from Joel.

A woman answered on the second ring.

'Hi,' Christina said. 'Um, I was sent some flowers from you, about a month ago now, and I was hoping you might be able to tell me who ordered them.'

'I'm afraid I can't give out any personal details about customers.'

'No, I appreciate that.'

In the back seat, Elise started screaming. Christina turned; Edward had taken her bag from her, and Elise had wriggled so far beneath the harness of her car seat that she was half hanging out of it, writhing in protest.

'I need you to be a good girl for Mummy,' she said, her hand over the phone. 'Please, Elise.' She returned to the call. 'Sorry, I know you can't. I mean, I just...' She stumbled over her words, not really sure what she was hoping to gain from the call. She knew who had sent the flowers. Or did she? Might it be possible that she had got things wrong? 'There was a second bouquet sent to me,' she said, remembering the shredded petals she had pulled from the box after speaking to Ollie that day. 'I know you can't give me a name, but would you just be able to tell me if the same person sent them?'

She was sure she heard the woman sigh. 'Can you give me your address?'

'Mummy!'

Christina turned sharply to her daughter. 'Stop it.' She wrangled the bag from Edward and thrust it at Elise before reciting the address to the florist.

'We sent a delivery to you on the twentieth of February.'

'Yes. And then there was another, a couple of weeks later.'

The woman made a clicking noise with her tongue as she searched her records. 'No. We only sent one order to the address you've given me.'

Christina thanked her, the words barely audible as they left her lips, before hanging up. Elise's screaming filled the car, despite the bag having been returned, and now Edward was crying too. Putting her hands over her ears, Christina pushed back against the headrest, swallowing a scream of her own.

They were the same flowers, she was sure of that. There was no chance that two different people might have purchased the same bouquet – one an online order for delivery, the other bought in person – and coincidentally chosen the exact same arrangement. Either Joel had gone to the shop in person, bought the same bouquet again and then destroyed it before having someone else deliver it to her home, or there was another possibility, one she had never considered until now.

He hadn't sent either of them.

DS Jones escorts me to the front of the station, where the desk sergeant returns the items that were taken from me yesterday. I have been kept here for as long as he was legally able to detain me, once again hoping to break my resolve and force me into a confession. The duty solicitor who attended the interview advised that I say as little as possible, so that was what I did. That jacket. They have no physical evidence, no eyewitnesses: nothing but hearsay, and fibres from a coat they will never be able to locate. But DS Jones knows, and he doesn't want to let it go. He doesn't want to let *me* go.

As I had known it would be, the night of the assault all those years ago was brought back up. I told him what I had told the police then, exactly as it happened; I was sixteen years old again, the girl that no one believed. A liar. It was used as a motive for murder, as the reason why I may have wanted Lewis dead, but when I began to argue that if I had wanted to seek revenge, I would have done it long before now, the duty solicitor's hand on my knee prompted me to silence. She reminded the detective that they had no physical evidence; that there was nothing to suggest I had even been up on the coastal path that day. Knowing the solicitor was right, DS Jones reluctantly let me leave.

I am turning on my phone to check for messages when I see him. He is a slight young thing of maybe fourteen – no older than sixteen – and he is wearing jogging bottoms that look too short and a hooded jacket that looks too big. He has a narrow face, a prominent jawline that gives him the look of someone who is always angry, as he is now, engrossed in some exchange with a uniformed officer. When I turn back to the front desk, DS Jones is still there, watching me. He looks to the teenager, then back at me, and I realise he is watching my reaction to the boy. But why? Should I know who he is, or why he is here?

I get a bus back to the village. The break in the bad weather was a temporary one, and a couple of miles from home, the rain begins again. I check my phone: two messages from Oliver and five missed calls, two from him and three from Sylvia. He must have gone to the house to tell her what had happened, to let her know where I was.

Call me when you can. I know a couple of solicitors – I can get you help. You're not on your own x

The next message reads:

And I'm sorry. More than you know. I should never have given you that necklace – it was a stupid thing to do. I don't know why I did it. Let me know when you're home. Please can we talk properly?

I don't want to talk about it. My sleep-deprived and anxious night in the police cell yielded little thought for Oliver and the necklace, not when my thoughts were consumed with clearing my name and proving my innocence. I should have told the truth from the start; I should have gone straight to the police and told them that I was there on the cliff, explained to them what had happened. The longer the secret has been kept, the more damning it has become. No one will ever believe me now.

But there were moments when I allowed thoughts of Oliver to seep into my consciousness, desperate for an escape from Lewis and the haunting last image of him that I am unable to escape. Through every scenario and every plausible outcome, nothing good ever came of a widower offering his dead wife's necklace as a gift to another woman. He lied to me, and I know from experience that if he can lie once, he can do it again.

With no idea what I will say to Sylvia when I get back to the house, like a coward I avoid it. I head for the coastal path, for a spot I have not returned to in years. I walk through a section of broken wire fence along a grassy ridge to the edge of the clifftop. The wind screams past the hood of my rain jacket, and I stumble forward, too close to the brink. Fifty feet below me, the sea crashes against the rocks, spurting spray upwards as the tide draws back and rushes forward again, repeating its angry ebb and surge. One false step and I would fall to my death. Lewis's face is behind my eyes once more. I think of Delta at the top of that wet and crowded staircase, oblivious to the fate that awaited her. I think of Bethany, making a choice between life and death, her mind so altered by whatever demons plagued her that she saw no other option than to swallow those pills. I put a hand to the scar on my temple, remembering how frighteningly easy that single step had been. The wind pushes me, and I fall backwards, my heart pounding.

After a while, I get up from the ground and head back to the village, pressing against the noisy wind. By the time I reach Sylvia's, I am soaked to the skin. Sylvia isn't home. I shower and change, desperate to be free of the clothes I have worn since yesterday. Once my hair is dry, I go back outside and head across to the gallery. There are builders finishing up for the day, packing tools into a van, and I hang back and wait for them to leave before letting myself into the building.

It is eerily quiet inside the gallery. The space has been cleared and work has begun; perhaps it won't take as long as I had feared. Yet there is nothing here that feels like home any more.

I am jolted from my apathy by knocking. When I go to the

front door, there is a young woman standing on the pavement, her hands thrust into her pockets and her head lowered as she fights to keep the wind from her face.

'I'm sorry to disturb you,' she says, spluttering rain with her words. 'I was hoping to order a painting from you.' She is soaked through, her jacket shiny with rain and her cheeks red from the bite of the wind.

'You're welcome to come in, but...' I gesture behind me, move aside to allow her to see the state of the place.

'Oh gosh. What happened?' She scans the room. 'I'm so sorry. I've seen this place online.'

'There was a fire. How did you come by it?' I ask, wanting to move on from the subject as quickly as possible. 'The website, I mean. I always wonder how people get to see it. I can't imagine it's that easy to just stumble across.'

'I prefer to support local businesses. I was looking for landscape painters and your website came up. The paintings on there...'

'Gone.'

'I'm so sorry.' Her sympathy sounds sincere, not merely the passing comment of someone who believes the words are expected. 'It's Brooke, isn't it?' she asks. 'I noticed your name on the website,' she adds. 'How long have you lived here?'

'Here in this place or here in the village?'

'In the village.'

'Always. I grew up here.'

'It's remote, isn't it? I can't imagine you get many visitors.'

'More in the summer. Rare at this time of year. What sort of painting did you want to order?' She almost seems to have forgotten the purpose of her visit. If she wants to pay for a painting, I am more than happy to accept the commission; I need the money, and it will give me something to focus on while I wait for whatever move DS Jones and his department have planned next.

'I'm not sure,' she says, her expression apologetic. 'I was hoping to see some of your work.'

'I wish I had something to show you. Do you want to have a

look at the website again and get back to me? My mobile number is on there – you can give me a call and we can talk through an idea after you've looked at some examples.'

'Sounds great. Thanks. I hope you can get this place sorted out soon.'

'Thanks. Me too.'

The rain has eased, and I watch her leave. Shortly after I return inside, there is another knock at the door. I open it without checking who it is, assuming the woman has forgotten to ask something and returned, but it is Oliver, and I immediately wish I hadn't gone back to the door.

'Who was that?' he asks.

'Just someone wanting to buy a painting.'

He glances up the road. 'Can I come in?'

'I don't think that's a good idea.'

'What happened at the station? Are you okay?'

'Nothing much. And other than being a suspect in a murder inquiry, I suppose I'm fine.'

'I can still get you that help,' he offers. 'You don't have to go through this alone, Brooke. It's madness. They'll realise the mistake they're making, trust me.'

'Trust you?'

He sighs. 'I deserve that. Look, Fin and I are going to put the Christmas tree up later.'

'We've not spoken about the tenancy,' I remind him, ignoring what I suspect is an invitation to join them. 'I've still got that booking in January.'

The thought of Christmas is too much, though it is now looming just around the corner. I can't play happy families with him, not now; not ever.

He nods but says nothing, which offers me no answers.

'What shall I tell the people who've booked?' I ask.

'What do you want to tell them?'

'This isn't going to work, is it? Not now.'

'Us at the house, you mean? Or you and me?'

'Both.'

His mouth twists. 'I'm sorry. I wish things were different.'

Me too, I think. I wish that he was the person I had thought he was. I wish he hadn't done such a stupid and irreversible thing.

'Can you give us until the new year?'

'I'm not going to turn you out on the street with nowhere to go, Oliver.'

'I know that. Thank you. We'll be out of your way by the end of the first week of January.'

When he turns to leave, a part of me wants to call him back, but I don't. I wait before locking up the gallery, then go to my car, my only company my phone. I try to access the internet, with no luck. I am tempted to throw the phone in frustration; instead, I drive to the familiar spot where signal returns reliably. I don't want to be alone any more today. I want to be with my sister. I want to see her face. I would gladly hear her voice, even if it meant another call from someone intent on hurting me.

Running an internet search on her name is something I have avoided. The latest articles relating to her all concern her death, and I have already read them far too often. I don't want to be reminded of how she died; I want to be reminded of how she lived, and so I am drawn back to her Instagram account, a profile I have stalked on numerous occasions in the past year. Most of her posts were filtered, making every moment more perfect than it must already have been. In every photograph she looks beautiful and happy, unblemished by hardship or life. The restaurants where she ate, the people whose company she kept, the countries she visited – everything is pulled straight from the glossy pages of a lifestyle magazine, as though she was a social media influencer rather than an actress.

And then I am reminded. This is all appearances. Filtered, carefully selected moments in time. And Delta was an actress. A good one, as I witnessed not long before she died.

As I scroll through her posts, travelling back in time through the years since she left Aberfach, the absence of us, her family, becomes more and more obvious. Was she ashamed of us? Did she want to be free of the associations we held, the ones she no doubt blamed me for? Everyone has skeletons in their closet, but most of us keep the door shut to prevent them from escaping. Perhaps that was how Delta viewed leaving this place, with one door shutting behind her and another opening, leading to a world that was far more exciting and glamorous.

I stop at a video. I haven't seen it in so long, probably not in the four years since she sent it. I check the date, making sure it is the same one. My birthday. Delta is at a swim-up bar, the phone positioned to make the most of the background, the quiet hotel grounds that suggest she has somehow managed to secure the whole place for her own personal use. Her bare skin is glistening with water, her hair piled high on her head to keep it from getting wet. I press play.

Hi, Brooke, she says. *Happy birthday, big sister! Sorry I can't be there to celebrate with you. Whatever you're up to, I hope you're having fun. As you can see, I'm working hard as always! I'll be back in the UK in a couple of weeks, so let's catch up then. Anyway, for now* – she raises a drink, a lurid-coloured cocktail with a striped straw and an array of fruit slices resting on the edge of the glass – *cheers to you! Love you, big sis. Byyyyeeee.*

I'm not on Instagram; she had sent it to my email address. If I hadn't had such a bad night with Mum the night before, I might have had the energy to be annoyed, but I was too tired to think of anything other than getting through the day without any accidents or upset. The video wasn't for me, it was for Delta; for her followers to see what an exciting and glamorous life she was living. Even her accent had changed, as though a few years in London had been sufficient to obliterate her Welsh lilt.

I watch it again, torturing myself with it. I both loved and loathed Delta: loving her for the daring girl she had been when we were growing up; resenting her selfishness and the way she had allowed herself to change. Hating her for lying, and for never admitting to the lie.

Hi, Brooke. Happy birthday, big sister!

I pause the recording, a single syllable standing out against the others. I drag my finger along the bar at the bottom of the clip, returning it to the start to play again. *Hi, Brooke.* And then I hear nothing but that word, my name repeated over and over as though she is here in the car beside me, nagging me about something.

Brooke.

Brooke.

Brooke.

After taking the twins to Leighton and Alice's flat, Christina drove straight home. Matthew would be out until the morning, which gave her plenty of time to do what she needed to. She had to go back into the attic and return to that secret compartment. She had only had time to look at the first of the collection of albums, and she needed to know what was inside the rest. Would Matthew have gone upstairs and removed everything? Sarah Dickinson's words rang like a klaxon in her brain. She knew that whatever lay within the covers of those books would unsettle her, but she couldn't leave until she had the truth, and Matthew was unlikely to offer it to her himself.

It would have been better if he had been having an affair with Delta, she thought. With proof of his infidelity, she could have left the marriage, taking the children with her. It was a sign with implications she couldn't ignore. She had been looking for a way out. She couldn't have loved Matthew, not really, not if she had been searching for reasons to leave. How long had she been looking for the exit route, never realising that this was what she wanted?

When she got back to the house, she looked for his car. It was gone. She hadn't made it as far as the attic when her mobile started to ring in her pocket. The noise startled her, and for a moment she was consumed by a feeling of paranoia, as though Matthew was somehow watching her and knew what she was planning.

She looked at the screen. Leighton. Her heart stuttered as she answered the call; he rarely phoned while the children were with him. Something must have happened.

'I'm sorry, Chrissie, it's Elise. She's been sick. She's okay now, but neither of us can do anything with her. She's inconsolable, she's just asking for you.'

'I'm coming straight over. I won't be long.'

She went to the hallway and retrieved her keys from the table, feeling guilty at having left the children. By the time she got to Leighton's, he had called her again to see whether she was on her way.

'I'm so sorry,' he said when he greeted her at the door. 'She hasn't been sick again, but it's really unsettled her. She just hasn't stopped crying.'

Her brother looked anxious in a way she hadn't seen him for a long time. He usually handled the twins with no problem, but the severity of Elise's emotional outpouring had obviously proven too much for him this time.

'Mama.' Elise wriggled from Alice's arms and ran to her mother, her face red and blotched with tears. She clung to her leg, and when Christina put a hand to her daughter's forehead, it was hot and sticky. She scooped her up, and the little girl snuggled into her shoulder, exhausted from crying.

'Edward's fast asleep,' Alice told her. 'I don't know how he's managed to sleep through the crying – he must have been exhausted.'

'Why don't you leave him here?' Leighton suggested. 'Wake him now and you'll have them both screaming on the way home.'

Christina was unsure. The twins liked to be together; they had never spent a night apart.

'He'll be fine,' Leighton said, reading her mind. 'I'll bring him straight home after breakfast. You can concentrate on looking after Elise.'

'I can bring him over on my way to work,' Alice offered.

Christina gave a small smile as she held her daughter to her. 'Thank you both so much. I mean it, you're such a help to me. The kids love coming to you.'

And we might be back sooner than you realise, she thought. By the time Matthew returned from his night shift tomorrow morning, she and Elise would be gone. She had seen enough, and yet she needed to know more. Sarah Dickinson's words echoed once again. There were so many questions, and nothing would be answered until she saw the truth for herself.

Leighton's eyes narrowed. 'Is everything okay?'

'I'm just tired,' she said, tightening her hold on Elise. 'I'll have an early night with her, I think.'

'Good idea. And please,' he said, putting a hand on her arm, 'don't worry about Edward. He'll be fine.'

Elise fell silent in the car, the whimpering that had continued after leaving her uncle's flat quickly evaporating once she knew she was on her way home. Christina kept checking on her in the rear-view mirror, knowing that before they got back to the house, she was likely to have fallen asleep, exhausted by her emotions. As predicted, two streets from home, Christina turned to find her daughter snuffling softly as she slept, so she changed direction and lengthened their journey, giving Elise a chance to fall into a deeper sleep before she carried her into the house.

As soon as the little girl was tucked in, sleeping soundly, Christina headed up to the attic. The ladder was still down, so either Matthew hadn't seen it before he went out again, or he had just left it where it was. Neither seemed to matter now; all that mattered was finding the truth.

FORTY-NINE

BROOKE

The following day, I go into Fishguard for some art supplies. When I'm done, I stop at a café on the high street, delaying having to go back to the village. I have yet to hear back from the woman who came to the gallery yesterday, so have nothing to make a start on to keep myself distracted, and the weather is still too terrible to do anything but stay inside. I am still trying to avoid Sylvia as much as possible, guilt making any attempt at regular day-to-day conversation impossible.

The high street is decorated with Christmas lights, the same garish bells and angels that have been dug out from the council's storage every year since as long as I can remember strung up on lamp posts and telephone poles. The whole thing manages to be even more depressing than it was last year.

In the café, I take out my phone and reply to a couple of emails. When I'm finished and look up from the screen, I sense a woman watching me from the far side of the café. As soon as we make eye contact, she gets up from her table and comes over to mine, and then I realise it is the woman who came to the gallery yesterday. I put my phone back in my pocket.

'Hi again,' she says, though the way she looks at me tells me that her being here is no coincidence. She drops into the chair opposite, uninvited. 'Is it okay if I join you?'

'You already have.'

'Look,' she says, pushing her hair behind her ear and leaning forward conspiratorially. 'When I came to the gallery yesterday...' She glances around as though worried someone might be listening. 'I need to speak to you.'

'Have you been following me?'

'Yes, but it's not what it seems.'

I'm not at all sure what it does seem. I had never laid eyes on this woman before yesterday, and now she is following me around town, stalking me in cafés.

'I need to talk to you,' she says again.

'About what?'

'Your boyfriend.'

My eyes narrow. 'I don't have a boyfriend.'

She bites her lip and glances around again, although no one is paying us any attention. 'My name is Alice,' she says quietly. 'I'm a police officer.' She reaches into her bag and pulls out ID, placing it on the table between us. DC Alice Fielding. Metropolitan Police. 'There are things you need to know,' she says when I look at her questioningly.

There is an urgency in her voice that I cannot ignore. When she takes her mobile phone from her bag and scrolls through it, looking for something, I find myself transfixed by her, with no idea what to expect. She is obviously referring to Oliver, though I have never referred to him as my boyfriend. I have no idea how she knows him, or what she might know about me.

She puts the phone in front of me. There is a photograph of Oliver and Fin, though Finley is much younger, perhaps not much more than a year old. 'Who is this, Brooke?'

She speaks my name as though she knows me. Perhaps, in a way, she does. She has searched me out, come to my home, followed me here, and all for what?

'Oliver and Finley,' I say, holding her gaze. There is a twitch at her temple, a flicker at the corner of her mouth that betrays a reaction to the names. 'What is this all about?'

'That's what he told you?'

'Just get to the point, please. What do you want?' Beneath my coat, my heart is racing, hammering in my chest. I take a deep breath, try to calm myself, achieving little effect. He lied to me once. He can do it again.

'I knew it,' she said, with a shake of her head, talking more to herself than to me. 'I knew what he was up to, but no one believed me.'

'Believed you about what?' I ask, not sure I want to hear the answer.

She reaches into her bag again and pulls out a handful of papers. Between them she finds a photograph, which she places in front of me. Bethany. I recognise her instantly, from the photograph that appeared on the GoFundMe page. Beside her sits a young man, broad and strong, his left arm decorated with an array of tattoos. On his lap lies a baby wrapped in a tiny white blanket, no more than a few months old.

'Bethany,' I say quietly. I look at Alice, who nods. Her eyes widen as though questioning mine, waiting for me to ask the obvious, because if this is Bethany, then who is the man beside her?

'Bethany and her husband, Oliver,' Alice says. 'And their son, Finley.'

My throat tightens. A member of staff moves to the side of us, clearing used cups and plates from the next table. She forces me to fall into silence, though in my head I am screaming. When she is gone, I find myself still unable to speak.

'Then who the hell is living in my house?' I finally manage.

Alice studies me apologetically, as though already regretting what she is about to do. 'His name is Matthew. His son's name is Edward.'

I laugh awkwardly, a nervous reaction. None of it makes sense. I don't know him, so why would he lie to me about who he is?

Alice shuffles through the papers and finds two that are stapled together. 'Here,' she says, smoothing them flat with the palm of her hand. 'I'm sorry to do this, really I am. I don't have the answers to everything, but you need to know that he's lying to you.'

I don't want to look at whatever this might be, and yet I reach across the table for the papers, a compulsion for the truth overriding my reluctance. With hands I cannot stop from shaking, I take my first glance at the lies I have been allowed to consume.

A birth certificate. Edward Finley Hale. Born in Barnet General Hospital on 13 April 2016 at 19.39, weighing 4 lb 2 oz.

I look up at Alice, who is watching me with sadness in her eyes, taking no pleasure in the task she has come here to undertake. There is still an apology in her expression, underpinned by determination.

'What is this?' I say defensively. 'It's not even an original document, it's just a photocopy. This could be anybody's.' Yet I move to the next page with a heavy heart and an inexplicable shame I can feel creeping to my cheeks like nettle rash. I have been foolish, naïve, yet I still don't know to what extent.

Elise Bethany Hale. Born in Barnet General Hospital on 13 April 2016 at 19.51, weighing 4 lb 13 oz. Twins.

'What is this supposed to prove?' I ask, denial trying to force its way past common sense.

'He lied to you about who he is. Oliver is my brother-in-law. So is Matthew. I think he's used Oliver's name to hide himself from you.'

'Why would he do that?'

Alice raises an eyebrow. 'Have you run an internet search on him yet?'

I feel my face grow hot, and it gives away the answer. It is a strange world we live in where we stalk our new acquaintances on the internet, and yet with Oliver I fell straight into that trap, wanting to find out the things he had not yet revealed to me.

'Exactly,' she says, reading my expression. 'He wouldn't have wanted you to search for Matthew Hale. You might have found out too much. Oliver keeps a low profile – he always has done.

Matthew must have felt confident enough that you wouldn't find out too much, not too soon, at least. He was prepared to take the chance, anyway.'

I run three steps ahead of the conversation, taking myself through questions I have not yet had a chance to voice. The more I think, the more improbable things become. We met by chance, Oliver and I, an encounter on the beach that led to him living in my house, which led to me entering their lives, which led to me sleeping in his bed. Chance. A chance encounter, that was all.

And yet at the time, all those months ago, hadn't I remembered seeing him on that beach before?

The room seems to spin, my vision blurring as though I am about to faint. The fire. The burglary at Jean Miller's. So many things happened following Oliver's arrival at the village to send my life descending into chaos.

'Are you okay?' Alice asks, though her words sound as though they are coming from underwater. 'Brooke?'

What if none of the last few months occurred by chance?

I stand quickly, the chair legs scraping on the tiled floor. A couple on the other side of the café are staring at me, but as I hurry from the building, I pay them no attention. I gasp as I fall through the door, gulping down a lungful of cold air. Traffic roars past, the noise of the road too loud and too close, and I lean against the wall to steady myself.

'Brooke.' Alice is behind me, a hand placed upon my back. 'Please. I don't want to do this, but you need to see the rest.'

I stand straight and gather myself, aware of people passing on the pavement. I must look a mess. 'Not here,' I say, and she follows as I make my way along the high street, turning left towards the cenotaph, where there are a couple of benches. I stop at the first and sit down, unable to look at her. She is carrying the papers she laid out on the table in the café; now she sifts through them, looking for something specific.

'Here. I'm sorry.'

I am looking at a family of four: a mother, father, son and

daughter. Finley is older in this picture, maybe two, and the girl is the same age. Of course she is. A twin.

'This is my sister-in-law, Christina,' Alice tells me. 'I'm married to her brother, Leighton. Bethany was their sister. She killed herself... you probably already know that.'

I can't talk. My words are strangled in my throat as I look at the photograph, a happy family smiling back as me. Am I the other woman? Is Oliver – Matthew – living some kind of double life that I have been blinded to? It's impossible, I tell myself. For nearly three months now he has been in the village, never spending a night elsewhere.

Alice hasn't taken her eyes from me, watching my face for every reaction.

'I don't understand,' I tell her. 'If this is Matthew and his family, where is Christina? If Finley is Edward, where is Elise?'

For the first time, Alice's composure slips. Her eyes glisten with tears she manages to hold back, but as she speaks, I find myself less strong, unable to stem the sadness that is wrenched from me by her words. The story unfolds in a blur, weighting me to the bench. When she finishes, Alice wipes her thumb beneath her eye.

'Look for yourself,' she says, gesturing to my phone.

I don't need to – I believe every word she has spoken, for why would she lie? – yet I type their names into the internet search engine, instantly finding repetitions of the story Alice has just shared with me.

'Now you see why he didn't want to give you his real name.'

As I sit on the bench near the cenotaph, my phone held limply in my right hand, the truth stares at me from its screen, in print and inescapable. Alice's words float around us, haunting. My eyes have blurred with tears, though there is still so much I have yet to understand. I am crying for someone else's story, for another family's tragedy.

'He preys on the vulnerable,' Alice says, her words muffled as though I am hearing them through a thick cloud of resistance. 'He did it with Christina – Bethany had only just died when Matthew reappeared in her life. He searches for grief and then he feeds off it.'

All the conversations Oliver and I have shared – all those late-night exchanges that lasted long into the dark hours of early morning – roll back into my consciousness, the admissions and the truths gathering weight with their return. I had thought we understood each other, that our grief offered us a common experience from which we were building a friendship, and something that might become so much more.

'Look at Christina,' she says, jabbing a finger at the photograph. 'Look at her, Brooke. Please. Why won't you look at her? You've already seen it, haven't you?'

The photograph is back with Alice now; I can no longer bear to look at it. I know what she is referring to, though I don't want to acknowledge it, not when the implications are so vast and so complicated. We are a similar age. We have the same colour hair, the same colour eyes; we are similar in size and shape.

'Look at her,' she insists again.

And I do. I look at Christina and a horrifying truth settles upon me, crushing me beneath its suffocating weight. She looks just like me. I look just like her.

'It's more than a passing resemblance, isn't it?' Alice says, holding eye contact. 'And if she looked so much like you, you must realise who else she looks like.'

She pushes another photo in front of me. I don't want to look. I don't want to have to see her.

'No,' I say, shaking my head. 'This is nothing to do with her.'

'I don't want to do this,' Alice says, moving closer to me, her voice thick with desperation, 'but no one else will listen to me, not even my colleagues. I've broken every rule to get to this – I'm currently under suspension and I'm probably going to lose my job. But you're not safe, Brooke, I just know it. He's not who everyone thinks he is... he wasn't who Christina thought he was. I'm not going to stop until I get to the truth.'

'I don't want to hear any more.'

I stand hurriedly. The papers and photographs fall to the floor, scattered at our feet. Delta's face looks up at me from the ground, an image I have never seen before: a one-hand-on-hip full-smile pose as she leans into an unseen person who escapes the focus of the camera. 'You don't know anything about my sister. I don't know what you're trying to do, but whatever you think you know, you don't. Just leave me alone.'

When I turn to leave, Alice grabs me by the arm. 'I saw something in his room when he was staying with us – something I wish I'd taken when I had the chance. By the time I went back for it, he and Edward were gone, all their things gone with them. It was a book filled with photographs. Photographs of Delta. I had no idea who she was at the time, but when I saw reports about her death, I realised I remembered her. I need your help. I think he killed her, Brooke. I think he killed Delta.'

FIFTY

CHRISTINA

The photograph album she chose when she returned to the attic was an older one, one that looked like something she might have bought years ago and then forgotten about. It was a pale pastel blue with a small turquoise bird embroidered on the front. She was forever promising herself that she would print out old holiday photographs – swiping a screen for memories would never replace the feeling of viewing them in a physical form – but time was always against her, and she had never got around to it. Her chest ached with the expectation of what she would find within the book's pages, but when she turned the front cover, the face that greeted her was not the one she had expected.

A face smiled back at her. Not Delta's, but her own. A seventeen-year-old Christina looked out from the page, a montage of photographs cut, stuck and labelled. *17 March 2002* was the caption next to one – a photograph of her in her sixth-form uniform, standing near the school gates as she waited to cross the main road. *Year 13 leaving do* read another, and there she was, Christina as she had been fifteen years earlier, sitting at a table and laughing with a couple of school friends.

Find someone who looks at you the way Matthew Hale looks at Christina Finley.

She turned the page, and her stomach sank further. Matthew had been legitimately present for the events she had been reminded of so far, there with good reason, the leaving party and the school grounds as much a part of his past as hers. But he hadn't been with her at the fireworks display where she had next been snapped, nor at the shopping centre where she had been photographed with an arm linked with her best friend. There she was in the images, young and oblivious, and there he had been too, somewhere right behind her where he had managed to go unseen.

She turned another page, chilled and compelled by the collection of images. There were old social media profile pictures – some as far back as the ones taken from her Myspace page – then a gallery of others, all uploaded long before she had been reunited with Matthew that day in the park. They had never been friends on any social media, not before that afternoon. She had never followed him, but he had been following her.

She sat back in the chair and tried to rationalise how this album had come into being. It was just a photo album. A photo album of a woman made by her husband. It was a memory book. Perhaps it was a gift. She desperately tried to tell herself that it was anything but an indicator that their entire life together had been built upon a lie, but no matter how hard she tried to convince herself that it could be explained away with a reasonable excuse, the truth remained louder and more vivid. He had been stalking Delta Meredith.

He had been stalking her.

These were her memories. Not theirs. Not his. For many of them, he shouldn't even have been there. And he had been there without her knowing. Following. Watching.

He was never going to give up, was he?

Sarah's words sounded in her head like a scream. She didn't want to think it, it was impossible. And yet it was here in front of her, the truth of it unavoidable. Other people had noticed it, years earlier, yet she herself had remained blind.

She snatched up the next book, flipping frantically from page to page as her life of the past fifteen years was replayed in front of her in a series of images. He had collected bus tickets, greetings cards, receipts – things she must have discarded without thought and that he had been there to retrieve. When she got to the final book, she heard her own breath escape her in a sharp gasp. There were no pages inside, just a hollow that housed a small collection of memorabilia: pens, a key ring, a trainer bra, small and pastel pink, rolled up into a ball. She was sixteen years old again, searching the changing rooms after a swimming gala. She had already been flushed after an embarrassing defeat in the butterfly stroke, a race that no one else in her team had wanted to enter and she had been bribed into taking part in. *Very funny*, she had said to the friends who were already dressed and ready to catch the bus home. *Now tell me where you've put it.*

She never had found that bra. She had gone home on the bus feeling embarrassed and self-conscious, worried that the cold might harden her nipples and they would be seen through her top. The girls had continued to deny any involvement, and she had never really trusted any of them in the same way after that day, convinced that they had made a mutual pact to humiliate her.

Along with the bra, there was something else. A packet of pills. She turned the box in her hand, not recognising the name. Then she noticed another word. *Laxative.*

Her heart pounded in her chest. Her ears had filled with white noise, an electrical buzzing that threatened to deafen her. The headaches, the nausea, the sickness. The weight loss. Kind, attentive, patient Matthew. A good man. She had thought he was one thing, but it appeared now that he was something very different. Everything was a lie. She had to get out of that house. She had to get herself and Elise away from there.

She stood and grabbed a couple of the albums to take with her. If Matthew realised that she had been up in that room and found what he had been hiding all these years, he might attempt to destroy the evidence that told the truth of what he was. She needed to protect herself and her children. And now, it occurred to her, Delta too. She had thought the woman an enemy, but they shared more in common than either could ever have imagined.

She hurried to the hatch, her descent down the folding ladder interrupted by a sound from the ground floor. She paused midway, the rushing waves of noise washing between her ears and drowning her other senses. Taking a deep breath, she attuned herself to the sounds of the familiar: a click of the front door; a jangle of keys. Matthew had come home.

FIFTY-ONE

BROOKE

Delta. Delta. Her name circulates in my brain, Alice's accusation echoing like the memory of a recurring nightmare. Late at night, when I have found myself unable to sleep, I have played the possible events that led to her death through my brain, repeating them over and over – each time with a tweak in the detail – to try to make some sense of what happened to her that evening. She left the theatre after the performance. She went to the Tube station; the same station she went to after every show to make her way home to her one-bed flat. I had imagined her life far more glamorous than this, as though a chauffeur-driven car would have waited for her at the entrance to the theatre, the driver on hand with an umbrella should there happen to be rain. In my mind, my sister had led a life of after-show parties and promotional events, when the reality, it was later revealed, was something quite different.

It had been busy that evening, the West End awash with crowds that had poured from bars and pubs, all rushing for the last Tube home. The rain had started at ten fifteen, about forty minutes before Delta had made her way from the theatre. The entrance to the station had been glassy with water, witnesses said. Everyone was in a rush that evening, desperate for shelter from the downpour.

People had rushed to help her. One of the women in the crowd was a retired nurse, heading home with her husband after an evening out. She had felt for a pulse but there wasn't one; Delta had died instantly. The post-mortem report later stated that she had broken her neck in the fall. The heeled shoes she had been wearing were a bad combination with the wet concrete. A freak accident.

But what if it hadn't been?

My hands tighten around the steering wheel as I try to fight back tears. The scene that I have replayed so often changes in my imagination, Oliver's face appearing in the crowd. He watches Delta, darting effortlessly and unnoticed between people as he follows her to the head of the staircase. A single shove to the base of the spine – might that have been all it took?

There were no suspicious circumstances surrounding her death. CCTV had showed nothing untoward. Delta had had a weakness in her calf – a dance injury that she had been having treatment for – and perhaps that had also hindered her when she slipped and fell.

Despite everything that had happened between us in the years leading up to our mother's death – the angry words and the bitter exchanges that would create an uncrossable canyon between us – she was always my little sister. From childhood I had been reminded that it was my responsibility to look after her, protect her. When she had needed protecting the most, I hadn't been there for her. No one had. It is this thought that has haunted me during the long sleepless nights that have passed between then and now: that Delta died alone, surrounded by strangers, unknown hands touching her skin in their search for signs of life.

I couldn't be there for her then, but I can now. If there is any truth in Alice's words, it is my responsibility to seek out the proof of it. As I drive into the village, I feel sick at the sight of the house ahead of me, perched on the hillside. For years now I have let strangers into what was once my home, but never like this. I have no idea who Matthew is, or the true extent of what he might be capable of.

I drive to the square and park in the car park by the harbour, not wanting Matthew to see me if he happens to be home. I go to Sylvia's first to get my spare keys, grateful that our paths don't cross while I make my brief visit. If Matthew has anything connected to Delta in the house, there are few places it could be hidden. As a holiday let, the furniture is minimal. He and Finley – he and Edward – have few possessions. Surely if he still has the book that Alice claims to have seen, it won't be difficult to find.

As I near the top of the path, I see that his car isn't outside the house. With no idea where he might be or how long he'll be gone, I have little time to spare. With a hand I cannot stop from shaking, I unlock the front door. The house is silent. Edward's toys have been pushed against the wall near the sideboard; a blanket is draped across the sofa. Matthew's trainers are on the carpet by the door.

In the corner of the room, near the television, there is a Christmas tree. It is decorated with red and gold baubles, wooden figures on skis and sitting on sleighs, multicoloured string lights wrapped in loops. There is a star at the top. It should be a cheerful sight, yet here amid all I now know, it looks gaudy and cheap, an artificial show of happiness to distract from the horrors that stand in its shadows.

The house smells of burned toast, and for a moment I panic, fearing that I am not alone.

'Hello?'

My voice is met with silence. A thought sneaks up on me, making my breath catch in my throat. The little girl at the end of Edward's bed. What if he hadn't imagined her after all?

I start opening cupboards: the one beneath the television, the ones in the sideboard on the wall to my left. I move on to the kitchen, both hopeful that I will find something and hopeful that I will not. When my search of downstairs proves futile, I head upstairs to Matthew's bedroom. It is not his, I remind myself. It is my mother's. My father's. This house is mine. The thought fuels me with a renewed energy as I search the wardrobe, opening his suitcase to find it empty. I check above and below the wardrobe, fumbling amid the dark corners in the hope that my fingers will touch upon something, yet they don't.

I have no idea how long I have already been here. Ten minutes... half an hour? Every second feels precious, but I know I am running out of time. I go to Edward's room, sickened at the thought that Matthew may be hiding something so incriminating and perverse in the place his young son sleeps. I search quickly, careful to leave everything as I found it, not wanting my presence here to be sensed later on.

There is nothing to be found in Edward's room. I return to the landing, and am about to leave when something makes me turn back to the other bedroom. For a moment, I don't feel like myself. My legs seem to move separately from the rest of my body, my eyes searching the spaces ahead of me as though someone else is responsible for leading me to them.

The bed is in front of me, neatly made with the striped sheets I chose online when I was preparing the house for rental. I run my hand along the wooden frame, leaning to smooth the undisturbed duvet. Somehow, in my heart, I already know it is here. The secrets of our pasts – secrets I hadn't even realised I had – are under this bed, beneath the mattress where we slept together and on which we've had sex.

A wave of nausea rushes through me. I kneel on the carpet and feel beneath the bed, my fingers groping between the slats. There is nothing there, so I lie on my back and edge my way further under, seeing straight away what I knew I would find. A hardback book, like a photograph album or a scrapbook. I slide it from the wooden slats, having to push some up to free it from its hiding place. Claustrophobia engulfs me, and I wriggle back out from under the bed, pulling the book open before I have time to change my mind.

The world dissolves around me, the floor melting beneath my

back; I put out a hand to steady myself despite being unable to fall, then I sit up, try to compose myself, though I know I have no hope of doing so. From the pages of the book, the same face looks back at me, dozens of eyes staring from a montage. Delta eating in a restaurant, Delta walking past a shop; Delta sitting on a Tube, engrossed in her phone. Each new page reveals yet more images of her: press releases for the show she was appearing in, magazine articles, posts taken from her social media profiles. The photographs blur as my eyes fill, at the realisation of... what, exactly? Nothing is as I thought, and yet everything remains unclear. Alice was right. Everything is a lie.

A wet night. A slippery floor. A staircase.

Tears escape me silently, staining my cheeks as they slide to my chin. My beautiful sister is alive within these pages, happy and carefree; oblivious. She never knew who was just behind her. If everything Alice said is true, then Christina never knew the person who was living right beside her all those years.

I turn the page and my blood runs cold. I have seen this photograph before, somewhere on the internet: Delta attending the opening night of some fancy restaurant in Mayfair, invited along by one of her theatre colleagues. She had mentioned it during her last visit home, using her own success to highlight my failings, and curiosity led me to google it. I wanted to see her happy, to see her enjoying the success she had so desperately craved, and yet I remember looking at this same photograph and wondering whether any of it was real, or whether the smile she wore like an accessory was all a continuation of the performance.

She is wearing a beautiful floor-length dress with a sweetheart neckline, the gold fabric cinching in her waist and accentuating her flawless figure. She is standing beside an older man – her co-star, I remember reading at the time – who has an arm draped around her back, his fingers resting lightly on her bare arm. Her hair falls softly to her shoulders, swept back at her temples. She is perfect, and my heart cracks a little more at the thought of everything she was and all the things she had yet to become.

And then I notice it. I want to push my fingers across the image, zoom in on the details as I would if I were looking at it on the screen of my phone, but all I can do is peer closer and narrow my eyes to make sure I am not imagining what I think I see. What I do not want to see. A silver necklace rests around her throat. Hanging just below the dip between her collarbones is a pendant, its aquamarine teardrop jewel sparkling as it catches the light.

I stop breathing.

I continue to turn the pages, urgency speeding my search. When I reach the end of the book, I find a pocket inside the back cover. I slip my fingers inside it, and they meet with something soft: a two-inch lock of hair that sits in a curl on my palm. Brunette. Perfect. Hers.

My beautiful sister, alive within these pages.

At that moment, I hear a sound downstairs. I close the album quickly and return it beneath the bed, careful to place it as near to its original hiding place as I can get. I push the lock of hair beneath a bed slat and then leave the bedroom, rushing downstairs to the cupboard where the vacuum cleaner is kept. Matthew stops in the doorway when he sees me there, Edward following him in a moment later. When our eyes meet, I feel certain mine must betray me. Just how much does he know?

He saw Alice outside the gallery, a voice in my head reminds me. *He knows that she is here and that you have spoken to her.*

'What are you doing here?'

'I came to clean.' The lie is a terrible one. I haven't done that since he moved in ten weeks ago, so why would I start now? 'And to say I'm sorry for not replying to your messages.' I smile at Edward. If Matthew intends me harm for any reason, surely he won't do anything to me with Edward here.

I am conscious of the fact that I must keep referring to Edward as Fin. If there is so much as a flicker of doubt on my face, I believe now that he will see it there. I mustn't let him know that I am suspicious of him.

And yet, of course, he knows. I have refused to respond to his messages or to talk to him about what happened with the necklace, or what happens next. I've made it clear that I think it is probably best that he leaves the house. Why would I now be cleaning it unless I was preparing to invite somebody else in to stay?

'I was wondering, actually, whether Fin might like to do some painting once I'm finished?'

I need to get the child out of here, I think. No matter how skilled Matthew's performance of doting father is, Edward isn't safe with him.

'Fin's tired,' Matthew says, something shifting in the air between us. 'Aren't you, Fin?' He asks the question without even looking at his son, his eyes still fixed on mine as I loiter uselessly at the vacuum cleaner, trying to maintain the pretence that I am here to clean.

'Go up to your room, Fin.' Edward looks about to protest, but the hand on his shoulder, likely planted there with greater force than is visible, puts an end to any imminent objection. 'I'll be up in five minutes.'

Edward's lip wobbles, but he follows his father's instruction and heads up the stairs to his room. As he passes me, I put a hand on his arm, an attempt at a silent reassurance that everything will be okay.

'Why are you here, Brooke?' Matthew asks, once Edward is out of sight.

My eyes scan the room, looking for something I might be able to use to defend myself with. I take a deep breath. 'Why are *you* here, Matthew?'

FIFTY-TWO
CHRISTINA
APRIL 2018

She couldn't remember getting from the attic stairs to the living room. She seemed to have floated there, ghost-like, the impossible truth that had been thrust upon her rendering her weightless. He was standing with his back to her, facing the mantelpiece and the framed photographs of the twins that were lined up there. He must have sensed her there in the doorway; her breathing was ragged and noisy, and it seemed impossible that he wouldn't have heard the roaring swell of her heartbeat as it thundered up through her chest and filled her head.

The albums were still in her hands, still clutched between sweating fingers. Her palms were hot, yet the rest of her was cold, as though ice had been injected and was threatening to turn her to stone.

'You've been up to the attic,' he said, without turning to look at her. 'Why?'

She had never anticipated that he would question her, not when every answer that demanded a voice should have been spoken by his.

'What are these?' She placed the photo albums on the coffee table and waited for him to look. The question sounded so inappropriately innocent, as though she was wondering about the contents of some unopened mail. There was one book of Delta, one of her. When Matthew turned to acknowledge her, his focus sliding effortlessly to what should have shamed him, she saw what might have been there all along had she only known to look for it. He saw nothing wrong in what he had done. What he was doing.

His eyes remained fixed on the albums for a moment before he looked up at her. There was no panic on his face, no surprise at the books being in her possession. He had already known that she had found them; he had known it when she had seen him earlier that day.

'Memories.' He answered the question so simply, as though that single word explained everything.

'We weren't together when a lot of these were taken. I barely knew you. They're not your memories, Matthew – they're mine.'

'But it was only ever a matter of time.'

Christina stared at him, any response she might have offered strangled by the tightening in her throat as she recalled Sarah's words once more. *He was never going to give up, was he?*

She took her book from the table, feeling her hands shake as she opened it to a random page. Her own face looked back at her, smiling on a night out with university friends, a photograph she had used as a social media profile picture. Alongside it, there was another image of her, this one taken from a distance. She was standing at a long table filled with rows of bottled water, her head tilted back as she laughed at something with the young woman standing next to her. She had volunteered as a marshal for the Birmingham half marathon, and she could recall that day so vividly – the weather, the crowds, the runners – that the photograph transported her back in time to a different life, one that had worn the glow of so much future possibility.

'I was at uni here,' she said. 'Why were you even there?'

She thought back on everything he had told her in those early days of their relationship, the getting-to-know-you conversations in which favourite films and favourite music were revealed amid details of family and life experiences, achievements and aspirations. It had become true for them, as Christina imagined it did for so many couples, that the more that was learned, the fewer questions were asked.

The half marathon had been in 2005. He had been in London that year, or so he had told her.

'I was there for you, Christina. I've always been there for you, haven't I?'

She thought of their reunion in the park that day, of how Matthew had been there when she had most needed him. Had he known that she would be there?

Of course he had. Bethany's need for routine meant that she and Christina would walk on the same day every week, at the same time, on the same route, with no alteration to the pattern. It was the only way Christina was able to get her sister to leave the house.

The album fell from her hands, its weight too much to bear. 'You already knew about Bethany, didn't you? That day at the park. You already knew she'd died.'

Christina hadn't bothered much with social media, but Leighton had. He would have posted about Bethany, letting people know what had happened before gossip spread and the truth became distorted. It would have been easy for Matthew to find out, though to have known where Christina would be that day, he must have been following them much earlier, watching them, learning their routines, using everything they had unknowingly offered him to forge a plan to get himself into her life.

'Everything is a lie,' she said.

'That's not true.'

'Of course it is. You lied to me. None of this is real.'

Matthew shook his head. 'We're married, Christina. We have a lovely home together, two beautiful children... a good life. Are all those things a lie?'

He spoke so calmly and with such reason that had the photo album not been open on the table in front of her, she might almost have believed what he said to be the truth.

'I love you. I've always loved you. You love me too, don't you? Or you did once, at least. Why else would you have married me?'

'I married the person I thought you were,' Christina said, blinking away angry tears. 'I married someone kind and good, someone I thought was honest.'

'I thought those things about you, too. But you still slept with someone else, didn't you?' He folded his arms across his chest as he waited for a reply that never came. Christina couldn't speak, words failing her as the truths of those past couple of months fell into place to create an image that was worse than anything she could have imagined.

Of course he had known. He had always known.

'Tick. Tock.' He spoke slowly, the single syllables spat at her. 'Time was always going to run out.'

She had been so convinced that it was Joel who had been tormenting her; Joel who couldn't let go, refusing to accept that it was the end. Her mind flitted back to the day she found the bloodied scarf in the bed she shared with her husband. She had thought it impossible that there was anyone else inflicting this cruelty upon her, and yet there had been Matthew. There had always been Matthew.

FIFTY-THREE

BROOKE

'You've seen Alice,' he says. He sits on the sofa, and I am disconcerted by how casually he is behaving. I had expected anger, denial; something. Not this. 'What has she told you?'

'Everything.'

He shrugs, as if that – as if everything – means nothing.

'I know your name's not Oliver,' I tell him, my voice shaking and betraying my fear. 'I know that your son's name isn't Finley, and I know about Christina.' *I know about Delta*, I add in my head, but I am not yet ready to go there. I don't know whether it is true, whether any of this is true, and yet there is that necklace, and it is enough to confirm too much.

'Alice hates me. She's trying to turn you against me. Don't let her poison what we have.'

I feel my face contort. 'We don't *have* anything.' I turn to look up the stairs, wondering whether Edward has come back out of his room. I don't want him to hear what is bound to be said. 'I don't know why you're here or what you want from me, but it's probably best that you pack up and leave.'

I didn't expect him to move, and he doesn't. He looks at me impassively, his expression unflinching, and I realise I have nowhere to go. There is a back door that leads from the kitchen, but I doubt I would have time to make it there without him reaching me first. He is blocking the way to the front door.

'I don't want anything from you, Brooke,' he says. I flinch when he stands, and he sees it in my reaction. When he moves towards me, I step back towards the stairs. 'I'm sorry, I don't mean that. I'm lying to you. There is one thing I wanted. I was hoping I could make you love me, and you do, don't you?'

I shake my head. It's the truth. I fell in love with the idea of a different life, with the possibility of an escape from the tedium that has become my existence here in the village. Delta was right all those years ago when she told me that I would dwindle into nothing.

'I don't love you,' I tell him. 'I don't even know who you are. I was lonely and it was fun while it lasted, but that's all it was.'

'Don't say that. You know who I am, Brooke. I'm only myself when I'm around you. Christina never made me the person that you make me. She was unfaithful, did Alice tell you that? She gave the appearance of being one thing, but she was something very different.'

He cannot hear his words as I do. They are the words of a mind unravelled, the hypocritical, narcissistic words of a person who says what he wants and does as he likes, as and when it suits him. There is no one whose true self is so different to its appearance as his.

'Am I supposed to feel sorry for you?'

He is feet away from me, yet I feel as though his hands are around my neck, the air being stolen from me. 'I gave her everything. Christina was perfect. I thought she was perfect. I thought she was the one. Kind and beautiful. And loyal. I loved her from the moment I first saw her. She was broken, but in a good way. Like you. Broken things can be mended, can't they? Made better again.'

I step back, almost falling as I hit the bottom of the staircase. 'What did you do to her, Matthew?'

He reaches out and touches my face, something flashing behind his eyes when I bat his hand away. 'You don't believe that anyone could love you, do you? But I do, Brooke. I've always loved you. We were meant for each other.'

I need to escape from this house, but there is no way I can get past him. Even if I could, I am kept there by Edward, fearful for his safety. My only option is to try to talk Matthew around, to pacify him with a pretence that his fantasy is a reality and that his feelings are reciprocated.

'You're not her, Brooke,' he says softly. 'You're not your sister. You're not Christina. Don't become them. You're the best of all of them, but you don't know it, and that's what makes you so special, can't you see that? Don't become like them. Don't listen to Alice. She's angry at me for taking Finley away, and I understand that, but she's trying to poison you against me. Don't let her do it.'

His words leave him faster with every breath, his pitch changing, becoming more desperate as he tries to convince me of his version of events. He believes himself some sort of hero, as though he was sent into my life to rescue me. But to rescue me from what? From the fire? From Lewis?

'His name is Edward. Your son's name is Edward.'

Matthew has told himself so many lies that he has started to believe them. It is really quite simple once you start; all you need to do is repeat yourself. Allow your voice to grow a little louder every time.

I am happy here, I have told myself, the words repeated on an endless loop. *I don't want anything more than I have.* Eventually I believed the lie.

'He needed a fresh start. Is that such a bad thing?'

'You're lying to him, and you've lied to me. Just what is real? Who was that boy I saw you with in the car park that day in St David's? He didn't scratch your car, did he? Did you do that yourself? I saw him at the police station. He was there with the detective,' I add, embellishing the truth to unsettle him. 'The one who came here with the search warrant.'

Something in Matthew's eyes has changed; there is a nervous flicker, some recognition that things are unravelling around him.

Yet all I hear are his words, reverberating: *You're not your sister*. I have made no mention of Delta or questioned whether or how he knew her, yet he has drawn attention to her, inadvertently acknowledging another of the secrets that has sat between us for these past few months. Just like that time he referred to her as an actress, and I overlooked it as a turn of phrase.

'He's nobody,' he says, the word inflected with resentment.

'Did you send him to start that fire? What did you do – pay him for it?' I choke on the words as a sob escapes me. 'Did you get him to start that fire so you could rescue me from it? You knew I wouldn't be there – you knew I'd be with you. Was it all planned so that you could be there when I went home?'

I think of Finley – Edward – sitting at the kitchen table, his small hand producing a painting that seemed mature beyond his years. His voice echoes in my memory, his childish tone taking on an implication that is suddenly so much more heartbreaking. *It's on fire*. I had thought him troubled by his mother's death, by the fire he had glimpsed at the gallery that evening – by all the things he didn't understand and those he possibly had a greater comprehension of than any adult had given him credit for. Perhaps that remains true, though not in the way I had thought it.

In my mind, I return to the room upstairs – once Delta's and mine, for the past few months Edward's. He is in bed, tucked beneath the duvet in his pyjamas, his night light casting a soft glow across the carpet. *Hell is on fire*. But now I know that's not what he said. He remembers more than anyone realises, the memories there, floating beneath the surface, struggling to rise for air. No doubt he has picked up the dropped fragments of conversations heard before he came here with his father, his young mind piecing them together in the only way he knew how.

El is on fire.

Elise.

'You weren't happy in that little cottage, were you? That place would never have made you happy, not like you've been here.'

He preys on the vulnerable. Alice's words echo, haunting me.

He searches for grief and then he feeds off it. He knew my sister had died. He probably knew about my mother. He started a fire, he made me a victim, and in my uncertainty, I ran to him.

'Those phone calls,' I say. 'It was you. Her birthday message to me. Why would you put me through that?'

I knew when I found that video on Delta's Instagram page that it was the same clip of her voice I had heard played down the phone all those times. It was posted online for everyone to see and anyone to access, but what I couldn't understand was why someone would use it in such a cruel way, or want to cause me so much pain.

'I only gave you what you wanted to hear.'

'Why Delta?' I ask, my voice shaking, though I already know the answer. With Christina's affair exposed, Matthew's illusion of her as the perfect one was shattered. Her infidelity left a void where a replacement was needed.

His jaw tenses. 'I was grateful to her to begin with. The first time I saw her, it felt like the moment I'd first seen Christina. I was being given a second chance at happiness. I already knew by then that Christina wasn't who I'd thought she was. She was an illusion really, right from the start. I put her on a pedestal where she never deserved to be. But then Delta... Delta seemed perfect too. So many people do from the outside, don't they? The more I saw of her, though, the more I realised it was all a facade. She was too self-ish... too ugly on the inside. But I believe in fate, and I believe that Delta came into my life for a reason, and that reason was to bring me here to you.' I cringe as he puts his hands either side of my face, at the thought that these same hands were the ones that might have pushed my sister to her death. 'Delta was just like Christina. Self-ish. Disloyal. But you're different. We were meant to be together, Brooke. They brought me to you.'

'Why did you do it, Christina? Wasn't I enough for you?'

She wasn't going to discuss Joel, not now that the truth of Matthew was staring her in the face. For all those months, she had carried such guilt, feeling herself indebted to him, when all the time this was who he was. Their marriage was a farce, a sham built on an obsession that she had failed to recognise as anything other than love. Everything was a lie.

Might she have found happiness with Joel? she wondered. She had been searching for something, never too sure of exactly what, and her affair had made her face the uncertainties of her own existence. She had thought her problems were contained within herself, some sort of deep-rooted ingratitude; she should have been happier, shouldn't she? She had so much to be appreciative of, didn't she?

But Joel wasn't the answer, any more than she had been the problem. The catalyst of her restlessness had been much closer to home, here within these four walls, a ticking time bomb disguised in beautiful gift wrap.

'All those excuses you made about being tired,' he said, pushing for a reaction. 'The headaches. The sickness.'

'All of it true,' she said. 'Because of you. Have you been putting those laxatives in my food?'

He ignored the question, preferring to keep his focus on Joel. 'Were you thinking of him when you were with me?'

'It was never about sex.'

'Liar,' he spat. 'Even now, you're still lying. I'm not the one who's guilty of deceit here.'

He reached to the sofa for his laptop, and she watched, rigid with anticipation, as he accessed a file. She recognised the room instantly, even seeing it from an angle she hadn't been accustomed to. The image was grainy, yet it showed enough. She felt her body flinch as she watched herself enter the bedroom, Joel following closely behind her. On the screen, she turned to him, and he kissed her before beginning to undress her. She looked away, unable to watch any more.

'But it wasn't about sex?' Matthew picked up the laptop and shoved it in front of her, forcing her to look again at the scene playing out. 'I'd have done anything for you, Christina. Anything for us.'

Christina felt tears dampen her eyes. How was he still managing to make her feel so guilty and ashamed when his own secret was staring up at them from the coffee table? He was playing the martyr so effectively that she almost believed the lie, still caught in the charade that he had created for her and their family.

'How did you get into his flat?' she asked, not sure she wanted to hear the answer.

He shrugged. 'Nice place. Thought I might make an offer. It was definitely worth a second viewing.'

Joel's flat had been on the market for months by the time she had ended their affair. Did estate agents even leave viewers alone when they were inside someone else's home? She couldn't think of a scenario in which this might happen, and yet Matthew was charming enough and manipulative enough to orchestrate anything, apparently. She had read of things like this before. She had read about women whose partners had controlled their lives without ever appearing to do so, and now she remembered wondering just how anyone could miss the signs that must have been there, so obvious to anyone who was on the outside looking in. Had the estate agent turned their back for a moment, long enough for Matthew to plant that camera in the bedroom? Had he made an excuse about forgetting something and needing to pop back in? Why would anyone think twice about trusting him? Charming, dependable, handsome Matthew. It was easy to fool other people when you were as skilled and experienced at it as he was.

'Were you thinking of Oliver when you were with Joel?'

Christina felt herself burn with anger. 'What's the matter with you? That's sick, you know that.'

'But is it true?'

She laughed bitterly, near disbelief. Matthew had always behaved strangely around her brother-in-law, but never once had she considered that this might be the reason. Had he been jealous of him? She and Oliver had been close, like brother and sister, made closer by the circumstances of Bethany's death, but could Matthew really have resented a relationship that had been grounded in mutual grief?

'Oliver is like a brother to me, you know that.'

'Makes your little infatuation with him even more weird then, don't you think?'

'Oh my God,' she said, realisation settling upon her. 'Have you spoken to him? Have you told him to stay away?'

Matthew said nothing, but his expression answered the question for him. He looked nothing like himself; nothing like the person she'd thought she had married. But in the face of her husband's deceit, nothing looked as it once had. Just like the physical ailments that seemingly had no cause, the psychological traumas now took on a different shape. The postnatal depression she had suspected but had never been diagnosed with, the feeling of being trapped and isolated, the desperation to be around other adults, people like Janet Marsden, who had inexplicably made her feel more normal. Like her old self.

This was the truth of it: that Matthew had isolated her. He had done it over years, bit by bit, taking away her independence by reducing everything she had and did to the confinement of these four walls. Hadn't it been his idea for her to leave the clinic and set up from home? Think of the benefits, he had said, before pointing out that she would have more money, more flexibility, more control over decision-making. What he had never pointed out – what Christina had never once considered – was that it would be another step towards a life condensed within their home, closer to him and further away from the contact of others. Yes, she had her clients. They talked – sometimes with her, sometimes at her – but never in the way she might have spoken with colleagues, people she would then have gone on to forge friendships with outside of work hours.

Little by little, she had lost everyone. Hadn't he succeeded in putting her off having Ollie and Fin to stay, despite them being the closest living memory she had of her sister? Hadn't he feigned concern for her poor health – an illness he was responsible for – by suggesting she take time off work? He had been breaking her physically and emotionally, removing her from every lifeline that had kept her *her*.

Even Leighton had become little more than a babysitting service. With a heavy sense of shame, Christina realised that she spoke no more to her own brother than she did to the women who worked at the twins' nursery. When was the last time she had gone anywhere with him and they had talked together about something more than whether she had packed enough nappies? It saddened her that she couldn't remember. Even on his birthday, back before Christmas, all communication had been done through Edward and Elise, as though in having children, Christina had ceased to exist as a person in her own right. But it wasn't the children, she thought – they hadn't chosen this, or even done so inadvertently, their dependence rendering her sense of self altered. It had been Matthew, all of it, his agenda quietly executed from the sidelines while he delivered the appearance of loving father and supportive husband.

She choked back tears at the thought that everything had been there right in front of her, hiding in plain sight. 'Did you put that scarf in our bed?'

Matthew looked down at the carpet, his silence ringing louder than any admission.

'Did you put it in our bed?' she asked again, repeating each word slowly, deliberately, taking a step closer to him. He didn't answer. 'Did you send those flowers? Was it you who sent the chicken hearts?'

Still he said nothing. She wished he would speak. She would rather have him shout at her than endure this endless silence, as though he was enjoying dragging out her punishment for crimes he had committed.

A memory came hurtling back to her, sending her off balance. Her hands wet with blood from her scarf. 'Where is he?' she asked quietly. 'Where's Joel?'

'It shouldn't matter to you now. We're what matters. Me, you, the kids. We should have been the only people who ever mattered.'

Christina choked back tears at the thought of what her husband might have done. He hadn't denied any wrongdoing. He couldn't, not when he was guilty.

The blood, she thought. Not the blood of an animal, but the blood of a human. A warning. Oh God. Joel. She took a tentative step backwards, a thousand possibilities presenting themselves in an instant like the memory of a nightmare.

'I need to know what you've done. If I matter to you, you'll tell me the truth.'

Matthew stepped towards her, his face close to hers, and she felt her body stiffen. 'I felt a bit sorry for him, right at the end. The sad thing is, I think he might have been in love with you. But you can't love back, can you, Chrissie? Not in the way you're supposed to.'

Christina sobbed for the life that had been taken and for the one that had never existed: her own, never really what it seemed. Might she have been happy with Joel? Had she heeded Janet's warning, could there have been a chance to save him – and her – before it was too late?

'And what about Delta?' she said, managing to regain composure. 'Does she know you've been following her?'

He lunged at her and grabbed her by the shoulders. 'I gave you everything, Christina. My entire life. I would have followed you to the ends of the earth to keep you safe, but all you've done is throw it back at me.' He was shaking her now, his voice louder and angrier with every word. She felt his fingertips dig into her flesh; felt drops of spittle land on her cheek as his rage expelled in her face. She had never seen him angry before, never like this. 'And what about the kids? Did you think of them in any of this, or did they just disappear while you were fucking him?'

She had to get out of that house and get away from him, but she couldn't go without Elise. What exactly was Matthew capable of? She had just found out. Joel had found out.

She raised a leg sharply and kneed him in the groin, and his grip on her shoulders loosened. She turned to make a run for the hallway, but he was too quick, upon her before she neared the living room door. He grabbed a length of her hair and pulled her back to him. As she felt his hands close around her throat, she struggled desperately to free herself. She had never realised he was so strong, nor that she might be so terrified of him.

As she twisted to try and break free, Matthew let go and she lost her balance. He shoved her in the chest, a push so hard that she fell back, tripping over one of the children's toys left out on the carpet and cracking her head against the sideboard. She dropped to the floor, the room spinning around her, the colours blurring at first before fading into grey.

He stood over her for a moment as the room continued to blur and refocus, blur and refocus, as though she was under the influence of some mind-altering drug. Pain cut through her skull like a knife plunged into her brain. She watched, unable to react, as he reached down to her. She felt herself being dragged through to the hallway, his arms beneath her own, moving her as though she was weightless. Every fibre of her body wanted to react, to fight back, to resist, and yet nothing moved, as though some circuitry in her brain that gave instruction to her limbs had been severed, rendered useless. The colours around her were fading, the details of her surroundings blurring at the edges. She tried to speak Elise's name, but nothing came out.

He looked down at her impassively, dead behind the eyes. Whatever she might have seen there once was gone, the person she had thought he was gone with it. He touched his fingertips to her cheek, though she felt nothing. 'You did this, Christina.'

He stepped over her as he made his way to the staircase. He was going to get Elise, she thought. He was going to take their daughter away from her. And then she realised that no, he wasn't. He thought Elise was at Leighton and Alice's flat with Edward, staying there for the night. Listening to his footsteps on the landing, she realised he was going to attend to something far more important than that, because amid everything else, one thing had always been the true focus of his life. He was going up to the attic to protect himself, to remove his lifelong secret.

FIFTY-FIVE

BROOKE

I put my hands over Matthew's, gently moving them from my face. The thundering of my heart betrays my pretence at calm, and I am sure he must hear it cutting through the silence. 'I'm going to go home now,' I tell him evenly, knowing there is little chance he will allow this to happen. 'We both need time to think about things, don't we? Go and be with Finley now. We can talk tomorrow.'

I don't dare refer to his son as Edward, though calling him Finley now seems as alien as it should have always done to Matthew. What lies must he have told his child to convince him that his old life was over and another begun, to persuade him that he must say goodbye to his name and his identity and adopt new ones without question? And what about Matthew's identity? It was only a matter of time before I found out, one way or another, that he had lied to me about who he was. I imagine this was why he was so reluctant for me to go to the bank with him that day in St David's. He couldn't possibly have believed that he could maintain the lie forever, so what was he planning to do once I found out?

'You know I can't let you go, Brooke.'

'You can. I won't tell anyone about any of this, I promise. Just pack your things and take Finley – you can start a new life somewhere else. You can go anywhere you want.'

I listen to my own words with disgust in my heart; they sound like the snivelling, grovelling words of a coward. Alice believes that this man killed my sister, yet here I am offering him promises of silence and loyalty if only he will reward me with my freedom. What I should be doing is fighting for her, making sure he pays for his crimes. I once accused Delta of running away from her problems, but staying inert and saying nothing is no more an attempt to face them than that.

'I want to be here. I want to be with you.'

His words sound more snivelling and grovelling than my own, and if it wasn't for everything that I now know him to be, I might find him pitifully pathetic.

'Why Oliver?' I ask, though I don't really care; I am trying to stay calm, trying to keep him talking while I think of a way to get myself and Edward out of here.

'What do you mean?'

'You could have told me your name was anything. Why did you use Bethany's husband's name?'

He is standing too close to me, so close that my heart feels as though it only registers every third beat. Upstairs, Edward remains silent, and its emptiness is terrifying. I wish he would cry, scream – something – so that I would know he is all right.

'He doesn't matter. Not to you. I think I could have been anyone, couldn't I, and you would still have understood me.' He places a cold hand on my arm. 'All I've ever wanted is for you to stay here with me. I just thought that if you believed I'd lost someone to suicide, you wouldn't do anything to hurt yourself again.'

Lies, I think. All of it lies. Only Matthew understands why he chose Oliver. 'But you didn't lose anyone,' I remind him, flinching from his touch. 'Not to suicide, at least. You had someone who loved you, and you killed her, didn't you?'

'She didn't love me,' he says, as though if this were true it would justify his crime. 'And it was an accident.'

'Then why didn't you call for help?' I ask, hypocrisy sticking in my throat at the thought of Lewis. 'If it was an accident, why didn't you help her? You have a choice, remember? Isn't that what you told me before? You always have a choice.' *You didn't kill him, Brooke*, I tell myself. *You and Matthew are not the same.* 'Understand this – you are nothing to me. You are a liar and a murderer, and you deserve nothing. That little boy upstairs deserves a million times better than you. So did his sister.'

At the mention of Elise, Matthew lunges at me. I try to dodge past him, but he is too fast, and when he throws his weight on top of me, we both fall to the floor. His body crushes mine, my cheek pressed to the carpet.

'Don't you ever speak of her,' he whispers threateningly in my ear.

His arm tightens around my throat. His face changes, growing younger, different, and I find myself back in the woods behind this house, no longer Matthew's face in front of mine, but Lewis's. I am silent, silenced, paralysed by fear. I will not be that person for a second time. My mouth finds the bare flesh where Matthew's sleeve has risen, and like a woman possessed, I sink my teeth into his arm, numbing myself against the awful metallic tang that coats my tongue when I break the skin.

'Bitch!'

I hurt him enough to make him pull away, and when his weight eases, I reach up to grab the mug that has been left on the table. I swing it around and it glances off his temple, disorientating him enough to make him lose his balance. I stumble as I get up and rush for the front door, but as I reach the hallway, he is upon me again, one arm around my waist, the other hand around my throat. As we struggle, we fall back into the living room.

I am unsure who sees Edward first: Matthew or me. He is standing at the top of the staircase, clutching a teddy bear to his chest. He looks terrified, and my heart breaks for everything he has been subjected to.

'Go back to your room, Edward,' I tell him, my words strangled beneath Matthew's grip. He reacts to the sound of his real name, as though realising he doesn't have to play this game any more, and I think he might start to cry.

'Stop it, Daddy,' he says, the words so quiet, so pitiful that I want to cry for him.

'Do what Brooke told you,' Matthew says, and I feel the grip around my throat loosen slightly. 'Everything's fine. We're just playing a game.'

But Edward is a bright child, not fooled by his father's lies. He stands still, refusing to follow Matthew's orders, and even when Matthew shouts at him, he stays where he is, whether rooted through bravery or fear.

Edward's defiance forces Matthew to a decision. He must either hurt me while his son watches on, or let me go. He does the latter, and when he rushes up the stairs towards the little boy, fuelled by a rage that I know he can't contain, I am offered a choice of my own. I can run now, escape this place, or I can save Edward.

I dart into the kitchen and go to the cutlery drawer, pulling out the sharpest knife. Edward's screams pierce the air, and I rush upstairs. Matthew is in my childhood bedroom; Edward is nowhere to be seen, but his cries can be heard, as can his fists, beating on the door of the walk-in wardrobe. Matthew has added a lock to the outside and has bolted him within the small space. I wonder how many times he has done this before. Was this how he forced Edward to become Finley, punishing him every time he made reference to his real name or his past life?

'Let him out.'

He looks at the knife in my hand, apparently undeterred.

'You're not going to use that, are you?' he says matter-of-factly. 'You can't, Brooke. It isn't in you. It's not who you are. Although you were there that day with Lewis, weren't you? Did you push him?'

Edward's cries grow in intensity; he is going to have a panic attack if he is left in there much longer.

'Don't do this to him,' I beg, the knife shaking in my hand.

'Please. He's just a baby. Are you really going to be responsible for the deaths of both your children?'

I prepare myself for the assault, knowing that my words will trigger a reaction. Matthew's face tightens, crimson rising from his neck to his face in a wave of rage, and I raise the knife, brandishing it towards him. 'I will do it. For Christina,' I tell him. 'For Elise. For Delta. You pushed her down those steps, didn't you? Why did you do it? She had never done anything to you.'

I step back as he advances on me, less sure of myself than I claim.

'My little girl would still be here if it wasn't for her.'

Breath catches in my throat. 'What do you mean?'

'I was supposed to be with her. We were supposed to be together. But she'd made other plans, just like Christina. You're all the same, aren't you? I thought you were different, Brooke, but it's all lies. If I'd been with Delta that evening like I'd planned, Elise would still be—'

He stops short, but I know I must keep him talking.

'Elise would still be what?'

Edward has stopped screaming. I want more than anything to hear him.

'You killed her, didn't you, Matthew? You killed Elise.'

The expression that pulls at his features tells me he has never yet admitted this to himself. Could he really have believed that it was somehow Delta's fault, that if she had been somewhere else or behaved in a manner that was more pleasing to him, he wouldn't have done what he did that night? But I'm not sure Delta even knew he existed. She couldn't have done anything differently.

'I didn't mean to,' he says. 'I didn't know she was in the house.' His face crumples with his confession. Tears flow from his eyes, yet I can feel no sympathy for him; I feel nothing but a swell of sickness at the thought that my sister died because this man could not accept the blame for what he himself was guilty of. Far easier to carry hatred for someone else, as though one death might in some way cancel out another.

'I know what you did,' I tell him, remembering Alice's words as though I am hearing them again. I recall the news reports I read while we sat at the cenotaph. Matthew had managed to convince everyone else of his innocence, but not Alice. 'What really happened in the house that night, Matthew? That fire wasn't accidental, was it? You started it. You killed them.'

'I didn't know she was there.'

'But you killed her all the same. You killed your wife and your child and then you staged it as an accident, and I don't understand how any of that was Delta's fault.'

At the mention of her name, his face changes. 'Because she was nothing but a cheap slut, just like Christina.'

I try to work out what he might be referring to, or whether there is any reference to something real, but there is too much noise in my head and too much silence still from Edward, and the room around me is swimming with all the truths that are revealing themselves, making a place that was for so long my home now feel like the least safe place on earth.

Did Delta reject Matthew at some point? Did he see her with another man, shattering his illusions of the future relationship he had imagined he might have with her? Matthew is a dangerous fantasist; the only person that could make any sense of his infatuation must surely be him. Or perhaps not so. Perhaps, by now, even he is unsure where one lie ends and another begins, of what is real and what is not.

There are a million questions I want him to answer, yet I don't want him to say a word more.

'You pushed her,' I say quietly. 'Didn't you? You pushed Delta down those steps.'

'I'm sorry.' He looks at me with the eyes of the man I met months ago, the one whose life I entered in the belief that he was a struggling single father, mourning the loss of his wife. A good man. The look is there, as bright as it was then, and then it is gone, its light diminished, and with its fading, I realise that the apology was not for what he did to Delta but for what he is about to do to me.

With movements that are too quick for me to respond to, he lunges forward, his hand slicing through the air and knocking the knife from my grasp. I hear it clatter down the stairs as he grabs me by the throat. He pushes me along the landing, and we fall into the other bedroom. I manage to claw at his face, cutting his cheek, but it only makes him angrier, and his grip around my neck tightens. He drops his weight on me as we fall onto the bed, and pinned beneath him, I feel the room around us start to leave me.

'Stop!'

Air floods my lungs, and I see Alice behind him, the flash of a blade. Matthew lunges for her, and the knife is knocked to the floor. The struggle that follows is brief – she is too slight, and he is too strong – and his hands wrap around her throat as they did around mine, her feet barely touching the floor. Hearing me get up from the bed, he throws her aside as though she is weightless; her head hits the chest of drawers, and she falls to the carpet. I scramble for the knife as I hear her groan, and when Matthew comes back for me, I am ready for him.

It happens quickly, my hand moving as though detached from the rest of my body. He reaches for my shoulders as his face contorts with the pain, and when he steps back, I see nothing but the handle of the knife, and the burst of blood that seeps through his shirt in a macabre crimson flower. He falls back against the wall before sliding to the floor, his face contorted in horror as he moves his hand to his stomach.

FIFTY-SIX

CHRISTINA

MAY 2011

'There's a little café just a few streets away,' Christina told him, leading the way out of the park. 'We could get a coffee there?'

'Sounds perfect.'

They walked the rest of the way in silence. The sky was heavy, distant clouds bringing a threat of rain, and Christina was grateful that the sun had come out yesterday when they had said their goodbyes to Bethany. Not that she had said goodbye, no more than in the ceremonial sense that everyone had expected of her. She would never say goodbye to her little sister. Bethany would be beside her in everything she would go on to do, a shadow that she would take with her everywhere she went.

She had never been inside the café before, but this was what she needed: to sit in places where Bethany had never been; to talk to people Bethany had never known. Leighton and Alice were too close, immersed in a grief of their own. Talking among the three of them seemed to deepen the others' wounds, and she didn't want to be responsible for making their suffering any worse than it already was.

They went to the counter together to order drinks before finding a quiet table in the corner.

'So what brings you back here?' Christina asked, as she took off her coat and hung it over the back of her chair.

'Just started a new job. Made sense to be closer.'

'Where are you working?'

'Heathrow. Air traffic controller.'

'No way?' she said, genuinely impressed. 'Wow. Not your everyday type of job, is it? How did you get into that?'

'I'm not sure really. Just fell into it.' He laughed when she pulled a face. 'I know – it's not the type of job you usually just fall into.'

'Must be stressful.'

'At times. But actually, it's mostly a bit boring. We have to take regular breaks. There's a lot of time spent hanging about, waiting for something to happen.'

They were interrupted by a member of staff, who placed their coffees on the table.

'Thanks,' Christina said. She reached for a sachet of sugar, a habit she was trying and failing to break. 'So how do you fill it? All your free time hanging about?'

Matthew shrugged. 'I do a lot of reading. What about you?'

'I qualified as a physiotherapist a few years back. I'm working at a clinic in High Barnet.'

'Do you enjoy it?'

She nodded over the top of the steam that rose from her coffee cup. It was nice to be talking normally like this, about everyday things, though there was nothing that could keep her mind from Bethany. She missed her so much already. It felt as though a weight had been lowered onto her chest, putting increasing pressure on her heart. 'Nice people,' she said, trying to steel herself against the thought. 'Interesting. Bet it's not as interesting as your job, though.'

'Honestly, you'd be surprised. Some days really can be boring. You can't be at the desk for more than ninety minutes at a time, you see. Not good for the mind to wander when you're responsible for an aircraft twenty thousand feet in the air, apparently.' He smiled, but the expression quickly fell from his face, as though it was somehow misplaced. 'You can talk about her if you like. Your sister. There's that thing people do, isn't there, when someone's just died and nobody mentions them for fear of upsetting you. But actually, when they change the subject and avoid mentioning them, it makes it more painful, because all you want to do is talk about them.' He held her eye, waited until she looked away. 'Sorry if I've said too much. I just remember it when I lost my dad.'

'I'm sorry about your dad. When did he die?'

'Three years ago. But look, that happens, doesn't it? The natural order of things, as they say. But your sister... I'm sorry, what was her name? I don't remember her from school.'

Christina shook her head. 'Bethany. There was three years between us,' she explained. 'She was only in Year Nine when we started sixth form.'

'Those were the days,' Matthew said with a smile.

'I don't remember you much from school. Sorry... I don't mean that to sound rude.'

'I was quiet, you mean?'

She felt her face flush, and lifted her cup to her mouth to try to hide it. 'That's no bad thing, is it?'

'It's worked for me. You get asked fewer questions when you're quiet. Do you miss it?'

'School?' Christina asked. 'God, no. You?'

'Never. I know they say school days are the best days of your life and all that, but no one really believes that, do they? I think most people are pretty miserable there.'

'And what about now? Are you happier now?'

Matthew looked up from his drink. 'Getting there. I always try to believe that the best is yet to come.' He smiled, the gesture reaching his eyes. He was handsome, she thought. She hadn't noticed it until now, though she had never really looked at him properly before. 'I remember you,' he said. 'You were pretty quiet too. In a good way.'

'Is there a bad way?'

'To be quiet?' He sipped his coffee while he contemplated a response. 'Depends what you're plotting, I suppose.'

'So what were *you* plotting, back at school?'

'Ah... that would be telling. I'll share my secrets if you share yours. Hey, it's a shame we didn't have this conversation eight years ago – we could have plotted together.'

Christina's phone began to ring in her pocket. 'Sorry,' she said, looking at the name on the screen. 'It's Oliver, my brother-in-law. I'd better take this.'

She took the call outside, and when she returned, Matthew had finished his drink.

'Everything okay?' he asked. 'I mean, as okay as it can be?'

'He needs me. Sorry, I'd better go.'

'Of course.' He stood and put on his jacket, watching Christina as she buttoned hers up. 'I'm so sorry about your sister. I just can't imagine.' He put a hand on hers, his fingers warm against her skin. 'It's been lovely to see you, Christina Finley. If you ever fancy doing this again, we could, you know, just sit and be quiet together.'

She nodded. 'Thank you. I'd like that.'

FIFTY-SEVEN

BROOKE

Sylvia takes my hand in hers as we leave the court building. The sky still hangs heavy above us, charcoal and overcast, the merest shard of blue sky visible in the distance. I have just been handed an eighteen-month suspended sentence for perverting the course of justice, but the truth is finally out, and I feel lighter for it. I had wondered whether Jean might make an appearance today, but after her admission during my trial, she has avoided being seen. Almost fifteen years ago, as a drunken twenty-one-year-old returned home for the summer, Lewis had confided in her what had really happened that night. I think of her outside Sylvia's house, spitting venom for my 'lies', and can only assume that she remained in denial to protect herself from what her son really was. All those years, she could have spared at least a portion of my suffering, but she shielded him by keeping the truth silenced. In his absence, the guilt finally overwhelmed her.

'This is a fresh start now, love,' Sylvia says, squeezing my fingers.

There were no charges brought against me for Matthew's injury. He awaits trial now, the complexity of the multiple murder charges brought against him and the delays of a world tipped on its head by a virus meaning it could still be some time before he faces justice for his crimes. The teenage boy he paid to set fire to the gallery and break into Jean's house – a fourteen-year-old from a children's home, the son of a drug-addicted mother and a dead father – finally agreed to give evidence against him, having been terrified by the consequences Matthew had threatened him with. Once again, Matthew had searched for the vulnerable, preying on someone who might be easily manipulated into believing his lies and enabling his crimes.

By the time we get back to the village, it has started to rain.

'I think I'll go for a walk,' I say.

'I'll come with you.'

'No,' I reply, too quickly, then put a hand on Sylvia's arm, anxious that I may have offended her. 'I'd like to go alone. You don't mind, do you?'

'Just promise you'll come over for a cup of tea when you get back.'

'I promise.'

I walk her to the steps that lead up to her house before heading for the coastal path. Light rain dampens my skin, and I raise my face skywards, allowing it to wash over me. When I reach the top of the path, I stop to take in the view. The ocean, pale grey and angry, stretches into the distance, waves crashing at the rocks below. A cawing gull passes overhead, anxious in its search for food. Beside me, I sense the ghosts that have remained with me these last few years, their presence now as light and unobtrusive as the air.

In the months that followed the confrontation at Hillside Cottage, I was exposed to the realities of the life I had become inadvertently entangled with. I returned over and over to the reports of the fire that killed Christina and Elise, each time picturing a new course of events that led to what happened in their home that day. The coroner confirmed that Christina had suffered a head injury, initially believed to have been sustained when she had fallen down the stairs and hit her head on the hall table. In the various versions of the events that had led to the fire, it was suggested that she had run from the landing at the smell of burning and lost her footing on the stairs. A toaster had been left too close to the water that was boiling in a saucepan on the stove; the electrical lead had caught alight, and the resulting fire had engulfed the kitchen within a matter of minutes. Matthew had been returning from work when he was contacted by a neighbour who had called 999.

That day I went to the house in search of the photo album, I thought I could smell burning toast. I continue to wonder about that now, in the same way that I have lingered over thoughts of the little girl by Edward's bed, and I believe in my heart that in some way, Christina and Elise were there with me that evening. Perhaps Delta was too. They are with me now, gentle whispers on the wind, and I owe it to them all to keep their memory alive.

Above the sounds of the sea and the wind, I hear my phone ringing in my pocket. Alice's name flashes up at me. I had known she would call to find out the results of the sentencing; we have remained in contact, finding comradeship in the shared experience of what happened that night, and she has looked out for me as I have for her, checking in regularly to help one another work past the nightmares.

'Eighteen months suspended,' I tell her, and I hear her sigh of relief.

'Are you okay?'

'Getting there. How are things with you?'

'Fine,' she says, which I know means the opposite is true.

'How is Edward doing?'

Her voice changes. 'As well as can be expected, I suppose. He has good days and bad.'

'And you and Leighton?' I ask. 'Have you two worked things out yet?'

There is a pause. 'Things are still difficult.'

'I'm sure you will, in time. What you've both been through...'

The wind hurtles through the hedgerow behind me, pushing me forward towards the cliff edge. With the sea below me and the rain on my skin, I feel more alive at this spot than I ever have.

'Have you read about Joel Cooper?' Alice asks.

Joel's story has been all over the papers, following on from the tragic revelations about what really happened to the Hale family. He lived alone and had no family other than a sister who lives in New Zealand, but a colleague contacted police when he hadn't turned up for work for a while and no one could get hold of him. His disappearance led to a police investigation, but he's never been found.

'Do you think they'll get any closer to finding out what happened to him?' I ask.

'I hope so. I always wondered about him,' Alice admits. 'Christina's number was stored in his phone, but then she was his physiotherapist, so it didn't raise any suspicions. There were messages from him to another number, though, someone he had obviously been in a relationship with. It was an unregistered pay-as-you-go phone. We never found out who it belonged to, and none of Joel's friends or colleagues knew anything about a girlfriend. If he was in a relationship with someone, why not mention her to anyone?

'There was something else as well, something that only occurred to me after the fire. I went over to the house to babysit for Christina one evening. She implied that she was organising a surprise for Matthew's birthday, but there was something about her that just seemed off. I did wonder afterwards whether she had gone to meet someone else, but it seemed so unlike her. Then those messages on Joel's phone – they suggested that things with this mystery woman hadn't ended well.'

'What did they say?'

'He was obviously upset at the way things had finished between them. And then the woman, whoever she was, threatened to go to the police if he didn't stop what he was doing.'

'What *was* he doing?'

'Good question. We don't know. We may never know. But I

always wondered after those messages surfaced... What if Christina was this secret woman that he hadn't told anyone about, and what if Matthew had found out? It gave him a motive for both their murders.' She falls silent for a moment, revulsion pausing her words. 'My superior said I was too involved, that I was letting my emotions overrule my judgement. He took me off the case. Anyway, Matthew changed after the investigation into Joel's disappearance became public knowledge. Within weeks of Joel's face appearing on the news, he moved out of the flat. I had my suspicions, but there was never anything to substantiate them.'

Perhaps Matthew's involvement in Joel's disappearance may never be proven, in the same way he may never face justice for Delta's murder. He'll have to live with his conscience, and if there is any justice in this world, he'll face a life sentence for what he did to Christina and Elise.

'You didn't tell Leighton any of this?'

'I couldn't talk to Leighton about anything back then. Matthew and Edward were the only family he had left – he would never have believed there was anything amiss. Leighton's a good person. Good people sometimes only see goodness in others.'

'Talk to him,' I tell her. 'You can survive this.'

'There's been too much pressure on us both. First Bethany, and then Christina and Elise.' Alice's voice breaks on a sob. 'I was there when they told Matthew about Elise. I knew something wasn't right, but no one else would believe me. He played the grieving husband so well, you see. But not the grieving father. He didn't have to play that part – there was no performance needed.' She stops talking, and I hear her trying to catch her breath. 'He had no idea she was there when he started that fire. I don't know whether he ever accepted his own guilt, or whether he blamed someone else to avoid admitting what he'd done.'

I feel a lump in my throat, and it threatens to choke me. Matthew told me as much when he claimed that his daughter would still be alive if it hadn't been for my sister. He had become so lost in his lies, so blinded by the fantasy that he had created for himself, that to him the claim was real.

Alice has sent me photographs of Elise, most of them with Edward beside her. She has haunted me, as my own sister has, but now I know that the little girl next to Edward's bed, the one who remained alive in his dreams, was not my sister, but his. Elise will stay with him always, as Delta will always stay with me, wherever I go.

'But surely when Matthew left as he did, Leighton must have found it unusual?'

'Oliver had done the same when Bethany died. There's no textbook for grief, is there? No right or wrong way to react. Leighton believed Matthew when he told us that he just needed time. He believed him when he said he'd come back.' She stops and takes a deep breath. 'I thought having Edward home might help him, but I don't know any more.'

I feel a knot of jealousy and something that feels strangely like grief twist inside me at the mention of the child's name. He will never hold my hand again; I will never learn anything else new about the world through his innocent eyes. He was never my child, though. He belongs with his family, and I believe in my heart that Alice and Leighton are the best people to care for him.

'The three of you need to be together. Now more than ever. Alice?'

'Yes.'

'Thank you. For everything. You saved my life. If you hadn't followed me to the house that day...'

Alice says nothing; it has all been said before. We allow the silence to linger between us for a while; there is something strangely comforting in just having her there at the other end of the line. Sometimes I wish we could be closer, that we could see each other occasionally, but perhaps the distance is for the best. She has her life to get on with now. I have mine. We will remain friends, I think, at least until one of us is ready to let go. Perhaps it will happen mutually, that we will one day find ourselves able to break free from the hold that Matthew has over us; we will end a phone conversation with our usual goodbye, neither realising that we have reached the point at which we will no longer need each other.

'You take care, won't you?' she says to me.

'And you. I'm always at the end of the phone if you need me. Remember that, won't you?'

'You too. Bye, Brooke.'

'Bye,' I say, and then, quickly, hoping to catch her before she hangs up, 'Give that gorgeous little boy a hug from me, won't you?'

With the wind in my ears and the noise of the rolling ocean beneath me, I hear the child's voice in an echo of recent memory – *Hello, my name is Ted* – and his mantra is haunting. I had thought he was introducing his soft toys to one another, but now that I know the secret he carried, I believe he was introducing himself. Did he understand what he was saying, or was he digging in his subconscious, in the recesses of his memory, for the relevance of the name, repeating it in an unknowing attempt to keep his former self – his former life – alive on the surface?

Hello, my name is Ted. My name is Ed. My name is Edward. I'm still here.

I step back from the cliff edge and take a deep breath of sea air into my lungs. I think of Edward, alone and terrified in the wardrobe; of Elise sleeping peacefully in a home that should have been her sanctuary. I think of Christina, lifeless at the bottom of a staircase. I think of Delta, beautiful and glowing beneath the spot-lights on that stage as I watched her all those years ago. I wish yet again that I had told her how brilliant she was, and how brightly her star shone.

A ship appears on the horizon, blurred and distant, and I wonder where it is heading and who might be on board. A gull soars and swoops to snatch something from a rock ledge just feet from where I stand, turning its head up to assess me, wondering whether I am a threat. I offer it a smile.

Hello, I want to say. *My name is Brooke. I'm still here.*

A LETTER FROM VICTORIA

Dear Reader,

I want to say a huge thank you for choosing to read *The New Family*. If you enjoyed it and would like to keep up to date with all my latest releases, just sign up at the following link. Your email address will never be shared, and you can unsubscribe at any time.

www.bookouture.com/victoria-jenkins

I have loved writing *The New Family* as much for its setting as its characters, and I hope you have enjoyed the almost Gothic undertones of the landscape depicted in Brooke's rural Pembrokeshire – a place I love and have missed during lockdown. Like so many of us stuck in towns and cities for over a year, I yearned for the sea while travel restrictions were in place, and this book has sometimes felt like a love letter to the coast. Aberfach is based on the real village of Porthgain in Pembrokeshire, and Brooke's tiny studio and gallery is inspired by the home of a real artist there. I have one of his paintings in my dining room – a watercolour of Fishguard harbour.

As with my last book *The Playdate*, *The New Family* is not set during lockdown, yet it has a claustrophobia that is reminiscent of it. The isolation experienced by Christina has been felt by so many people during the past twenty months, and the statistics regarding domestic abuse and its increase during lockdown are shocking. Details of the emotional abuse and coercion Christina endures were inspired by a real-life case of a woman whose husband had been gradually poisoning her with laxatives, his hold over her life and her finances so subtle that it was years before her adult children suspected that something was wrong. I was keen to write this type of character, as I find those who are outwardly good and respectable – those who manage to keep their dark intentions hidden from even the people they live with – far more terrifying than the antagonists who are openly bad.

Christina and Brooke are women whose lives are polar opposites: one a married mother, financially secure and with a successful career; the other single and living on her own, struggling to make ends meet. Though they never meet, their lives are entwined in ways neither can imagine, and their grief for their sisters gives their differing stories a parallel theme. Like so many of the books I have written, *The New Family* is at its core a story about the relationships between females – sisters, mothers, friends – and the ways in which family ties shape our lives.

I hope you loved *The New Family*; if you did, I would be very grateful if you could write a review. I would love to hear what you think, and it makes such a difference in helping new readers to discover my books for the first time.

I love hearing from readers – you can get in touch on my Facebook page or through Twitter.

Thanks,

Victoria

facebook.com/victoriajenkinswriter

twitter.com/vicwritescrime

ACKNOWLEDGEMENTS

Thank you to my editor, Helen Jenner, for taking the chaotic ramblings of an idea and making them into something I'm now happy to put my name to. Thank you to my agent, Anne Williams, to my publicist, Noelle Holten, and to the brilliant team at Bookouture who put so much time and effort into each of my books. I am so lucky to work with such a great group of people, and I hope it will continue for many books to come.

As always, thank you to my family, who continue to put up with me. I owe a big thank you for this one to the Stay Safe WhatsApp group, who have patiently endured my Wednesday questions and returned some brilliant (and sometimes bonkers) ideas. Thank you to Steve, Gaynor, Clint, Mark, Ryan, Delyth and Crystal (also Crystal's friends) – you have given me enough plot lines for a series, and it has been insightful (and a little worrying) to discover just how dark your minds are. Gaynor, if you don't mind, I will bypass some of your book title suggestions!

To my little girls, Mia and Emily, who are somewhere in everything I write – thank you for being you. And lastly, to Dave Webber (also known in the Jenkins house as Deeeeeeee) – thank you for letting me write in your lovely home, with that view of your beautiful garden. This one is for you.